The Darcy Brothers

Monica Fairview
Maria Grace
Cassandra Grafton
Susan Mason-Milks
Abigail Reynolds

White Soup Press

Published by: White Soup Press

The Darcy Brothers
Copyright © 2015

For information, address
 Maria Grace at Author.MariaGrace@gmail.com

ISBN-10: 0692370307
ISBN-13: 978-0692370308 (White Soup Press)

Authors' Website: JaneAustenVariations.com

Dedication

To all the Readers who supported us during the
creation of The Darcy Brothers,
whose many comments, Poll votes and plentiful
feedback not only helped us to shape this
tale but also gave us so much
encouragement along the way.
Without you, this story would not be what it is!

Acknowledgements

Our thanks to the authors of Jane Austen Variations whose support and encouragement throughout this journey has been priceless; to readers David McKee and Evie Cotton whose enthusiasm and weekly Reader's Perspective posts nourished our creative energies; to Jan Ashe and Ruth whose help as a beta reader has been invaluable; and to Regina Jeffers for her participation in early plot discussions.

CHAPTER 1

"SO TELL ME AGAIN, why am I going to Rosings?" Theophilus Darcy stretched his long legs across the floorboards of the traveling coach until his feet were not quite touching his brother's impeccably polished boots.

Fitzwilliam Darcy grunted and shifted in his seat until his feet were free once more.

Theo grinned. So predictable. Why did he take so much pleasure in this?

Darcy clamped his jaws together and swallowed back his sharp words. Theo would not provoke him to intemperate speech, not today. Not again.

He drew a deep breath, savoring the fragrance of the newly refreshed leather upholstery. He would never admit it to his brother, but he delighted in the scent. Simple, elegant, and made to last, exactly as it should be.

"I asked you a question, Brother dear." Theo tapped his boot against Darcy's.

Darcy jumped. "Stop that. There is plenty of room in this coach without you crowding me."

Theo chuckled and pulled back just enough that Darcy

would have to concede he complied, but not an inch further. "So touchy. Always have been, as I remember. You never liked sharing a seat with me, even when we were children." He tapped Darcy's boot again.

How was it Theo never acted his age? Now six and twenty, he displayed less decorum than Bingley or even Georgiana. Would he never behave as a responsible gentleman ought? He was finally a barrister in his own standing now. How would he ever gain the confidence of the solicitors who would bring business his way when he continued to play the role of an ill-bred adolescent?

Darcy stared at the side glass. His brother's reflection stared back at him. Theo was a handsome fellow, with a ready smile and easy manner, much like Wickham's. Darcy's stomach churned. No wonder he found it so easy to make friends.

Theo's reflection grinned as he twitched his eyebrows into the expression he knew most rankled Darcy's nerves. Blast and botheration! Could a man not even enjoy the scenery on a long journey? This would be a long three days indeed.

"I ask you again, why am I going to Rosings?"

Darcy huffed and the side glass fogged. "Apparently, to punish me by making this trip as unpleasant as possible."

Theo barked out a full-bellied laugh. "Oh, I have not even begun. If that is my purpose, then I must apply myself more whole-heartedly to the task." He slid down in the seat and parked his feet on the squabs beside Darcy.

Now he was going to scuff the new seat covers! Darcy swept Theo's feet off. Boot heels thudded on the floor boards. "Enough!"

"Then answer me."

"We are going to Rosings because Aunt Catherine expects us. We have a duty to her as family. She requires assistance in instructing her Steward and land managers and relies upon Pemberley to provide such assistance."

"That is why *you* are going. I—as you know—know next to nothing about estate management, and if she needs contracts drawn up, a broker for another mortgage or an arbitrator for her disputes with her local tradesmen, she requires a solicitor, not my services. There is simply no need for me to be here."

"We have a family duty to call upon her."

"*You* might. But I do not. Have you forgotten she cannot stand the sight of me?"

"Who is responsible for that?"

Theo rolled his eyes. "It is not my fault the Old Bat has no sense of humor."

"Old Bat? That is how you refer to our aunt? Such disrespect—"

"You cannot tell me you have not thought the self-same thing. Just because you are too proud to admit to your baser feelings—"

"Proud? You consider self-control and good manners marks of pride? No wonder you cannot be permitted in polite company! You give offense—"

"*I* give offense?" Theo leaned forward and planted his elbows on his knees. He laced his fingers and balanced his chin on his hands. "No, you have it quite reversed, dear Brother. *You* are the one who gives offense wherever you go."

Darcy's eyes bulged, and he coughed back the ungentlemanly invectives.

"Why else would Fitzwilliam Darcy keep company with one of the *nouveau riche*? Bingley is a jolly fellow, I grant you, but he is decidedly below you. Not only that, but apparently he is unable to control your offensive nature any better than the rest of us. I recall hearing that in Hertfordshire—"

"You are in no position to criticize my friends." Darcy snorted. Hertfordshire was not a topic to be discussed with Theo. "Hypocrisy does not become you."

"Hypocrisy?"

3

"My friends look to me for insight and advice. Yours seek you for money."

"That is not hypocrisy. I call it generosity, of which I have been the beneficiary in the past. I am only too happy to return the favor in equal measure. One never knows when one might be in need of a generous friend or three."

Stubborn, foolish, maddening…would he never see? "Need I remind you, *my* friends never had me sent down from school?"

"Wickham and I—"

Darcy lifted his hand. "Stop. I have heard this far too many times. No more excuses. Why can you not accept responsibility for what you did and be grateful I was able to persuade the Governors to reinstate you? Without that—"

"Yes, yes, I know, *Prince William*." Theo flourished his hand between them and bowed from his shoulders. "Without your timely intervention, your stellar reputation, and a generous quantity of your blunt, I would never have graduated. Without your pull and your support, I would never have attended those three years at the Inns of Court. You forget however that it was *I* who applied myself—"

"To socializing and revelry and cards—"

"With the most notable barristers at those dinners, who have in turn set me up with connections to solicitors—"

"With whom you would never have contact, except that *I* pay your Bloomsbury rent."

"What do you want me to say? That I owe all my gentlemanly standing to you?"

"You mean to tell me you would rather I withdraw—"

"No, just acknowledge I could indeed have made my way without you."

Darcy leaned back, arms crossed tightly over his chest. "And what exactly would you have done?"

"I could have done very well for myself in the army."

"I suppose you could have scraped together the four hundred pounds for a commission in the infantry, but where would you come up with the money to rank up? Or would you be content to spend your life as a lowly Ensign?"

"Which would not have been nearly smart enough for you. Your pride could not tolerate the possibility that I might fail to distinguish myself. You had to dictate—"

"I have never dictated—"

"You dictated I accompany you to Rosings. You know I hate it there, and Aunt Catherine hates having me."

Darcy grumbled deep in his throat.

"You do not trust me."

If he clamped his teeth any harder, Darcy feared one might crack. Yet, if he did not, there was a very real risk he might finally speak his mind.

"What, no response?" Theo laughed, a coarse, derisive sound. "I must be correct. You always refuse to engage me when I am right."

No, this cheap ploy to bait him into conversation was not going to work. Darcy turned to face the side glass, even if it meant he still stared into Theo's smug reflection.

"You could have left me behind at Pemberley easily enough. Or have you forgotten I am quite used to keeping my own establishment? Georgiana and I would have been perfectly fine on our own at home, without you."

"Not after Ramsgate." Darcy muttered through clenched teeth.

"So *that* is what this is all about? I have already told you—"

"Enough."

"Yes, your Highness." Theo bowed, this time touching his head to his knees.

Darcy rapped on the ceiling and jumped from the coach before it had stopped moving.

In just a few moments, his horse was readied and their journey resumed. At last, relief from Theo's mindless droning and constant needling. He had been too much in Wickham's company no doubt, and had picked up some of that rake's worst traits.

At least *that* was finally at an end now. Not that Theo had much use for Wickham anymore, but still, the cad was safely away from the entire Darcy family and things were finally as they should be.

Now all Darcy had to do was forget one Elizabeth Bennet, and his world would once again be set completely to rights. He huffed out a heavy breath and resettled in his saddle. His horse shook his head and glanced back at him. Darcy clucked his tongue and his mount returned to his walk.

How did one young lady—one bewitching, maddening, enticing young lady—manage to discompose him so? She crept into his thoughts when he least expected. Each book he picked up, he wondered if she had read it and what her pert—or impertinent—opinions might be on it. Each trail he walked, he wondered if it would be to her liking. Each time he heard tell of an assembly or ball, he cringed, re-membering again his ungentlemanly words spoken in the hearing of a young woman who was well worth pleasing.

He winced, those fateful words echoing again in his mind. ...*not handsome enough to tempt me*... How could he have said something not only so ungracious, but so utterly and completely untrue? Surely those words would haunt him until his dying day.

Darcy had to get her out of his head. Time with his Aunt Catherine—and cousin, Anne—was just the tonic to do it. How could a woman like Anne exist in the same world that contained an Elizabeth Bennet? The two were unalike in every imaginable way.

Lady Catherine still expected him to marry Anne.

He gulped back the bitter tang coating his tongue, the same one he always tasted whenever his aunt brought up the topic of marriage. How would he disabuse her of the notion he would marry according to her will?

Perhaps he could recommend his brother as a fitting substitute. That would insure Theo a secure source of income if he failed as a barrister, which he might do simply to vex Darcy.

But Theo was right—Lady Catherine barely tolerated him and that only for Darcy and Georgiana's sake. She could never accept him as a son. Blast and botheration.

A cold raindrop hit his nose. He glanced over his shoulder. Dark clouds gathered on the horizon, whipped together by a chill wind. The next posting station should be close, maybe a quarter of a mile off. Perhaps—

Thunder cracked. Heavy, cold drops pelted his face. Perhaps not.

It was two days before the rains ceased. Much as Darcy wished to escape his brother's baiting, he had been obliged, long before the next watering stop, to return to the carriage, and the remainder of the first day's journey passed much as it began. The ensuing four and twenty hours drew to a close at a coaching inn in Watford, and as the third and final day dawned, Darcy woke unrefreshed. Spending the night in Hertfordshire had not been conducive to sleep, and even when he had finally drifted into a restless slumber, his dreams were haunted by memories of the previous autumn and a pair of fine eyes.

Theo had made a late night of it, joining a card-playing group of young men at a table in the public bar, and Darcy had thrown him a warning look before retiring to his room. The flagons of ale lined up on the table did not auger well for his brother who was, in Darcy's opinion, a little too fond of imbibing and then making rash decisions.

Though the rain clouds had gone, dispersed by a strong wind, the condition of the roads did not advocate riding, and thus they faced a third day of confinement within the carriage. With Darcy's lack of proper sleep and Theo's late night, neither was in a frame of mind to tolerate the other's failings, and this soon led to the resumption of an old argument.

"Something preys upon your mind, Brother." Theo raised a hand as Darcy began to shake his head. "I am a grown man of six and twenty; why will you not confide in me?"

"There is nothing to tell, and even if there were, I doubt you would be my confidante."

Theo grunted. "No; being of royal blood, you consider yourself above the needs of the humble mortal and yourself the only counsel you require." He leaned forward, resting his elbows on his knees and fixed Darcy with a stare. "When are you going to get off your high horse and realize you can trust me?"

"*How* can I trust you?" Darcy blew out a frustrated breath. "Did you see through Wickham after the Cambridge debacle? No; then you are once more in collusion with him over the study of the law—and I use the word 'study' lightly."

Theo's normally genial countenance darkened and he sat back in his seat. "You cannot compare me to him. I completed my studies; I have a profession."

Darcy ignored him. "Yet I foolishly placed Georgiana under your protection in Ramsgate."

"Ramsgate was not my fault!"

"How can you absolve yourself so easily? When will you start to accept responsibility for your actions?"

"Because, I repeat, it was not my fault! I was not to blame at the time, and I am unlikely to lay claim to it several months later."

"Yet you fell in with Wickham's scheme."

"I told you before, it was not by design, and I had no idea what he and that Younge woman had afoot. You should be thankful I was there. If I had not been, you probably would not have followed, and Georgiana would be lost to us." Theo's voice faltered, and Darcy observed his troubled countenance. No doubt his mind had travelled down a similar road to his own: it would not be the first sibling they had lost, though to different circumstances.

A heavy silence ensued which neither brother seemed inclined to break, each staring out of opposite windows. Eventually, the movement of the carriage was sufficient for Theo's late night to catch up with him and he slept, and Darcy pulled out his watch. Georgiana and her companion should be on their way to Town now. He sighed as he tucked the fob away. He had not wanted to leave her when they set off for Kent and though the journey to London from Derbyshire was a long one, it was worth it to know his sister would be only a few hours' ride away. With all that had happened, he could not face leaving her so far away. He glanced at his brother's slumbering form and his expression darkened. Theo's suggestion he remain at Pemberley with Georgiana was quite ridiculous in the circumstances.

He turned to stare out of the window, wishing to push Theo from his thoughts, but though he did not regret the cessation of their bickering, he now found his mind falling towards that which he would forget: Elizabeth Bennet.

Resignedly, Darcy stared at the passing countryside. They had skirted London now and were entering Kent, and with little persuasion, his mind flew back to the last time he had seen her—at the Netherfield ball.

It had been a night of mixed emotions: his determination to secure her hand for a set had not delivered the pleasurable half hour he had hoped, yet the antagonism stirred by their conversation had kept him enthralled. The behavior of her family throughout the evening—her elder sister excepted—soon followed upon this reflection and he sighed.

As if her immediate family did not present sufficient challenge, her more distant connections afforded likewise. What was the name of that peculiar man, her cousin? He was dashed if he could recall it, yet he could picture without hesitation his appalling dance with Elizabeth—the all-significant first set—and his constant shadowing of her throughout the evening.

Caroline Bingley had amused no one but herself during their journey to London over the likelihood of seeing Eliza Bennet wed to her cousin. Yet was she so far from the mark? The heir to her family estate... though his insides churned at the notion, Darcy could not deny its validity.

Within seconds, Elizabeth's face was before him—chin slightly raised, lips almost pursed, as though struggling to contain a smile, her eyes full of intelligence and light. A familiar tight sensation grasped Darcy's chest, and he closed his eyes. When? *When* would he ever forget her?

"Hey ho! What now?" With a start, Darcy looked over at Theo, who had awoken as the carriage drew to a precipitous halt. "Do we arrive so soon?"

Frowning, Darcy dropped the window, but before he could question the driver, a footman appeared at the door.

"'Tis the ford, sir, swollen by the rains and impassable just now." He waved a hand back down the lane. "There is an inn back along the way. I will enquire for another direction."

Sitting back in his seat, Darcy glanced over at his brother, who had resumed his usual slumped position, his feet stretched out in front of him. Thankfully, he had not returned them to the squabs.

"Dash it." Theo sighed dramatically. "And I was *so* anticipating our imminent arrival. Let us hope the diversion takes several days, hey Brother?"

"Aunt Catherine expects us to arrive today; if we do not, she will be displeased."

"Surely the Old Bat cannot object to delays caused by the elements; they answer to none of us." Theo turned to stare out of the window. "She will hardly be contemplating my arrival with any pleasure. She will bemoan the absence of the good Colonel, and I will be at the receiving end of her displeasure from dawn until dusk, as is her custom." He threw a keen glance at his brother. "I am her whipping boy, you know, for I favor the wrong side of the family."

Before Darcy could muster a response to this, the footman reappeared at the window. "I am sorry, sir, the nearest bridge is a ten-mile detour. As the waters peaked some hours ago, the ford should be passable fairly soon. The innkeeper suggests you tarry a while."

Theo snorted. "Aye, and we are likely not the first, nor the last, traveler the innkeeper has managed to turn into good business as a result of this storm!"

With little option, however, the coaching inn was where they were bound.

Theo, soon in possession of a flagon of ale, joined some local men near the hearth and took little time in settling down to enjoy their conversation, his open countenance and his ready smile more than overcoming the brevity of the acquaintance.

Unwilling to be witness to Theo charming yet another room full of strangers, Darcy walked into the inn's dining room, picking up a newspaper as he went, and before long he was engrossed in its pages in a corner of the room. Yet his peace did not endure. Before long a party, hindered likewise by the swollen waters at the ford, came into the room to partake of a meal, and try though Darcy did to focus on the political news, their voices would intrude. With a frustrated sigh, he turned his attention to the financial reports but then his attention was caught by the mention of his aunt's name.

Lowering the paper, he peered over it. A middle-aged couple, accompanied by an elderly lady with a wizened face, and a young lady of indiscriminate age, were sat to table partaking of their fare and freely discussing their business aloud.

"Aye, under her patronage at Hunsford parsonage." The man continued. "Mr. Collins has done well for himself."

Darcy frowned. That was it! Collins was the ridiculous cousin's name. He turned back to his reading. There was little of interest for him in that person's concerns.

"Indeed. There was much speculation when he brought home a wife," added the lady. "And Mrs. Collins very kindly invited me and Sarah here to take tea with her. She showed us great courtesy, but then she was raised a gentleman's daughter."

Unable to prevent it, Darcy's interest was stirred, and he slowly lowered the paper again.

The man nodded. "Aye, she is a good soul is Mrs. Collins. You do not see the like in this neighborhood often; the air of Hertfordshire must be agreeable, to breed such a fine woman!"

Darcy's attention was fully caught as the sickening sense of doubt in his mind took firmer hold. Could it be? Had Caroline Bingley been correct after all? The uncomfortable lurching of his insides vied with the distaste in his mouth at such a conjecture. Yet it was not impossible...

"There you are!" Darcy started and dropped the paper into his lap as Theo appeared in the room. "The water has receded sufficiently; we may proceed. What joy!"

Theo's intelligence was of interest to the party at the table, and they dropped any further conversation in favor of their repast, and Darcy had no choice but to follow his brother from the room.

Though Theo cast him a curious glance every now and again as their journey resumed, he refrained from speaking for some reason or other, and Darcy welcomed the respite. They had soon negotiated a careful crossing of the ford and before long they approached Hunsford and the lane leading to the entrance to Rosings Park.

He had never paid any mind to the modest parsonage before, but now it drew his gaze immediately. Before he could study it with any purpose, however, his eye was caught by the sight of the aforementioned Reverend Collins who hovered in the lane and, as the carriage passed him by, made several low sweeping bows in its general direction.

Darcy blinked rapidly; Theo was staring out of the other window, looking somewhat morose as they passed through the ornate gates, and he glanced back at the parsonage before it disappeared from view. The figure of a woman had emerged from the shadow of the doorway, unbeknownst to the parson who continued to bow as the coach faded into the distance.

Turning back, Darcy swallowed hard on the sudden constriction of his throat. It was impossible to say at this distance, but he had an awful suspicion he had just seen Elizabeth—at the home of his aunt's parson, who had found himself a wife in Hertfordshire.

Lady Catherine's greeting had been all Theo expected. The look of distaste she threw him as he entered the drawing room was sufficient to have him greet her as briefly as politeness allowed and throw himself into an armchair near the fireplace. As always, Darcy was her only object, and once she had learned of the call to duty preventing Colonel Fitzwilliam from making his annual visit, she seemed oblivious to anyone else's presence.

The heat in the room was oppressive, with a roaring fire blazing at both ends and the lamps burning even though it was still several hours until dusk. As his aunt and brother talked, Theo slumped down in his seat. What with his late night, the long days in the carriage, the heat from the fire and the droning of his aunt's voice, he knew he was set for oblivion before long.

Lady Catherine's next words, however, quickened his interest. "I am led to believe you were in company with my parson last autumn, Darcy, when he visited Hertfordshire. Is it true, or did he take a liberty in implying it?"

Theo threw a quick glance at Darcy, quickly noting his drawn countenance. What was it with Hertfordshire? How frustrating he forgot to mention his curiosity to his sister in his recent letter to her; after all, she was the one who

13

had first drawn his attention to something affecting their brother's spirits since his return.

Conscious Darcy had thrown him a wary glance, Theo pretended a yawn and stretched out his booted feet, placing his arms behind his head as he wriggled down in his seat. He would feign interest in the fire but continue to listen.

"I am not certain I would say we were 'in company' precisely, though the man did have the gall to come and introduce himself."

Lady Catherine narrowed her gaze. "Under what pretext?"

"He wished to assure me of your and my cousin's good health when last he had seen you."

With a nod, Lady Catherine sat back in her seat. "It was a little forward of him, I will grant you, but you cannot fault his purpose, Darcy. The Reverend Collins is a good man."

Darcy inclined his head, and Theo shifted his position so that he had a better view of his brother's countenance.

"Mr. Collins found himself a wife in Hertfordshire."

"Er—indeed?" Darcy cleared his throat and tugged at his neck cloth as though its restriction caused him some discomfort, and Theo was torn between amusement at this and an avid curiosity over what caused such a reaction in his normally inscrutable brother.

In the meantime, his aunt seemed to have noticed Theo.

"I will thank you, Theophilus, for not lounging in such an ungainly fashion!" She turned back to Darcy and fixed him with a beady eye. "Yes—I expressly told him to. 'Find a wife, Mr. Collins,' says I before he departed for Hertfordshire 'and a gentlewoman at that'. And of course he could not return until he did, though I understand it was not difficult. The neighborhood seemed to contain all too many single young women."

Lady Catherine got to her feet. "It is a good match for

her. Her father has visited of late, though he is now returned to Hertfordshire. Mrs. Collins seemed most attached to him."

Darcy sank lower into his seat, his skin paling. "And he brought one of her sisters with him—a very sweet girl—along with a close friend of Mrs. Collins. They remain at the parsonage yet; you may meet with them at some point. I have condescended to have them dine here before now, and I may do so again." She walked over to pick up her closed fan from a side table and turned about. "I was most put out to learn from Mrs. Collins she has also already made your acquaintance, Darcy. Is this true?"

Theo had lost interest by this point, but he looked up again as a small sound escaped his brother. Darcy seemed lost for words, but before he could conjecture any further, Theo let out an "*Ouch*" as his aunt rapped him hard on the shin with her fan.

"Sit up, Boy! You do your spine and the upholstery an equal disservice!"

She turned away and resumed her seat, and Theo rubbed his shin, his gaze still upon Darcy. If his brother's skin paled any further, he would have to call for the apothecary. Before he could consider the matter further, however, a loud knock came upon the door and a servant entered.

"Excuse me, Ma'am," he said, fetching up before Lady Catherine. "Your steward is here on urgent business that cannot be delayed."

Lady Catherine rose majestically to her feet. "Send him in." She turned to Darcy. "His timing is opportune; you can assist me with whatever it is."

Robert Farrell entered the room, greeting Darcy as he did so, and came straight to the point.

"We have a dispute in the village, Ma'am, and it looks set to get out of hand. The notices over the enclosure of the south and west pastures were posted in the church porch but two days ago, and already Clayton is objecting.

He is unlikely to muster sufficient support, but he is causing unrest. I fear there will be retribution."

Darcy frowned. "What paperwork has he?"

"Nothing in writing, sir; it was a gentleman's agreement."

His interest caught by the name, Theo got to his feet, walking over to join them. "I heard something of this at the inn; I may be able to assist." He had spoken to the very tenant they referred to as he aired his grievances loudly to all who were prepared to listen.

Lady Catherine glared at him. "Of course you cannot assist! What do *you* know of Estate matters?"

Theo turned to Darcy. "This predicament was spoken of and why this Clayton felt obligated to obstruct. I think—"

Darcy threw him an exasperated look. "Idle gossip is not going to solve this matter. You would make better use of your time in perusing a book." He turned away from him dismissively. "Come, Farrell, let us repair to the estate office to consider our options."

Lady Catherine swept after them, and Theo glared at the door as it closed. He was genial by nature, but nothing could push him further than his brother treating him like he was of no value to the world. He would be damned if he would wait for them with nothing to do but twiddle his thumbs and kick his heels like a schoolboy.

He sprang to his feet and went over to the window. Clouds had gathered to blot out the weak Spring sunshine, and a squall of a shower was now sending water to stream down the glass. Even the weather, it seemed, was against him. There was no chance of going out.

He wandered over to his aunt's escritoire. It was painted in the Oriental fashion, with Chinese dragons, intended, no doubt, to intimidate those sufficiently foolhardy to approach. Theo opened the desk and sat down, opening each of the small drawers and peeping into the corners. Perhaps he would unearth some terrible secret of his aunt's. He found nothing of the least interest, however, beyond a few walnuts that could not be cracked.

Presently, he took out a sheet of paper. It gave off an unpleasant scent—a blend of dusty lavender and rotten oranges—perfume to his aunt, no doubt. Dipping a quill in ink, he began a sketch of his aunt with fangs and bat wings, then neatly labeled it 'The Old Bat'. The sound of a movement outside the door led him to scrunch it up into a ball and throw it into the wastebasket.

Then, he recalled he owed his great friend, Montgomery Preston, a letter. Monty had just succeeded to his title, and Theo knew he was overdue in acknowledging it.

Dear Sir Montgomery,

No, no, that will never do. I am sorry, my friend, Baronet or no, I cannot call you anything but Monty.

My deepest condolences on the loss of your father. Though I know you have expected the unhappy event for quite some time, I know it is difficult to step into his place nonetheless. I watched my brother endure that transition and uniquely understand the weights you must feel right now.

In your last letter, you asked me to recommend a new solicitor in London since Lyman's untimely demise. I have several men whom you might consider to take his place. I will introduce you when next I am in Town. Sadly, I cannot say precisely when that will be, as I have been condemned to visit my aunt at Rosings by Prince William himself.

Yes, I can hear you scolding me now for calling him that. But truly, when he slips into his haughty, overbearing Master-of-all-he-surveys manner, there is simply no other way to refer to him. He still refuses to leave Georgiana in my care. I cannot begin to tell you how that infuriates me. But you well know it, so I shall not waffle on about it.

Theo dipped his pen in the ink again and reflected on his brother's brooding silence in the carriage. A great deal of it was, naturally, Prince William playing the older disapproving brother, but not all.

Something more than his usual irritation with me is troubling my brother, though, and I mean to get to the truth of it. To be entirely frank. I am worried about him. He has not been himself since his trip with Bingley, and I cannot make out why. Something happened in Hertfordshire, but what?

He does not gamble on anything—cards, horses or sport of any kind. He hardly drinks and would never meddle with anyone's daughters. I can only imagine some business dealing went sour. If that is the case though, why the secrecy? If you hear anything in Town, you will let me know of course.

Theo paused and glanced over towards the window. The patter of rain against glass had ceased, and a patch of pale blue sky had reappeared, flanked by angry grey clouds. Could he risk going out? He longed more than anything to saddle Theseus and ride with the wind, but the horse had already trudged through some appalling muddy roads and deserved a rest. With a sigh, he returned his attention to his letter.

I have not forgotten about your dream of a matched team for your four-in-hand. I continue to look for such beasts as I am dragged through the countryside by His Highness. Are you really certain you wish to proceed? I know horses are your single indulgence, but still, you may wish to review your situation again before taking on such an expense.

Yours,

T.D.

He sealed the letter and strode over to fling open the window. The musty air of the room was making him irritable, he was quite certain. After days of being cooped up in a carriage with his brother, he was in desperate need of distraction. What use was the country if one did not have a chance to breathe the fresh air?

His mind made up, Theo went in search of the sour-faced butler.

"See that this letter is sent, will you?" he said as he handed it over, and, grabbing his hat and walking stick, he set out for a walk.

⚘CHAPTER 2

THE COOL AIR DID little to soothe Theo's frustration at first, for Darcy's dismissal had cut him more than he cared to acknowledge. Out of temper, he strode down a well-worn, familiar path cutting across the park, intent upon the grove where he had spent many a happy hour as a boy. A strong wind continued to blow, and he lowered his head, holding his hat in place as he walked, his other hand swiping his cane against the long grasses bordering the graveled path through the trees. A stream bordered it on one side, normally barely a mere trickle, but now it remained swollen to twice its usual width, and he contemplated stopping to throw some stones into its depths, keen to shed the aggression that lingered yet.

He had gone but a few paces further, however, when the sound of a voice caught his ear, drifting towards him on the breeze, and a flash of color ahead soon led him to the owner of the voice, a young lady. Halting his pace, thoroughly diverted, he stepped behind a nearby trunk to watch her, for she made a delightful picture, her skirts buffeted by the wind, her chestnut curls, unadorned by any hat, bouncing around her glowing cheeks as she turned this way and that, seeking something on the ground.

"Aha!" she finally exclaimed, and stepping towards the tree behind which he stood, grasped a fallen branch.

Feeling the inappropriateness of his seclusion, and thus his spying upon her, Theo made sure to step noisily forward, his boots crunching on the gravel path, and she looked up instantly with a gasp.

"Forgive me; I did not mean to startle you."

With a quick smile, she shook her head. "Pay me no mind, sir. I was too fixed upon my purpose to pay heed to my surroundings."

He indicated the aforementioned find. "Were you intent upon playing beater? I fear the shoot is under-manned if a lady is required for such actions!"

She shook her head, her curls bouncing against her cheeks. "Indeed not! My quarry is out of my reach, and this," she waved the branch, "shall hopefully be sufficient aid."

"It is a singular weapon, Madam. I am not certain it will suit."

"I do not seek game, sir, though it is a prize nonetheless; yet it is at present caught in a snare." She pointed across the stream, and a wide grin overspread Theo's countenance as he caught sight of a bonnet fixed in the lower branches of a tree.

"A rare specimen indeed, and the like of which I have yet to bag!" He flourished his cane. "May I be so bold as to take a shot?"

She nodded, and he walked to the water's edge, but even with his longer reach, the bonnet remained aloft and beyond him.

Theo studied the ground before him. "I believe there is but one solution, Madam. I shall brave the high seas for you and duly restore you to your bonnet." He made an exaggerated bow before removing his hat, looking about for somewhere to rest it that it might not become too soiled, only to realize the lady was offering her gloved hand.

"I would not wish to intrude upon your leisure, sir, but if you are to come to my assistance, permit me to support you as best I can."

He inclined his head. "It is my pleasure. I do, after all, possess the traditional accomplishments of an educated gentleman, not least of which is coming to the aid of a lady in distress."

With a grin, Theo met her sparkling gaze, before handing his hat over for safe-keeping. She stepped aside as he took several paces back, then leapt across the stream, landing with a squelch on the other side. Flecks of muddy water patterned his trousers as his boots sank ankle deep into the soft mud at the water's edge, and he tugged them free, slipping and stumbling his way, effectively but with little elegance, to the safety of the grass verge.

"Hey ho! I am in safe harbor—do not be alarmed, Madam!" He glanced over to where the lady stood; there was no sign of concern on her features at all, merely an impish smile enticing him far more than he wished to acknowledge. How he wished to know more of her!

Clearing his throat, Theo turned his attention to the recalcitrant bonnet, lodged somewhere above him.

"Shall I throw you the branch?" The lady indicated the discarded item which he had not thought to take with him, but he shook his head.

"I shall make do!" He raised his cane and stretched up in an attempt to dislodge the bonnet.

The lady clapped her hands together. "You are almost there, sir. One more prod should do the trick."

Theo grasped his cane more firmly and, with a small jump, finally managed to dislodge the bonnet from its leafy hold and it tumbled down through the air straight towards him. Before he could take evasive action, it landed with perfect precision upon his own head.

A burst of laughter from the lady was, however, sufficient encouragement for him to leave it in place.

"I am tempted to retain it, Madam. It is a fine fit, and I trust you are out of countenance with it as you had tossed it aside."

Clearly struggling to contain her amusement, she shook her head. "Indeed, I did not. It was Mother Nature's desire, for as I entered this clearing, a gust of wind whipped it from me before I could prevent it."

With a more successful leap this time, Theo crossed back over the stream and came to stand before her, performing his best attempt at a curtsey. Smiling widely, she held his hat out to him.

"Much as the color becomes you, sir, I believe we should trade. Gallantry must be rewarded with more than muddy boots! I am gratified I was able to preserve your hat from a similar fate."

Theo laughed, thoroughly delighted with her, but then she too curtseyed. "And now I must repeat my thanks and say farewell for I am past due at the parsonage. Mr. Collins always expects me to return directly, and I will not be thanked for keeping him from his supper."

She turned away as Theo inclined his head in acknowledgement. He was conscious of a twinge of disappointment; did her reference to Mr. Collins mean he had come across the wife he had so serendipitously secured in Hertfordshire? He turned his feet back towards the house, mulling upon the good fortune of some.

Not being prone to the depression of spirits, the chance encounter had restored Theo's natural enthusiasm and, despite his reluctance to be at Rosings, he bounced up the stone steps to the front door with a much improved air and countenance.

He made a perfunctory attempt at scraping some of the mud from his boots, then shrugged and let himself into the house, closing the door carefully so as not to alert anyone to his return.

To the either side of the doorway stood two highly polished suits of armor; these had stood in their silent positions for as far back as Theo could remember and, moreover, presented a temptation he was loath to resist. With a quick glance about to ensure he was undetected, he grinned, removing his hat and balancing it on top of the helmet of one of the figures. Pleased with his efforts, he rested his cane across the extended arms and turned around, looking for inspiration.

He was just threading two large flowers, extracted from a vase on the table in the center of the hall, into the mouthpiece of the helmet when a voice behind him made him spin about.

"What the *devil* do you think you are doing?"

An ominous creaking behind Theo hinted at the disaster to come, then time seemed to stretch as the helmet toppled off the suit of armor, bounced with a loud clang, then rebounded into his brother's shin. Theo winced at Darcy's grimace of pain. "I was merely attempting to add a little cheer to the decor."

Darcy bent over and rubbed his abused shin, then carefully picked up the helmet, its visor now dented and dangling loose. "This survived intact for four hundred years until you came along," he said coldly.

"Had you not startled me, it would have been there for another four hundred," Theo shot back.

"Had you merely respected a historical artifact, it would not have happened."

So much for his improved spirits! Theo managed to smile despite gritted teeth. It was a skill he had practiced often. "Whatever you say, Your Highness."

"Oh, stop that nonsense!" Darcy snapped. "Where have you been? Your boots are covered with mud."

"I went for a walk, not that it is any of your business.

My boots became muddy when I rescued a damsel in distress."

"I hesitate to think what you might have demanded in return for whatever slight service you offered."

"None. I came upon the parson's wife, whose bonnet was caught in a tree. I retrieved it for her."

Darcy's shoulders tightened. "Why was her bonnet in a tree?"

"She said it had blown off." Theo dropped into one of the chairs lining the wall. "It was my pleasure to help her. She is a lovely girl—all chestnut curls, bright eyes, and a lively expression. A quick wit as well. A pity she is wasted on the parson."

His brother turned away to look out the window. "It was likely a prudent match for her," he said coldly, then added briskly, "As it was for him. Apparently, he only sought a wife because our aunt instructed him to do so."

"And prudence is the only important thing, is it not?" Theo said mockingly. "Heaven forbid a man should choose his wife because he finds her attractive, or even worse, because he loves her." Despite his tone, he was watching his brother carefully. Once again, a mention of the parson had angered Darcy. What could the man have done in Hertfordshire to discompose his normally stoic brother to this degree?

"Love!" Darcy snapped. "Love is only for poets. It will not keep a roof over your head, nor will it feed your children, nor establish them in society. Love cannot keep the Pemberley estate intact for future generations. It is not the person who marries for love who suffers, but his children and their children after him."

Theo sat back in his chair and studied his brother. "Every man owes something to his children," he said mildly. "He also owes something to himself."

Darcy's lip curled. "That is what selfish men would say."

It was time to take a risk. Cocking his head to the side,

Theo said, "What is troubling you, William? You are not yourself."

He could almost hear the mask snap back into place. "Nothing is troubling me. Nothing at all." Darcy turned on his heel and strode away.

Theo tapped his cheek. His best hope of discovering what had happened between William and the mysterious Mr. Collins was to observe them together. A plan began to take shape in his head. True, it would mean undertaking several of his least favorite things—awakening early in the morning, attempting to be polite to his aunt, and avoiding annoying his brother—but sometimes sacrifices must be made.

Darcy trudged down to breakfast in uncharacteristic low spirits. He had tossed and turned half the night haunted by images of his Elizabeth in Mr. Collins's bed, giving him a leaden feeling in his stomach and a decided distaste for company.

Why could he not have remained in ignorance of her fate? Leaving her behind in Hertfordshire had been hard enough, but at least he had the minor consolation of believing she was happily engaged in life at Longbourn, and perhaps giving his memory a wistful thought from time to time. But no—he had to have his loss rubbed in his face, to see his beloved Elizabeth's spirits ground down under the weight of life with that fool Collins. He had not expected to enjoy his stay in Kent, not when he had to deal with both his aunt and Theo, but now it had turned into a nightmare.

If only he could skip breakfast and go for a gallop over the countryside, perhaps he would be able to breathe again. He quickly squelched the thought that he might come across Elizabeth, or at least see her at a distance. Even an early morning ride was impossible, though. Theo already seemed to suspect something was troubling him, so

Darcy could not afford to alter his routine. Why did his wastrel of a brother have to possess a moment of perception right now?

It had seemed a good idea to bring Theo to Rosings with him, now enough time had passed since Ramsgate to allow his fury to abate sufficiently he could speak to his younger brother without shouting at him. Darcy had even hoped Theo might have finally learned his lesson about Wickham, and the two brothers could have a rapprochement. Unfortunately, that had been wishful thinking, born of his own foolish desire for a brother who could understand him. Theo was as shallow and annoying as ever.

At least he would not have to face Theo over breakfast, since he rarely troubled himself to rise before noon. That was something for which to be grateful.

It turned out his luck had failed him in this matter as well. When Darcy entered the breakfast room, he found Theo seated beside his aunt, apparently engrossed in something she was saying. Fighting the impulse to turn on his heel and leave, Darcy instead gave them a cool greeting. The furthest seat from Theo was next to Anne, but Darcy took it anyway. At least she would not chatter at him.

The first bitter sip of coffee awoke him to the realization that something was decidedly amiss. Theo was listening to Lady Catherine. Not only that, but he was asking her opinion—and sitting up straight in his chair. And Lady Catherine, usually fulsome in her welcome to Darcy, had barely acknowledged his arrival. Darcy's lips tightened. Theo was plotting, and whatever his goal was, it would undoubtedly have unpleasant results for Darcy. He began to attend to the conversation he had deliberately ignored until now.

"…And mark my words, Theophilus, if you wish to be a Judge some day, you will have to change your ways. The Darcy name grants you a certain degree of credibility, of course, but you will have to prove yourself worthy of other men's trust before they will bring you their business. First you must join a club."

"Fortunately, I already have the honor of being a member at Brooks," said Theo deferentially. "I hope that meets your approval."

Lady Catherine frowned. "Whites is superior to Brooks."

"Ah, but I cannot afford the fees at Whites, so I must make do with Brooks."

Darcy fumed. Theo could not afford Brooks either. If it was not a flat-out lie, then Theo must have been gambling or going to moneylenders. No doubt it had never occurred to him to apply that money to the rent Darcy paid for him.

With a sniff, Lady Catherine said, "I suppose you will at least meet some politicians there. It could be a start. But you must work to be invited to the finest social events."

Theo took a sip of his chocolate, his brows furrowed. "How shall I determine which events are appropriate for me? So often I go to a Venetian breakfast or a musical soiree expecting good company, and instead it turns out to be the sort of people you have warned me to avoid."

"I will give you a list of those on whom you may depend. If Anne's health would permit, I could go to Town and introduce you to the proper sort of people myself, but that is impossible. You must cultivate friends who will not lead you into the way of temptation, for we have seen where that leads, young man! You will also need to learn to practice moderation. Although you must never refuse a game of cards, you must never be seen to play for high stakes. And no practical jokes! Remember, once you have earned a bad reputation for yourself, there will be no possibility of remedy. Memories are long in the *ton*!"

Theo was nodding solemnly. "I will have to search out men of good character, then. I shall start as soon as I return to London."

"You must not wait so long, or you may lose your resolve as you have so often in the past!"

"Perhaps I should practice while I am here. I heard you praise your clergyman yesterday—is he the sort of fellow I should spend more time with?"

Darcy's head shot up. What knavery was Theo planning, and why was he spouting this utter nonsense? As if Theo would ever voluntarily spend so much as a minute in the company of a fool like Mr. Collins!

"Hmm. He can do you no good in society, of course, but I suppose you could do worse than to have him as an influence on you. He understands the importance of deference to his betters."

"I shall call on him today, then." Theo frowned. "But no—I will have to wait until Sunday, for I have not been introduced to him."

Lady Catherine brushed this objection away. "It is no matter. I would take you to his house and introduce you myself, but I do not wish to be away when the doctor calls on Anne. Darcy can take you. He has met Mr. Collins."

Theo smiled as if she had granted the wish nearest his heart. "An excellent thought! I say, William, would you do me the great honor of introducing me to this paragon of parsons?"

"Of course he will! I have said so," said Lady Catherine crossly before Darcy had time to frame a response.

Darcy's suggestion of riding to the parsonage earned him an odd look from Theo, who noted it was just across the lane from Rosings Park. That was hardly the point; it might take only a quarter hour to walk there, but if they rode, he could avoid talking to Theo. He could barely think straight as it was, given his dread of seeing Elizabeth turned into Mrs. Collins, not to mention the effort of fighting to deny the part of himself that was euphoric to have the opportunity to see Elizabeth, no matter her circumstances.

There was no help for it; Darcy and Theo set forth on foot, the former in grim silence, the latter speaking cheerfully about the weather and the state of the Kentish roads. Even when Darcy failed to respond to his direct questions, Theo continued to talk as if he had not noticed, but a mocking light appeared in his eyes.

Darcy, in no mood to tolerate his younger brother's nonsense, finally said, "What is it you want from our aunt? Money?"

Theo had the gall to smile. "Just answers."

"What is that supposed to mean?"

Shrugging, Theo said, "It is what barristers do—seek answers. If I cannot get my information from one witness, I try another."

"She is not a witness in a courtroom. It is disrespectful of you to manipulate her as you did."

Theo shook his head, laughing. "Only you would think so, Darcy! She will treasure the memory of this morning, when she finally made her wayward nephew see the error of his ways. There is no greater gift I can give her than to ask for her advice!"

"It would not hurt you to take a little of that advice." Good God, he was starting to sound like Lady Catherine himself!

Theo snorted. "Really, William, that is rich."

All the hurt and anger he had felt since hearing of Elizabeth's marriage to Mr. Collins erupted. "I do not know why I still attempt to help you when I know full well you will simply ignore me and waste my money!" He strode ahead, refusing even to look at Theo, not pausing until he reached the parsonage gate. If Elizabeth was inside, she might be only a few dozen feet away from him.

Theo ambled up, his face unreadable. "William," he said softly, "how many cases have I argued since being called to the bar? How many of them have I won? Who do you suppose hires me for those cases?"

Something about Theo's voice made Darcy pause.

Then a curtain in the window of the parsonage twitched, riveting Darcy's attention. Could it be Elizabeth? "Later, Theo. They have seen us; we must not dawdle here."

Darcy's heart pounded as a maid showed them into a crowded sitting room. His gaze was immediately drawn to Elizabeth as she placed a bookmark in her book, the sunlight from the window beside her dancing over her chestnut curls and illuminating her expressive lips.

His breath caught in his throat. She was every bit as enticing as she had been in Hertfordshire—no, more enticing, because now he knew what it was to live without her. How could she have married a man like Collins?

He tore his attention away as one of the other young women, her hair drawn back under a simple cap, approached him with a smile. He recognized her vaguely from Hertfordshire, but what was her name? He had to say something. With a bow, he said, "Miss…um…"

Elizabeth's voice rippled with amusement as she came to his rescue. "Mr. Darcy, Miss Lucas is now Mrs. Collins."

The woman in the cap was Mrs. Collins? Did that mean…could it mean his Elizabeth was still free? He glanced at her left hand. No wedding band! The surge of relief almost robbed him of words.

"I… allow me to offer my best wishes on your marriage, Mrs. Collins." He managed a formal bow, somehow, scarcely able to control his joy. "This is an unexpected pleasure, Miss Elizabeth." He sounded like a schoolboy stumbling at his lessons.

Behind him he heard Theo clearing his throat. In the shock of being in Elizabeth's presence, he had almost forgotten he was not alone. "Pray allow me to introduce to your acquaintance my brother, Mr. Theophilus Darcy."

The ladies curtsied and made the appropriate sentiments. Elizabeth, her eyes sparkling, offered her hand to Theo, a privilege she had not given to Darcy. Sick jealousy filled him as his younger brother said smoothly, "I trust your bonnet is no worse for its adventures yesterday."

"Not at all, since you were so gallant as to rescue it," she said archly.

Heavy footsteps in the passageway heralded the arrival of Mr. Collins, his hands rubbing together in apparent pleasure at discovering the nephews of his patroness. "Mr. Darcy, how kind of you to condescend to call at my humble abode! It is a great honor. I trust my dear wife has already made you welcome. Lady Catherine has spoken of nothing but your upcoming visit for weeks. And this gentleman must be your cousin, Colonel Fitzwilliam, of whom I have heard much praise. It is a great honor to make your acquaintance."

Did the foolish man always insist on introducing himself to his betters? Darcy said icily, "*That* is my brother. Theo, this is Mr. Collins."

Theo turned his warm smile on the man. "I fear I am but a poor replacement for my cousin, whose duty prevented him from making the journey. You cannot imagine, sir, how I have looked forward to this meeting."

Yes, Theo was definitely planning mischief of some sort, but Darcy could not bring himself to care. He was with Elizabeth again, and she was free. Even if he could never have her himself, at least no one else did.

Though Theo's intention for this visit to Hunsford had been to learn more about Mr. Collins and observe his brother's interactions with the parson, he was quickly distracted from his purpose when he learned that Miss Elizabeth Bennet of the dark hair and fine eyes was *not* the new Mrs. Collins after all. What a relief that was! He shuddered to think of such a beautiful creature wasted on the simpering parson.

When Mrs. Collins urged the group to be seated, Theo hung back a moment expecting his brother to claim the chair next to the young lady, as they shared a prior acquaintance, but he did not. Instead, Darcy moved to the far end of the room where he sat slightly apart from the others. Well, if his brother was not going to sit by Miss Bennet, then he would!

Theo was quickly absorbed by the lady's expressive eyes, dancing with humor as she told the story of her recent encounter with Lady Catherine's favorite porcine princess, who had escaped from her pen and come calling at the parsonage unannounced. At the time, Mr. Collins was out on his daily parish visits along with his wife and, therefore, unavailable to offer refreshments to their guest. Miss Bennet had been forced to chase the stubborn pig out of the kitchen garden unassisted. Theo noticed how she had shown no hesitation in making light of herself as she described in great detail the strategies she had used to trick the wily pig into leaving. Her complete lack of self-consciousness in making herself appear less than perfect utterly and completely charmed him.

Several times during this story, Theo saw Miss Elizabeth glance in his brother's direction. Each time Darcy was staring at them with a vaguely disapproving look on his face. Surely, His Highness could not object to Theo talking to this young woman? She was just the sort Darcy was always telling him he should seek out in contrast to some of the other less reputable women with whom he tended to spend his time. Elizabeth Bennet was a gentleman's daughter and clearly a person of intelligence and good character. So why the sour look?

"What else have you enjoyed during your visit?" Theo inquired, turning his attention back to his companion.

"Of course, visiting with my dear friend Charlotte has been most enjoyable," Elizabeth said, tilting her head thoughtfully, "but I believe my walks in the park would rank a close second to her company."

"Then you must have come across old Watling, the gamekeeper, on your excursions," Theo said, a hint of mischief in his voice.

"Do you mean that darling old man who cannot see past the length of his arm?" Elizabeth inquired.

"That would be the very one."

"You will forgive me, but your aunt does not seem like the sort who would pay good money to continue the employment of a man who can barely tell a sheep from a deer."

"You are both forgiven and correct." Then, lowering his voice, Theo leaned closer, but soon realized his mistake. The hint of lavender emanating from her was intoxicating, but he quickly roused himself and managed to continue. "Poor Watling's position here dates back to the days of my uncle, Sir Lewis de Bourgh. The story goes that he once saved my uncle's life with the result being Sir Lewis had it specifically written into his Will that the gamekeeper could never be dismissed. He also granted him a generous pension to commence when he wished to retire."

"But he continues to work?" Elizabeth looked a little uncertain.

"Since my aunt has never been one to give something for nothing, she has encouraged Watling to stay on. Thus, my aunt has a nearly blind gamekeeper."

The corners of the lady's mouth turned up slightly at this. Good Lord, she was lovely! The brightest spot in an otherwise bleak landscape of endless evenings of listening to Lady Catherine expound with great authority on matters about which she knew absolutely nothing at all. For the first time since Theo's arrival, he began to think his entire stay here might not be a complete disaster. Surely, his aunt would invite the inhabitants of the parsonage for tea and for supper at least several times a week.

"I would hope then he has adequate assistance in his duties from younger men with much sharper vision?" Elizabeth's eyes glowed in good fun as she spoke.

"Yes, and those younger men make certain Watling never carries a loaded shotgun," Theo assured her.

"But how do they accomplish that without being discovered and wounding his feelings? Although wounding his feelings is certainly much better than wounding something else."

Theo found himself grinning at her like a mischievous boy. "I believe after much trial and error and the near loss of that very pig who invaded your garden, they acquired a second identical shotgun which is loaded with blanks. Before he leaves on his morning rounds, they find some way to make the switch."

Elizabeth erupted into laughter. This was not the silly giggling of a girl, nor the false tittering of a woman who was courting his favor, but a light, sweet sound like music drifting in the air. Her conversation, her humor, and oh, the sound of her laughter had drawn him in so quickly. Glancing at Darcy, Theo saw his brother was scowling again. Yes, the minute Elizabeth's laughter made its way across the room His Highness began to look as if murder was on his mind.

Suddenly, Theo had a rather unsettling thought. Could the stormy looks from his stodgy, staid brother signify *he* was attracted to Miss Bennet? The idea nearly made Theo spill his tea. She was lovely but not at all the sort of woman one would expect Darcy to have any interest in. The irony was too rich. This attraction, however, could explain Darcy's low spirits ever since returning from his visit to Hertfordshire last autumn, his continued lack of good cheer during the normally pleasant Christmas season, and even last night's tryst with a bottle of Lady Catherine's best brandy, for had they not both been under the mistaken assumption she was the new Mrs. Collins?

Theo's keen legal mind was forming a theory, but like any good barrister, he needed to gather further evidence before making a final judgment. To do this, he would have to give up the pleasure of Elizabeth's company and seek additional witnesses.

"Mr. Collins, I understand you have a special interest in

horticulture. Might I prevail upon you for a tour of your garden?" Theo asked, turning his attention to the parson who had just taken an over large bite of his scone. With his face reddening, he began to bob his head up and down vigorously.

Surprisingly, the quiet Miss Lucas came to her brother's rescue. "Yes, Mr. Collins takes very particular care of his garden, a healthy activity which my sister encourages at every opportunity."

Theo was surprised. The young lady had not spoken a word for the entirety of their visit thus far, but clearly she could exert herself when she wished to.

"Is it also an interest of yours, Miss Lucas?"

She blushed as Theo turned to look at her and promptly lost her voice again, merely nodding slightly.

Elizabeth intervened. "Oh, yes, although Maria would take no credit for it herself, it was her idea to plant the most sweetly scented flowers closest to the front door so visitors who must linger after knocking will be enveloped in the delightful fragrances."

"Then, Miss Lucas, perhaps you would join Mr. Collins and me on our little garden tour?" Theo's suggestion was met with a girlish giggle.

As they excused themselves to go outside, Theo noted with satisfaction that Darcy was slowly making his way over to take the now available seat beside Miss Elizabeth Bennet.

Walking around the garden, Theo encouraged Collins to talk about his stay in Hertfordshire, hoping to hear more evidence to support his theory. With several not so subtle comments by the parson himself, Theo patiently drew out the story of how Lady Catherine had sent him to Hertfordshire to mend the rift with the Longbourn family and choose a bride from amongst the Bennet sisters. Theo could not believe his luck. His companion was so ridiculously indiscreet.

"What kind of flower is this?" Theo asked. As soon as Mr. Collins began to ramble on about the plant, Theo threw in another question hoping the man would just keep talking and never notice the change of topic. "Are all of her sisters as pretty as Miss Elizabeth Bennet is?"

Collins seemed to muse upon this, then spoke quietly. "The eldest, Jane, is the loveliest creature I have ever beheld. And so quiet and modest, too."

"The perfect wife for a parson," Theo exclaimed. "Did you not offer for her?"

Collins put a finger to his mouth as if contemplating how much to reveal, but Theo could tell the man wanted to say more. Since all that was wanting was a little encouragement, Theo nodded his head and smiled, a trick he had learned in the courtroom.

"I was told in confidence by Mrs. Bennet that Miss Bennet was soon to be engaged. To a friend of Mr. Darcy's, as it happens," Collins informed him.

"What about this shrub with the little yellow flowers?" Theo asked, as if his very existence depended upon the parson's answer.

"Forsythia, a particular favorite of mine. I transplanted it here after Lady Catherine's gardener decided to replace it with something new," Collins said as proudly as if they were viewing his first-born child.

"If the eldest Miss Bennet was not available, then it would seem logical to seek the hand of the next oldest. Miss Elizabeth is also very comely."

At this, Collins blushed and turned to his sister-in-law. "Maria, would you fetch me the watering can? This poor little darling looks thirsty." Once Maria was out of earshot, he continued. "Oh, Miss Elizabeth would have been a very unfortunate choice for me. She is so headstrong, and your aunt would never have approved." Leaning in he confided, "It was very fortuitous she refused me, though I believe she is sorry now she has seen my charming abode here and witnessed the generosity of your aunt."

Surprised though he was to learn of the lady's rejection of her cousin's hand, Theo concealed it as best he could and continued his cross-examination of Mr. Collins until Maria returned, struggling under the weight of a full watering can.

"Thank you, my dear sister," said Collins. He took it from her and immediately became engrossed in tending to his plants.

Sensing he had extracted as much as he could from his host, Theo turned his attention to Maria. Offering his arm, he began to stroll with her to the other side of the garden away from the Reverend Collins.

"I believe you met my brother when he was in Hertfordshire last autumn," Theo ventured.

Still a little intimidated, Maria managed a nod. Getting any information from this young woman was going to require more work on his part. He tried again.

"I am certain you must find great enjoyment in soirees, concerts, assemblies and such. Were there any events of that nature when my brother was in your neighborhood?"

"Oh, yes, sir! My parents hosted a party, and Mr. Darcy's friend Mr. Bingley gave a ball at Netherfield!" Maria's eyes grew dreamy.

"Do you like to dance, Miss Lucas?"

At that, Maria went into raptures about the Netherfield ball, the number of partners, the music, the food and even the new ribbons for the dress she wore that night. From his experiences with Georgiana, Theo knew how to listen to a young lady and just what to ask to put her at ease and keep her talking.

"Did my brother dance with many ladies at the ball?" When Maria looked at him quizzically, he explained, "I like to tease him about such things from time to time."

She smiled and informed him Darcy had danced only with Mr. Bingley's sisters.

"Only Mr. Bingley's sisters when all evidence indicates

there are so many beautiful ladies in Hertfordshire! He led me to believe he enjoyed himself immensely at the ball. Surely, he must have partnered other young ladies?"

"Yes! Yes, now I remember. He did stand up with Miss Elizabeth Bennet once!" She frowned, then added, "Though neither of them looked as if they enjoyed it very much."

Fascinating! Partnering Bingley's sisters was a courtesy since they were hosting the event, but his brother had also danced with Elizabeth Bennet!

Just then he heard Collins calling to him. "Oh, Mr. Darcy, Mr. Darcy! I have picked some of the loveliest blossoms in my garden for you to take to Rosings for your aunt, if you would be so kind, sir."

Theo turned his attention back to the parson. Meanwhile, Collins was so caught up expounding upon the generosity and condescension of his remarkable patroness that he lost track of where he was putting his feet. Stepping on a rock, he lost his footing, and before either Theo or Maria could cry out a warning, Mr. Collins lost his balance. His arms shot up into the air as he fell, all the flowers intended for Lady Catherine flying up into the air before they rained back down on his head to spectacular effect as he landed in the midst of a prickly holly bush. His squeals of pain put Theo in mind of the pig Elizabeth had chased from the garden, and he struggled to suppress his laughter as he turned to see the ladies and Darcy rushing out of the house.

After extracting Collins from the holly bush and wishing him a speedy recovery, Theo helped Elizabeth to gather up the flowers that could be saved and his brother then indicated they should take their leave.

As Theo bent over Elizabeth's hand in an intentionally exaggerated fashion, he whispered, "If your bonnet ever finds itself in a desperate situation again, it should not hesitate to call upon me for rescue."

"My bonnet will keep that in mind, sir," she said with

just a hint of a smile.

When Theo looked up, Darcy was glowering at him. Again.

"Really, Fitzwilliam, you look positively wretched," Theo said, as they started back to Rosings together. "Are you feeling ill? A little too much brandy last night?"

At Theo's mention of brandy, Darcy threw him an imperious look. "Whatever makes you think something is amiss? The only thing that comes to my mind is the pain of tolerating your ceaseless questions!"

Theo's eyes narrowed thoughtfully. The last time he had seen Darcy overindulging was just after Ramsgate, was it not? But no, it was more recent—it was after returning from Hertfordshire last autumn. Again, the connection to Hertfordshire.

Past experience always led Theo to assume Darcy being out of sorts must be his fault, but he could think of nothing he had done this time, at least nothing more than his usual pranks, to cause his brother distress. As much as he enjoyed tormenting His Highness, Theo's love for his brother was just as fierce and protective as it was for Georgiana, and as it had been for... no, he would not allow himself to think on that now.

After his unfortunate remark about Darcy's brandy consumption, Theo remained silent as they walked back to Rosings together, his mind occupied with considering what he had learned from Collins and Miss Lucas and his own observations. Oh, yes, the evidence was mounting. Darcy's intemperate mood, his thunderous looks while Theo was conversing with Miss Elizabeth Bennet and his excessive imbibing last night all seemed to be adding up to one thing. His brother, who had rarely made a misstep in his entire life, may just have fallen for a young woman of whom no one in their family would approve.

Based on his new discoveries, Theo tried to determine

how he might smooth things over. If his brother was truly interested in the lady, then he must be very upset at this moment because of the attention Theo had paid her during their visit.

Theo cleared his throat. "I know you and Aunt Catherine have been urging me to settle down and marry, but I do not believe it would be a prudent course for me until I am better established in my profession. I have my earnings as a barrister, and of course, an allowance from you—for which I am truly grateful—but marriage? That will be out of the question for me for quite some time."

Darcy looked at him with some surprise. Encouraged, Theo continued pursuing his strategy.

"I had a pleasant conversation with Miss Elizabeth Bennet today. She was telling me about Aunt Catherine's prize pig, who got into the garden at the parsonage, and I was explaining to her how Rosings came to have a nearly blind gamekeeper."

Darcy said nothing, but Theo could see the corners of his brother's mouth turning up slightly even though he was pretending not to be paying attention. Just as they reached the wide stone steps to the house, Theo said, "Mrs. Collins seems a genteel lady of good sense, but Collins is another matter altogether."

The image of the man sitting in the holly bush with flowers on his head came to mind. "I hope the cuts and scrapes from his unfortunate tumble do not prove too painful. Despite everything, though, he does seem to have all the right qualifications to be the recipient of our aunt's patronage." Unable to resist, Theo took one of the flowers from the bouquet, balanced it on his head, and grinned at his brother.

Darcy shook his head, "Yes, he was absolutely the perfect choice."

They looked at each other, Theo rolled his eyes, and they began to laugh. Their mirth died down as soon as Lady Catherine's butler opened the door, but for just a

moment, they had shared something other than recrimina-
tions. Theo realized it was the first time they had laughed
together since before Ramsgate.

❧CHAPTER 3

THE BUTLER MET THEM at the door with a look of profound relief. "Her Ladyship has been asking for Mr. Theophilus this last half hour."

Theo laughed as he handed over his hat and gloves. "And no doubt blaming you and everyone else for your inability to produce me instantly for her convenience. Never fear; I will go to her immediately before she abuses anyone else for my absence." He winked at Darcy before striding off toward Lady Catherine's throne room. Even the prospect of a tongue-lashing from his aunt for some imagined sin could not suppress his high spirits. He had not realized how much he had longed for his brother to see him in a light disconnected to disapproval.

Astonishingly, Lady Catherine did not seem to be angered with him either, but instead had remembered several crucial pieces of advice she had not given him that morning. Or perhaps it was several hundred pieces. It certainly took her long enough to tell him her thoughts, but he stopped listening after the first few minutes. As long as he nodded, looked thoughtful, and occasionally agreed she had a point, his aunt was perfectly content to dispense her wisdom. Instead, Theo contemplated all he had learned at the parsonage. Elizabeth Bennet might indeed be just what his brother needed.

Finally, Lady Catherine wound down, and Theo thanked her for her fine advice and condescension. Even Collins could not have done better.

He had not yet exited the room when she said, "And one more thing, Theophilus. Tell your brother I want to see him. The settlement has waited quite long enough."

Theo decided he might just wait a little before giving Darcy that message. It would put him in a foul mood, and he wanted to enjoy a little more pleasant time with his brother first. The settlement had waited for years already; it could hold a little longer.

He found Darcy staring into the fire in the sitting room, a glass of brandy in his hand and a dark look on his face. He narrowed his eyes at the sight of Theo.

Theo's gut clenched. What could William possibly be angry about now? He could not have done anything wrong in the brief time they had been apart. Even if his brother had watched his behavior with their aunt, he had behaved well. But Theo knew that look. He had seen it far too often.

Since there seemed no hope of companionable time together, Theo said, "Our aunt wishes to see *you* now."

Darcy ignored him. "There is a letter for you." His voice dripped scorn as he gestured to the small table by his side.

So that was it. William disapproved of many of his associates, usually for the wrong reasons, but this seemed excessive. How much damage could an unread letter do? He stepped forward to take the envelope, then shook his head when he recognized the handwriting.

This particular one could do a great deal of damage. Why did George Wickham have to decide to write to him at this particular moment and why had his staff forwarded it here? Especially since Theo had made it quite clear to him their friendship had ended.

"You said you were no longer in contact with Wickham." Darcy's tone was accusing.

There was no point in prevaricating. He would rather get this over with quickly. "I have not been in contact with him since Ramsgate, but he persists in sending requests for money. I ignore them."

"I do not believe you."

It was too much, after his earlier hopes that someday he and William might settle their differences. "Believe what you like. You always do, in any case."

William held out his hand. "Give me that letter."

Theo bit down on a scathing retort, then forced himself to speak calmly. "You may be the head of the family, but that does not entitle you to read my personal correspondence."

"So you *do* have something to hide. Give it to me."

Theo fingered the letter. There would be nothing of importance in it. He always threw Wickham's letters away without a response. Well, this time he would not even read it.

"I have nothing to hide, and no need or desire to know what Wickham is about." He held the envelope out, but his brother's satisfied look was more than he could tolerate and, turning quickly, he tossed the unopened letter into the fire.

"Damn you!" Darcy dove for the hearth and snatched it out, but the parchment was already alight, a merry flame dancing from the end of it. Darcy, forced to drop it, stamped on it as he blew on his burned fingers. Smoke curled around his boot.

Theo crossed his arms. "There is an ember on your waistcoat. Playing with fire is dangerous, you know."

Darcy glared at him as he brushed away the offending ember, leaving a black spot behind on the fine green silk.

"You would know. You spend your entire life playing with it." He picked up the charred letter and unfolded it, causing nearly half of it to drop away in ashes. His eyes moved across the remaining portion, then he grew pale.

Despite his resolve to keep his distance, Theo could not help himself. "Is something the matter?"

His brother folded the charred letter with what seemed like unnecessary care. "Nothing *you* would have concern about. It seems I will be leaving for London shortly, and I expect you to remain here and out of mischief."

What had been in the letter? But Theo could hardly ask after having thrown it into the fire. "As you wish." He opened the door and strode out, forcing himself not to look back.

Georgiana knew the minute she opened her eyes that her brother had returned from Rosings. There was something about the way the servants moved through the house. They walked more quickly and spoke in softer tones so as not to disturb the master.

After dressing in a pale pink muslin morning gown, she descended the stairs to investigate. With each step she took down the long stairway, she wished she were older, old enough to wear bolder colors. The pink made her appear even younger than her sixteen years and that was the last thing she wished for these days. William still saw her as a child, but she supposed that was at least partly her own fault for exhibiting such poor judgment last summer over Wickham.

Just as she set her foot on the last step, William came out of his study with a man whom she did not recognize.

"I want to know where he is before the end of the day," her brother was saying. She recognized that look of intensity he wore. Others might not see the worry lurking beneath it, but she could.

"I will do my best, sir, but London is a large city," said

the man.

"That is not my concern. Your job is to find him and..." Darcy stopped mid-sentence when he saw her. He only faltered a moment, but it was long enough for Georgiana to read a world of emotions on his face. Then his mask of control fell back into place.

"Good morning, sweetheart. I will join you in the family dining room in a few minutes."

She sighed. Everyone was always telling her to go somewhere or do something.

As Darcy and the man walked toward the front door, her brother continued speaking but kept his voice so low she could not make out the words. Georgiana considered moving closer to listen but thought better of it and made her way to the family dining room to wait. After rejecting the morning offerings from the kitchen such as eggs and ham, she chose a pastry. It was one of her favorites, and Cook had undoubtedly made it especially for her. In spite of her lack of appetite this morning, she would have to force herself to sample it. The next time she met with Mrs. Cotton, the housekeeper, she would certainly be asked how she liked it so word could be passed to the kitchen.

After one of the footmen had brought her fresh tea, she sat quietly poking at the pastry, waiting for William. It seemed she was always waiting—waiting for one of her brothers or her cousin, waiting for something to happen...waiting for her life to begin. Taking out her frustrations on the pastry, she stabbed it repeatedly with her fork until the delicate layers fell apart leaving flakey debris around on her plate. Just then, William appeared. He kissed her cheek and busied himself at the sideboard fixing a plate for himself.

"I thought you would be at Rosings for another fortnight, William. Has something happened?" she asked, trying to keep her voice even and calm.

"You are up and about early, my dear!"

Another evasion. Georgiana set down her fork and

crossed her arms resolutely. She would have to try again. "What are you doing in Town? I did not expect you for another fortnight." He was always very precise, staying exactly the same number of days at their aunt's, so coming home early alerted her something out of the ordinary had happened.

"Does that mean you are not pleased to see me?" he asked.

"William, I am not a child. I know when something is wrong. Please tell me."

Joining her at the table, Darcy indicated to one of the footmen to pour his coffee. As soon as the young man completed his task, Darcy dismissed him. "Georgiana, we do not discuss private family matters in front of the servants."

"We do not seem to discuss family matters, private or otherwise, at all, let alone in front of anyone," she challenged, looking him straight in the eye. "Now what are you not telling me?"

He frowned at her. "It is nothing. I was called to Town to see to some matters of business. It should only take me a few days, and then I will return to Rosings. I thought perhaps I would take you back with me."

Georgiana could scarcely hide her surprise. "You want me to come with you?"

"I think it would be good for you to spend some time with your brother and me. With Anne, too."

"If that is what you wish," she replied. "Of course, I will come, although you know I do not like listening to Aunt Catherine's endless lectures on comportment." As she spoke, she watched her brother closely. In spite of his reassurances, something still did not seem quite right. He had never asked her to come along with him to Rosings for his annual Easter visit.

"You look surprised," he said between sips of coffee.

"I thought you were planning to spend time with Theo."

"I will be spending time with him, but I would like you there, also. Could you be ready by the end of the week?"

"Yes. How long do you think we might stay?" She absentmindedly added more sugar to her tea and stirred. The clink of her spoon against the china was the only sound in the room.

"I am not certain. About a fortnight, perhaps." He raised an eyebrow in her direction.

"Very well, I shall begin preparing. I will go out today with Mrs. Annesley and purchase some gifts for Aunt Catherine and Anne."

He gave her a disapproving look that carried a hint of something more. Fear? Whatever could he be afraid of?

"No, I do not want you going about on your own!"

Taken aback by the strength of his reaction, she said, "Mrs. Annesley will come with me. I will hardly be alone."

"You are not to go out without me. Do you understand?"

She nodded reluctantly.

"Would tomorrow suit you?" he asked.

"Yes, that would be lovely." Georgiana picked up her fork again, took a bite of the delicate pastry and chewed thoughtfully. She was determined to discover whatever it was he was not telling her.

Darcy found Wickham at the tavern on Chestnut Street just as his agent had described. Rather than confront him in the public rooms, Darcy arranged a private meeting and asked someone to send Wickham to him. Wickham's curiosity and the thought of possible easy money would encourage him to stay and talk instead of simply disappearing. Darcy watched in silence as the bar maid brought in a bottle and two glasses. The minute she turned to leave, Darcy picked up one of the glasses and examined it. Finding it disgustingly smudged and dirty, he drew out his handkerchief and wiped, first around the rim and then over the rest of the glass. He was so absorbed in his task that he did not hear the sound of someone approaching. He started when he heard Wickham chuckle.

"Darcy, Old Man, what are you doing in this part of town with the great unwashed? Surely this little establishment is beneath your notice."

Looking up, he saw Wickham standing in the doorway, leaning indolently against the doorframe. He did not bother to stand or speak but merely gestured to the chair opposite him. Seeing a bottle of brandy on the table, Wickham's look brightened, and he sidled over. After settling himself, he poured himself out a healthy measure of the amber liquid.

"Are you not drinking?" Wickham asked.

Darcy's response was to push his glass, now much cleaner, across the table. He began without preamble. "You will leave Georgiana alone. I do not want you within miles of her. Do you understand me? A different town altogether would be satisfactory; a different country even more preferable. At the very least, I trust your stay in Town is fleeting. Why are you not with your regiment?"

"All officers are permitted their share of time away; not something you would appreciate, being without a profession, is it Darcy?" Wickham smirked. "Besides, whatever makes you think I would have anything to do with Georgiana, especially after Ramsgate?"

Without a word, Darcy laid the charred and tattered remains of the letter to Theo on the table. Wickham went slightly pale, and his eyes slid away. Clearly, he recognized it.

Recovering quickly, he laughed. "Oh, that little jest? It was nothing. Only a way to tease your brother. He and I often exchange such…"

Wickham's words were stifled when in one motion, Darcy reached across the table and grabbed his old enemy by the cravat.

"I do not find it amusing in the slightest," Darcy

snarled in Wickham's face.

"Well, it was not intended for you, now was it? Is Theo so under your control that you read his post now?"

Darcy yanked at the man's cravat again, bringing them almost eye to eye over the table. Deep in his heart, Darcy felt a flash of satisfaction when Wickham's eyes widened with alarm.

"Let me go!" Although Wickham put his hands up to break free, he was unsuccessful as Darcy held on with an iron grip. "There is no need for violence! See here, you have made me spill some of this lovely brandy."

Darcy's civility had worn paper-thin. He wanted nothing more than to make Wickham hurt—for mistreating Georgiana, for deceiving his father about his true nature, for stealing Theo's friendship from him. Releasing his hold on the cravat as suddenly as he had taken it, he pushed Wickham away, causing him to fall back into the chair at a strange angle and with such force that for a moment it looked as if the chair might topple over backwards. After scrambling to regain his balance, Wickham's fingers again went immediately to his cravat. Darcy's keen eyes did not miss the way the other man's hands were shaking as he straightened his clothing.

"I thought you invited me here for a *friendly* chat," Wickham said, clearly trying to cover his discomfort.

"I am not your friend," Darcy said flatly.

"Yes, but Theo still is. Some people are more loyal than others."

Darcy stabbed a finger at the letter on the table. "Is this the kind of letter one friend writes to another? Does a friend threaten a *friend's* sister?"

"I told you it was a joke. I like to tease Theo. It is so easy to get him riled these days." Then under his breath, he added, "But apparently not as easy as it is to excite you."

Darcy stiffened as he heard a rough sound emanating from deep inside himself. Had he truly just snarled at Wickham? All the anger and frustration, all the wrongs

Wickham had perpetrated on his family seemed to rush at him with such rapidity that he was almost dizzy. He shook his head to clear it and knew he was dangerously close to laying his hands on the man again.

Wickham took a large swallow of brandy, and that familiar smug smile spread across his face again. So apparently while Darcy felt himself unraveling, Wickham was regrouping, his bravado returning. Darcy, usually cool and calm in most any situation, fought for control.

"You still owe me for keeping silent about Georgie's near elopement. It would not do to have any rumors about her out there bandied around, now would it? Ruin her chance at a good match on the marriage mart."

"I owe you? I would say it is the other way around. You should be glad I did not let my cousin hunt you down and run you through with his sword. He was very keen to do it, too."

Wickham's eyes narrowed. "We both know you would never allow that. Fortunately for me, you are too...too *honorable*." He spat out that last word as if it left a bad taste in his mouth.

"I think you might be rather unpleasantly surprised at what I will do to keep you away from my sister. Now you listen while I tell you how this will go." Darcy stood and looked down at Wickham. "You will keep away, far away from Georgiana, or I will find some way to have you transported. And you will cease all contact with Theo." When Wickham looked skeptical, Darcy added, "You know I do not make idle threats. Do you really want to risk it?"

Wickham leaned back in his chair and lazily raised the glass to his lips. He actually had the temerity to look bored. "Whatever you say, Darcy." He took another sip. "This is really good stuff. Did you already pay for the bottle? If you did, I will just take it back to my room and ponder my sins."

Darcy grunted in disgust and made his way out of the

room, through the tavern and back into the street. Good Lord, he could not wait to be back home so he could change his clothes and take a bath. The encounter had left him feeling positively unclean. When the footman dutifully opened the door, he gathered his coat about him and slipped into the vehicle. Once inside where no one could see him, he put his head in his hands. Threats did not seem to work very well on Wickham. He had to find some other way to protect his family from further damage at that man's hands.

The next morning at breakfast, Lady Catherine announced her intention of sending a messenger to the parsonage to issue an invitation for tea for the afternoon.

"It is not the first time," she stated. "I have graciously invited the Collins's and their guests already, but while Darcy was here, I did not require their company."

"I am sorry you do not find me entertaining enough, Aunt."

"As you well know, I hardly see anything of you. You are either risking your life riding madly about the estate on that great brute of a horse or you are sulking in the library. For the life of me, I cannot imagine why you have an interest in those dusty old books of mine. I was informed by one of the maids that you even took a whole stack of books off the shelf and were searching through them as though your life depended on it."

So the Old Bat's maids were carrying tales, were they? Well, his life *had* depended on it, or at least his peace of mind. Fortunately, Cousin Richard had responded to his recent letter and told him the name of the volume in which he had drawn yet another incriminating cartoon of their aunt, and he had been able to put the issue to rest.

"You have a very valuable collection, Aunt," he said.

How was it that Lady Catherine always drove him to utter barefaced lies, like a boy of eight caught stealing a custard tart?

"I would have thought you would be pleased to see me engaged in harmless pursuits."

His aunt gave a most unladylike snort. "Your behavior has certainly improved since the last time you were here, but I am not such a fool as to believe that you now prefer books to other entertainments. Besides, I do not approve of bookishness. Too much reading can have a detrimental effect on one's health. It can make one excitable."

How fortunate it was that not everyone agreed with this perception of reading, or the human race would not have advanced beyond its primitive origins. However, this was a perfect opportunity to appease his aunt. She had handed it to him on a silver platter.

"Perhaps, now that you mention it, I have been spending too much time indoors with dusty books. It cannot be good for my health, particularly since the weather is improving." It occurred to him that he could kill two birds with one stone. "I could call on the parsonage if you wish, Aunt, and give them your message. If I cannot entertain you, at least I could be useful."

"You will do no such thing," said Lady Catherine, severely. "I will not have you playing errand boy. It is quite beneath your dignity. But since you are being so obliging, I have another task for you."

Theo groaned. He could not imagine what it was, but he doubted he would like it.

"I hope it can wait until after I take Theseus for a ride. He will break down the stable door if he is not exercised."

"Mark my words, that brute will be the death of you," said Lady Catherine. "Do not come running to me to say you are sorry when you have been tossed to the ground with your neck broken."

"I doubt I will be in any condition to do so, Aunt Catherine."

"Enough of your insolence!" said Lady Catherine. "Go. But be back before luncheon. I will be expecting you."

Things were not looking promising. Not at all.

The hours until the guests arrived passed painfully slowly. Not only was Theo impatient to find out more about Miss Bennet, but since there was little to keep him occupied, his mind dwelled too often on Wickham and his letter. What had he written about? It could not solely be a demand for funds, as was his wont, for that alone would not draw his brother so rapidly to London. Had it been an attempt at blackmail, an underhanded way of convincing Theo to lend him the money he had requested? What harm might the bounder threaten if not complied with? Had Theo done the right thing in allowing Darcy to go to Town in his place?

As if his brother had given him any choice in the matter! Obviously, Theo was still the bad boy, and Darcy did not trust him enough to deal with the problem. Would he ever redeem himself in his brother's eyes? At this moment, the chances of that happening were about as good as the chances of Theseus winning a race at Haymarket. Theseus was a fine specimen, but he could never compete against the racing thoroughbreds.

Theo was feeling decidedly glum. The heavy chains tying him to Rosings seemed to be growing shorter and heavier by the hour.

To make matters worse, his aunt had called him to the drawing room in the afternoon and made him read some ghastly book of sermons. Lady Catherine was clearly deluded enough to think that they would be instructive, but since after two or three sentences he had been bored to tears, he no longer paid any attention to what he was reading, allowing his thoughts to drift.

When the footman announced the arrival of the party from Hunsford, Theo had to stop himself from jumping up and dancing a jig.

Even prisoners were allowed out for the occasional

walk.

He rose and, putting as much space between himself and his aunt as possible, sought out Miss Bennet's vivacious figure. The sight of her was like a whiff of fresh air in the moldy confines of his aunt's living room.

First, though, he was forced to give his attention to Collins' kowtowing. Theo's good humor returned as he heard the clergyman's long-winded expressions of pleasure at being invited to spend time in their august company. Having already discovered Collins to be an unintended source of entertainment when the clergyman had become entangled in the holly bush at the parsonage, Theo was all anticipation that something similar would happen today. However, for the moment at least, nothing untoward did.

Once the irritating parson had finished expressing his effusions, Theo turned his attention to the rest of the party. Mrs. Collins was as he expected—politely deferential. Her sister, Miss Lucas, appeared quite overwhelmed in Lady Catherine's presence and hardly raised her gaze from the ground, despite Theo's attempts to put her at ease.

Miss Bennet alone of the group did not seem at all awed by his aunt, which confirmed Theo's positive opinion of her. She was not easily intimidated, and she clearly delighted in anything ridiculous. Her eyes danced as she gave him her hand in greeting and he laughed back.

"Any mishaps with your bonnet on the way here?" he asked.

Elizabeth's eyes sparkled as she shook her head, the chestnut curls framing her face bouncing merrily.

"None at all, I assure you," she said. "I was particularly careful to hold onto it, knowing you would not be available to come to my rescue."

Theo had not intended to flirt with the young lady he suspected his brother admired, but he really could not help it, not when she was looking at him expectantly, a mischievous smile hovering on her lips. The words slipped out of their own accord.

"You have only to say the word, Miss Bennet. I would climb the highest tree, if it meant earning your gratitude."

She pressed her lips together, trying not to laugh. "I do not believe there are many tall trees at Rosings, and even if there were, I do not think my bonnet capable of sailing quite so high."

He was about to answer when Lady Catherine turned a disapproving eye on him. Normally, he would have ignored it, but under the circumstances it was a timely reminder. He was not supposed to engage with Miss Bennet on his own behalf but on behalf of his brother. His only purpose in talking to her was to discover as much as possible about her.

For once, he was glad of his aunt's intervention.

"I see that you, like your brother, have a prior acquaintance with Miss Bennet," said Lady Catherine.

He opened his mouth to respond to the implied reproof in her tone—though why a prior acquaintance was something to feel guilty about, he could not fathom—but Miss Bennet forestalled him.

"Not at all, Lady Catherine," said the lady, oblivious to the fact that his aunt did not look happy at being contradicted, "I did not have the pleasure of being introduced to Mr. Theophilus until two days ago, when Mr. Darcy himself introduced his brother to me."

Theo noted that she did not mention their earlier encounter.

"That was when Mr. Darcy condescended to visit our humble abode to offer me and Mrs. Collins his congratulations," said Mr. Collins, "and to express his pleasure at my fortunate choice of a bride. "Mr. Collins," he said. "You are to be congratulated—."

"Yes, yes," Lady Catherine interrupted, "unfortunately, my nephew has been called away to London. However, he will not stay long. He is excessively devoted to me and will wish to return as soon as possible."

Theo watched Miss Bennet closely to see the impact this information had on her, but she gave no indication of the news interesting her, one way or the other.

So is that the way the wind blows, then? Is the lady indifferent? Poor William. No wonder he was in such a state.

Theo found it hard to believe. True, his brother was arrogant and abrupt at times, but that did not seem to stop the ladies from fawning over him. In fact, Theo could think of few occasions in which his brother was not being actively pursued by some young lady or the other. It was quite blatantly unfair. Theo himself had his share of ladies who expressed interest, but that was because he made every effort to charm them. William, however, did nothing at all. His brother's ten thousand a year helped, of course, but it was not simply that. Viewed objectively, Theo supposed his brother was quite handsome, but Darcy seemed to possess some other mysterious quality that appealed to the ladies.

Yet here was Miss Bennet, seemingly indifferent to his brother. Of course, it was too early to tell. She could simply be very good at concealing her feelings. He tried to remember if she had looked around the room in search of his brother when she had first entered, but unfortunately he had been too caught up in conversing with her to notice.

Well, if he wanted to help his brother, Theo had to discover how she felt. It was really most fortuitous that he had come to Rosings with Darcy at the very same time as Miss Bennet was visiting. Fate had practically thrown the young lady into his lap. Metaphorically, of course. Determining the level of her interest in his brother was a task which required the utmost delicacy if he was to avoid revealing Darcy's attachment, but Theo was something of an expert on affairs of the heart.

He cast a quick glance around. This was as good a moment as any to begin. Lady Catherine was engaged in conversation with Mr. Collins and his party. Theo would have Miss Bennet to himself, for a few minutes at least.

"I am all agog, Miss Bennet. How did you come to meet my brother?"

She threw him an amused glance, almost as if she knew what he was up to.

Tread carefully, Theo. Miss Bennet is no fool.

"You may well ask that question, since it seems your brother is not fond of making new acquaintances. I was introduced to him at an assembly, through a friend of his. Do you know Mr. Bingley?"

"Yes, he has been a particular friend of my brother's since their school days."

She frowned. "Is not Mr. Darcy older than Mr. Bingley?"

"It is common at boarding schools to have older boys take charge of younger ones."

"Did *you* have an older boy as protector?"

"Yes, I did." He shied away from the memory. Wickham had been the older boy. "Not all of us are so fortunate, however."

"You think Mr. Bingley fortunate? Perhaps it was the other way. Perhaps it was your brother's good fortune to be associated with such an amiable companion."

Was it possible Miss Bennet admired Bingley rather than William? She certainly seemed to think highly of Darcy' friend. Theo pounced on the opportunity to interrogate her.

"Is Mr. Bingley a particular acquaintance of yours?"

Miss Bennet's countenance took on a more guarded expression. *Aha.* He was on the right track.

"I have not known him for long, but I was fortunate enough to stay at his country estate—Netherfield—for four days."

She was being evasive. He sensed Miss Bennet would not make it easy for him to extract information. She was too quick-witted to be fooled into any inadvertent admission.

He decided to change the direction of his questioning.

"I am surprised my brother attended a local assembly. Normally, he avoids such situations like the plague."

"I assure you, Mr. Darcy made it abundantly clear he did not wish to be there. In fact, he might as well not have been, because he refused to dance with any of the young ladies present, other than with Mr. Bingley's sisters. I wonder that he made the effort to put in an appearance at all! In fact, he later implied quite openly he considered dancing akin to savagery."

A bark of laughter escaped Theo. "My brother said that? He must have been in a particularly disagreeable mood. He does not easily express his opinions to strangers. Darcy is generally rather shy. It takes him some time before he feels comfortable in a social situation with people he does not know."

He was on the verge of sharing his nickname for his brother—*Prince William*—when he thought bitterly of yesterday's letter from Wickham. He had relished when Theo had used the nickname and had used it himself openly. With disgust, Theo realized it had become forever tainted by its association with that man, and he would never find it a source of amusement again. More was the pity, because he sensed Miss Bennet would have appreciated it.

"I detected no shyness in him," said Elizabeth, readily. "His attitude was one of superiority. It was clear he found the company beneath his notice."

Though she said it in a half-laughing manner, there was a degree of intensity on Elizabeth's countenance that surprised Theo, and no mistaking the sharp gleam in her eye. Had William said something in particular to her to trigger an aversion?

Whatever it was, one thing was unfortunately clear. The lady did not think favorably of his brother.

That being the case, Theo was at a loss. Would it serve any purpose for him to make a concerted effort to interest Elizabeth in his brother? There were ways he could nudge her into thinking better of him, but would that amount to love? It was not unusual for many of their class to marry without their feelings being engaged, but such marriages were usually arranged because they were beneficial to both parties. Charming as Elizabeth was, it was by no means certain that marrying her would be beneficial to his brother.

Theo caught the direction of his thoughts and almost smiled at the irony. Only two days ago, Theo had argued with Darcy in favor of love as a foundation for marriage. Now, he was not so certain. What could a one-sided love bring to a marriage other than pain? If Elizabeth did not care for his brother, surely it would be undesirable for Darcy to be shackled to a woman who did not return his regard?

Would it not be better to find a way to discourage Darcy from his interest in Miss Bennet altogether? Although in his experience, it was impossible to convince anyone in love to change his or her course.

It was deuced difficult to decide what to do under the circumstances, but then, he did not really *have* to do anything. He could wait for a response from Cousin Richard, to whom he had written asking him to unearth what he could about Miss Bennet's family. Perhaps the Colonel would discover some crucial information about her circumstances. Meanwhile, there was no harm in furthering his acquaintance with the young lady. He would discover more about the type of person William had developed a *tendre* for and, at the same time, relieve some of the boredom of his visit, for if there was one thing that was certain in this rather muddled business, Elizabeth Bennet was more amusing company than his aunt.

As though the Old Bat guessed his intentions, Lady Catherine chose that very moment to call Elizabeth to her side.

"Come sit by me, Miss Bennet. I cannot converse with you from across the room. I wish to ask you a few questions."

The lady threw Theo a laughing glance and rose to her feet, her teacup showing its protest by clattering loudly against its saucer. Theo wanted badly to laugh, but under the withering glance of Lady Catherine, he managed to smother it.

"Should I submit calmly to the inquisition," murmured Elizabeth, as she stepped past him, "or should I show some resistance?"

"I believe submission might be the best course of action for the moment, Miss Bennet. It is too soon to organize the forces of resistance."

"Then you must promise to come to my rescue shortly," she said, setting her cup down firmly on the table.

"What are you saying to Miss Bennet, nephew? You are delaying her. I wish her to sit here. I wish to speak to her."

There was more to her imperious tone than her usual desire to take charge of the situation. He knew the Old Bat well enough. She suspected him of conducting a flirtation with Elizabeth, and she meant to prevent him.

"I am sorry, Aunt. Miss Bennet was reluctant to relinquish her tea." Yet another barefaced lie. Staying at Rosings was not good for his heavenly credit.

"And so she should be," said Lady Catherine. "The tea in this household is of the very highest quality. At least it shows she has good taste."

"Everything in this household is of the very highest quality, Lady Catherine," interjected Mr. Collins. "When I was in Meryton, I took every opportunity to extol the grandeur of Rosings and to impress a sense of its magnificence upon those who have never had the fortune of seeing it. I was able to describe at length the refinement of your drawing rooms, the fine proportions, the ornaments and, in particular, the exquisite quality of the fireplace, but I feel mere words cannot do it justice."

Theo could barely restrain himself from snorting at this blatant sycophantic behavior, but his aunt lapped it all up.

His gaze met Elizabeth's across the room. It was brimming with laughter. He felt in her a kindred soul. *She* at least understood what it was like to be forced to endure day after day of Lady Catherine's presence. *She* did not condemn him as Darcy did.

He turned away. He could not allow himself to become susceptible to Miss Bennet's charm, simply because he was languishing of tedium in the countryside. He was tempted, of course. Oh, why could William not see that forcing him to spend so much time at Rosings was not conducive to harmony, but rather led to the opposite? How could William think that removing him from Town and forcing him to spend an extended time at Rosings would temper his ;wildness,' when in fact it made him quite desperate with boredom? Being inactive was abhorrent to him, but even more so now, left to his own devices, not knowing what had been in that damned letter to cause his brother to head back to Town directly.

Frustration mounted inside him. Everything seemed to be conspiring to hem him in, and he knew himself all too well. So far Theo had towed the line, because he felt a need to atone for his past mistakes with Darcy and to attempt to bridge the chasm that had sprung up between them. He knew there was a great deal in his past to forgive. Lord knew he could never forgive himself, not for what had happened to Sebastian, not for his disastrous friendship with Wickham, and not for the carelessness that had almost destroyed Georgiana at Ramsgate.

He had much to answer for, but he did not think Rosings was the best place to do it.

All said and done, the wisest thing for him to do at this moment would be to take Theseus and ride as far away from here as possible, and as soon as the guests departed, he would do just that.

CHAPTER 4

THEO'S SKIN CRAWLED, itching as if he wore a wool coat on a hot day with no shirt. Only motion, rapid motion, would ease his suffering now.

Just how many months could it take to saddle a bloody horse? Next time, he would do it himself. The groom finally brought Theseus. Theo took to his back without a word.

Theseus understood—he always did. The glorious creature sensed his mood and quickly went from a walk to a trot. At least all the fine grounds around Rosings were good for something.

Wind, with just a hint of spring chill, buffeted his face. Road dust scoured his cheeks. A passing crow laughed at him, ghastly bird. At least he was free—free from the oppression of his aunt, the expectations of polite company, and from the—no—wait, that would never leave him.

Guilt would be his constant companion. Even Theseus could not outrun his most powerful, ever-present companion.

No matter how many insisted Sebastian's death was not his fault, it was he, favorite big brother, Theo, who taught

63

Sebastian to dive off the rocks. Had he never learned, Sebastian would still be with him, tormenting Prince Will—Fitzwilliam with him and their mother would not have withered away in grief.

He swallowed back the familiar bile, the one that rose every time he thought of that day by the stream, his younger brother, his mother...

Theseus increased his pace along the open field.

...and Georgiana. He gritted his teeth against the burning pain that filled his belly. His dear, innocent little sister. How he had failed her! Had he just danced that set with her instead of finishing that deuced game of cards. Had he not suggested Wickham as a partner, they would never have—

Enough! Enough! He blew out a labored breath. This path of self-recrimination had been trod many times over and it never led anywhere useful. All those things were in the past and nothing, absolutely nothing he might do, would ever change them.

He guided Theseus through a small copse and along a smooth path by a stream—the one where he first met Elizabeth Bennet.

How was it Darcy managed to pick the one woman in England who would not immediately throw herself at his feet? Either she was a fool, or exactly the sort of woman *Prince*... no, not that... the sort Fitzwilliam needed to disabuse him of his self-important musings and make him sympathetic to those lesser creatures around him.

Her fine eyes certainly suggested the latter.

He ducked a small branch that strayed too near his face. The past was already written, but he might chart the course for the future. He would keep Darcy from losing the first woman in his acquaintance worth winning.

Theo laughed heartily. That was exactly the thing, the good turn his brother most needed, though he might never admit it to anyone. No one else could give Darcy the assistance he did not even know he needed. Theo would help his brother woo—and win—the lady. Whether or not Darcy was ever grateful for it, Theo would—

A woman screamed.

Theseus skittered and jumped. The back of Theo's head collided with something very hard. The world dimmed, and he slipped from the saddle.

Pain.

His head throbbed. His ankle…and dear God! His shoulder! Shooting pain centered in his shoulder and shot through his torso. His muscles clamped down against it, driving the agony deeper. He clutched his left arm.

"Mr. Theophilus!"

Elizabeth Bennet? What the devil was she doing here?

"I am so sorry, sir. I fear I startled your horse."

He groaned and rolled to his right. Searing pain tore through his upper body. Were those horrible, high pitched cries coming from his lips? What a lovely way to comport himself in front of a lady.

"Where are you injured?"

"Shoulder." He pulled his arm tight to his chest and rolled up, hissing through his teeth until he sat straight. How was he to get back to Rosings when he could barely sit up?

She knelt in the dirt beside him. "I fear it may be dislocated. I must remove your coat to see."

A string of invectives fell from his mouth as she eased the coat down and off. Poor girl, she had probably never heard such language, but she was merciful enough to give no sign of it now.

He glanced at his left shoulder. The unnatural angles of the joint twisted his gut. He had never cast up his accounts before a lady, but today might be the first.

"I can reset the joint. It is not a pleasant thing, but it will relieve the pain and the sooner the thing is done the less likely there will be permanent damage."

"Do it—quickly," he muttered through gritted teeth. For all his mishaps and injuries, nothing, absolutely nothing compared to this agony.

"My father has put his shoulder out a number of times. The surgeon showed me what to do." She scooted behind him.

Would she simply stop talking and do whatever it was—*now*?

Elizabeth slid her hand into his armpit, hard, strong and excruciating. He groaned and bit his lip until he tasted blood.

"Press your arm to your side." Thankfully, she guided him. He could not manage the simple movement alone. Another high pitched squawk escaped. How humiliating!

"Right. Now, just a moment here." She rotated his lower arm away from his body.

He felt more than heard the resounding pop that roiled his stomach. The scream that followed was just a reflex. He hunched over, balanced on his right hand, panting to quell the churning in his belly. When the wave passed and he could breathe normally again, he did so without the searing, blinding misery of a moment before.

"I thought I would never draw a proper breath again. How can I thank you?"

"Do not be so excited just yet. You must rest that shoulder and do very little with it. It should be tied up to support it, but I have nothing—"

"My cravat? Will that do?" He fumbled with the knot.

"Yes, I believe it will."

He pulled at the knot with his right hand. Normally, he could work it loose in a single fluid motion. Not so today when he had a lovely audience and a shredded dignity to repair. His hand trembled and stubbornly refused to obey his command.

"Ah, sir?" She bit her lower lip.

Had she any idea what an enticing maneuver that was? Had he not already settled that Miss Bennet was for his brother or been in so much pain, he might have done something very, very foolish.

"Are you in need of assistance?" Her cheeks flushed a pleasing rose.

How could a woman be so bloody attractive at a moment like this? "I am afraid so. It seems my valet has done a particularly good job on this knot…"

"My father often has the same trouble after he injures his shoulder." She reached for his cravat.

Her fingertips brushed his jaw. How lovely and cool they felt. One could easily imagine—but one should not. One definitely should not!

"There, I believe I have the knot out." She tugged the cravat and it slid easily around his collar.

He closed his eyes. This scene—well some of it at least—was the stuff of heady daydreams. Torture! Pure torture!

She knotted the cravat into a sling and adjusted it behind his neck, no hint of discomfiture upon her face. Never had he left a woman so unaffected, yet she was calm and steady in crisis, knowledgeable and quick to act. Just like his brother. How ironic, a woman as quick to rescue Darcy's family as Fitzwilliam himself, yet she had little interest in a man who could truly appreciate her nature.

"Is that comfortable?" she asked.

"Yes, as much as is possible under the circumstances. That is a most useful skill you have developed."

"My father has deemed it so as well, although, all things considered, I would prefer not to be called upon to use it. Please forgive me for startling your horse."

"I should have been paying better attention."

"You seemed distracted when you left tea. Can you stand?" She pushed to her feet.

"I do not know. The ankle hurts, though not like my shoulder."

"I wish that were a more reliable gauge of your injury."

He stretched his leg tentatively. The dull ache intensified, but not into the severe sharpness that heralded a serious injury.

"That looks hopeful." She cocked her head and lifted her eyebrow in an expression so like his brother that Theo laughed.

"Are you well, sir?"

"I am, forgive me. Your expression, it reminded me of Darcy."

"Indeed. How singular." She offered her shoulder to help him stand.

On his feet, he tottered a bit, the world somewhat wobbly around him. Thankfully, it soon settled into a dull ache and exhaustion.

"If you think you can get in the saddle, I can lead—"

"You, lead Theseus?"

"You can ride him on your own?"

"Ah, no, I doubt it."

"Then what alternative is there? If I leave to get help, the moment I am out of your sight, you will be on his back trying to ride and doing further injury to yourself and quite possibly your horse." Elizabeth planted her hands on her hips and seemed to grow several hand spans taller, just as his mother had when she scolded.

He snickered; it just would not be silenced.

"Laughing at me again—"

"You look and sound like my mother."

"First your brother, now your mother. Shall I take on the likeness of every member of your family?"

"I see nothing of Aunt Catherine in you."

"That is a great relief."

Oh God, it hurt to laugh, but he could not stop. He leaned against Theseus' shoulder, peals of laughter shaking his body.

"We must get you back to—the parsonage is closer, but Rosings is more—"

"Stuffy and prone to lecture." He snickered.

"I was going to say comfortable."

Another spasm of laughter gripped him, groans hidden amidst the guffaws.

"If you will oblige me and try to mount, your horse and I shall get you to the parsonage."

Mounting his horse after the celebration the night he was admitted to the Inn of Courts was far easier to accomplish than getting in the saddle today. Four attempts! What kind of clod took four attempts to get on a horse? He gripped the saddle with his right hand and panted heavily. He had run from Pemberley to Lambton and back with less effort.

"Are you ready?" She took Theseus' reins.

"Are you certain you can manage—"

She patted the horse's cheek. "Quite sure. Just because I like to walk does not preclude a comfort with horses." She encouraged Theseus into a walk. "When one must share the horses between farm and carriage, and with four sisters besides, walking is often the most agreeable option."

Each of the horse's gentle steps pounded his body like a full on gallop. How far was it to the parsonage? "I cannot imagine a household of five sisters. Are they all very much like you?"

"Are you and your brother very much alike? You laugh quite freely while your brother, I should think, never so indulges."

"There are those that consider him rather somber."

"I should be surprised to hear there are those who do not."

A laugh welled up, but he squelched it, his balance on Theseus precarious. He would not fall from his horse twice in one day. "You might be surprised. He has his unguarded moments in which he can be quite easy—with his friend, Bingley, or our cousin, Colonel Fitzwilliam."

"Indeed? I would not call those unguarded moments easy."

What had William done? "I take it you witnessed such a

moment?"

She shook her head. "I should not have spoken so. Please—"

"No, I must and you must indulge me, if only out of deference for my weakened condition."

"It is really of no matter. I do not wish to discuss something so improper—"

"If you remember it this long, then it is of consequence. My brother is apt to give offense wherever he goes. He is not mean-spirited by any imagination, but he has shocking little sense for how he appears to others. It is his greatest flaw, in an otherwise impeccable character."

"Indeed, I thought it was that once his good opinion was lost, it was lost forever."

Great heavens! "He said that?"

She tipped her head.

"And he speculated upon your flaws as well?"

"I am apt to willfully misunderstand people." She touched her chest and arranged her face to look far too much like William.

Was she trying to make him laugh and disgrace himself again? "He is socially inept in a society that needs the lubrication of pretty words and insincere speeches."

"They are helpful in their place, I suppose."

"But as inaccessible to my brother as it is a lame man to run. Try as he might, his best efforts are halting and limping."

She glanced over her shoulder at him, tongue in cheek. She was considering his words, mulling them carefully, but her eyes were unconvinced, even guarded. Blasted, foolish man! William must have gone beyond his normal bounds of awkwardness. "I take it then, he said something rather awful to you."

"Not *to* me."

"But in your hearing."

She nodded.

When? William went with Bingley just after Ramsgate.

That would surely account for a foul mood and unguarded speech. He could have muttered any number of unpleasantries in a fit of pique. Apparently William did not exhaust his supply on Theo.

"Was it your appearance he maligned or your character?"

"I have not had the pleasure of hearing him opine on my character."

It would probably be easier to repair the situation had it been that. A woman's vanity was fragile and difficult to repair. "Was he complimentary to anyone?"

"No. I believe he found our entire company equally disagreeable."

"Would it make a difference if I told you he came to Meryton following a…a…grievous situation in our family. A disaster had been narrowly averted, but he was deeply taxed by the entire affair."

"So you say he was of no mind for company at the time?"

"Not at all." He pressed his temple, head pounding in time to Theseus steps.

"Then he should not have come."

"Probably not, but Bingley insisted he needed Darcy's help with the property and, with Bingley's gregarious nature, I am sure he thought new company the best remedy for melancholy."

"I take it you agree, company is an excellent remedy?"

He grimaced. This woman was far too perceptive.

"You were amongst those who faced your brother's disapproval?"

"Yes…but it was not undeserved." His cheeks flushed.

"You have lost his good opinion?"

Gah! How had she turned the conversation?

"And you wish it restored."

"Yes," he mumbled. Why did he answer such an inquiry?

"Why does it matter to you?"

"My brother is…a good man, whom I respect. He has been a rock to our family in difficult days. I…owe him a great deal…and admire him." A sizable lump in his throat silenced him, thankfully. Where had that speech come from?

"His good opinion is worth the earning?" she asked in that same maddeningly innocent tone.

He grunted something affirmative sounding. No wonder William was on his way to Bedlam over her.

"Perhaps you should tell him that. If he is the man you believe him to be, I think he would be honored to hear it." Elizabeth glanced back at him and blinked as if she had merely commented upon the weather.

Vexing woman! She knew full well the weight of what she suggested. He had never said anything of the like to William—they never shared such things. It was not done.

Could she be right?

He pinched the bridge of his nose. What an entirely disruptive, discomposing woman, this Elizabeth Bennet. She had just managed to blithely cut to the heart of the matter and insert herself into the middle of an affair no one else dared venture into. Even if she did not know it, she understood William and Theo like only one other—their mother—had.

She must marry William, it had to be. So great a need required a great sacrifice. He licked his lips. "I will tell him—"

She looked at him, eyes wide, a lovely smile blossoming.

"On one condition."

"That the sun move backward in the sky or the seas part before your command?"

He laughed and immediately regretted it. "No, nothing quite so dramatic. I will tell him, if you will give him another chance."

"Excuse me? Another chance?" Her wide eyes and dropped jaw were a picture to treasure.

How nice to finally regain the upper hand! "Forgive him his trespass on your feelings and allow him a fresh start. Give him an opportunity to show you a better side of himself."

"Why? What you propose seems hardly a fair trade, a very small favor that hardly balances—"

"Let us just say, I do not like knowing you are out there in the world and thinking ill of him."

She chuckled and shook her head. "You are an unusual man, Mr. Theophilus Darcy. But, in the interest of restoring your filial harmony, I will make every effort to do as you ask."

If his head—and every other part of his body—did not ache so badly, he would have urged Theseus into a joyous gallop.

Darcy pressed his heels into his horse's side. The familiar borders of Rosings were finally visible on the horizon. Bless Richard for arranging his obligations so he could accompany Georgiana to Rosings later in the week, enabling Darcy to leave within an hour of receiving Collins' Express describing Theo's injuries.

The annoying little parson had a penchant for exaggeration to be sure, but he said that Theo was not grievously injured from his fall the previous afternoon. What did a vicar know about serious injury? The ankle and shoulder were troublesome to be sure, but Theo also struck his head. Darcy's gut knotted tighter and he pressed his horse for more speed. He lost one brother to a head injury. Dear God, let him not lose another!

How could Theo be so careless, so foolish? That horse—no, no he could not allow his anger to run loose in foolish thoughts. Theseus was a fine horse, and Theo a finer horseman. Had Darcy even told him that? No, he had not—nor any number of other encouraging things. He rarely spoke anything but criticism to his younger brother.

Why?

Theo's reckless irresponsibility had caused so much—

Darcy gulped back the lump in his throat. Theo was not truly to blame for anything that had happened. It was so much easier to blame Theo than delicate Georgiana or departed Sebastian. Theo was there to weather his disapproval and rebuke. But it was neither right nor fair for Theo to bear the brunt of Darcy's anger against himself.

A ragged cry of anguish tore from his throat. There was the terrible truth of it. Darcy blamed himself for everything:. Sebastian's death, Georgiana's near elopement, even Theo's near dismissal from school. Only Theo was strong enough to bear the full force of Darcy's turmoil.

He needed to tell Theo that, before any more tragedy could befall the Darcy family and leave those words forever unsaid.

Darcy knocked on the parsonage door, heart thundering in his ears. Collins himself opened the door so quickly he must have been sitting in the foyer waiting.

"Mr. Darcy, welcome to my humble abode. We are so very grateful that you have graced us with your presence." He bowed and ushered Darcy inside.

"Yes, yes. Thank you. My brother—"

"He has had the best of care. The surgeon just left, the very man my esteemed patroness, Lady Catherine de Bourgh recommended—"

"He is doing well, Mr. Darcy." Elizabeth peeked over Collins's shoulder.

Had more welcome news ever been borne by a lovelier herald? He stepped past Collins. "Please, tell me everything."

"Indeed, sir." She gestured toward the parlor.

He shrugged off his coat and doffed his hat, handing them to a waiting Collins. Had he not been a vicar, he would have made an excellent butler.

Elizabeth sat on the edge of the settee nearest the fire. Darcy pulled another chair as close as he dared. She peered into his eyes, studious lines across her brow.

"I do not know what Mr. Collins said in his letter, but I feel quite certain your brother will fully recover. I saw the accident and—"

"Saw the accident?"

"I fear I was at fault. I was walking and startled his horse causing his fall. He struck his head on a branch, but he was only dazed for a moment. He dislocated his shoulder when he fell. That was the more serious injury. I was able to reset it—"

"You?"

"My father has suffered that same injury several times and our local surgeon taught me to assist my father."

"We are deeply in your debt, Miss Bennet." She was so close. Her lavender scent draped around him. Her eyes were filled with such concern, compassion…All the cross, ill-tempered things he had said to her flooded his mind. He ran a finger along the inside of his cravat. "I…I…said some things…in Hertfordshire…that I am not proud of…" He clutched his temples. Blast the slowness of his tongue.

"I appreciate that you recognize it, sir."

His head snapped up and he stared slack jawed. What did she mean by that? Was it absolution or condemnation of his abhorrent manners?

"I…I…" he stammered. So like his tongue to fail him when he most needed it to craft appealing words.

"I believe I should take you to your brother."

Getting to her feet, Elizabeth brushed past Darcy as he stood up and led the way out into the flag-stoned hallway, speaking to him over her shoulder as she walked.

"It was the surgeon's advice your brother remain here last night to rest; the parsonage is of more than adequate size, but with myself and Miss Lucas as guests, Mrs. Collins had no option but to accommodate him in her own sitting room."

She stopped outside a pine-paneled door and turned to look up at him, surprising an intense look upon his countenance. He seemed quite distracted and, when he made no response, she prompted: "Mr. Darcy?"

With a start, he blinked. "Forgive me; you were saying?"

Elizabeth gestured towards the door. "Mr. Theophilus Darcy is within."

Before Darcy could take hold of the handle, however, the door opened, and Mrs. Collins appeared before them.

She smiled reassuringly at the gentleman, pressing a finger to her lips. "He sleeps, Mr. Darcy. The surgeon has administered more laudanum this morning but is confident your brother will be fit to be moved later in the day—though he must, of course, continue to rest. I shall arrange for some tea." Charlotte turned to walk away but Darcy stayed her with his hand.

"Mrs. Collins, I—we, are greatly in your debt. Thank you for your kindness and care of my brother. It is much appreciated."

It was Elizabeth's turn to blink in surprise, and she turned away slightly to conceal her reaction as Charlotte spoke to him before heading along the passage towards the kitchen. Mr. Darcy's tone was respectful and almost warm with gratitude. Had she truly, as his brother implied, not seen the best of him?

Though she had considered overnight Mr. Theophilus Darcy's words, Elizabeth had taken them lightly, along with her promise to give Mr. Darcy another chance; her ill opinion of the gentleman was too ingrained to be swept away with such ease. Yet she must give him merit. His prompt return, his blatant concern for his sibling and his consideration of her friend's inconvenience had shown facets of a character she would not previously have given him credit for.

Disinclined to indulge such charitable notions, she stepped away as the gentleman made to enter the room, but then he turned back to face her.

"I would be much obliged if you would stay, Miss Bennet. I have had too much time in the saddle alone with my thoughts and to sit here with only they as companions will not serve me well."

Though she had quite her fill of the Darcy brothers as of late, Elizabeth nonetheless pushed aside her reluctance and preceded him into the room.

Theo was reclining on a makeshift bed fashioned from the leather chaise lounge under the window, his strapped ankle resting on a strategically placed footstool. The temporary sling Elizabeth had formed from his cravat had been replaced with a sturdier, more professional support, the arm resting across the gentleman's chest, which rose and fell with his breathing. His cheeks were flushed, no doubt from a combination of the laudanum and the heat from the blazing fire in the nearby hearth, and Darcy strode to the window, throwing it open to admit a blast of fresh air.

He then indicated to Elizabeth to take the seat placed near Theo's side, but before pulling forward another for his own use, he stared down at the prone form of his brother. All the fears haunting him on his journey returned, though he knew he should trust to what he had been told. Theo was not in any danger and would make a full recovery.

Yet he had taken a knock to his head; he had lost consciousness. Could there be damage yet to manifest itself? Darcy closed his eyes and drew in a deep breath.

"Mr. Darcy?"

He started, then turned to look down into Elizabeth's face.

"Do not take it too hard, sir. It could have been so much worse."

Little did she know how well he comprehended the sentiment; so much worse…

"Sit down, sir." Her voice was gentle and encouraging. "You have had a long night and a trying journey; you must take some relief from seeing your brother is well and in safe hands."

How was it she could determine what was going through his mind? He turned to pull forward a chair, and for a moment, silence reigned, the only sounds in the room the ticking of the long case clock in the corner and the crackle of logs in the hearth.

Then, Darcy recalled himself. He had asked the lady to bear him company; he was duty bound to attempt some conversation, and recollecting their brief exchange the last time he had been at the parsonage, he comprehended his omission.

"I—er—I trust your family is in good health, Miss Bennet?"

He sat back in his seat, relieved when she smiled—not at him, it must be owned, but into the distance as though recollecting something or someone. Then, she turned her eyes upon him.

"I believe they are, sir, though I have seen but little of them these few weeks." Her gaze narrowed. "My eldest sister has been in Town for several months—have you never happened to see her there?"

Feeling a little uneasy, Darcy shook his head. "No—I have not had the pleasure of coming across Miss Bennet." The lady raised a brow, and he added, "London is a vast city. I am not surprised our paths have not crossed."

Elizabeth nodded. "Oh, I think where there is no *common* acquaintance, one might happily venture into Town for any considerable length of time and avoid all manner of people—deliberately, or by accident." She paused, studying him with a thoughtful air for a moment and Darcy stirred in his seat. "Yet I understand my sister and Mr. Bingley's sisters exchanged calls?"

He stared down at his feet for a moment. *Well, Darcy*, his conscience murmured, *you brought this upon yourself. You would have company, and you would have* hers. *Distraction is what you sought, and now you have it. So answer her, Man. Find some words to satisfy her!*

"I do not reside with the Hursts when in Town. Thus, I am not privy to who their callers might be at any given time."

Elizabeth's smile did not quite reach her eyes. "It is strange it was not mentioned in passing when you next met—but then, perhaps you do not see much of them either when in Town." She tilted her head to one side as she looked at him. "From Miss Bingley's correspondence with my sister, we understood you all to be much in company with each other."

Darcy frowned at this gross exaggeration on Miss Bingley's part. "We have met on occasion, I cannot deny it. Yet surely it is all relative; what seems a great deal of time to one party might be very little to another."

The lady seemed to consider his words for a moment. "Yes, you do not strike me as someone who willingly seeks the company of others."

Uncertain how to respond, Darcy stared at her, but a sudden groan from the sleeping form beside them was sufficient to redirect their attention.

"Fsssh." The sound that fell from Theo's lips could hardly be called a word, but a frown now marred his brow.

Elizabeth picked up a cloth from the table and, dipping it in a nearby bowl of water, she proceeded to mop Theo's brow, lifting the curls upon his forehead as she did so.

Darcy fought against a wave of jealousy; hard upon its heels came the desire to gain his mount and, as soon as practicable, fall from his saddle, that such kind ministrations and concern might be his due.

Before he could allow this ludicrous notion any purchase, however, further distraction came at the sight of Elizabeth leaning over his brother to adjust his pillows.

Dear Lord, if Theo should open his eyes now, what would he think?

"Miss Bennet, I do believe –"

"Do hush, Mr. Darcy." She waved a hand at him. "He is trying to say something."

Darcy stood up and the lady stepped away, her face almost as flushed as his brother's. Theo was restless, his head turning to and fro on the pillow, and she was quite correct: he was trying to form words.

"Fish," he then said, quite clearly. Then, he groaned, and mumbled, "I need fish—I want fish...help me..." before falling silent again and his movement calming.

Darcy caught his breath, but Elizabeth frowned as she retook her seat. "Do you think he suffers from hunger?" He barely registered her words as she continued. "Is he becoming distressed?"

Pulling himself together, he shook his head. "No—it is merely the laudanum. He is deep in dreams that can assume outlandish proportions." He chose not to enlighten the lady further, despite her questioning gaze and turned to resume his own seat, his gaze fixed upon his brother's face. Yet another memory from childhood took hold, a very young Theo running after him, his little legs unable to keep up; a Theo desperate for his elder brother's company. They had been so close back then, when there had just been the two of them.

"You and your brother," Elizabeth's voice drew him back into the present. "You are not very alike."

Attempting to marshal his thoughts, Darcy shook his head. "No, we are not."

"He has—if you will forgive me saying—such easy manners."

"And I do not."

Elizabeth sighed softly and shook her head. "I do not know. Perhaps it is just you are more—reserved."

"I do not have the talent some possess, including my brother, of conversing easily with people I do not know."

Darcy got to his feet and walked over to the open window. Then, he turned around to look at Elizabeth. Her air and countenance spoke of confusion, uncertainty.

Then, she gestured towards Theo. "Your brother believes I misunderstand you."

Darcy frowned. The notion Theo had been discussing him with Elizabeth was unsettling.

"And you, Miss Bennet? Is this your continued attempt to try to make out my character?"

With a small smile, she shrugged her shoulders lightly. "Of course, for I have not been in company with you since the Netherfield Ball and thus there has been little enough opportunity."

He held her gaze, and she raised her chin slightly as though anticipating his response. The last thing he felt in need of just now was to be reminded of that evening, nor a repetition of the awkward conversation they had endured during their set.

Fixed as their attention was on each other, neither of them noted the flickering of Theo's eyelids and the slow opening of his eyes. His startled gaze, once a little more focused, took in the lady beside him, then travelled to his brother and, as he lowered his lids again, a slight smile lifted one corner of his mouth.

Fortuitously, a light knock came upon the door heralding the return of Mrs. Collins and a serving girl bearing a tray of tea things, and Darcy let out a slow breath. Relieved by the timely interruption, he took the opportunity of resuming his seat. His request for Miss Bennet to bear him company had been to distract him from his memories and regrets but in its place had come all the force of his longing for her, and a renewed suspicion she did not hold him in much favor.

"Mr. Darcy?" He looked up quickly and took the proffered cup of tea from Mrs. Collins with a smile.

"Thank you."

She smiled in return and turned to leave, resting a hand

upon her friend's shoulder as she passed her. At the door, she turned to face them.

"I have dispatched Mr. Collins to Rosings, sir, with the most recent intelligence of Mr. Theophilus Darcy's condition and of your safe return." With that, she left them alone once more.

Darcy took a sip of his tea, letting the hot liquid ease the growing restriction in his throat. Why did the maddening woman always reduce him to the idiocy of a schoolboy? He raised his eyes only to find Elizabeth studying him intently.

Clearing his throat, he returned his cup to the saucer with a clash and quickly placed it on a side table.

"She is an admirable woman, your friend."

Elizabeth smiled. "Indeed, she is."

The smile was endearing and no help whatsoever to his floundering heart; earlier, he was dashed if all he could focus on was that damnable curl dancing above the pale smooth skin of her neck as he followed her along the hallway. Now, he struggled to prevent his gaze from drifting to where the amber crucifix she often wore nestled on the same soft skin just above the hollow of her neckline.

Tugging at the restraint of his neck-cloth as he felt warmth rising in his cheeks, Darcy sought desperately for a fresh topic of conversation.

"This is a generous living." He waved a hand to indicate the parsonage. "I believe Mr. and Mrs. Collins are comfortably placed in the neighborhood."

With a light laugh, Elizabeth nodded. "Indeed they are; though perhaps a little *too* close to the source of their good fortune."

He could not help but agree, but all the same, felt the need to defend his relation. "My aunt has her faults, Miss Bennet, but they are not of generosity. She is a good patroness to those dependent upon her."

A strange expression filtered over the lady's countenance, and he frowned. Then, she spoke, "Having patronage over dependents—it is a solemn responsibility, is it not? One you would take as seriously as your aunt?"

"Indeed. Why do you ask such a question?" Darcy knew he would regret it the moment the words passed his lips.

"I had heard of an instance whereby such benefaction—one under your jurisdiction—was not bestowed where it was due."

Her tone was not censorious but neither was it conciliatory and, agitated, Darcy got to his feet once more. "You speak of Wickham."

A noise emanated from the reclined form of his brother, but neither turned towards him.

Darcy held Elizabeth's gaze firmly. "I wish I could oblige you, Miss Bennet. I hold secrecy in little favor, but some things must remain private in my family's dealings with that man, things I am not at liberty to divulge. Forgive me."

The lady rose from her seat slowly, though what she may have said next he was left to ruminate upon, for a louder groan came from his brother, and as the lady turned her attention to him, Darcy blew out a frustrated breath.

He had little time to dwell upon what Wickham may have told Miss Bennet, however; as the lady turned to dampen the cloth in the nearby bowl again, a movement caught his eye. Theo, his eyes now open, gave him a distinct wink before dropping his lids and letting out another pronounced groan, drawing Elizabeth back to his side in an instant.

Darcy's fixed attention upon the lady was disturbed by the sound of approaching wheels and, glancing out of the window, he was surprised to behold his own equipage pulling up outside the parsonage. Without delay, the Reverend Collins clambered down from his lofty perch beside the coachman, a great deal of self-importance in his air and countenance.

"My dear Mrs. Collins!" he exclaimed as he tripped over a stone in the path. "Is it not extraordinary? How fortunate are we in our esteemed neighbor and patroness?"

"Fortunate indeed, sir," the lady replied, as she joined him outside.

As this did not appear to satisfy Mr. Collins, he dragged his wife to the gate, gesturing wildly. "Can you not *see*, my dear? Lady Catherine was so good as to permit me to travel *outside* with the coachman! 'Mr. Collins,' says she, with great kindness, 'Mr. Collins. Take Mr. Darcy's carriage directly and return both my nephews to Rosings forthwith. For expedience, I insist you travel with it."

He drew in deep breath and puffed out his chest. "Is she not quite *the* most admirable woman of our acquaintance?"

Charlotte nodded. "Indeed, she is, Mr. Collins. Come then," she turned back to walk along the path. "Let us apprise Mr. Darcy of his aunt's wishes and see if his brother is fit to be moved."

"Oh, but he must be, my dear," exclaimed Mr. Collins as he scurried behind her. "Lady Catherine will not stand for anything else."

Suppressing a grunt of distaste, Darcy turned his gaze back to Elizabeth, hoping she had been too preoccupied to hear her cousin's words, but the pink upon her cheeks and her defiant gaze as their eyes met proved otherwise. There was no chance to speak, for a rap came upon the door as it opened, but he had time to ponder whether he or Elizabeth felt the most discomfort over the ridiculousness of their relations.

CHAPTER 5

FINALLY FREED FROM THE challenging and alluring presence of Miss Elizabeth Bennet, Darcy thankfully turned his attentions to his brother. The only way to transport him with minimal discomfort and cushioned from the movement of the carriage was to permit him to lean back against Darcy, his strapped foot—for once not a source of annoyance—resting upon the opposite bench.

Thus it was the carriage made its slow progress along the lane and through the gates into Rosings Park.

Theo appeared to have drifted away again, and Darcy sighed, turning to stare out of the window. Had he accomplished anything other than confirming what he already knew? He was besotted with Miss Elizabeth Bennet. He had suspected it to be so for some considerable time, and the more he learned of her, the longer he spent in her company, the deeper embroiled he became.

That his interest had no future preyed equally upon his mind, and he could ill determine at this precise moment where the weight he bore in his chest for Elizabeth ended and that for Theo began. He glanced down at his slumbering brother. When had he last held him so? When had he last offered him comfort?

Theo stirred briefly, then nestled his head against Darcy, his hair brushing his brother's chin, and as though struck by a sting of lightning, Darcy was thrown back in time, back to that awful day by the lake, cradling not Theo against his chest, but Sebastian.

Theophilus and Sebastian—close in temperament, like two peas in a pod, inseparable despite Theo being the elder. Theo and Seb...wishing he could push away the memories, Darcy suppressed a groan. He had been nearing twelve years of age when the accident happened, but even then he had begun to grow apart from his siblings. They were not being groomed to run the estate, to take on the mantle of guardianship for future generations. Their time was for freedom, for play, for innocence...

He released a shallow breath and stared more fiercely at the passing parkland as the memories would persist in flooding his mind. His grasp upon Theo tightened as they hit a pot hole and the carriage jostled his brother's body... his brother's body... the familiar ache gripped Darcy's throat, and he fought to suppress a suddenly rising sob that threatened to choke him.

Darcy had cradled Seb's lifeless form at the water's edge, praying, begging someone—*anyone*—that his brother might awaken, that he was merely sleeping. The only sounds beyond his own labored breathing had been distant birdsong and the trickling of the benign stream as it fed into the lake. The watery rays of spring sunshine had cast an eerie light over the scene, with no hint of a breeze stirring the newly formed leaves of the surrounding trees, nor the damp curls upon his brother's forehead.

And then he had seen her—his mother, only so recently returned to her latest confinement. Theo had fled to find someone, and now Darcy saw her running towards them, several men from the estate in her wake, and behind them, his brother. At nine years of age, Theo's legs were not up to the return at such speed, but he labored on, the tears coursing down his face apparent, even through Darcy's own.

It was when his mother fell to her knees beside him, covering her face, her body shaking, and sobbing—deep, wrenching sobs that made no sound—that Darcy had known there was no hope...

Theo stirred, then let out a yelp of pain as his elbow connected with the seat, jarring his shoulder. Darcy shifted his position, careful not to cause him more discomfort and glanced out of the window, swallowing hard on rising emotion.

Had what happened to Sebastian had an effect upon Theo's character—was it a contributor to his constant recklessness? Was this his escape? Did he feel—as did Darcy—the blame was all his, guilty to still be alive? Before he could consider this further, the carriage came to a halt with a jolt.

"They are..." Theo's voice was weaker than normal, no doubt due to the medication keeping him subdued, and Darcy leaned down to try and hear his words.

His eyelids flickered and opened, and he stared up at Darcy as though not entirely sure who he was. Then his gaze narrowed and he nodded slowly. "Yes. That is the way of it."

Darcy frowned. "What is the way of it?" He slowly eased his brother into an upright position. "Are you fully awake?"

Theo turned awkwardly in his seat and squinted at him like a cat, then rubbed his eyes with his free hand before concealing a yawn. He shook his head. "They really are—I can see why they hold your attention..." his head lolled forward for a second and Darcy feared he had lapsed into unconsciousness and grabbed his good arm to steady him, but then Theo shook his head again and raised it to meet his brother's confused gaze.

"Miss Elizabeth Bennet. She has—do you not think,

she has the finest pair of…"

"Theo!"

Theo blinked; then, he fixed Darcy with a stern look. "If you would only let me finish, Brother! She has the finest pair of eyes I have ever seen on a woman."

Eyes. Yes, of course, she had fine eyes. What else could his brother have possibly been going to say? Closing his own for a second, Darcy rubbed a hand across his brow, then opened them as a servant lowered the steps.

As two footmen assisted his brother from the carriage, Darcy stared after him. What had been Theo's meaning? Was the laudanum speaking for him, or did he truly admire Elizabeth? Was he too falling under her influence? And how the devil had his brother detected his own interest in the lady?

His insides twisted uneasily, but unable just then to give the matter his full attention, he stepped down from the carriage and waved the hovering footmen aside. "I will support him."

He turned to Theo. "Take my arm, put as little pressure as possible upon your ankle."

Supporting the weight of his brother, he managed to get him up the steps and into the entrance hall.

They had gone but a few slow paces towards the staircase, however, when Lady Catherine appeared in the doorway to the drawing room.

"There you are!" she pronounced. Her gaze flickered briefly over Theo's wan face as he leaned into his brother's side. "Did I not say that horse would be the death of you?"

"Always has to be right," muttered Theo.

Darcy did not trust Theo's tongue when he was this heavily influenced by laudanum, especially in Lady Catherine's company. "Come, Theo; can you hold the banister as we climb the stairs?"

"I can climb them perfectly well by myself," said Theo,

leaning heavily against Darcy's shoulder.

"Of course you can." Darcy's voice dripped with irony. "How much laudanum did they give you?"

"Too much. I think….I think I would like to sit down." Theo's knees began to buckle.

Darcy grabbed his brother's uninjured arm before he could fall. "I would be obliged if you would wait until there is a chair to sit in. The parlor, I think." The fainting couch was much closer than Theo's bed. Somehow he managed to urge Theo into shuffling in that direction.

"Theophilus Darcy, you are slumping again! I will not have it," proclaimed Lady Catherine.

Theo rolled his eyes. "About that chair…"

"Here you are." Darcy gently lowered Theo onto the fainting couch.

Theo heaved a sigh of relief as he leaned back, then winced as he swung his feet up on the end of the couch. "Blasted ankle feels fine until I try to walk on it." He sounded so aggrieved, Darcy was hard put not to smile.

Lady Catherine signaled to a maid who spread a blanket across his legs. Theo tried to kick it off and grimaced in pain. "I am not an invalid. I hurt my ankle and they gave me too much laudanum. I will be perfectly well directly."

Darcy sincerely hoped so. Unless they had given Theo enough laudanum for an elephant, he should not be so befuddled. He had heard of people with head injuries who seemed fine at the time, but grew worse over the following days and died. His throat tightened. Surely fate would not be so cruel as to take a second brother from him?

"You certainly shall be well, young man, once you take this medicine. It will have you fit in no time." Lady Catherine waved away the maid and held out a glass filled with a dark liquid to her nephew.

Lady Catherine was not the sort of lady who nursed invalids. She always gave orders for others to care for Anne. If she was taking matters into her own hands here, she must be more worried than she looked. She would not have forgotten about Sebastian either.

"I do not need more laudanum!"

His aunt looked down her prominent nose at him. "It is *not* laudanum, and you *will* drink it."

Darcy rested his hand on Theo's good shoulder. "Drink it."

Theo looked up at him, heaved a sigh, and said, "Very well." Taking the glass from Lady Catherine, he quaffed half of it in one gulp. His face screwed up as he pushed the glass away. "No more. That tastes terrible."

"Anne drinks it twice a day without complaint. Are you weaker than she?" demanded Lady Catherine.

"My respect for my cousin's courage has increased dramatically," Theo muttered. He looked at the glass with distaste, then swallowed the remainder. "Now give me some brandy to wash down that swill."

Darcy shook his head at a servant who approached with a snifter of brandy. "Some wine, well watered, instead." He gently took the empty glass from Theo.

"Killjoy," muttered Theo.

Was Theo *trying* to do himself damage? Darcy's fingers tightened on his brother's shoulder. "Brandy and laudanum is a bad combination."

Theo snorted. "And when did *you* take up doctoring? I truly will be an invalid by the time the two of you are done with me."

Lady Catherine snapped, "It is your own fault for taking foolish risks."

"Oh, fine. Next time a woman in my path screams, I will run her down instead. Are you satisfied?"

"Theo," Darcy said, his tone a warning.

"Remind me, why did you take me from the parsonage? The nurses there were kinder and far more pleasing to look upon." Theo sat up and gingerly moved his feet to the ground. "I am going to my room, where I hope to be left in peace."

This time Darcy allowed the footmen to assist his

brother. Despite his resolution to behave differently toward Theo, it had taken his brother only a few minutes to annoy him once again. Why did he have to argue with everything Darcy said? He was only trying to help Theo.

Darcy followed Theo's slow progress. Once they reached his room, the footmen arranged the feather pillows on the bed to ensure his comfort, but after that Darcy waved them away. "I will stay with him."

"There is no need," Theo said irritably, his speech slurring. "If I require assistance, I can ring for one of our aunt's astonishingly efficient servants. Do you suppose she beats them if they are too slow?"

Although Darcy had wondered the same thing, he said, "There is no need for disrespect. I am sure they have duties other than tending to you." He settled in the armchair beside the bed, wishing it did not hurt to hear Theo tell him to leave.

"If you insist upon forcing your company upon me, at least refrain from lecturing me until I can think clearly. I would hate to see your eloquent words go to waste— though of course they always do." Theo swiveled his head toward the window, and the mocking tone disappeared from his voice. "Oh, dear. That is *not* a good sign."

Darcy followed his gaze, but could see nothing unusual outside. "What is the matter?"

"Can you not *see* her?"

"See whom?"

"Mother, and Father beside her. He looks angry." Theo flinched and pulled up the counterpane. "Do not tell him I am here."

Darcy's heart began to pound. "Theo, you are imagining things."

"They are standing right there!" His eyes looked wild.

Nothing Darcy said could convince his brother to the contrary. Theo did not stop arguing until he fell asleep a quarter hour later, allowing Darcy to drop the façade of calm he had erected. The laudanum should have begun to wear off by now, yet Theo's confusion was growing worse. The injury in his head was clearly taking a toll.

Darcy crossed to the small writing desk by the window and rummaged through it until he found paper and ink. He wrote quickly, without his usual care, ignoring a drop of ink that stained the edge of the paper. After blotting the note, he folded it with trembling hands and addressed it to a well-known London doctor, marked Express.

Georgiana Darcy could always tell when her eldest brother did not want her to ask him questions. His brows would come together, his lips would tighten into a line, and he would not look her in the eye. She trusted William, but she had seen enough of his anger at Theo over the years to wish to avoid having it turn on her. So when William had that look on his face, she did not ask questions.

This one time, though, she truly wished that she *had* asked him why he had to hurry off to Rosings without her. He had said it was a matter of business, but what kind of business could he have at Rosings that was so urgent he would leave Darcy House before he even finished his breakfast and further, when he had only just returned home on alleged 'business' too? Or that he would feel the need to hide it from her? She found Lady Catherine intimidating—most people did, after all—but that was not a secret, and it would not keep William from speaking to her about their aunt.

What had been in that letter he received at breakfast? William had merely looked annoyed when he opened it and began reading, but then his face had grown pale and he was on his feet, calling to have his horse readied for the journey. And wearing that expression that told her not to ask questions.

The letter had not been from Theo, nor from Lady Catherine. She had seen enough of the spidery handwriting to know that for certain. So who at Rosings would send such an urgent request that William would obey it instantly? Had something happened to their aunt, or perhaps to Cousin Anne?

By midday, her anxiety was sufficient to cause her to take an action which certainly would anger William if he ever discovered it. She knew which drawer of his desk he usually kept his correspondence in, and if any of the servants noticed her in his study, she could always say she needed to consult one of his books. It was not as if she were forbidden to enter the room, after all. She had simply never gone in it when he was not there.

She did not have to search hard. The letter was right where she expected it to be, though it showed signs of having been crumpled. That was unlike William, who usually took good care to keep his correspondence neat. After a quick glance at the door, she unfolded it and began to read.

Theo picked at his blanket, sweat running down his face. "Fish?"

Darcy hurried to his side. "I am here."

His brother's face grew slack-jawed with relief as he turned his head toward the voice, but then he frowned and looked away. "No."

"Yes, it is I, Theo. Can I bring you something?"

Theo's eyes drifted closed. "You are not Fish."

"Yes, I am." As he said it, Darcy recalled the day he had told Theo never to call him by that baby name again and to stop following him everywhere. There had been a flash of pain in Theo's eyes before he turned away. Why had he been so harsh with his little brother? He knew the answer full well; it was because every time he saw Theo's dark eyes looking up at him, it brought back all those terrible memories of Seb's dead body. It had been easier to ignore Theo than to face those visions, and he had justified it by telling himself Seb's death was Theo's fault. "It is me.

I am Fish, just grown up now." He could not believe he had said that.

His brother looked at him again, then shook his head briefly. "No," he said, sounding disappointed. "Fish is not so…." He waved his hand in the air vaguely, then closed his eyes again.

Fish was not so… what? Old? Severe? Stern? Disapproving? Theo was right. Darcy was no longer his trusted childhood friend, but a distant, judgmental man who had ignored Theo and poured all his affection into the innocent Georgiana… then failed to protect *her* from danger. What had happened to him? He and Theo had been constant companions, two knights defending Pemberley from invading armies of marsh grass, lopping off the top of the stalks and comparing how many enemy heads they had collected. Theo had followed him everywhere, and Darcy had taught him to climb trees, to skip stones in the pond… and how to dive off the rocks, when Theo had been no older than Sebastian was that dreadful day. Theo might have been the one to teach Seb the stunt that led to his death, but Darcy had forged the path for it.

Darcy dropped into the chair and buried his face in his hands. *He* was the guilty one, not Theo. He had not tried to stop Theo from teaching Sebastian, even though he was old enough to know better. Seb had been begging Theo to show him how to dive, and Darcy was already jealous enough of Sebastian's preference for Theo's company that he had not wished to drive a bigger wedge between himself and Seb by forbidding him from diving. What a fool he had been! He had failed both his younger brothers, who looked to him for safety and wisdom.

Even at the time, he had recognized his own failure in forbidding the activity, so he had thrown himself into the task of becoming always responsible, always in charge, never softened by the desire to please someone he cared for. It could not bring Seb back. As their mother faded away and died after losing her youngest son, Darcy had responded by blaming Theo for everything, pushing him away and threatening to thrash him if he ever heard him say Fish again. The boy Fish was dead, replaced by the man Fitzwilliam. And he had ignored Theo's loneliness—sociable and friendly Theo who had effectively lost both his brothers on one terrible day.

Was it any wonder Theo had turned to George Wickham for companionship? Darcy had also left George behind when he turned his back on his childhood, then scorned Theo for his boyish pranks with his former friend. When Theo had finally listened and stopped calling him Fish, the childhood nickname was replaced by *Prince William* and *His Highness*, and Darcy had been glad of it because it set him apart from them. He had loftily ignored all Theo's attempts to get his attention, all the nights he had asked pointedly whether there would be *Fish* for dinner, the days when he would insist in midwinter that it was a fine day to catch *Fish* in the pond. *He* was Prince William, after all, trustworthy, responsible, and above boyish games and teasing.

No wonder Theo disliked him so. Darcy had made himself humorless and distant, and despised everyone who was not—at least until Elizabeth Bennet had come along. She had teased him and played with him, refusing to give up on him, no matter how serious he remained. And how her playfulness attracted him! Somehow she had managed to reach the innocent boy who had not yet been maimed by the loss of Sebastian and Theo, and touched the part of him that was still able to love.

He almost smiled at the thought until he remembered how she had received him at the parsonage. For once, he allowed himself to look the truth in the eye. She might tease him and flirt with him, but she had never given a sign of liking him, not the way she seemed to like Theo, who still knew how to play and find joy in life. He had told Bingley that Jane Bennet, no matter how happily she received his attentions, did not seem to care about him, and was no doubt only acting on her mother's orders. It was not true. Jane Bennet's eyes had lit up when she saw Bingley. It was Elizabeth who would tease and flirt with no evidence of affection in her eyes. *He* would have been the one risking a loveless marriage, not Bingley, and so he had stolen Bingley's chance of happiness along with Miss Bennet's. And Elizabeth seemed to know it. Now she had even more reason to dislike him.

"Seb, no! Stop!" Theo moaned, sweat dripping down his face. Mechanically, Darcy dipped the washcloth in the cool water, wrung it out, and wiped his brother's forehead—taking care of him, the way an older brother should, not by dismissing him and scorning him, but by being there when Theo needed him.

The cool washcloth awoke Theo, who looked at him questioningly. "What are *you* doing here?"

At least he recognized him this time. "Theo," Darcy said tentatively, half expecting his brother to turn away. "You are ill, but I will not let anything happen to you."

His brother looked dubious, but shrugged and closed his eyes again. Darcy could hardly blame him for his doubts. He had given Theo no reason to think he would care if he lived or died.

He had hardly even acknowledged his existence. Elizabeth had been surprised to discover he even had a brother. She had known of Georgiana's existence since he spoke of her often in Hertfordshire. Had he never so much as mentioned Theo? He knew he had not. He had preferred to forget about Theo when he could. He had not even wanted to bring Theo to Rosings; he had only done so because it was his responsibility to keep an eye on his brother, and he always did his duty, no matter how unpleasant.

But he *had* brought him to Rosings, and now Theo was as taken with Elizabeth Bennet as he was himself. It would not matter in the long run, since Theo could not afford to marry her, and Elizabeth could not afford to refuse a proposal from a man of Darcy's standing regardless of her feelings for him. Elizabeth might prefer Theo's company, but it would not affect the final outcome. Should he choose to make her an offer, Elizabeth would be his, regardless of her wishes or Theo's—if he could live with himself.

No. He had wronged Theo enough. If his brother developed strong feelings for Elizabeth, he still could not marry her, but neither could Darcy. He could not force his little brother to watch his happiness with her. It was a stark truth, but also one precisely calculated to make Darcy understand his own desires. But he had ignored Theo's needs for too many years now, and he would not do so again. If only God would spare Theo's life, Darcy would somehow find a way to live without Elizabeth Bennet.

"Theo?" he said tentatively, but this time his brother did not respond.

Georgiana glanced up at the clock on the mantel. Three hours since she had sent her message with a servant. Three hours without a reply. She froze at the sound of a knock on the front door, and held her breath until she heard a familiar voice.

Past caring about propriety, she hurried out into the front hall. "I am so glad you have come!" She threw her arms around her cousin Richard, who swung her in a circle just as he had when she was a little girl.

"Georgie!" His voice was a reassuring warm baritone.

When he set her down again, she stepped back and put her hands on her hips. "What has taken you so long? I was starting to think perhaps you had gone by way of Pemberley!"

The Colonel laughed. "My, but you are impatient! Now that I am here, tell me what could possibly be so urgent?"

"You must take me to Rosings immediately. How soon can we leave?"

Fitzwilliam put up his hands. "Whoa, little one! Slow

down! Your brother has already asked me to escort you to Rosings later in the week, but now you want me to drop everything, give up my tickets to the opera tonight, not to mention my evening with…well, never mind. You want me to take you to Rosings today? What is so urgent it cannot wait a day?"

Georgiana, who had been practicing emulating her eldest brother's icy stare, the one he used when things were not going as planned, leveled that look now upon her cousin.

"What is the urgency?" Fitzwilliam repeated.

"I think you know very well what has happened, and you are all conspiring to keep it from me. Theo is my brother, and I must go to him!"

"Something has happened to Theo?" Fitzwilliam's brows knitted together.

If he was feigning ignorance, he was certainly very convincing. Georgiana was in danger of tearing up and told herself she simply would not have it! She would not turn into another one of those silly girls who cried at everything. Taking a deep breath, she replied evenly, "Do not pretend you do not know."

Fitzwilliam put his hands out palms up. "Pretend? I have no idea what you are talking about!"

"William received a letter saying Theo was thrown from his horse. His shoulder is injured, and he…he…" Finally, it was all too much, and despite her best efforts, a sob that sounded something like a hiccup escaped.

Fitzwilliam pulled her close, his large hand stroking her back. "Hush now. It cannot be as bad as all that."

"He has hit his head!" she said into his coat.

"He what?" Fitzwilliam held her away slightly by the shoulders and looked into her eyes.

"As soon as William read the letter, he called for his horse and left for Kent," she said.

"When was this?"

"The letter came this morning."

"What else did he say about the injury? How did it happen?"

Georgiana looked down at the floor. Now she had worked herself into a corner. She would most certainly be in trouble for reading the letter, but that would have to be far less than the worry of not knowing if Theo would recover.

"Georgiana? How did you learn of this?"

She hesitated. Now she would have to confess she had been in her brother's study and read a letter intended for his eyes only. "I might have been looking for something in William's study and seen a letter there and…" she trailed off.

"Georgie?" Fitzwilliam raised a brow.

"Yes, I know I shall be in trouble with William, but I would do it again. Why does everyone always try to protect me? I am no longer a child!"

"Your brother made me promise to watch over you and bring you to Rosings later this week. I knew nothing about an accident." He pulled out his handkerchief so she could wipe her tears. "Let me see the letter."

Georgiana led Fitzwilliam to her brother's study where she retrieved the crumpled paper from his desk.

Her cousin's brow wrinkled in concern as he read.

"Please take me to Rosings, Richard. If something happens to Theo…I… must see him."

When Fitzwilliam finished, he looked up. "How soon can you be ready to travel?"

When Darcy wiped a cool cloth over his brother's face, Theo looked up, his eyes somewhat unfocused.

"Still here?" Theo mumbled.

"Of course," Darcy said.

"Why?" Theo asked, and then he closed his eyes and slept again.

Theo's question opened a fresh wound in Darcy's

heart. Did his brother truly think so little of him? Did Theo believe Darcy would desert him just when he was most needed? Darcy ran a hand through his hair, which was wild and unruly from the day's exertions. Theo had to get well so he could try to make up for all the harsh, judgmental words he had said over the years. And if it meant giving Elizabeth up to him, Darcy would do that, too, just to have his brother back. He would help Theo more, make it possible for him to marry. Whatever it took.

When Lady Catherine appeared to check on Theo, she insisted Darcy come down to supper. After trying all of her tricks to bully him into submission, she finally gave up and had one of the maids bring a tray for him. Just as he was finishing his meal, Mrs. Shafton, the housekeeper, appeared with another dose of Anne's medicine for Theo. When Darcy would not allow her to give it to Theo, she lingered to ensure it was administered.

"I will wait until he stirs and then give it to him. You may go now," Darcy told her.

At first she hesitated, as if she was uncertain whether it was better to defy her mistress or Darcy, but she finally relented after he promised a second time that he would see Theo took the medicine.

The minute Theo moved, Darcy propped his brother's limp body up against some pillows and held the glass to his lips.

Theo wrinkled his nose and looked at him fearfully through bleary eyes. Then he whispered something. Leaning down, Darcy put an ear closer to his brother's lips.

"Please...no." Theo's voice was barely audible.

"Lady Catherine says this will strengthen you. Anne drinks it twice a day," Darcy told him as he continued to press the glass to his mouth.

Theo raised his eyebrows as if to say, 'See how much it has helped Anne,' and kept his lips firmly closed against the liquid. Again he shook his head.

"Stop fighting me! You will spill it," Darcy reprimanded him.

Theo turned his head away and mumbled, "Feel…worse. No…please."

Darcy took the glass away and set it on the table beside the bed. "What are you trying to tell me?"

"Not good," Theo said with a little more strength in his voice this time. "Makes me feel…strange."

Darcy looked at his brother and then at the glass. Picking it up, he sniffed the liquid. "I see what you mean. This is vile."

Setting the glass on the table again, he dipped a cloth in cool water and wiped Theo's face. Suddenly, he felt his brother's hand on his arm and a look passed between them.

"Thank you," Theo said.

"Surely, it cannot be so bad." Darcy picked up the glass, looked at it again, and took another sniff. "What is in this?"

"Something like laudanum, but stronger. Too much…fatal," Theo told him.

"Very well. I will not make you drink it."

"Pour it out. Please."

"But Lady Catherine would hardly give Anne something that was harmful to her."

Theo raised an eyebrow again. "Perhaps she does not know."

"It must be that dreadful doctor of hers!" Darcy said. "I have never completely trusted him."

Theo shrugged.

"I have sent to London for our family physician. He should be here tomorrow. The man who attends Lady Catherine and Anne will not touch you. I promise."

Theo mouthed a "thank you" but was already drifting off to sleep again.

CHAPTER 6

ON THE WAY TO ROSINGS, Georgiana tried to distract herself by looking out the window of the carriage. The fear came in waves and with each swell she balled her hand into a fist in her skirts as if to hang on until she could get control again. When she realized what she was doing, she made a conscious effort to open her hand and relax it. Fitzwilliam must have seen her struggling as he arranged to exchange places with Mrs. Annesley, settled in next to Georgiana, and put an arm around her.

"Lean against me," he said. "All will be well." He kissed the top of her head.

"You and my brothers always say that even when you do not know if it is true."

"We cannot help but protect the ones we love."

Georgiana smiled weakly and looked out the window again. "I did not realize we were leaving so late. It will be dark before we reach Rosings."

"We are fortunate. The sky should be clear and the moon bright so it is a good night to travel."

Finally, exhausted with the strain of worry, Georgiana

laid her head on her cousin's shoulder and fell into a restless sleep, awaking some time later with a start. Confused, she looked around. "How long was I asleep?"

"We are almost there," Fitzwilliam assured her.

Up until that time, she had been so focused on getting to Theo she had not considered what she would say to William. How could she explain her presence when she should not even have known about the accident?

Fitzwilliam must have sensed her concerns. "I think the best strategy might be to simply say we decided to come to Rosings sooner than planned."

"Yesterday, I would have agreed with you in order to avoid conflict with William, but this has shown me I cannot allow him to treat me as a child, to shut me out of important things. Perhaps if I am honest about what happened, he will recognize I have grown up and can take responsibility for my actions."

"I promise you I did not know about the accident."

"How typical! He thinks he has to shoulder every burden, solve every problem all by himself. I must show him it does not have to be that way," she told him.

Fitzwilliam pulled her against him in a quick hug. "You, my sweet, have become wise beyond your years."

"If something has happened to Theo, William will never recover. I must be there for both of them."

When Colonel Fitzwilliam and Georgiana arrived at Rosings, Hastings, Lady Catherine's ancient butler, opened the door to them.

"Where is he?" Georgiana demanded immediately.

"We were not expecting you, Miss Darcy, Colonel Fitzwilliam," the butler intoned. "I shall announce you to Lady Catherine."

"No, I wish to see my brother first. Where is Theo?" Georgiana asked impatiently.

Hastings exchanged a look with the Colonel before he

responded. "He is in the Blue Guest Room. May I have someone take you to him?"

"I know the way. Richard, will you make my excuses to Lady Catherine, please? If I wait for her, I could be delayed for hours." Turning to Mrs. Annesley, who had been standing just behind her, Georgiana said, "Please see to my things and rest yourself. I will not require your assistance until later."

Before Mrs. Annesley could protest, Georgiana turned to her cousin, who gave her a nod, and she set off for the stairs.

"Hastings, you may announce my arrival to your mistress, but please take your time in doing so, if you know what I mean," said the Colonel.

"As you wish, sir." The butler set off very, very slowly for the drawing room.

Georgiana ascended the stairway as quickly as she could, keeping in mind that ladies never rushed. Once at the top and out of sight of her cousin and companion, she set off down the hallway to the guest wing at a run. Hang propriety! She had to get to her brothers.

After a quick rap on the door, Georgiana swept into Theo's room without waiting for an answer. Once inside, she stopped and looked from one brother to the other.

Darcy stood. "What are you...?"

Before he could even finish the sentence, Georgiana kissed him on the cheek and slipped into the chair he had just vacated. Setting a hand on Theo's forehead, relief sweep over her. "He is not feverish." She turned to her elder brother. "What are his injuries?"

Darcy, who seemed too stunned by her sudden appearance to protest, described what had happened.

Georgiana knew she had only minutes, possibly seconds, before he began to question what she was doing there and how she had learned of the accident.

Theo opened his eyes and squinted at her. "Georgie, is that really you or am I seeing things again?"

"I am here now. I will take care of you," she said. She turned to Darcy and looked at him as if daring him to contradict her.

Whatever Darcy had been planning to say died on his lips as he found himself on the receiving end of a very good imitation of one of his own severest looks. He blinked slowly as if he could not believe it.

"He has been seeing things?" she asked.

Darcy's lips tightened. "We think it is the medicine."

"Laudanum should not do that unless perhaps he was given too much. Were you careful about the dose?" she asked.

Darcy cleared his throat and exchanged a look with Theo. "Lady Catherine gave him some of Anne's medicine. We think it might have some…harmful ingredients."

Georgiana's eyes grew wide. She turned back at Theo who nodded.

"We were just discussing the best way to approach Lady Catherine. She must not allow Anne to take it any more," Darcy said.

"It is not that simple. If it contains even one of the ingredients I suspect it does, stopping suddenly would be more harmful than continuing to give it to her. She must be tapered off it," Theo responded. He was finally beginning to sound a little more like himself.

"What should we do?" Darcy asked.

"If we could find out where the medicine is kept, we could start watering it down with something. Tea, perhaps?" Theo suggested.

"And when Mr. Cox arrives from London in the morning, we can consult with him," Darcy added. "But how can we find out where she keeps it?"

Georgiana smiled. "I have a plan that might work."

Darcy put a hand on her shoulder. "We will talk later about what you are doing here," he said severely.

When she replied, "I think we should," she was pleased to note the slightly confused look on his face. It was clearly not what he was expecting to hear.

Darcy, Georgiana, Colonel Fitzwilliam, and Mrs. Annesley took turns sitting with Theo through the night, and by morning, his color was returning and no signs of further impairment from the head injury had appeared.

Before Theo's morning dose of Anne's special medicine was due to be administered, Georgiana sought out Mrs. Shafton and offered to take the medicine to her brother. Just as she had hoped, she was able to follow the housekeeper to the source. The bottle was kept in a cupboard in her little office. As Mrs. Shafton carefully measured out the dosage, she explained the exact proportions to Georgiana who listened intently to her instructions. She thanked the housekeeper and made her way back to Theo's room. Now all they had to do was steal the key to Mrs. Shafton's cupboard, sneak into her office unnoticed, and water down the medicine a little more every day. That should be simple enough. Georgiana laughed at her own boldness.

As Georgiana was reporting back to her brothers about the medicine, one of the footmen knocked at the door. "You have a visitor from the parsonage. She has come to inquire about Mr. Theophilus' health."

"Who is the caller?" Darcy asked.

"It is Miss Bennet, sir. What should I tell her?"

When Darcy froze, Georgiana said, "Richard is sleeping in. You will have to go down. I can manage here for a few minutes."

Darcy reluctantly left them to talk to Elizabeth. When she and Theo were alone, Georgiana asked, "Who is she? If she is a 'Miss' then she is not the parson's new wife."

"No, she is a friend of Mrs. Collins. She was both the cause of my accident and my savior. She fixed my shoulder, helped me onto Theseus, and walked me back to the parsonage. A very capable and lovely young woman."

"We owe her a debt of gratitude."

"It is more complicated than that, dear sister. It seems our brother is finally in love."

Georgiana's eyes grew wide. "Our brother? In love?"

"I have been watching him since we arrived and am convinced of it. Actually, they met last autumn when Darcy visited Bingley in Hertfordshire."

"And what about the lady? Does she return his sentiments?"

"You know how little William gives away. I doubt she has any idea."

"Perhaps I should go down and meet her after all," Georgiana said. "I will send for Mrs. Annesley to sit with you."

"Before you go, could you get rid of that vile stuff just to make sure no one tries to pour it down my throat while I am sleeping?"

Georgiana took the glass and dumped its contents out the window before she went to meet this woman who had broken down her formidable brother's defenses.

When Georgiana entered the parlor, she was somewhat dismayed at the scene. Miss Bennet was seated on a little settee while her brother was standing stiffly behind the protection of a tall-backed chair. The lady stood when Georgiana entered, and they both waited for Darcy to make the introductions. Finally, he seemed to realize what was required and stepped forward.

"I have heard so much about you from your brothers," Elizabeth said warmly.

"You left Theo alone?" Darcy said sternly to Georgiana, as if Elizabeth was not even in the room.

"No, he is not alone. Mrs. Annesley is there with strict instructions about what to do." Giving her brother her sweetest smile, she turned back to Elizabeth. "I am very pleased to make your acquaintance. Thank you for helping

Theo when he was injured."

"It was the least I could do since I was partly to blame." Elizabeth glanced at Darcy. She looked a little puzzled. "I have brought some soup for him. It is what my mother always makes when one of us is ill. I hope it will help. I gave it to one of the footmen to take to the kitchen."

As they talked, Georgiana watched, first her brother and then Miss Bennet. Darcy was silent but rarely took his eyes off their visitor. His face did not betray him, but there was something in his eyes that Georgiana had never seen before. Oh, yes, he was definitely interested in Miss Bennet, though his siblings were possibly the only ones who would ever be able to detect it. On the other hand, the lady did not seem to show Darcy any partiality and made little if any attempt to include him in the conversation although she did glance in his direction several times. Georgiana sighed inwardly. This was going to be very complicated indeed.

After a brief visit, Elizabeth rose. "I must go now. I am expected back at the parsonage."

Georgiana took Elizabeth's arm as if they had been friends for years. "I will tell Theo you called and inquired about him. Bringing the soup was so good of you. We all appreciate your thoughtfulness, do we not, William?"

Darcy and Georgiana thanked Miss Bennet again as they walked her to the front hallway. After more farewells and a promise to call tomorrow, Elizabeth departed. Georgiana and Darcy started up the stairs back to Theo's room.

"He is in love with her," Darcy said solemnly.

At first, Georgiana thought she had heard him incorrectly. "What did you say?"

"Theo is in love with Miss Bennet."

She tried to hide her astonishment at this revelation. "Oh, my, and does she return his sentiments?"

"I have observed some signs of it. She took great care

of him when he was first injured, and then she came all the way here to bring him soup and inquire after him."

"Surely, that was just common courtesy."

"There are other signs."

"Hmm…," Georgiana replied uncertain what else to say.

"She would be a good match for him although she does not have much of a dowry," Darcy continued.

"Then that would make it impossible."

"I have been thinking of ways I could help him, make it easier for them to marry."

"Oh, my," Georgiana said softly.

"Please do not mention this to Theo. Much depends upon what happens when they see each other again once he is feeling better," Darcy confided.

"I…uh…" Georgiana was too astonished at what she had just learned. Each of her brothers thought that the other was in love with Miss Bennet. What a tangle!

As they reached the top of the stairs, Darcy put a hand on her arm to stop her. "There is only one way you could have found out about Theo's accident. You know my study is sacrosanct."

Georgiana took a deep breath. "Yes, I have been meaning to talk to you about that. Shall we step into the small parlor? I do not want to disturb Theo."

She did not look at him as they walked to the parlor, knowing too well the look he wore. His brows would be drawn low over his eyes and his lips pressed into a hard disapproving line. It was a familiar enough expression. Why could he not listen instead of becoming so cross?

Darcy ushered her into the dimly lit room. The ornate parlor only caught the afternoon sun, making it dreary at best during any other hour of day. An ideal spot for their conversation.

She sat in a small, uncomfortable chair—the only kind

Aunt Catherine seemed to permit in her realm. Hard, lumpy and garish, a bit like her. Oh, Fitzwilliam would not approve of that thought, but Theo and Richard would laugh; they would probably think of it themselves.

"Now, let us talk about how you knew of Theo's injury." He stood before her, hands clasped behind his back. If he had a cane in hand, he would look just like a disagreeable school master.

"What would you have me say?" Her voice squeaked like a little girl's. *Why did it have to do that?*

"What would cause you to do such a thing? To abandon proper manners and respect? I have no doubt you have been taught better than to rifle through another's belongings, much less read their correspondence. I would not tolerate that behavior in a servant, yet now it seems I have to endure it in my sister. What were you thinking?"

"I...I...I was thinking you left me little alternative."

"I? You suggest I forced your hand? How do you blame me for your indiscretion?"

He looked so surprised—and so offended. *Was it possible he truly did not understand?* "I do not like to be spoken to in a loud voice nor do I appreciate being lectured."

"What has that to do with any of this?"

"If I ask you questions when you are wearing your 'do-not-dare-ask' expression, that is exactly what will happen." She clutched the arms of her chair to keep from running away.

"My what?"

"You know, it is the look you usually wear for Theo when he wants to talk about something."

That stopped him cold. His jaw dropped and eyes bulged as though words lodged in his throat. *Perhaps a sharp slap on the back would help. Probably not.*

"Georgiana!" That was exactly the tone she had hoped to avoid.

"You see, you are yelling at me now."

"Of course I am. I have every reason to be! You read

my post and now are blaming me for it."

She rose up a little in her seat. "If you would bother to talk to me, to tell me things, I would not have to do such a thing."

"I tell you what you need to know."

"No, you do not."

"Then you might ask."

"I cannot. You yell at me like you are doing now when I ask."

"You are behaving like a child."

She jumped to her feet, voice rising to meet his. "No, I am not. But you treat me like one!"

"I do not."

"Do you raise your voice to your peers? Do you withhold important information from them? Do you take offense when they ask needful questions?"

"Of course not."

"But you do that with me...and with Theo. We are both well grown, and both quite tired of it. Quite tired."

His face grew dark and contorted into the expression she feared. "You will not speak to me that way, Georgiana."

No longer would she be afraid. If Theo could stand up to him, then she could as well. "Very well, but neither shall you speak to me the way you have been. If you wish respect from me, you shall have to give it in kind. No wonder Theo is so very put out with you. You are a tyrant."

"What are you saying?"

"I am saying that I have had enough of your rule." She threw her hands into the air. "Richard is as much my guardian as you are. I shall apply to him and leave Pemberley to you."

"You would not dare."

"Watch me." She stormed past him and out of the parlor.

Just a few steps into the corridor, she ran headlong into Richard. He caught her elbows to keep her from falling.

"What is wrong? You look a fright? Is it Theo?" He clutched her arm, his face losing a little color.

"No, Theo is fine. Fitzwilliam is … impossible." The word itself was too mild to fit her pique, but anything stronger was unfit for a young lady of quality to utter. There were times, like now, when it would have been pleasing to be a man.

"He deduced you have been reading his post?"

She turned away from an all too penetrating gaze. "Yes."

"You had little doubt he would. You did not expect him to be happy about it, did you?" He tucked her hand into the crook of is arm and led her to the gallery.

The long, uninhabited hall, with somber rows of ancestors and kings staring down at her only echoed Fitzwilliam's sentiments.

"No, of course not. But he treats me like an empty headed bit of fluff, and I am not."

Richard chuckled. "You are too harsh with him."

"Not at all. And it is even worse since…since…"

"Ramsgate?"

She pulled her hand from his arm and turned away. *Must it always come back to that?* "I made a mistake and I know it. But must it brand me for life as too stupid…"

He stepped in front of her and took her shoulders into his large, strong hands. "You are not stupid. No one ever said that."

"But I am treated as such. I have learned from my mistake. I would like to think I deserve to be treated as though I had."

"I understand that, though it is still—"

"Do I not even deserve to be permitted to ask questions?"

"You should be." He handed her his handkerchief.

"And yet I am not. He glares at me, cuts me off, lectures me when I try, even as he does Theo."

"Shall I speak to him?"

She dabbed her eyes. "No. He and I must work this out on our own. Besides, there are more important favors I must ask of you. Come, sit." Grabbing his hand, she sat on a window bench.

He crouched beside her. "What do you need of me?"

"There are two matters weighing heavily on me, and I cannot manage either without your help. The first is Anne."

"Anne?" He shook his head and blinked. Such a dear little look he wore when he was surprised.

"Aunt Catherine tried to give Theo some of her medicine and he, Fitzwilliam and I are now convinced that those vile tonics are more the source of Anne's problems than her cure."

"How do you know?"

"Theo believes it contains…I do not know exactly what…but he believes it to be very bad. It made him quite ill and not right in his mind."

Richard knotted his hand in the back of his hair. "And Fitzwilliam agrees?"

"Yes, he does. They believe we must dilute her medicine, not discontinue it altogether, lest it cause even more problems. We need your help to accomplish all the necessary subterfuge."

Richard snickered. "The reputation shall never leave me, shall it? You can count on my assistance. I have seen the damage those tonics can do. If Theo and Fitzwilliam both agree, then far be it from me to cause dissention in the ranks."

She exhaled heavily and sagged against the window. The sun left the glass hot in its wake. "Thank you."

"You said there were two things?" He laid his hand on hers.

His hands were so callused and so heavy. A meandering scar trailed across the back of his hand into his sleeve.

That must have happened in France.

"Yes, but the second is a bit more sensitive." She bit her lip. Would he become angry at her mention of it?

"I am all ears." He winked. Somehow he always knew the right thing to do.

"Both Fitzwilliam and Theo have confided in me that they believe the other to be attracted to the same woman."

Richard coughed, but he was probably trying not to laugh. "Miss Bennet?"

"It is not funny."

He snorted into his hand. "No, I suppose it is not."

"I need your help to determine which of my brothers, if either, has found her appealing."

"And you want help furthering the match?" His eyebrow arched so high it nearly touched his hair.

"She is a suitable match for either of my brothers. I should very much like her as a sister."

His lips wrinkled into the funny little half smile he had given her since she was small. "As long as you promise me that we shall not attempt to match-make where no real interest lies, then I will help you, Little One."

"How do we—"

"I think it simple enough. The denizens of the parsonage and their guests are here regularly enough. We simply watch your brothers the next time they are in Miss Bennet's company. Neither one of them is so artful as to be able to hide his interest from purposeful observation."

"You think it so simple?"

"Smitten men are rarely subtle enough to go undetected and Darcy men doubly so."

"I hope you are correct."

"Trust me, I am. Now," he pulled her up. "What shall we do to reconcile you to Fitzwilliam?"

Darcy stalked away and straight out the garden door. He needed air, fresh air and in vast quantities. What had overcome his sweet, gentle little sister? She never spoke to him—or anyone—that way before. How was it she was acting like...like Theo!

He raked his hair and turned down the gravel path that led to the woods. What was happening to his neatly ordered life? Ramsgate, Theo's dubious career, Anne poisoned by her medicine and Miss Bennet here in Kent! How much could a man endure? What had he done to so torment the fates that they would unleash this upon him?

Reading his post—she had read his *post*! After all that had taken place at Ramsgate, had she learned nothing? Had she not matured?

He stopped near a large tree and leaned against the trunk. Rough bark bit into his hands. A bright ladybird crawled over his finger and along the back of his hand, tiny legs tickling as it went. Georgiana loved ladybirds, ever since she was a little girl. He and Theo used to catch them for her. She would laugh so as they crept along her apron.

She was not a little girl anymore. Georgiana was a young woman. A lovely young woman. It was so hard to remember that. As difficult as recalling Theo now allegedly had a gainful, respectable career.

The ladybird flew away. Just like Georgiana would someday fly away from him when she married. Or when he chased her off with his ill-temper. She was right; he had yelled at her, just as one might yell at a servant. Perhaps he had treated her as poorly as...as Theo.

He bumped his head along the tree trunk, savoring the sharp pain. Foolish, foolish! When had he become a man his own siblings would choose to avoid?

No, this had to change.

Soon.

Now.

He pushed off the tree trunk and turned back for Rosings. When he cleared the woods, a movement in the garden caught his eye. Georgiana and Richard. He tugged his coat straight and strode to them. No sense in dragging things out.

"Darcy!" Richard waved him over.

Georgiana's face flushed, and she looked at her feet.

"These gardens never change, do they?" Richard plucked a sprig of leaves.

"I do not think they do. Aunt Catherine's tastes are nothing if not entirely predictable." He pretended to smell a nearby blossom.

"Georgiana wishes to speak to you." Richard pushed her a step towards him.

She glared and stumbled. Darcy caught her elbow.

"I should like to speak to her as well."

"Excellent." Richard nodded and trotted off, far too content with the situation. He had all the subtlety of a charging stallion, but perhaps that was helpful this once.

Georgiana tugged her elbow out of Darcy's grasp and turned her face away.

"You are still angry with me." It was at best a stupid question, but it was something to say.

"I imagine you are angry with me as well," she mumbled at the ground.

"Not so much as I am angry with myself."

Her face lifted and she met his eyes. Why did it hurt so much to see the surprise on her face?

"I should not have spoken to you as I did. And if you are afraid to ask questions of me, then there is something very wrong indeed…with me."

"I…I…"

"You are surprised to hear me say such a thing?"

She nodded just a tiny bit, almost as if she were afraid to agree too heartily.

"I am sorry for that, too."

She touched his fingers. "Fitzwilliam, I am sorry. I should not have read your correspondence."

"I agree, you should not." He took her hand. "But I can understand why you did it."

Once more, that excruciating look of surprise. What

kind of ogre had he become?

"It was still wrong of me."

"Yes, it was. But I forgive you. Will you forgive me for driving you to do so?"

She squeezed his hand. "I will."

"I cannot promise I will be able to change immediately, but I will try. In the meantime, please, stay at Pemberley."

"I would like that very much. And I will not read your letters or go into your study uninvited again."

"I am sure you will not." He pressed a kiss to the top of her head. If only dealing with Theo were so easy.

CHAPTER 7

THE COLONEL'S WORDS WERE prophetic. The following morning, as they broke their fast, Lady Catherine declared her intention of permitting the party from the parsonage to take tea with them at the soonest opportunity, and the following day at three o'clock was soon fixed upon.

It was a remarkably fine day for so early in spring, and the lady of the house lost no time in instructing the servants to lay out the necessary paraphernalia in the conservatory in preparation for the arrival of the guests.

"How are you bearing up?" The Colonel settled on a chair beside Theo whose arm remained strapped, his injured ankle resting on a small stool.

Theo stared longingly at the open door to the gardens. "I suppose I must take comfort—this is almost outside, is it not?" He turned to his cousin, lowering his voice. "Did you manage to unearth anything of interest regarding the Bennets of Longbourn?"

Richard shook his head. "Naught beyond what you told me in your letter: Miss Elizabeth Bennet is a gentleman's daughter, one of five sisters, with the estate entailed upon

Collins. There is no dowry to speak of but the only disgrace against the family seems to be their lack of good connections; the lady has an aunt married to a country attorney and an uncle in trade, albeit very successfully."

With a grunt, Theo shifted against the cushions. "There are those who would find that sufficient disgrace to discount her, and my brother, I have always assumed, would be one of them. He must be in deep."

"She must be quite a woman."

Theo grinned. "Indeed; as you will find directly. Now," he fixed his cousin with a serious eye. "Georgiana told me she spoke to you about Anne the other day. How did you fare with the medication?"

The Colonel grinned back. "Mission a complete success; did you doubt it?"

Theo grunted. "No!" He looked over to where Anne sat. "Our cousin approached me after breakfast—a rare enough occurrence—chose to sit with me for close to half an hour. She spoke very little, but she fidgeted a great deal! Her words on leaving me were, "I confess I feel a little strange." He chuckled. "I did not like to say it, but she looked a little strange too—do you not see it?"

He nodded towards Anne, and the Colonel studied her for a moment. "There is some animation in her features and she is, as you said, restless." Richard frowned. "I hope she bears no discomfort as the effects wear off. I diluted the open bottle with cold tea, but the full bottle behind it on the shelf now contains far less potion and a vast deal of Earl Grey!"

"Then, we shall see a fairly swift alteration. We must hope her recovery is not so rapid as to be detected too soon."

"If it is, we shall have to consider a diversion."

"Speaking of diversions—" Theo nodded towards the door where the party from the parsonage were now entering the room.

Keen to finally meet this Miss Bennet, with whom his

three cousins seemed entranced, the Colonel got to his feet, amused to note Darcy—who had been loitering near the door ever since they came into the conservatory—had now decamped to the opposite side of the room.

"Excuse me whilst I accept the inevitable," he said to Theo as their aunt rose majestically from her chair to greet the visitors, and he walked over to join her.

The introductions were made abruptly by Lady Catherine who, despite having condescended to extend the invitation in the first place, now seemed to wonder at her own generosity and the need to introduce yet another member of her family to such people.

The Colonel had no difficulty in assessing which of the three ladies present might be Miss Bennet even before she was presented, and he enjoyed a few words with her before she excused herself to pay her compliments to the others present. Darcy, he noted from the corner of his eye, remained by the window, the only acknowledgement between him and the lady a distant bow and a brief curtsey in return.

Once the formalities were over, the Colonel was quick to note how soon the lady made her way over to enquire after Theo, and by the time he had managed to conquer the Reverend Collins' onslaught of complimentary greetings and turned to survey the field, she sat by his side. Theo's face was wreathed in smiles, his confinement clearly all but forgotten.

Securing a cup of tea for himself and Georgiana, the Colonel walked over to join her, prepared to do as they had agreed and observe the players.

She frowned as he sat down. "What is Theo about? He told me he believed our brother to be in love with Miss Bennet! Why does he persist in showing such interest himself?"

The Colonel grunted and took a swig of tea from his cup. "Perhaps he cannot help himself."

"Oh Richard! Not you also?" She looked quite dismayed, and he put his cup on the table and laughed.

"Have no fear, my dear. Miss Bennet is an attractive and charming lady, and I can see it would not be difficult to find oneself ensnared without due intent, but this old soldier is made of thicker skin!" He patted Georgiana on the hand. "I think we have sufficient on our hands discerning the interest of your brothers! On which matter, where the devil is Darcy now?"

Georgiana inclined her head towards a corner of the conservatory housing a small collection of books, and the Colonel snorted. "True to type. Skulking in the shadows rather than center stage like Theo. This will not avail us of much." He turned to Georgiana and grinned. "Though we have a well-chosen observation point here. Well done! We can oversee the entire battlefield and observe each opponent without detection!"

Georgiana bit her lip and looked over to where Elizabeth could be seen helping Theo by adding lumps of sugar to his tea and stirring it, their conversation clearly delighting them both. "I do not think our aunt is happy with Theo paying so much attention in Miss Bennet's direction."

Looking across the room, the Colonel observed Lady Catherine's thunderous expression. "Well, at least it keeps her attention from her daughter for now."

"But what of Fitzwilliam?"

"She would be even more unhappy if she saw that." He nodded towards the gentleman in question, whose gaze, despite the book in his hand, was fixed upon Miss Bennet and his brother, his air and countenance conflicted.

"But how are we ever to determine who has the right of it—all we see is Theo's interest openly displayed, when he claimed Fitzwilliam was the one enamored."

"You are full young, Georgie, if that is all you see!"

She looked over towards her elder brother, but he had turned to stare out of the window into the grounds.

"How is Fitzwilliam ever to speak to her if Theo demands her attention so—we will discern naught from this!"

The Colonel patted her on the arm and got to his feet. "Perhaps we need a little alteration; leave it with me. Oh—wait! Our aunt has risen!"

Lady Catherine swept majestically across the conservatory to where Theo reclined, and Miss Bennet got to her feet.

"Miss Bennet. Do me the honor, I beg you, of keeping my daughter company. I wish to remove to the garden, and her companion has her day off."

The Colonel's gaze flew to the lady's face to see how she would take such an incivility, but though her eyes flashed, she smiled down at Theo. "Excuse me, Mr. Theophilus."

"Anne." Lady Catherine waved her fan at her daughter. "Put on several shawls before you venture out of the door. Miss Bennet will assist you."

"But what about me?" Theo made to get to his unsteady feet.

"Stay!" thundered Lady Catherine. She jabbed him in the chest with her closed fan and he scowled, dropping back against the cushions and then wincing.

He threw an exasperated look at his brother across the room, but though Darcy had turned to observe the commotion, his visage was without expression.

The Colonel sighed. "Excuse me, Georgie; I need to speak to your brother."

"Poor Theo! It is so unfair. Why must he stay indoors?"

"Not that brother, my dear!"

Georgiana looked surprised. "Oh—I see." She glanced over to where Darcy once stood, but he had already stepped outside. "Then I shall remain here with Theo to bear him company."

Once all of the party, with the exception of Theo—he refused to have Georgiana trapped inside just for his sake and said he would go and rest for a while—were settled outside, and the servants had refreshed cups and plates for those who wished it, the Colonel looked around for Darcy, soon espying him on a stone bench over by one of the ornamental fountains.

He walked over to join him, smirking as he passed Anne and Miss Bennet, the latter of whom was hiding a copious number of shawls under their chairs as his cousin held her face up to the sun, clearly relishing its feel upon her skin.

"Why so distant?" He sat down next to Darcy on the bench.

"You know I have no time for this sort of thing."

"Yes—we all know. Yet there is some company worth indulging in, surely." He turned to look over to where Miss Bennet now sat at Anne's side.

Darcy cleared his throat. "I am not... I do not have a natural propensity for pleasantries."

"No indeed; your bent is more towards *unpleasantries*, is it not?"

This comment merely earned him a scowl, and the Colonel laughed. "Come, Man, do not waste this opportunity, for what are we to do in life but improve ourselves. Tell me," he fixed Darcy with a compelling eye. "How did you become such a master of fencing?"

Darcy glared at his cousin. "How should I know? Lessons? Repeated exercise until it became instinctive?"

"And riding? You are a fine horseman, as well you know. Your performance on the pianoforte, though rarely displayed in public, is almost equal to Georgiana's, and we are all fed up to the gills of hearing from our aunt about the neatness and evenness of your lettering."

"To where does all this tend, Richard?" Darcy's tone was impatient. "All accomplishments must be studied, be they menial or otherwise."

"Precisely. So what do we ascertain from this? To be certain, you did not emerge from the womb brandishing a sword in one hand and a pen in the other—you were not born a horseman or a musician. All these accomplishments you were prepared to learn and—above all—*practice*."

Darcy grunted. "One does not practice making pleasantries—one either has the talent or one does not. It is a tiresome aspect of social commitment.

"Now that, my friend, is where you are wrong." Darcy, however, refused to be drawn, and the Colonel, deciding it was time to change tactics, got to his feet.

"Well—if you persist in remaining aloof, I shall leave you to it. I have far better things to do with my time." With that, he left his cousin as he had found him and strode across the lawn to where Anne and her new companion sat.

"Miss Bennet." He bowed, and then met her amused gaze. "Would you do me the honor of taking a turn about the garden. I am in need of some levity!"

Elizabeth smiled, but then she glanced over his shoulder to where Darcy remained staring into the fountain. "And this you do not find in your cousin?"

"Come," he tucked her arm in his and, excusing them both from Anne, led her to a path bordering the garden which would take him in Darcy's direct line of vision. "My cousin is many things, Miss Bennet, and has many good qualities, but levity is not one of them. Now, let us enjoy some pleasant conversation before my aunt takes it into her head to move the entire party down to the lake!"

Georgiana looked quite despondent as she and the Colonel made their way along the hallway to the small sitting room where the footmen indicated Theo had been taken to rest.

"I do not see we learned anything from all of that." Her voice was equally flat, and the Colonel stayed her with his hand.

"Do you not? I must own I disagree. I have no doubt

which of your brothers is truly smitten with the enticing Miss Bennet!"

Her eyes widening in surprise, Georgiana let out a small gasp and grabbed Richard's arm. "Truly? Then which is it?" Then, her countenance sobered. "I fear you are to say it is Fitzwilliam."

"You fear?"

"Oh, Richard, could you not *see*? Miss Bennet's preference is clear, for only one of my brothers receives her smiles and her laughter and the willing presence of her company."

"I saw plenty to convince me of Darcy's preference. His behavior is quite remarkable. Despite his displeasure in social occasions such as these, he has the breeding and manners to handle them with finesse. Though he is never quite himself at Rosings as he can be in other places, even you must see his air and countenance are conflicted beyond anything and his distancing himself from the company is almost absurd."

"Is this sufficient to believe him enamored of Miss Bennet?" Georgiana looked hopeful. "Perhaps Theo is still confused from his fall and mistakes it all."

The Colonel snorted. "If we are to speculate, Darcy could simply have had enough of the sycophantic parson's company, but I am confident I have the right of it." His countenance took on some seriousness. "Did you not see his reaction to my walking with Miss Bennet? I deliberately led us to and fro across his line of vision, and he was ensnared. I have never seen such fixation in his gaze, and..."

"Oh!" Georgiana exclaimed. "I recall it too! When I first met Miss Bennet the other day, it was not only his attention fixed upon her, but his eyes—I remember they never left her, even though he left the conversation to myself and the lady."

"Precisely—but even more, it is the expression within them. He attempts to conceal it, but twice I managed to surprise a look which leaves me in no doubt of the depth of his infatuation."

"Then it is as Theo supposed: he is in love with her."

"It does appear to be the way of it; when all these things are put together, they present a convincing picture." He frowned. "I remain, however, as uncertain as you over the lady's opinion of Darcy."

Georgiana sighed. "Did you not see the formality of their greeting earlier? It was in stark contrast to that exchanged between Miss Bennet and Theo; if Fitzwilliam has lost his heart to a lady whose interest is in our brother, how shall it atone? How shall *any* of them ever be happy?"

"Do not take on so, Georgie! We have yet to establish the truth of Darcy's assertion over Theo's feelings." The Colonel took her arm and urged her forward. "Come; let us go to him."

"Thank heavens!" Theo raised his head from the cushion as they entered the room and then lay back again. "It is bad enough having to rest this blasted ankle without being made to take to my chair like an old lady each afternoon to rest my shoulder."

"Well, we are here now to entertain you."

Theo squinted up at them; the shutters had been drawn at his aunt's instruction and only a thin trickle of sunlight filtered into the room.

"And the party from the parsonage?"

Georgiana threw her cousin a knowing look, but the Colonel gave a slight shake of his head and pulled forward a chair, indicating she sit before pulling one forward for himself and straddling it, leaning his arms on the back rest as he stared at his prostate cousin.

"On their way home, thank the Lord."

Theo let out a splutter of laughter. "Aye, even the delightful company of Miss Bennet is overshadowed after several hours of the Reverend Collins. I swear, if he had paid me his compliments one more time, I would have taken his hat and rammed it up his—"

"Steady, old man!" The Colonel warned him with a glance at Georgiana, but she was staring intently at her brother and seemed not to comprehend the direction of his words.

"Theo!" Georgiana burst into speech. "Do you recall what you said to me—about our brother and his… interest in Miss Bennet?"

Shifting awkwardly in his position, Theo turned his eye upon his sister, a brow raised in question. "Of course. Why do you ask?"

"It is just… earlier… you seemed—well, you appeared quite taken with her." A wave of pink filled Georgiana's cheeks as she uttered these words, declaring her discomfort in speaking so to her brother.

The Colonel patted her reassuringly on the shoulder and turned to his cousin. "Is it the truth? You have no intentions? I know it would not be an easy match, for I understand she has little dowry."

Theo shrugged. "If you wish to know my interest, then it is for the lively companionship Miss Bennet offers. There is no denying she is an attractive woman—almost beautiful once you are swept away by those lovely eyes—" he stopped and looked first to his sister, then back to his cousin. "But I stand by my words to you, Georgie; I believe Fitzwilliam is enamored of her, and though we have fallen out over many things over the years, competing with him for the one person who may be able to redeem him is beyond me."

A look of relief spread across Georgiana's features, but Theo shook his head.

"Your concern should not be for which brother has lost his heart to the lady, more what the lady thinks of *him.*"

The Colonel nodded. "Indeed. Hence my seeking out her company earlier. It is impossible to say what her true feelings are. Though Darcy has clearly not impressed her in the past, there is little indication whether her opinion has improved, for she is resistant to questioning, however covertly put."

Theo laughed. "Yes, I discovered that for myself. She is not easily fooled into revealing what she truly thinks."

"Fitzwilliam did not look at all pleased when you were walking with Miss Bennet, Richard." Georgiana looked to her cousin.

"Darcy has not sported a pleased air and countenance for some time."

Georgiana looked mournful. "But then—what is to be done?"

Theo leaned back into the cushions and pinched the bridge of his nose. "Must something be done? Can we not simply enjoy watching him squirm for a while longer? As a man confined in his activities, I must have some amusement!"

The Colonel laughed but Georgiana frowned. "Theo! That is unkind!"

He laughed. "I am not serious, Georgie—it is merely a jest!" He reached over and squeezed her hand. "If it is your wish, so be it. I shall join forces with you and Richard in trying to find a way to help bring them together."

The next morning, Darcy arose early even by his own standards. The early hours where none made demands on him nor needed him were too precious to waste.

He dressed without his valet. Even that intrusion was too much right now. What did it matter? No one but the servants would see him until after his ride and subsequent ablutions.

The single groom in the stables said little—good man—saddling his horse quickly and disappearing back into the morning shadows. Perhaps he should ride Theseus instead. The poor creature was becoming restive in Theo's absence. But no, riding that high-spirited equine was more work than he wanted right now. Theseus would have to wait for his exercise until Darcy found his patience.

The wind on his face and his horse's steady hoof beat lulled him into quiet meditation. This was what he escaped for, a quiet and peace offered nowhere else.

How could this spring trip have become so immensely complicated? Every year he visited Rosings and nothing out of the ordinary ever happened—ever! This year made up for all the rest.

He pinched the bridge of his nose and urged his horse faster. Theo's accident, Elizabeth and all her presence here meant; now Georgiana, Richard and their suspicions about Anne. Where to begin sorting this dreadful tangled web? Mr. Cox should return in a day or so to check on Theo's recovery; that would make a start of it. But he would do nothing to sort out the issue of Elizabeth.

How could Richard… He grumbled deep in his throat and twitched his shoulders. Richard was not a callous man; he would not toy with a woman's affections, nor would he knowingly injure Theo. But his marked attentions had to stop. Somehow he—

Hoofbeats thundered behind him. Who? He looked over his shoulder. Richard waved from atop Theseus, grinning as though he had no cares at all. At least the horse would be properly exercised today.

"Good morning, cousin!" He pulled Theseus alongside Darcy's horse.

"You are up early this morning. I thought you preferred to keep gentleman's hours when on your leave."

Richard laughed. How did he do that so easily? What would it be like to have such an easy temper?

"As much as I would like it, some habits are more difficult to break. Besides, this fine beast's plight could not be ignored. He veritably called me to exercise him."

Darcy snorted. "More likely, you thought this the only opportunity you would have to ride him. I do not recall Theo ever granting you permission—"

"True enough. No doubt he fears the creature might become accustomed to a true horseman." He stroked Theseus' neck.

Darcy chuckled and shook his head.

"What say you—a race to that folly over there?" Richard pointed.

Darcy leaned forward. Richard dropped his hand and they took off. How long had it been since they had done this? Years, surely that long. Too long.

The pounding gait, scent of the morning and wind in his face took him back to mornings long ago when his need for solitude had not become so demanding, when he might still share the morning with someone else. Would that he could return to those times again, even for just a little while.

Theseus pulled ahead and easily won the contest.

Darcy passed the folly and eased his horse to a walk. It was easy to let Theseus, and by extension, Theo, win here. Somehow he would have to remember this when he next saw Miss Elizabeth. His gut clenched. No, he would conquer this, he must. He owed Theo that.

"I say, he is a fine creature!" Richard patted Theseus' neck, panting still. Sweat trickled down the side of his face.

"Theo is an expert where horseflesh is concerned."

"I would much rather tear up the ground with a fine horse under me here at Rosings than on the continent, running from the French!"

Darcy shifted in his saddle. How did Richard maintain his easy manner whilst enduring so grim a profession? Even if he understood, would it be something he could duplicate? Not likely.

"Do you think Theo might be willing to sell him to me?"

"Hardly. That horse is his prize. Little would make him willing to part with it."

"I had a feeling you might say that. Too bad. I could use a steed like this one. I suppose I should consider myself lucky that he is not equally fond of the lovely Miss Elizabeth Bennet." His eyebrows rose suggestively.

"What?" Darcy pulled his horse up short.

"I said I need a horse very much like this one. Do you know from whom—"

"Not about the horse!"

"What then?" Richard chuckled. "Miss Bennet?"

"Yes."

"Oh, her." He shrugged.

Darcy's heart barely beat. Would Richard not answer the bloody question? "What did you say?"

"You are tenacious, are you not? Very well, I simply noted that your brother is far fonder of his horse than the young lady in question."

"That is not possible." It could not be. Could it?

"What makes you say that?"

Darcy's hands clenched the reins so tightly his fingers cramped. "It was clear, in the way he spoke of her, in the way he looked at her—"

"Perhaps you are not so wise and all-knowing as you think." Richard snickered and grinned.

Was he being so maddening intentionally or did it just come as naturally to him as it did to Theo? No wonder those two always got on so famously. "On what grounds do you contradict me? Wishful thinking? I did not miss the way you shamelessly flirted with her last night."

"Good. I hope she did not either."

"Have you no shame? To compete with Theo for a woman you cannot afford—"

"I am not in competition with him."

"I cannot believe you would deny it. Were you not working to attract her attention last night?"

"Of course I was. But that does not mean I am competing with him." Richard nudged Theseus to continue his walk.

"How do you know that? It is obvious to anyone with eyes—"

"You will not just let it rest, will you? I know because I asked him."

Darcy wheeled his horse about to follow Theseus. "You what?"

"I asked him his interest in her. I have no desire to duel with a cousin over a pretty woman. There are far more pretty women in this world than I have cousins."

"What did he say? Surely you misunderstood. How could you expect him to answer such a question?" Darcy's heart thundered louder than the horses' hooves.

"Not everyone is so circumspect with their intentions as you. Not all of us play everything so close to the vest. I hardly think there is much to misunderstand in 'go to it man and may you enjoy great success.'"

"I cannot believe he said such a thing."

"Believe it or not. It matters little to me. I have Theo's approbation and shall not fail to act." He threw a quick salute Darcy's way and rode off toward the stables.

Darcy watched his back for a long time. His horse snorted, and he turned it away from the house.

How could Richard ask such a question? But would Theo prevaricate on such a matter? Blood rushed to his face and roared in his ears.

Was it possible he might have both his brother *and* Elizabeth—if, of course, she could be convinced? He chewed the inside of his cheek. Not even the regular hoof beats of his horse could quiet his disordered thoughts.

Richard flashed Georgiana a wink and a salute as he sauntered past the morning room, and she suppressed her smile and sipped her tea. He had certainly wasted no time. That was one thing about Richard, he did not hesitate either in coming to a decision or in acting on one.

She reached for a still warm scone. Aunt Catherine's cook did make these visits to Rosings much more bearable, though the scones and other dainties she offered were generally the only thing she missed when she returned to Pemberley. Perhaps she might ask after the receipts.

"Georgiana?" Anne peeked into the morning room

"You are up quite early this morning."

"I am, am I not?" Anne smiled a funny little crooked smile Georgiana had not seen in years. "I actually feel quite well today." She looked better than usual this morning. The color in her cheeks was brighter and some of the shadows under her eyes had faded.

"You look positively spritely."

"I feel that way, and I am hungry too."

Georgiana passed her the plate of scones and a bowl of jam. "Let us hope this propitious turn of events continues."

"Indeed yes. But in case it does not, let us do something—something fun. I do not wish to waste such a rare, energetic sort of day."

"What have you in mind?"

Anne chewed a large bite of scone. "Oh, this does taste very well indeed. My gracious, have they always been this good?"

"I believe so."

"I cannot imagine how I have missed that. I must have another!" She reached for another scone. "As to something fun—let us go driving in my phaeton! It has been ever so long since I have taken it out. I forgot how much I used to enjoy it."

"That does sound like a lovely idea. Perhaps you might teach me a little of driving. I ride at home, but there is an old phaeton in the carriage house that I would love to use to call upon the tenants."

"Have you not a driver for that?"

"I do, but there is something so delightfully freeing about driving oneself."

"Too true. That is exactly what I love best about driving. I will take just one more scone and we may be off."

Of course a change of clothes was required and the

grooms had to ready the equipage, so it was nearly an hour before Anne perched on the phaeton, reins in hand, ready to be off.

Georgiana climbed in beside her. "Is it difficult to manage? I have heard stories—"

"Not this one. The high flyers are death traps. It takes so little to upset them. But this one is so low to the ground it is quite stable. With a gentle horse, it is no trouble at all." Anne clucked her tongue and flicked the reins. The phaeton creaked and protested just a bit until the wheels finally rolled smoothly down the lane.

"So tell me, cousin, what do you think of our new additions to Rosings Park?"

"You mean the vicar?"

"And his guests—yes."

"Well, he is just the sort of man I would have expected Aunt Catherine to choose for the parsonage." Georgiana licked her lips and watched Anne from the corner of her eye. They so rarely spoke, it was hard to predict what might offend.

Anne bit her lip and peeked at Georgiana. "He is a bit ridiculous, is he not?"

Georgiana giggled.

"Do not mistake me, he is a good sort of man, but I wonder if he is too much in awe of Mama."

"Ah...I..." Georgiana gaped. Who knew Anne had such decided opinions—who knew she had any at all?

"Oh, do not look at me that way, Cousin dear. I know you have thought the same thing. You are just far too well-mannered to say anything so direct."

"I...but...she..." What was she trying to say? She should reply, but what did one say to such disarming frankness?

"I have shocked you, I fear."

"A bit, yes."

"You are surprised I have thoughts and opinions?"

"Well, no...just that they are rather different to what I

expected them to be." Georgiana squirmed in her seat.

"You expected me to be a mousey version of Mama—echoing her sentiments with little alteration?"

"Well…yes…I suppose so."

"I fear then I will continue to disappoint you for as long as this unusual burst of energy lasts. Just because I rarely have the strength of interest to express myself does not at all imply that my mother speaks for me. I just rarely feel equal to the task of doing something about it."

"I had no idea."

"Of course not." Anne chuckled and guided the phaeton around a gentle curve in the lane. "That is one of the reasons I have enjoyed Miss Elizabeth Bennet's company so much recently."

"You have?"

"You have not? Though I have not said it, I have reveled in each of her delightfully impertinent yet utterly polite responses to Mama's outrageous conversation. I have never encountered anyone who dares speak so boldly, yet with complete courtesy. It vexes my mother so that she cannot call Miss Elizabeth out for her lack of manners. Have you noticed the shade of purple Mama turns—"

Georgiana sniggered. "It is quite a sight to behold."

"Oh, oh! I have a splendid idea! Let us go to the parsonage and invite the lady to ride with us. I know the phaeton is only built for two, but we are all small and, if we squash up, we can all fit."

"Oh, what fun, do!" Georgiana clapped softly. How perfect! Perhaps she ought to let Anne in on their plans for her brother and Elizabeth. She opened her mouth to speak, but shut it quickly. Lady Catherine had always maintained Anne should marry her brother. How did Anne feel about it? Oh dear, this could become quite problematical.

They arrived at the parsonage. Mrs. Collins and her friend stood in the garden, near Mr. Collins's roses. Mr. Collins burst from the house, overflowing with eloquence which he poured liberally upon Anne.

Anne glanced at Georgiana, rolled her eyes and nodded toward Elizabeth. Georgiana hopped down and approached her.

"Good morning, Miss Bennet."

"Good morning, Miss Darcy."

They all curtsied.

"This is a very fine morning, is it not?" Mrs. Collins smiled. She was such a sensible woman, an excellent balance for her silly husband. Just like Elizabeth's levity and open nature would be an excellent balance for her brother—if they were successful.

"Are you and Miss de Bourgh enjoying your drive?" Elizabeth asked.

"Yes, we are, thank you." Georgiana glanced quickly at Anne. "My cousin is having a rare day of good health and wishes to enjoy it to the full. She wished me to ask you if you would like to join us for a turn about the park."

"Oh do go on, Lizzy. I must go into the village with Mr. Collins to pay calls soon and Maria has gone to call upon the apothecary's daughters. So you will not be abandoning us."

"Are you sure, Charlotte?"

"It will do my heart good to know you are in excellent company. I am certain Mr. Collins would not have you turn down such a delightful invitation for any reason." She winked.

"Then I thank you very much for the invitation." Elizabeth smiled.

Oh, she was very lovely when she smiled. No wonder Fitzwilliam was so tongue-tied around her. It was a wonder he could form a coherent thought at all when she was present. That certainly explained how he might have offended her so deeply.

Moments later, they had climbed back into the phaeton, packed very close together, and set off to a chorus of gratitude and well wishes from Mr. Collins.

"You bear decidedly little resemblance to your cousin,

Miss Bennet." Anne's eyebrow quirked exactly the same way Fitzwilliam's did when he was amused.

Elizabeth's eyes narrowed as she studied Anne. "I believe you mean that as a compliment, so thank you."

Georgiana giggled and Anne laughed, a high pitched, bird-like trill few had ever heard. "You see, I told you she would be excellent company."

"You flatter me, Miss de Bourgh."

"I flatter no one, Miss Bennet. I have far too much of my mother in me for that. I only speak the truth."

Elizabeth's brows rose. "Then, thank you."

"I suppose it is a family trait, from the Fitzwilliam side. We are frank and truthful, perhaps to a fault."

"So you say your family only speaks the truth?"

Georgiana grimaced. Oh dear, this line of conversation would not flatter Fitzwilliam at all. "As a rule, yes, that is true, but we can, occasionally, allow a cross word to escape that is quite the opposite of what we do mean." Oh, please, do not let Anne argue!

"Oh, how that is true!" Anne rolled her eyes. "I think perhaps your eldest brother to be the worst among us at that."

"It is only because he feels so deeply but expresses so little."

"Indeed, but when he feels deeply, he also offends deeply. Remember when—"

Georgiana clapped her hands to her mouth. "Oh yes. Your mother was utterly mortified."

"I have never seen her so offended!"

"What happened?" Elizabeth asked.

"It is not flattering to my brother, so I shall not be a tale bearer. However, the important point is that he spoke those hurtful words in the midst of his grief over…over Sebastian's—our youngest brother's death." Georgiana's throat tightened. She cleared it and sniffled.

"I am sorry."

"It was many years ago; I am afraid I never knew him,

but I believe Fitzwilliam has grieved more than anyone. The anniversary of the event affects him heavily. But since he is not very well spoken, his grief comes out rather badly."

"You are being easy on him, Georgiana. He tends to offend whenever he is worried about you or Theo, which is quite often. Why, the last several months—"

"Please, Anne!" Georgiana gasped. Her face grew cold. Had Anne no notion of what she should or should not say? Probably not, given her mother. But still.

Anne snorted. "There is no need to be so sensitive about the imperfections—"

"I think I understand enough. There is no need to detail it all." Elizabeth said softly.

What a dear lady. She would understand Fitzwilliam once she knew him a little more. "The important point is that he does not mean to offend. I am not even sure he understands when he does it. And when it is pointed out to him, he will not rest until he makes a situation right. Especially for someone he cares about."

"Indeed?" Elizabeth's brow quirked.

"Yes. I will grant you that. He is one to deeply feel his error. I am sure there are few men of his character in all of England." Anne clucked her tongue and the pony quickened his pace.

Elizabeth blinked, her bottom lip between her teeth, and her brow furrowed.

Theo groaned and shifted his leg on its pillows. His confinement in these stuffy, dusty rooms was definitely the worst of his trials right now. The pains in ankle, shoulder and head were nothing to this bloody imprisonment. At least no one was pouring laudanum and God-knew-what-else down his throat any longer.

The door creaked open admitting Prince Will—Fitzwilliam himself, bearing a tray of something that smelled utterly delicious. Theo licked his lips and swallowed. He pushed himself up straighter on the chaise lounge. How had his brother managed to bring in real food instead of that unnamed mush that kept being sent under the guise of nourishment? Did he go into the kitchen himself?

"I see you approve then?" Fitzwilliam set the tray down and dragged a small table closer to Theo.

"How could I not? A man can only eat so much pap before his mind starts to resemble the vile stuff."

Fitzwilliam chuckled. "I cannot disagree. But do not express your appreciation too loudly as our aunt is quite convinced a meal like this might be detrimental to your recovery."

Theo grabbed a plate and heaped it with cold ham, kippers, potatoes and cheese.

"You do not need to eat it all at once, you know."

Theo glanced up. There was no criticism in his tone, this time at least. How odd and unexpected, and appealing. "Perhaps not, but with a very real chance she might burst in at any moment and snatch it all away, I am disinclined to take the risk."

Fitzwilliam leaned back in his seat and watched Theo eat, an odd contemplative look in his eyes. "Anne was very well today. She even took our sister out for a drive."

"Indeed? That is good news."

"Perhaps you were correct about her medicine."

Then Georgiana had been successful. Good on her. "I am cautiously optimistic for her then. One good day does not a recovery make, but it is a start."

"True. Mr. Cox will be here soon. I shall be interested to hear his evaluation." Fitzwilliam nodded, his eyes drifted somewhere beyond Theo and the familiar awkward silence unfurled between them once again.

Theo finished his plate and began refilling it.

"Richard took Theseus out today."

Theo rubbed a napkin across his mouth. "And he did

not break his bloody neck? The army has improved his horsemanship."

"He would buy that horse from you, if you would part with it."

Theo laughed and nearly choked on the mouthful he had failed to swallow. "You set him straight on that account I imagine?"

"He did indeed." Richard sauntered in and closed the door behind him. "So you brought the prisoner a proper meal? Quite merciful of you, Darcy."

Fitzwilliam shrugged and dragged a chair in closer. Richard dropped into it and plucked a roll from the generously laden tray.

"There now, that is mine!" Theo stretched across the table, not quite reaching Richard.

Richard slapped his hand away. "There is plenty to share with a poor underfed soldier."

"Underfed my arse. You can barely get those breeches on. Another generous meal and you will be splitting those seams—"

Fitzwilliam passed Richard a plate. "I will bring more if it is needed."

They both turned to stare at Fitzwilliam.

"Why do you stare at me like that?" He pulled back a bit, the familiar glare returning.

"Oh, do stop that." Richard crossed his ankles and leaned back. "It is just odd that you would not send a servant but rather do it yourself."

Fitzwilliam snorted. "A servant might be detained by our aunt for questioning and forced to bring back an approved meal, I on the other hand will not. I am sorry my efforts do not meet with your approval."

"Now why would you assume such a thing?" Richard winked.

"That is not what you intended to convey?"

"Not at all—I rather like this side of you."

Fitzwilliam twitched his head and shifted in his seat. He

never was one who liked to be closely examined.

"You do leave yourself rather open to misinterpretation, Richard. I heard it as Fish did." Theo refilled his plate. Those roast apples looked quite appealing.

Fitzwilliam glowered.

"Is that so?" Richard crossed his arms over his chest.

"Yes indeed. You know, at the Inn of Courts—"

Richard laughed and looked at Fitzwilliam. "Here it comes, we are about to be treated to another 'How I made barrister' story."

Odd. Fitzwilliam said nothing. He did not even twitch his eyebrows. He leaned in a little closer as if to listen. Very strange indeed.

"It is good to know you find me so amusing. But I insist you hear me out. My tale has direct bearing."

Richard extended his hand. "By all means, continue."

"I will. This is a tale of two judges, with both of whom I regularly dine. Both are well respected among their peers and excellent in their profession. However, they are esteemed very differently."

"One is secretly a scoundrel, no doubt?" Richard chuckled.

"Hardly. Both are quite similar in character, quite upstanding men."

"But one gregarious and the other taciturn." Richard's gaze flickered to Fitzwilliam who frowned and turned aside.

"No, no, not even that. Neither is so open a temperament to be called gregarious. They are both essentially quiet, formal men."

"Then what is the vital difference, oh wise one?" Richard bowed low from his waist, forehead almost touching his knees.

"The difference lay in what they approve—or rather in their ability to express it clearly. I know from conversations with them both that they are equally quick to approve something—or someone—"

"Or not?"

Theo flashed a strained smile. "Or not. As I said, they are both discerning men."

"No, you had not said that." Richard smirked.

"It was implied."

Fitzwilliam sniffed—was he hiding a chuckle?

"In any case, being equal in discernment, one is apt to express it well and clearly whilst the other is rarely heard uttering a word of approval to anyone. The former is well-liked and sought after, the latter is merely well-respected. Poor chap assumes people know when he approves and has no idea why people flock to the other judge instead of him."

"Indeed?" Darcy leaned forward just a bit.

"Absolutely."

Richard leaned back and stroked his chin. "I have seen the same thing in the army. Those who liberally show approval and generously praise what is praise-worthy, their men will almost always out-perform those commanded by dour and critical officers."

"You see, it is true." Theo crossed his arms over his chest.

"I confess, I discovered myself not nearly so adept in the practice as I thought myself to be."

Fitzwilliam turned to Richard, wide eyed.

"It is not as though either of our fathers offered much example to follow in that arena." Theo sneered, though he probably should not have. Fitzwilliam still refused to acknowledge the hurt Father's dour ways inflicted upon them all.

"No, they did not." Richard scratched his head. "But as a young Lieutenant, I had a Captain who provided an excellent model to follow. He could inspire the men to do things I could not. So I began to study his tactics, how he spoke to them and what he would say."

"Was it not difficult to use another man's words? Did you not feel yourself insincere, saying things you did not mean?" Fitzwilliam asked.

"It was awkward in the beginning, but so was learning to ride or shoot or fence at first. I saw it little different from any skill requiring practice." Richard's eyebrows flashed up. "But I would not perjure myself with insincere, empty flattery. I learned first to look for what was worthy and then to speak it openly."

Fitzwilliam rubbed his fist across his lips. "Was it—"

"Difficult? Yes. Uncomfortable? Yes. Effective? Astonishingly so. In truth, I still find it difficult to believe the power a little honest approval has in changing a man's opinion of me."

"I have seen the same myself and so have you. You just do not recognize it. Your friend Bingley is quick to express his approval—look how many friends he has."

Fitzwilliam huffed. "I hardly think that—"

"Do not be so quick to judge. I know you think him a bit cakey at times—and you may be right. However, consider how close are his ties to trade—his father was in business, was he not?"

Fitzwilliam grunted.

"And already see how well respected he has become in society. True, some will not see past his connections, but how many already welcome him since you began introducing him?"

"He has many supporters." Fitzwilliam nodded and pushed up from his seat. "Your tray is empty. Do you care for more?"

"If you are willing, yes, enough for three, perhaps?" Theo glanced at Richard who nodded curtly.

Fitzwilliam picked up the try and inclined his head. "As you wish."

They watched him leave.

"Interesting." Richard said.

"Quite." Theo smiled.

CHAPTER 8

THE UNPREDICTABLE SPRING WEATHER brought two days of persistent rain to southeast England and thus none of the inhabitants of Hunsford Parsonage to Rosings Park.

Darcy awoke on the third day from yet another night of poor rest, his dreams haunted by his brothers, his recent fears over Theo's condition interwoven with painful memories of Sebastian. Lying awake served him little better, for as he lay in the darkness of yet another long and lonely night, thoughts of a certain lady would persist in filling his mind.

Despite his cousin's avowal Theo had no intentions towards Elizabeth, Darcy was unable to fully dismiss the notion. Yet even were it so, how could he compete against his cousin, who had made it as plain as the Fitzwilliam nose upon his face he was quite taken with the lady? And had not Elizabeth made it equally clear she preferred his brother or his cousin's company to his own?

Darcy had reflected upon much that had happened with Elizabeth since coming into Kent. Had she accepted his attempt at an apology over his slur at the Meryton Assembly? Was her manner towards him any less antagonistic than it ever was?

Everyone seemed to think he would do well to practice his social skills; did Elizabeth think so too, and did not this echo the barely concealed illustration by his brother over the two judges and their appeal to others?

Such thoughts rolled interminably round Darcy's head as he made his way downstairs to join his family. His silence went unremarked at the table; the lively banter between Theo and Richard, now they had an extended audience in Anne as well as Georgiana, knew no bounds, only tempered by their aunt when she felt things were becoming a little too loud.

A thankful intrusion came with the arrival of Darcy's physician from Town, and he quickly removed to the library with his brother and cousin to speak in confidence with him.

Barely an hour passed before a footman closed the door upon the doctor's retreating back, and Darcy turned away deep in thought.

Mr. Cox's report on Theo's recovery had been reassuring, yet still Darcy could not fully rescind the tremor of uncertainty that lingered. Perhaps it would always remain with him. He had also taken the opportunity to speak to Mr. Cox regarding Anne's medication, and the doctor had taken away a furtively acquired undiluted sample of the concoction. The affirmation of the gentlemen that Anne's condition appeared to be improving in direct proportion to the watering down of the liquid was sufficient for Mr. Cox to advocate they continue to administer it in weakened doses. Yet the doctor's severe countenance had unsettled Darcy—were there ramifications yet to manifest themselves? He could hardly credit the rapid improvement in Anne over recent days. What on earth did the potion contain, and what was its singular purpose?

"Darce! There you are!"

Looking up, he espied his cousin peering round the library door. "Come on, man. Theo is chomping at the bit—does he have a clean bill of health?"

"The rains have been in his favor. His enforced rest has contributed to a vast improvement, though he cannot yet ride." Darcy walked across the hall and into the library, and the Colonel closed the door behind him with a snap. "Not a mount such as Theseus."

A groan came from his brother where he reclined on a chaise longue, and Colonel Fitzwilliam laughed as he sat down and reclaimed his teacup.

"I do not doubt it!" He threw Theo an amused glance. "For all his rashness, I do not believe he doubts it either! It is clear his shoulder, though much improved, is not up to Theseus' speed and vigor."

"Yet he would do well to exercise his ankle," Theo chimed in, swinging his legs down to the floor and sitting up. "He is on a downward spiral into naught if he does not soon escape the confines of these walls."

Darcy studied his brother for a second, then nodded. "I agree."

Theo blinked. "You do?"

"Yes, within reason. The doctor says you have sustained a sprain, nothing more. It is well strapped and with a cane you should be able to take to the Park for a short duration."

"Capital!" said the Colonel, getting to his feet to replenish his cup.

Darcy walked over to one of the windows and stared out over the parkland. It was a beautiful spring morning with the return of a weak sun spilling soft rays from a pale blue sky. Would Elizabeth be out, thankful to be released from the confines of the parsonage? How he wished he could walk down towards Hunsford in hope of meeting her—but to what end? Had he not finally owned she did not find his company a pleasure? That was saved for his brother and his cousin.

"I will attend Theo if you have business with our aunt,

Darce." He looked over his shoulder, and the Colonel shrugged. "I know she made it plain earlier your presence is required this morning.

"The Devil may take Aunt Catherine on such a day as this! I would like to join you."

Theo failed to conceal his surprise at this, but Darcy chose to ignore it. He was steadfast in his intent to attend more to his brother—whether he welcomed the attention or not. His conscience tried to whisper it was merely a distraction, but he firmly silenced it.

"Fine by me! The more the merrier!" said the Colonel as he retook his seat.

Darcy walked back across the room towards the door. "I must speak to Farrell before we go."

"As you wish. So—how is our aunt's Steward faring? His continued presence implies he has mastered the art of pleasing her."

"Indeed." Darcy glanced at the clock on the mantel. "There is a pheasant shoot about to start, and he will be in demand, so I must not delay. Shall we meet by the East Front in a half hour?"

The Colonel smirked at Theo. "Perfect. We shall send Hastings to inform Aunt Catherine once we are safely out the door. At his tortuous pace, it should give us ample time to make good our escape!

Darcy took his leave, but barely had the Colonel raised his cup to drain it when the door swung open once more and Anne de Bourgh entered. She walked swiftly—that in itself sufficient for both men to exchange a satisfied glance—but there was also something different about her appearance. He had pondered upon it in the morning room, and the Colonel was damned yet if he could discern what it was.

"You look well this morning, Cousin." Theo stood and waved her into a chair, but she shook her head and walked instead over to the same window that Darcy had recently vacated.

"I shall not linger—I am merely come to ask about Darcy."

Theo frowned as the Colonel got to his feet. "What of him?"

Anne turned to face them, a smile playing about her lips. Before she could speak, however, Theo pointed at her. "Your hair is different."

Raising a self-conscious hand to her tumbling dark tresses, Anne's cheeks filled with color. "Yes—Georgiana's maid has been instructing mine." Her hand dropped to her side and she met their gaze warily. "Do you find me foolish?"

The Colonel smiled. "On the contrary, my dear. It is very becoming."

Theo rolled his eyes. "Yes. It is very shiny and has curls. Now, about Darcy?"

"I have just come from Georgiana—she told me of your plan regarding Miss Bennet. I wish to help but I cannot see what is to be done."

"Hah!" The Colonel laughed. "And did Georgie confide in you willingly?"

Anne looked a little culpable. "I can be persuasive when I wish."

Shaking his head, the Colonel placed his empty cup on the table. "Yes—or rather, you can be your mother's daughter when it suits you!"

There was silence for a moment, and Theo, keen to be in the fresh air, turned for the door, but a sudden exclamation from Anne drew his attention. "Oh, oh, oh!!!"

"What is it?" The Colonel hurried to her side. "Are you relapsing?"

Anne threw him an exasperated look. "No, you dunderhead! I have been struck by a notion!"

Theo walked over to join them, testing his ankle warily. "The first in a good while, I fancy, from your excitement!"

Anne nodded, her eyes sparkling in a way neither gentleman could recall ever having seen before—or at least not since she was a child. "I have the perfect plan!"

The Colonel stared at her. "You do?"

"Yes! But I cannot tell you—not yet." She clapped her hands together. "Oh this will be such fun!"

This interference in Darcy's affairs, much as he wished to see his brother happily settled, did not sit well with Theo. "I do not see how more schemes and stratagems will help matters."

Anne smiled. "You should have more faith, Theo. I am certain I can find a way to help Darcy and pique the lady's interest."

Theo's heart misgave him. "And that is?"

With a shake of her newly arranged curls, Anne placed a finger to her lips. "I shall not speak of it. You cannot persuade me. I shall leave you now—Georgiana and I are due to meet Miss Bennet for a stroll around the copse; she will be here directly."

"And what of Georgie?" Theo glanced from one cousin to the other. "Do you anticipate her being party to this?"

Anne shook her head again. "I think not. Georgiana has the sweetest temperament, but her feelings are writ clear upon her countenance. It is best she remains uninformed."

Still uneasy, Theo sighed. "And Darcy?"

The Colonel grimaced. "Darcy must remain in the dark too. He does not approve of subterfuge of any kind, even if it should work in his favor."

"Hmph!" Theo grunted. "*Especially* if it might work in his favor. His intentions are too noble for his own good at times."

Anne laughed. "Indeed. Well, we shall work for his good in his stead."

"Capital! If we join forces we cannot fail—there is a deal to be said for the unanticipated attack on all sides!"

Theo shook his head. "I still feel—"

"Nonsense, Cousin!" The Colonel escorted Anne to

149

the door. "You will thank us for our intervention, you will see."

With a frown, Theo turned to look out of the window and blew out a pent up breath. His apprehension was growing, not least for his brother—an unusual sensation. With Anne bent upon scheming and Richard paying marked attention to Miss Bennet, how was the matter ever to be resolved? It seemed a queer path to courtship in his limited experience.

Conscious the Colonel had rejoined him, Theo threw him a quick glance. "She has a meddlesome streak, our Cousin Anne. There will likely be no stopping her now she has made her mind up."

"What else would you have her do?"

"We could always put her back on her medication!" Theo raised a hand as the Colonel threw him a disbelieving look. "Do not look so out of sorts, Richard. I am in jest."

Colonel Fitzwilliam merely grunted and turned to stare at the now closed door to the library, and Theo wondered if his cousin realized how admiring his gaze was. Yet before he could speculate further upon this, the door opened once more and their aunt swept across the room towards them.

"Theophilus, I want you in the study directly. I am assured your health is little impaired now, and I wish to have some papers drawn up." She looked about the room. "Where is Darcy? He must attend also."

The Colonel waved a hand towards the window. "He has gone out into the grounds, Aunt. It will have to wait until he returns."

"It will not." She glared at the Colonel and then turned on Theo. "If you are so recovered, find him. Bring Darcy to me, and we will make use of your legal mind."

"Devious Old Bat!" Theo muttered as the door closed behind his aunt. He caught his cousin's eye and shrugged, then winced as his shoulder pulled. "She is intent upon free service. Never one to let an economy pass her by!"

"If her purpose is what I suspect, she will have no need of your service, trust me!" Ignoring his cousin's questioning glance, the Colonel grinned. "It can wait for another time, Cousin."

Theo grunted. "Good—I have no intention of acting as Clerk to the Court of Aunt Catherine!"

Darcy's business with his aunt's steward was soon completed, and the distant sound of beaters calling to one another in the woods indicated the shoot had commenced. He drew in a deep breath of the refreshing spring air as he waited on his brother and cousin, pacing slowly to and fro on the gravel sweep. It was time he ceased dwelling upon the past; spring was a time for newness, beginnings. He would stop asking for further advice on Theo's condition and trust to faith all was well. He would strive to mend the rift that had developed between them, and he would also turn his attention to aiding his cousin, Anne.

His gaze upon his feet, he thought back to the physician's visit earlier. When had his cousin been assailed by her condition? As a young child, she had run and skipped and played as much as anyone. Even into her teenage years, she had driven out in her pony and carriage, ridden with verve and delight. What had brought about the need for medication?

"Good morning, Mr. Darcy."

With a start, he raised his head to behold Elizabeth.

"Good morning, Miss Bennet." He bowed in response to her curtsey, but beyond greeting him, she said nothing, and an awkward silence ensued.

Racking his brains for some form of pleasantry, Darcy recalled the conversation of the previous day, of how approval should be expressed if one was to find favor. He could no more emulate his brother or his cousin than fly from the highest tree tops; yet Elizabeth liked Bingley, did she not, and she was taken by an easy manner. Was there truth in Theo's words? Dare he attempt it?

He swallowed hard on the sudden restriction in his throat. "You look—you look well—are you—well?"

She appeared a little surprised by this question, but smiled briefly.

"As you see, sir, all limbs functioning satisfactorily and able to take my daily exercise without any undue duress."

She had taken him literally; why must she willfully misunderstand his meaning? Did she not know a compliment when it was made? What else could he say to indicate his approval? Theo had complimented her upon her eyes, and he had long acknowledged their hold upon him. Would it be too forward? What else could he speak of—her pleasing figure? No; that way led to all manner of pitfall. The liveliness of her mind? She would likely scorn him for singling out a woman's intelligence...

"You have—I have long admired—err," feeling his face warm in his embarrassment, he bit his lip. What could he say? Everything about her was lovely. He cleared his throat. "You have nice... hands." Nice *hands*?! Darcy gave himself a mental slap on the back of the head. "When you play the instrument, I mean. Slender—nice..."

A spurt of laughter greeted this, but the lady quickly sobered. She studied him silently for a second, then inclined her head. "Thank you. I think I may safely say that is the first compliment they have ever received. I shall treasure it."

Was she sincere? Darcy knew not, but he did know he could make no further attempt whilst she looked at him like that. It was best he revert to more traditional civilities. Before he could summon a comment on the weather, however, she spoke.

"May I enquire after your brother?"

"My brother is well, I thank you." He paused. "Were you calling to ask after him?"

"Not directly. Your sister sent a note inviting me to walk with her. And you, sir? Are you confined to walking in circles upon the driveway? I can assure you the mud is not too dire if you keep to the given paths."

He shook his head. "I am waiting upon my brother and cousin to join me."

"Mr. Theophilus Darcy's ankle is sufficiently recovered to walk upon? That is good news."

"Yes—the physician was here earlier and advocated some gentle exercise."

Elizabeth threw him a thoughtful glance. "You take prodigious care of him, sir." Then, she laughed. "Though I would imagine your brother does not take kindly to being confined indoors! I am sure he is longing for his mount."

A little disconcerted by how well she seemed to understand Theo on such short acquaintance, Darcy nodded. "You are quite right; his first thought was for a gallop across the fields. I suspect he was disappointed by my suggestion he make use of two legs rather than four!"

Shaking her head, Elizabeth smiled. "Siblings, Mr. Darcy—they can be such a worry, can they not? Oh!" She stopped, color flooding her cheeks.

Darcy frowned. "What is it?"

"Forgive me, dear sir. I spoke unconsciously just then. I was given to understand by your sister you sadly lost a younger brother in your youth. I am so sorry, Mr. Darcy."

Darcy blinked, then glanced down at her. Her cheeks were still infused with pink but it was undeniably becoming, and he realized with a shock that, entranced as he was with her company, his mind had not—as it had a thousand times before—naturally fallen towards Sebastian.

"Do not be disturbed. I thank you for your sympathy; it was a long time ago." He drew in a deep breath. "Though I will own the pain lingers."

She nodded as though she understood and, conscious he wished to prolong the moment, Darcy waved a hand. "Would you care to join me in my circling? It fills the time well enough when one is waiting upon others."

Elizabeth looked a little uncertain, but then she smiled.

"I am ahead of time. Of course I will join you."

They walked slowly, making a large circle around the sweep of stones, their boots crunching on the gravel. Neither said anything for a while, but it was a comfortable silence.

Then, Elizabeth threw him a quick glance. "I was told recently, sir, you only ever speak the truth." He threw her a startled look. "An admirable trait; yet, not if the truth is painful."

Cursing his foolish blunder in Meryton, Darcy sighed. "Sometimes, Miss Bennet, what one may perceive as a given at one moment, may be proved otherwise. Perhaps what matters is to realize the genuine from the false—that is when one owns the real truth."

Elizabeth smiled at this, but said nothing, and determined to prove to himself he meant those words, he drew in a breath before saying, "You said the other day your eldest sister had been in Town these few months?"

"Indeed I did."

"And does she remain there yet?"

Elizabeth nodded. "Yes—she is staying with my aunt and uncle in Gracechurch Street. Why do you ask?"

Darcy came to a halt and turned to face her. This was perhaps a mistake, as looking down into her face was a pleasing distraction and it was only when her lips began to twitch into a bewitching smile and she spoke that he pulled himself together.

"Mr. Darcy?"

"Er—yes, quite. Forgive me." He swallowed and then spoke in a rush. "I have been considering—I mean, if Miss Jane Bennet remains in London, I feel I should advise my friend of it." A raised brow was the only response to this, and he cleared his throat. "Yes—well, I had planned to write to Bingley, and as I will be able to share the intelligence of old acquaintance in the neighborhood, it seemed only fitting I also advise him of your sister's being in Town."

A strange expression filtered over the lady's face, but before he could discern its implication, she gave him a wide smile, one he had seen often in his careful observations of her, but it had always been reserved for those who had her approbation, and his heart swelled with delight.

Unable to stop himself, a smile overspread his features too. "I wonder, in the circumstances, whether I might request the direction, that he might put right the oversight and pay a call?"

"I am certain my sister would be honored to receive him, Mr. Darcy." Elizabeth's expression sobered and she bit her lip. "But surely Miss Bingley has the direction? She has called upon Jane before now?"

Darcy faltered; what was he to say that did not implicate others? How he hated disguise of every sort, yet complete honesty was beyond him at this point. In the end, he opted for prevarication.

"My friend does not reside with his sisters when in Town—Bingley prefers the comforts of a hotel, or he will make some stay with me. He will receive the information more directly should it come from my hand."

Elizabeth stared up at him. "Then I will leave the direction with Miss Darcy, if I may?"

Darcy nodded, then turned about as he was hailed. His cousin and brother had rounded the far end of the building, making slow progress towards them, and he turned back to catch the traces of a smile on Elizabeth's face as she acknowledged their shouted greetings.

"I will bid you farewell, sir." She curtsied, but before she could mount the steps to the entrance, he stayed her with his hand.

She gave him an enquiring look, and he released her quickly, desperately seeking words, something, anything, that could be considered approbation.

"It has been a pleasure, Miss Bennet."

She eyed him warily. "It has?" Then, she laughed lightly. "Yes—I suppose it has. It is a fine day for taking the air, is it not?"

He shook his head quickly. "No—I mean, yes, it is. But I did not mean—I speak of—you. I—it is most enjoyable to be outdoors, but the greater pleasure was in the company."

He bowed deeply, unable to say more, and unwilling to see mockery in her eye, he turned away, but this time, she stayed him likewise.

Darcy stared at the small, leather-clad hand on his arm, then raised his eyes to hers as she removed it. A strange look settled over her countenance, but she met his earnest gaze with an open expression. "Indeed it was, sir."

With a small smile, she turned and soon disappeared inside, and Darcy turned to join his brother and cousin, a glow of something close to contentment warming his breast.

The three gentlemen walked for some distance at a gentle pace along the path towards the small copse of trees bordered by the stream. Conversation was sporadic as they all took enjoyment from the fine weather and the opportunity for exercise.

Allowing Theo to set the pace, Darcy and the Colonel let him walk on ahead for a while, his enjoyment in his release from Rosings apparent in his face and his step.

"Darcy." The Colonel slowed his pace and spoke quietly. "You do realize, I trust, Aunt Catherine wishes to draw up the settlement."

With a sigh, Darcy nodded. "Aunt Catherine wishes to draw up the settlement every time we visit. I have no intention of permitting her any such license."

"And one day, you will have to tell her this!" The Colonel hesitated. "What of our cousin? Now the Anne of our youth returns to us... will it alter your intentions?"

"Not now, Richard." Darcy nodded towards Theo who had stopped just ahead of them. "Naught has changed with me, and I doubt very much Anne is that way inclined either. She certainly never was."

"Yet she is now eight and twenty—and I suspect seeking a life free of the shackles of Rosings."

"But not with me," Darcy muttered as they reached his brother.

"How I relish being outdoors once more!" Theo held his face up to the sun, removing his hat and closing his eyes.

"You had best heed the dangers of walking blindfold outside, Cousin, else you will end up getting wet!"

Theo did as he was bid with a laugh, duly noting the stream as he replaced his hat, and they made their way under the boughs of the first trees. They had gone but a few paces further when the Colonel, who now led the way, stopped.

"There is someone up ahead."

Darcy looked up quickly; he had hoped their paths might cross with the ladies at some point, but he was to be disappointed.

Theo narrowed his gaze and followed the direction of his cousin's hand. "Oh, it is just Watling."

"The old gamekeeper? Hah! So it is," laughed the Colonel. "I forgot he was still retained despite his near blindness! He is well removed from the shoot!"

Darcy frowned. "He must have lost his way, though it is probably best for Farrell and his guns that he has."

"I say, Watling!" The Colonel stepped forward to greet the elderly man, who turned in the direction of the voice hailing him.

"Is that you ag'in, Ma'am?"

Theo burst out laughing. "You must have need of changing your cologne, Richard!"

"Good morning, Watling," Darcy said formally as he joined them, ignoring the rolling of Theo's eyes. "You are not shooting, I trust, without your young assistant's aid?"

The old retainer squinted up at Darcy, then shook his

head. "No, no, no—not I, sir." He waved his shotgun in the air. "Stray pheasants seen down yonder." He pointed into the undergrowth ahead. "Them poachers will be at 'em if someone don' track 'em down. Just tryin' to rouse 'em."

"Good. Well, we will leave you to your duty." They took their leave and returned to the path, soon entering a small clearing.

Though he knew his brother would not wish to own it, Darcy could detect some weariness in Theo's gait now and, reluctant though he was to end their foray into the park, he did not wish his brother to face a setback.

"We have come sufficient distance for today, Theo. Let us turn back."

Theo raised a hand. "Wait! I recognize this spot!" He turned to face Darcy and the Colonel. "This is where I first encountered the delightful Miss Bennet!"

Darcy's interest was caught as Theo continued. "Yes— see there." He pointed across the stream. "Those very branches caught her bonnet after it sailed through the air."

Theo removed his hat with a flourish. "Shall I see if I can snare my own in such a manner? We shall have some fine sport retrieving it!"

Before Darcy could protest, Theo had flicked his wrist and tossed the hat skywards. It did not gain much height, but before it had chance to secure a perch or return to its master's hand, a loud bang shattered the peace of the day, and the hat fell to the ground and rolled towards his cousin.

Laughing loudly, the Colonel stooped and retrieved the hat, now sporting a hole in its brim.

"Watling must have mistaken it for some sport! He will not make much of a meal from it!"

Theo found this highly amusing, and taking the hat from his cousin, he inspected the damage. "His aim is not half bad for one with such poor vision! He must have been a crack shot in his youth!" He held the hat out, ready to swing it skywards once more.

"Theo, no!" Darcy's warning tone drew his brother's attention. "Do not be so foolhardy. The man is a liability, even if the bullets are blanks."

With a challenging look in his direction, Theo tossed his hat a second time, but with little regard for his recent injury. All of a sudden, three things happened in rapid succession: a shot rang out close by, Theo let out a yelp of pain and a lady screamed.

Darcy rounded on Theo. "Are you hit? Of all the foolhardy stunts…"

"Not I," said Theo coldly. "Merely wrenched my injured shoulder. Look to the ladies."

He had not even finished the words before Darcy took off at a run in the direction from which the scream had come. Theo followed at his heels, disregarding the stabbing pain in his injured ankle as he dodged tree trunks and brush.

Georgiana's voice cried, "Oh, help! Someone please help!"

Not his sister! Was he to lose *her* this time? Or would it be his cousin, or the lady he hoped someday to call sister? As Theo broke out of the copse, he could see the familiar shape of Georgiana standing on the stream bank a short distance away, her hands over her mouth staring at a shape on the ground, Anne de Bourgh kneeling beside her. So it was Elizabeth lying half on the ground, half in the stream.

But even as he feared the worst, she said in a teasing voice, "Although I am very sorry to cut short our walk, I must request that one of you return to the house in search of assistance. And quickly! This water is *cold*."

A hand grabbed Theo's arm. He tried to shake it off, but it held like a vise. Turning, he said, "Damn it, Richard! This is not the time…"

"Stop." It was the Colonel's commanding voice, and Theo instinctively obeyed. More quietly he said, "Miss Bennet is in no immediate danger if she is arguing with Anne and Georgiana. Let William reach her first and be her rescuer."

"What is the point of that?" Theo demanded, then realized his cousin's meaning. "Oh, yes. Right." Stopping had its disadvantages, though. It gave him time to be aware of the throbbing pain in his ankle.

"Here, use me as a support," said the Colonel. "Pretend your ankle is hurting again. That will slow us down enough to give William time to play the hero."

"No need to pretend," grumbled Theo. "Believe me."

This had to be the most utterly ridiculous position Elizabeth had ever found herself in, even worse than the time a farmer's pigs had chased her up a tree near Longbourn. Lying half in, half out of the stream, her bonnet falling off, having been shot—shot! of all things!—right in the middle of Rosings Park.

Anne de Bourgh pressed a blood-soaked handkerchief to her shoulder. In a high pitched voice she said, "Please, Miss Bennet, do not panic! There is no need to worry, none at all. Someone will be here very soon, I promise you, and you will be perfectly well in no time!"

"I do not know why you think *I* am panicking," said Elizabeth. Having been shot ought to entitle her to a little rudeness, and Anne's terror was becoming tiresome, not to mention Georgiana's sobs. "If I could think of a way to stand without using either this arm or that leg, I would simply get up and walk back to the parsonage." A gratifying prospect, if not a terribly realistic one, given that her previous attempt had landed her in the stream.

"Oh, thank heavens!" Georgiana cried. "William is coming. He will fix everything! He always does."

Elizabeth grimaced. Now the proper Mr. Darcy was also going to be treated to an exhibition of her ridiculous position. And just when she was beginning to think he might not be the ogre she had believed him to be! She raised her head to see him sprinting towards them, his brother and cousin right behind him. Naturally, if she was to look like a complete fool, it would have to be in front of *all* the eligible gentleman! It was deeply unfair that she could not simply vanish from embarrassment.

And now Mr. Darcy was wading through the stream to reach her, soaking his perfectly pressed trousers. Maybe if she just closed her eyes, this would all disappear. At least she would not have to see that look on his face, the one that always seemed to censure. He would find no lack of things to criticize this time.

Georgiana cried, "William! Thank God you are here! Someone has shot Miss Bennet, and when she fell, her ankle made a terrible noise and now she can't move it. You must *do* something!"

"Elizabeth." A firm hand clasped her wrist—the one on her uninjured arm, fortunately. "Elizabeth, you must wake up. Please wake up."

She opened her eyes to find Mr. Darcy's face only a few inches from hers, her hand in both of his. "I am perfectly awake. I was simply meditating on whether it is possible to sink into the earth, or, if not, whether it is actually possible to die of mortification."

"Thank God," he breathed. Closing his eyes, he bowed his head, his forehead resting on hers.

What in heaven's name did he think he was doing? First calling her by her Christian name, and now *this*?

"Mr. Darcy, might I impose on you for some assistance in moving onto dry ground?" She decided not to add the part about remembering where he was and what he was doing.

He straightened immediately. "Of course. But first, you must tell me where you are hurt. I do not wish to injure you further."

"On my shoulder, but 'tis not so deep as a well or as wide as a church door, but 'tis enough, 'twill serve. Ask for me tomorrow and you will find I have died of embarrassment, but not of a gunshot wound. It is hardly even bleeding now." It did burn like the very dickens, but she was not about to admit that.

"Elizabeth, please." His eyes were round with worry. Why was he so concerned—so frightened he was calling her by her given name? She would have sworn he would never forget propriety to that degree.

Colonel Fitzwilliam materialized on her other side. "Miss Bennet, I beg you to pardon me, but I must check your wound." He was all business, as if this were a battlefield and she a wounded soldier. "Darcy, look away." With surprising gentleness, he removed Anne's handkerchief, then eased the shoulder of her dress a few inches down, making her desperately grateful the wound was no lower than it was. It was a good thing her mother was not here to make accusations of compromise.

Mr. Darcy sucked in his breath. Apparently he had ignored his cousin's injunction to look away. What would her poor mother do if she were compromised by *two* gentlemen? Elizabeth was half-tempted to laugh.

The Colonel restored her sleeve to its proper position. "I imagine it must be quite painful, but I am happy to say it does not appear to be dangerous. The shot must have been partly spent by the time it reached you since it does not appear to be overly deep. Still, we must get that bullet out."

Mr. Darcy spoke as if he had not heard him. "Richard, you must ride after Mr. Cox. He cannot have gone far yet. Take Theseus. He is the fastest."

"I will ride after him, but I assure you it is nothing to worry about. I have seen far more than my share of bullet wounds, and this one is minor."

"Richard!" Mr. Darcy snapped.

The Colonel held up his hands. "Very well. I am going." He stood and dusted off his knees. "Theo, do try to keep your brother from making a fool of himself. If you will excuse me, ladies."

He bowed and strode off. Elizabeth closed her eyes again. Apparently it *was* possible to feel even more embarrassed than she had before. For days now, everyone had been insisting, or at the very least implying, that Darcy admired her. Charlotte, Miss Darcy, Mr. Theo, even Miss de Bourgh just a few minutes ago. She had laughed at all of them. Apparently the joke was on her. Mr. Darcy, of all people? But after their odd conversation earlier, and now this, even she could not deny there must be some truth to it.

"Miss Bennet, we must get you to the house. Can you place your arm around my neck?" At least he had remembered his manners this time.

"There is no need to carry me, sir. I can wait for a cart to be brought."

"It would take too long to harness the horses and bring it here." Apparently Mr. Darcy was back to giving orders. This time he merely looped her arm around his shoulders, then slid his arms under her. "I will do my best to be gentle, but this is likely to cause some pain. I hope you can forgive me for it." He smoothly swung her into his arms.

He obviously had no intention of allowing her to refuse, so she might as well give in with what little grace remained to her, given that his every step sent a stab of pain through her shoulder. "I promise you I shall only blame the man who pulled the trigger," she managed to gasp out.

For some reason Mr. Darcy turned to glare at his brother. "Or the man who tempted him to pull the trigger."

"That is ridiculous!" said Theo indignantly. "How could my hat over *there* induce someone to shoot over *here*?"

"Enough, Theo. We will speak of this later." His tone changed completely as he glanced down at her. "I hope this is not too painful."

She would look even sillier if she denied it. "I will be glad when we reach the Parsonage."

"I am taking you to Rosings. It is much closer."

At the moment, she did not care where they went, as long as it was close by. She bit her lip to keep from crying out in pain.

❧CHAPTER 9

LADY CATHERINE STAMPED her foot. "Fitzwilliam Darcy, put that young woman down this instant! I will not have it!"

Theo inquired, "Should he put her on the floor, or is it acceptable to take her as far as the fainting couch?"

Darcy glared at his brother, then headed for the staircase with Elizabeth still in his arms.

"Stop! Miss Bennet, I insist you tell him to release you at once."

Elizabeth's smile was bewitching. "Mr. Darcy, pray release me at once," she said obediently.

"No." He smiled back down at her as he started up the stairs.

"My apologies, Lady Catherine," Elizabeth called. "Apparently he will not listen to me either."

He paused at the top of the stairs. His first instinct was to bring her to his own rooms. That was where she belonged, even if society did not agree. Still, society's rules must take their due. Unsure which rooms might be prepared for guests, he took her to Georgiana's room and placed her gently on the bed, leaving his arms around her soft form a few seconds longer than necessary. Propriety demanded he leave the room immediately, but Darcy decided he had paid enough attention to propriety for one day. "I hope the doctor will be here soon. In the meantime, is there anything I can bring you for your comfort? Some wine, perhaps, or tea?"

She shifted to sit up, winced, and lay back again. "If the kitchens can produce some willow bark tea, I would be grateful for it. Although I dislike admitting it, a tiny bit of laudanum might not be unwelcome."

He could see how much the admission cost her. He gestured to the maid who hovered just outside the door. "Some willow bark tea for Miss Bennet. And send someone to the parsonage as quickly as possible and ask Mrs. Collins for some laudanum."

Elizabeth said, "I would be very surprised if Lady Catherine's housekeeper does not have some laudanum among her supplies."

He hated to think how much pain she must be in to request that. "I think it a poor idea to ask."

"But…"

As if on cue, Lady Catherine bustled in, followed by a maid carrying a glass of the familiar dark liquid. "Darcy, you may go now. I will handle this from here. Miss Bennet, you must drink this."

Elizabeth reached for the glass, but Darcy was there first, knocking it out of the maid's hand so the contents splashed across the floor.

"Fitzwilliam Darcy, what is the matter with you today?" Lady Catherine stormed. "You are not yourself. Perhaps *you* would benefit from a dose of Anne's medicine as well. Well, do not just stand there, girl—fetch some more!"

Darcy spoke between gritted teeth. "Lady Catherine, with all due respect, I refuse to permit Miss Bennet to receive that so-called medicine."

"*So-called* medicine? How dare you! You saw how

quickly Theophilus was back on his feet, and you must admit Anne has been doing remarkably well of late."

"Anne has been doing remarkably well because we have been watering down her medication, and Theo never had a second dose after the first one left him raving and conversing with dead people. That *medicine* is dangerous."

"You have no idea what you are talking about! Anne has been ill for years, and she becomes worse when she does not receive her medicine on time."

"That is because she is addicted to it, not because it is helping her. That medicine is full of opium. Theo said he could taste it."

"I do not believe it!"

"Ask Theo yourself, then, and Georgiana, for that matter. They will verify what I have said." Before he said even worse, he turned his back to his aunt and spoke quietly to Elizabeth. "I am sorry you had to witness that scene."

"At least I understand your reluctance to ask for laudanum!" she said with a wan attempt at a smile.

<hr>

Theo should have known it could not last. William had somehow forced himself to be pleasant for a few days. And just when Theo had started believing perhaps their relationship might be changing for the better, the truth came out. How dare William blame him for Miss Bennet's injury! All he had done was to throw his hat in the air. It was not even in the same direction! And then William had scowled at him the whole way back to Rosings Park when Theo had tried to take Miss Bennet's mind off her injuries by teasing and making jests. He had been doing her a kindness by trying to distract her from her pain, and William had been angry at him for it. And the most damnable part of it was that it *hurt*.

William had disapproved of him since they were children, and it was never going to change, no matter how much Theo tried to be a loving brother, no matter how much he changed his life. It would never be enough for William. He should just accept it.

He was in no mood to deal with his aunt's furious demands about Anne's medication, nor Anne's cold fury on discovering her years of illness had been avoidable. Lady Catherine would never approve of him either, so why should he even try? Let her torment William instead. He deserved it. Theo derived great satisfaction from telling his aunt that William was the best person to answer her questions, then stalking from the room, the effect somewhat marred by his limp.

He threw himself down in the ridiculously ornate chair in his bedroom. How could his aunt possibly spend so much money on a chair that was so uncomfortable? Theo blew out his breath between his teeth. There was no point to this. His family was his family. Georgiana and Richard liked him, and that would have to be enough.

Time to think of something more cheerful. He pulled out the letter from Monty that had been waiting for him and broke the seal. Inside a page of Monty's scribbles was another letter in different hand.

Frowning, Theo opened it and began to read.

Theo found his brother and sister in the salon, William pacing the floor and Georgiana looking too cowed to say anything. If William was going to be in this much of a temper until Miss Bennet recovered, Theo was just as glad he would not be there to suffer through it. William would likely be pleased to see him gone as well.

"I have had a change of plans after receiving a letter," he announced. "Unfortunately, my presence is required in London tonight, so I will be departing Rosings as soon as possible."

William glared at him incredulously. "You are leaving with no warning, just like that?"

Theo shrugged. Why should he give William the satisfaction of knowing that his displeasure hurt him? "Business calls," he said lightly.

"Business?" William's eyes narrowed. "Permit me to guess. The letter was from your dear friend Monty, telling you of some absolutely not to be missed event. What is it? A horse race? A prizefight? A new gambling hell? Or is it a woman?"

"Perhaps it is all of those, and more." There was no point in defending himself. William would believe the worst of him anyway.

"How *dare* you even think of your little pleasures when our family is in disarray?"

"What better time to take my leave?"

Georgiana said, "William, Theo, *please*. Has there not been enough quarreling today?"

Theo's righteous fury melted away at his sister's miserable expression. "I apologize, Georgiana. You are quite right. I will write to you." He kissed her forehead, then nodded coolly at his brother. "William."

Not trusting his temper enough to bid Lady Catherine farewell, Theo left the house. The horses were still being harnessed to William's carriage. That would be another thing for his brother to be furious about, that Theo had taken the carriage without his permission, but it would be back in the morning. With his ankle shooting pain through his leg with every step, riding was not an option.

He paused to look back at Rosings. So much had happened here, and he was leaving with so much undone. He hoped Georgiana would somehow convince Miss Bennet to marry William, since she was probably his only hope to ever have a civil conversation with his brother, but at the moment he sympathized with her dislike of William. He had not even had the opportunity to say goodbye to her, since that would require entering the bedroom, and William would never approve of that. Of course, that had not stopped William from doing so, even though he was always blaming Theo for flouting propriety. Apparently it did not count when he did it himself.

Oh, devil take it! Why was he still trying to please William? Turning to the driver, he said, "I have forgotten something. I will return presently." He hobbled back into the house, using the banister to support himself as he climbed the stairs. He hoped whatever Garrow had in mind for him in London did not involve much walking.

The door was open to Georgiana's suite, so Theo passed through the small sitting room to the bedroom where Miss Bennet sat propped up with pillows. "Pardon me, Miss Bennet. I know it is quite improper for me to be here, but…"

"But you knew I was desperate for someone who could explain how in the world I came to be shot," Elizabeth replied promptly.

She could still make him smile. "Do you recall my telling you about the gamekeeper who is all but blind? Someone must have forgotten to switch his gun for one with blanks, and you, along with my hat, have suffered the consequences."

"Yes, of course! Old Mr. Watling. The poor man must feel terrible about what happened! I hope he will not be dismissed for it."

"Never fear; he cannot be dismissed, and even my brother is not unreasonable enough to place blame on him for something he could not help, though I doubt he will be permitted to carry a gun again. I would not, however, wish to be the man who failed in his responsibility to give him the proper weapon." No, William was only unreasonable in his blame when it applied to his brother. "But the reason I am so daring as to approach you now is because I will be leaving for London presently, and I wished to bid you farewell and to thank you for making my stay at Rosings Park much brighter than I had expected." He bowed extravagantly.

Her face fell. "So soon? I am sorry to hear it. I hope nothing is the matter."

Theo grimaced. "Nothing is the matter, at least not for me. It is a favor that has been called in. A gentleman who has served as my mentor has a case in Old Bailey very soon that he wishes me to handle personally. While you are enjoying a well-deserved rest here, I will be up all night reviewing the case with him so I can make a decent presentation to the Judge tomorrow."

"I wish I could see that! I imagine you must make a fine barrister. Well, under the circumstances, I will have to forgive you for abandoning me here."

If only William could have such an attitude! "I hope I will have the pleasure of your company again soon. And, on that subject, Miss Bennet…"

She arched an eyebrow at his teasing tone. "Yes?"

He bent down to whisper in her ear. "If you do not do the honorable thing in regard to my brother, Miss Bennet, I will see to it *everyone* knows how you compromised him by insisting on him carrying you all the way here."

She spluttered with laughter. "*I* insisted upon it, did I? Odd, that is not how *I* recall the event!"

With a broad smile he said, "I stand by my story, so you see, I do expect we will meet again."

The humor on Elizabeth's face disappeared abruptly. Theo followed her gaze to the doorway, where William stood with a black expression. "Dear me," Theo drawled. "I seem to have overstayed my welcome. Pray remember what I said, Miss Bennet!" Theo did not permit himself to favor his sore ankle at all as he brushed past William without a word.

Elizabeth sighed. What was Mr. Darcy angry about now? Had she done something, or was he angry at his brother or someone else entirely? And what was she to do about Mr. Theophilus' strange assumption she would be marrying his brother? "Do come in, Mr. Darcy."

He hesitated, then took the seat beside the bed. "I hope my brother was not imposing himself upon you."

Was that the source of his anger? "No, not at all. I was glad to see him."

"I saw him whispering to you, and you looked embarrassed afterwards. Theo, I am sorry to say, has been known to be quite improper in his speech to ladies. I apologize that he subjected you to that."

Elizabeth's eyes flew open. "Not at all! Truly, there was nothing improper in what he said to me."

"May I ask you what he said, then?"

Her cheeks grew hot. Mr. Darcy was the last person in the world she could repeat those words to! "It was just a bit of silliness. Nothing of any importance."

His jaw tightened. "It is kind of you to attempt to excuse my brother, but your blushes are testament to the impropriety of his remarks. You may be assured I will have strong words for him on the subject, and you will never be subjected to it again."

"No! Indeed, it was nothing of the sort!" But he would never believe her unless she told him some sort of convincing story, and she was in too much pain to think of a credible one. She covered her face with both hands to shut out the sight of him, ignoring the stab of pain in her injured shoulder, then said in a strangled voice, "Very well, if you must know, I will tell you, and you will see why I did not wish to do so. He was teasing me, saying I had compromised you by forcing you to carry me here." She could not bear to look at him. In fact, the idea of never uncovering her face again had great appeal.

"He said that *you*... but you did not...."

Neither of them noticed the soft snick of the outer door to the suite closing, nor the click that followed it. Outside the suite, Anne de Bourgh smiled in satisfaction as she tucked away a key ring.

With Darcy and Elizabeth safely trapped in the bed-chamber together, Anne hurried down the stairs to the front door, her original plan quickly succeeded by her actions. She only hoped she was not too late, for she had heard Theo give the order for a carriage to be brought round earlier and needed to catch him before he left. His presence was critical to the success of this sudden opportunity to bring Darcy and Elizabeth together. Locking them in the room alone and unchaperoned was only the first step. For the rest, she would need Theo's help. He had always been one to enjoy a practical joke and though this was a serious matter, she knew he would enjoy the subterfuge involved.

Not a moment too soon. The footman was just about to shut the carriage door when Anne managed to intercept him.

"Wait, Theo. You cannot leave yet."

"I assure you, Cousin," said Theo. "I am needed in London most urgently."

"You are needed here most urgently. Your brother's future happiness depends on it."

"I am not certain I care about my brother's *happiness* at this particular moment. In fact I would rather see him as *unhappy* as possible. Let him wallow in his own misery. Let him fairly drown in it for all I care."

"You need not turn sullen on me, Theo. You have obviously quarreled with him, *again*. However, I know you will not fail me in my hour of need."

"I fail to see how Darcy's happiness qualifies as your hour of need, Cousin," he said.

Anne fished for the key ring in the folds of her clothing and shook the keys back and forth like church bells.

"Darcy and Miss Bennet are as good as engaged," she announced.

"No," exclaimed Theo. "You would not be so wicked

as to——?"

Anne raised her brows.

"Good Heavens, Cousin Anne, I would never have thought you had it in you! Perhaps my trip to London can wait, after all, if only to see the expression on Darcy's face if your plan succeeds." His gaze narrowed. "Tell me, how could you anticipate such a chance arising?"

Anne shrugged. "I did not! I had intended to express interest in finally marrying Darcy myself, to pique Miss Bennet's interest." Then, she pulled a face. "I am relieved I did not have to go through with it!"

Grinning, Theo stepped out of the carriage, gave her an exaggerated bow, took her hand and settled it into the crook of his arm. Anne noticed that he had to lean on her so as not to put too much weight on his ankle.

"Have you considered carefully?" he said, as they stepped back into the house. "You know there will be the devil to pay."

Anne gave a haughty sniff.

"Extreme measures are required. My mother lives in hope of writing up the marriage settlement between me and Darcy any day now. Miss Bennet is so prejudiced against your brother; she will not learn to appreciate him unless she is forced to deal with him. As for Darcy, he is so torn with indecision it would take an earthquake to get him moving. He is too concerned about stepping on your toes or harming Fitzwilliam to stake his claim on Miss Bennet. A fine mess you made of that aspect of it. Whatever made you decide that making Darcy jealous would be useful? All he does is growl." She paused. "Besides, it is too late to express any doubts. The deed is done, and we must now follow it through to its natural conclusion, but we must make haste."

Theo let out a loud guffaw. "You are in fine mettle, Anne. I think I shall enjoy this plan of yours, if only to see what you make of it. Tell me what you need me to do."

"The only thing I have not worked out is how to prevent the servants from answering the bell if Darcy or Elizabeth were to pull it."

"That is easy," said Theo. "Just inform them that she has taken a strong dose of medicine which might render her delirious, and that she must not be disturbed under any circumstances."

Anne snorted. "Is that really all you can come up with? It seems a very poor reason to prevent them from obeying a summons."

"Not if I tell them," said Theo. "People are generally more likely to believe what is implied rather than what is said. Watch and learn, Cousin."

As it turned out, Anne had to admire his technique. By the time he had finished explaining the matter to the staff, even she was convinced that, somehow, it would be extremely improper to enter Miss Bennet's bedroom no matter how often she rang the bell. There were meaningful nods and exchanged glances. Anne fancied she saw one of the footmen wink.

She was not entirely happy about the conjectures that would inevitably follow, and the moment they were out of earshot she let Theo know it.

"I hope you were not implying that you were planning a tryst with Miss Bennet, Theo. I also hope you do not resort to such methods very frequently."

Theo stiffened. For a moment, he looked almost like Darcy. "I assure you, Cousin Anne, I do *not* resort to such methods, as you call it. Must everyone persist in thinking the worst of me? Even you?"

He sounded both angry and hurt. Anne felt sorry for thinking such a thing, but she really did not know him very well. The illness that had befogged her mind for so long had prevented her from forming a clear perception of the people around her. It had been like walking through a dream world.

"I am not your brother, you know. You do not have to account to me for your behavior. I was simply confused about what it was you were implying."

"That is entirely the point, Cousin. Even *I* am confused about what I am implying. It is up to everyone to think whatever they choose."

She still did not like it. She did not want to encourage speculation of any kind about Miss Bennet. It was too late now, however. The damage was done.

"Very well," she said, deciding to let the matter drop. As long as her purpose was fulfilled, there was no point in dwelling on it. There was no time. They had to move ahead with the next step of the campaign.

"If you will find the Colonel," she said, "I will collect Georgiana and galvanize my mother. Then the assault can begin."

Elizabeth's conversation with Darcy—which after the initial embarrassing questions had turned into a rather strained exchange of civilities—came to an abrupt end when Darcy stood up and began to walk around the room in an agitated manner.

Elizabeth looked on in bewilderment. Was it possible Charlotte and the others were right and Mr. Darcy did feel some affection for her? It was difficult to believe, if one took into regard his thunderous expression at the moment. At one point he stopped, stared at her closely, and looked as if he would ask her something, but then he turned away and resumed his pacing.

Finally, he came to a standstill and stood by the side of the bed, his hands clutched behind his back like a little boy reciting his lessons.

"It is presumptuous of me, but I cannot hold back any longer. I must ask you this, Miss Bennet. Do you entertain any regard for my brother?"

"That is certainly a presumptuous question, Mr. Darcy," said Elizabeth. "If you mean by it, do I find him agreeable, then I can safely say that I do."

Really, Elizabeth, this was no time to tease the man. She knew very well what he was asking, and the truth was that she liked Theo. As she liked Colonel Fitzwilliam. They were both charming gentlemen and she found them stimulating company. She did not think herself, however, attached to either of them, though her experience in these matters was limited. The closest she had ever been to falling in love was her connection with Wickham.

She realized with surprise that it had been some time since she had given Wickham any thought or even remembered him in passing.

Meanwhile, Darcy was gazing at her so intently that she had to look away.

"I have no special attachment to him," Elizabeth acknowledged, with a small smile.

Darcy's eyes blazed with a particular light. She shifted in the bed, conscious for the first time that she was alone with a man in a bedchamber, unchaperoned. She had not really noticed it before, but now she felt an unexpected flush of heat run through her. Turning self-conscious, she drew the sheet up all the way to her chin. When she tried to tuck in the sides, however, her injured shoulder protested with a sharp stab of pain and she gave out a small moan.

"Oh, you are in pain!" said Darcy. "Allow me to do that, Miss Bennet."

He rose and tucked the sheets carefully under the mattress, covering her injured shoulder and taking immense care not to jostle her.

It embarrassed her to see the grand Mr. Darcy serving her. What would her mother say if she saw it?

He leaned forward to straighten the cover over the bed. As he did so, his hand brushed against her forearm.

She drew back, startled at the way her skin tingled in response. She was at a loss to explain her reaction. Perhaps her nerves were shattered after being shot. Or perhaps it was Mr. Darcy's close proximity in a closed chamber. No wonder respectable young ladies were forbidden from entering gentlemen's bedchambers.

Elizabeth needed to put a stop to it. As he moved to the other side of the bed to tuck her in, she waved him away with her good hand.

"I do not need to be trussed up like a chicken, Mr. Darcy," she remarked with a little laugh, trying to dispel the strange feeling that was coming over her.

He straightened up into a standing position, looking as awkward as she felt.

"Do you wish for company, Miss Bennet, or would you prefer to rest?"

She wished for company, but at this particular moment she also needed to reflect on what was happening to her. A strong sense of longing to see Jane came over her. She wished Jane could have been there so they could have discussed Mr. Darcy's unexpected behavior.

She did not think it would be wise for Mr. Darcy to stay. "I would like to rest for a while, but perhaps later you can return and bring Georgiana or your cousin with you to prevent me from succumbing to boredom."

Darcy's face shuttered.

"Very well, Miss Bennet. I will give you a chance to rest. Try to get some sleep."

Bowing stiffly, he turned and strode to the door.

Darcy straightened his shoulders and tried not to show any signs of the turmoil that was surging through him. *Miss Bennet did not want him to stay.* She had made it quite clear that she did not care for his company. He longed for one sign from her, just one, however small, that would indicate she was interested in him, but there seemed to be none forthcoming.

At least she did not toy with his feelings. Thankfully, her playful nature did not extend that far.

Darcy pulled at the door handle, but the door refused

to budge. Puzzled, he tried it again. He pushed the handle down as far as it would go then, leaning his shoulder against the wall, he tried to use it as leverage, but the door remained stubbornly closed.

"The door is jammed," he said.

There was nothing like a closed door to make a man feel like an incompetent fool. He would have liked to talk to Elizabeth of lock mechanisms and springs, but he knew nothing at all about them. All he could do was jangle the handle up and down in the hope that it would loosen.

Elizabeth tilted her head to one side, her eyes dancing.

"That is a poor excuse for you to extend your visit with me, Mr. Darcy."

He felt his ears redden at the accusation. He knew it was only said in jest, but there was enough truth in it to sting. He *did* wish to extend his visit, but he had not jammed the door deliberately.

He started to bang at the door to see if someone would hear and come to his assistance. It was undignified, but it might do the trick.

"Shall I ring for a servant?" said Elizabeth.

Now *that* was a more sensible solution, but then, she was not the one seized with a sense of panic at being locked in.

"I will do it. I do not wish you to undo my work after I took the trouble of tucking you in," he said, surprised that he was capable of joking. He approached the bed again and tugged vigorously at the bell pull.

Elizabeth was sitting with her head against the head-board, her eyes closed. His gaze took in the long thick lashes that rested against her cheek, the soft swell of her red lips and the long extension of her neck that was inter-rupted by the sheet.

It was more than he could endure. He had not wanted to leave the room, but heaven forgive him, he was finding it more and more difficult to keep himself under control.

He would give anything to be able to go to her and take

her into his arms, to press his lips to hers and cover that long neck with kisses. Only an iron will prevented him from doing it. It would be despicable for a gentleman to take advantage of a lady's weakness when she was injured. Then there were Theo and Richard to worry about; he did not want a lady to come between them. Nor could he do such a thing unless he was sure of her feelings, until she looked at him with an ardor and feeling that equaled his.

Why was no one coming to let him out?

He began to walk up and down again. Then a thought struck him and he slapped his hand across his brow.

"Depend on it," said Darcy. "This is Theo's mischief. He left the room after I entered and must have locked it then. He probably thinks it is vastly amusing and is chuckling away as he rides to London."

Darcy went to the window as if expecting to see Theo bolting away on horseback.

"I do think it is strange that no one has answered our summons," said Lizzy. "It is not my impression that the servants are slovenly at Rosings."

"They are not. I cannot imagine my aunt would run Rosings with any less efficiency than a barracks. I am sure there is a perfectly good explanation for that." He opened the window and looked out. "I suppose if necessary, I can climb down the drainpipe."

"Surely you are not that desperate to escape my company, Mr. Darcy!" said Elizabeth. "Still, it is a spectacle I would like to witness. If you will help me to the window so I can watch, it would be a tale to tell when I return to Meryton. Mr. Darcy Descending Down a Drainpipe. I would make ample use of alliteration."

Darcy smiled. "I would rather not amuse the inhabitants of Meryton if I can help it, Miss Bennet. As for your first statement, you cannot accuse me of both wishing to escape you and plotting to stay in the room with you at the same time."

She was really bewitching when she smiled in that playful way, mischief written all over her face. It tugged at every heartstring he had. A few strides and he could be at her side. It was so very tempting to give up his scruples and gather her into his arms.

Do it, Darcy.

You must not. You are a gentleman. A gentleman does not accost injured ladies in their bedrooms.

He teetered on the precipice.

"Really," said Elizabeth. "It is very odd that no one has come."

Her remark brought him back to himself and he took a step backward.

"Prodigiously strange." He went to the door and looked through the keyhole. There was no key there. Theo must have pocketed the key, which gave Darcy another thing to worry about. Could Theo have taken the key with him to London?

Another suspicion raised its ugly head. Where did Theo get the key from in the first place? This was not a random action spurred by the moment. Theo had *planned* to do this, and there could be no explanation for it other than a desire to take revenge on Darcy by making him look like a fool in front of Elizabeth.

"I am providing entertainment for my brother even as we speak. He enjoys playing pranks at my expense. You would think he would have outgrown that by now."

All the pent-up frustration of the last few days—Theo's accident, his flirtations with Elizabeth, the irresponsible shooting, his sudden decision to leave for London—surfaced. It appeared the purpose of Theo's life was to torment his older brother, to make trouble for him at every turn. And now he had rushed off to get into yet another scrape with that good-for-nothing friend of his Monty.

Elizabeth saw only the charming side of Theo, as so many people did, but there was unfortunately another side to him as well.

"My brother is the bane of my existence, Miss Bennet."

Even as he spoke, he knew he was doing the wrong thing, but he could not help it. It would not endear him to Elizabeth for him to speak badly of Theo, but he wanted her to understand what he had been through as he struggled to raise a brother with a tendency to wildness. For the first time that he could remember, he wanted to speak about those grueling years after his father had died and left him with two younger siblings to take care of.

He badly wanted to give Elizabeth Bennet a glimpse of who the real Fitzwilliam Darcy was. Perhaps in time she might even come to like him.

Elizabeth listened to Darcy with astonishment. She had never imagined taciturn and reserved Mr. Darcy capable of such an outpouring of feelings and she had certainly never imagined herself as the recipient of his confidences. She did not want to hear them. He was painting such a dark picture of his brother, and the more he spoke the more agitated she felt. Any charity she had begun to feel for Darcy disappeared, especially since Mr. Wickham seemed implicated in a great many of the crimes Darcy was accusing Mr. Theo of committing.

"Perhaps, if were not for Theo, Sebastian might still be alive right now."

A horrified silence followed. Darcy seemed shocked that he had said such a thing. Presumably he realized how bad he had sounded, because he immediately turned contrite.

"No. That is not true," he said. "Theo had nothing to do with Sebastian's accident. Nothing at all."

But to Elizabeth, it was apparent that Darcy had harbored the thought or he would never have mentioned it.

"From what I heard of the story from Georgiana," said Elizabeth, feeling a strong urge to defend those maligned so heartlessly by Mr. Darcy, "Theo was a child at the time, no more than nine years old when Sebastian's tragic accident occurred. How could you lay the blame on him all these years later, knowing he could not have understood what was happening? I remember when we were in Netherfield; you told me then that your good opinion, once lost, would be lost forever. Theo is clearly guilty of having lost your good opinion, as is Mr. Wickham. In Theo's case, since he is your brother, the consequences are less dire. But I cannot imagine how badly Wickham must have offended, to have his living taken from him and to have been left destitute?"

"Wickham? Destitute? And you believe this destitution to be inflicted on him by me? This, then is your opinion of me?"

"They say that first impressions are generally correct. My attitude has been softening towards you since you and I spoke at the Parsonage, and I had even begun to think better of you these last few days, but it appears my initial perception was correct. If you are able to judge your own brother so harshly, then it is not surprising that you would be capable of tossing out the son of your steward by the wayside without a qualm."

"You take an eager interest in that gentleman's affairs," said Darcy, tight lipped.

Her temper rose.

"Is it so strange that I pay attention to someone who was a victim of circumstances? Someone who, by right, should have been granted a living near Pemberley? Who has been treated so abominably even though he has caused injury to no one!"

Darcy's expression darkened. She had pushed him too far now, she could tell.

"Hurt no one?" he said. "Hurt no one?"

In two strides, he had crossed the room and was at her side. To her astonishment, he kneeled next to her bed and took hold of her hand. "I do not wish to cause you pain, Elizabeth, if you have formed an attachment to Wickham, so I will not tell you of the many unfortunate situations I have had to rescue him from, but I must warn you that he is not what he seems. He—" Darcy peered into her face intently. "I cannot speak of it—but it concerns my sister Georgiana. You can ask her about her experience with Wickham, although it will give her great pain to speak of it."

Elizabeth's mind reeled, both from the revelation about Mr. Wickham—though she could only guess at what Darcy meant—and from the strange sensations she was feeling at having Darcy so close to her. She no longer knew what to feel. A moment ago, she would have said she hated him, but now—.

Oh, it was too confusing. It was all too much. Her shoulder was throbbing; she could not think straight.

"I am sorry if I have distressed you because of my revelations. I would not wish to cause you pain, dearest Elizabeth."

Darcy reached out with his hand to touch her cheek. The contact sent a strange shiver through her. His face was only inches from hers. Elizabeth's pulse began to race.

CHAPTER 10

THE DOOR FLEW OPEN.

"What is the meaning of this?"

The voice penetrated through Darcy's befuddled thoughts. His aunt!

Darcy sprung to his feet and turned to face Lady Catherine. Except she was not alone.

"How the mighty have fallen!" said Theo, in a smug, self-righteous tone. "I would never have thought it of you, William."

"Miss Bennet!" said Anne.

The worst was Georgiana. She stood there staring, her hand pressed to her mouth, an expression of horror on her face.

"Fitzwilliam, what were you *doing?*" she said, in a strange voice.

Her words rang out in a suddenly silent room. Tension filled every corner of it.

"I fear you are compromised, Miss Bennet," whispered Anne.

"I am afraid so," said Theo, lounging carelessly against

the door.

"When we came to your rescue, Miss Bennet, we little imagined—" Fitzwilliam peered over the top of everyone's heads. "The servants said they heard banging noises," he continued, by way of explanation.

Darcy knew guilt was written all over his face. He had been about to kiss Elizabeth when they had entered.

"There is nothing else to be done," said Anne, bluntly. "You will have to marry Miss Bennet, Cousin William."

"Nonsense," said Lady Catherine. "We are the only witnesses. No one need know about it." Her gaze came to rest on Elizabeth. "As for you, young hussy, you may leave Rosings right now. Have you no shame? Coming to Rosings for the sole purpose of trapping my nephew into marriage!"

"Now I know who shot at me," said Elizabeth, striving to make a joke of the situation.

"It is too late for all this, Aunt," said Colonel Fitzwilliam, ignoring Elizabeth's attempt at levity. "I am afraid nothing more can be done. The fact is, Darcy locked the door to the room and we have caught him red-handed. Miss Bennet is a lady, and Darcy has compromised her reputation."

"I?" said Darcy, suddenly realizing that this had all gone beyond a prank. "*I* locked the door? And pray, where is the key?"

"Over there on the table," said Anne, readily.

Everyone turned to look at the key. There was no doubt about it. There it was in plain view.

Darcy turned to Theo. His brother had not budged from his position in the doorway, so Darcy could not blame him for placing the key there. Was his mind playing tricks on him? Had he wished so much to stay with Elizabeth that he had failed to see the key?

Darcy looked towards Elizabeth, a bemused expression playing at the corners of her eyes. Fortunately, *she* did not think him guilty, and that was all that mattered.

He took a deep breath. "I suppose it is no use protesting that things are not what they seem?"

"No use at all," said Anne, firmly. "You will have to offer for Miss Bennet. You must do the honorable thing."

"If someone will allow me a word in edgewise," said Elizabeth, "The easiest solution is simply to ask all of you not to speak of the matter, and that will be the end of it. I cannot believe any of you will be malicious enough to spread gossip that will tarnish my reputation. In any case, I am prepared to take the risk."

"You cannot mean that," said Georgiana, of all people, in a small voice. "You have four sisters to think of. The reality of the situation is that there will be gossip, even if everyone in the room swears to silence." She looked towards the two footmen lurking just outside the open door.

"Servants in my employ do not spread gossip," said Lady Catherine, in a quelling voice intended to intimidate Georgiana.

Darcy bristled defensively, but his aunt had already turned her attention to Elizabeth. "I find your suggestion very sensible, Miss Bennet. I am willing to revise my opinion of you."

Sensible? There was nothing sensible about it. Did she not she realize the seriousness of the situation? Darcy clung to the only words that made sense in this madness. *The honorable thing.* Yes, there was only one honorable thing to be done. He did not believe for one moment that Elizabeth was not worried about her reputation.

Besides, it is what you wish, more than anything in the world, a voice whispered inside him.

He walked up to the bed calmly, even though he was shaking inside, went down on one knee and took her hand in his.

"Miss Bennet, will you do me the honor of becoming my wife?"

A collective breath was held as everyone waited expectantly. Elizabeth chewed on her lower lip. Her hand fluttered inside his.

"I am sorry," she said, "but I cannot."

Darcy stared at her in incomprehension. He could not get his mind around her response. Had she actually refused him?

"There," said Lady Catherine, in a voice filled with satisfaction. "The chit will not have you. She knows that nothing good will come of marrying above her station. Miss Bennet, I knew you were a prudent young lady the moment I laid eyes on you. *That young woman*, I thought at the time, *will not suffer fools gladly*. My opinion of you is confirmed. You have done exceedingly well. If you had a brother, Miss Bennet, I would have bestowed a living on him."

"Do not be ridiculous, Mama," said Anne. "Miss Bennet, I am sorry to say this but you have no choice but to accept my cousin. You need not be noble and self-sacrificing about it. My cousin is perfectly willing. Are you not, Darcy?"

Darcy did not think he could ever be more embarrassed than at this moment. To have his emotions discussed in front of everyone immediately after being rejected by the object of his affections!

"I am not prepared to discuss any of my feelings about anything or anyone in public. If you will allow me a few moments of privacy with Miss Bennet, I would like to speak with her about the matter alone."

"Certainly not," said Lady Catherine. "She has rejected you. What could you possibly have to say to Miss Bennet?"

"Mama!" said Anne, pushing Lady Catherine backward.

"I am shocked and dismayed," said Lady Catherine, her eyes bulging. "My own daughter! I have nursed a viper in my bosom. After all I have done to secure Darcy for you. Anne! How could you?"

Anne ignored her mother's remarks, continuing to push Lady Catherine backwards as the room cleared.

If Darcy's situation were not so dire, he would have

laughed to see his aunt being upstaged by her daughter. But there was no laughter inside him at all.

How in the world was he to convince dear, obstinate Elizabeth that it was essential for her to marry him?

Darcy stepped out of the room with everyone else and carefully closed the door behind him, taking a deep breath. He had never felt so humiliated and embarrassed in his life. He needed a moment to gather his scattered wits about him. He needed to *think*.

"What are you doing out here, Darcy?" said Fitzwilliam. "You are supposed to be in there with Miss Bennet, convincing her to marry you."

"It may have escaped your notice, Fitzwilliam, but the lady has just rejected my offer. I need a strategy before I go back in there."

"No doubt you will think of something to say, Fish," said Theo, using the childhood name, leaning against the wall and looking vastly amused. "You always do."

At Theo's words, the embarrassment changed to anger. Theo had engineered the whole situation for his own entertainment. Did he not realize that this went far beyond a prank, that he was in fact toying with people's lives?

"You have a great deal to answer for, Theo," said Darcy. "You have put me in an utterly untenable situation and—"

"It was not Theo who thought up the scheme, Darcy," said Anne, interrupting, "It was I." At his astonishment, she looked as pleased as a cat who had found the cream.

Lady Catherine stared at her daughter as if she had just announced she had two heads.

"You? You did this? *You?*" she sputtered, her face turning the color of beetroot. For the first time in his life, Darcy saw his aunt at a loss for words. Her mouth moved up and down but she seemed unable to find a way to express her outrage.

"Aunt Catherine, shall I send for smelling salts?" said Theo.

"I am not in need of smelling salts," snapped Lady Catherine. "I am in need of a cure to this madness! Anne, you do realize you cannot marry Darcy if he marries someone else? Have you any idea, child, what damage you have done?"

"Of course I have an idea. I have been sickly, Mama, but I am not stupid. I am more than happy to have someone else marry Darcy. I have no interest at all in marrying him."

As if he had not been humiliated enough today, now Anne was adding insult to injury. Darcy forced himself not to look at Theo. The impudent puppy was snickering in the corner, enjoying every moment of his discomfort.

"Nonsense!" said Lady Catherine. "You have no right to articulate your preference. Marriage is determined by adults, not by young girls who cannot be relied upon to know their own good."

"It may have escaped your notice, Mama, but I am eight and twenty and quite a few years beyond adulthood. In any case, it is useless to cry over spilt milk," said Anne. "Elizabeth Bennet and Darcy are as good as engaged."

"Not under my roof," said Lady Catherine. "I will go in and ensure that the conniving chit never agrees to an engagement."

She moved towards the bedchamber. Darcy stepped sideways to block his aunt's entrance.

"You will do no such thing, Aunt. This is no affair of yours," he said, his voice like ice.

Lady Catherine sent him such a cold look that for a moment he almost wavered. However, it was Elizabeth who was in that room. All his protective instincts rose to the surface.

"You will not step inside that room, Aunt Catherine."

"You cannot dictate to me in my own house, Darcy."

"I can and I will."

Lady Catherine sent him another poisonous glare. When he did not falter, she looked away.

"You have not heard the last of this," she hissed. "I had an agreement with your mother, and I will ensure you honor it." She turned on her heels and strode down the hallway.

Theo whistled in approval. "Bravo, Darcy! I never thought I would live to see anyone standing up to the Old Bat. My faith in you is fully restored; 'Prince William' is gone, long live the King!"

"Stop calling me that," said Darcy. "This is no time for humor."

"On the contrary, this is the best time for humor," said Theo.

"I think you ought to let Darcy focus on the issue at hand," said Colonel Fitzwilliam. "Your brother has been placed in a very awkward situation. Like it or not, the reputation of a young lady is at stake. I would say that is no matter for joking."

Theo had the grace to look abashed, and Darcy felt a momentary gratitude toward his cousin until he remembered Richard should not have been there in the first place.

"As for you, Richard, I thought you were on your way to bring back Mr. Cox. Elizabeth is in pain."

"I do not need to chase after him personally, you know, Darcy. I have sent someone reliable to fetch him. He should be arriving any moment."

"Still, I was relying on you—"

Theo turned away. "I must go. I am long overdue getting on the road."

The Colonel frowned. "It is growing late; will you not stay until morning?"

With a shake of his head, Theo walked off down the landing. "Not much point, Cousin." He glanced back over his shoulder as he paused at the top of the stairs. "No one is relying on me for anything." He threw Darcy a pointed glare and set off down the steps at a rapid pace.

"William," said Georgiana gently, touching him on the arm. "I do believe Miss Bennet is waiting. You ought to go in."

Darcy's heart began to pound. He had no better idea of what to say than he had had when he had left the room.

Well, delaying further would hardly endear his cause to her.

He straightened his shoulders, took a steadying breath and knocked on the door of the bedchamber to give Elizabeth fair warning.

Darcy entered and shut the door behind him, leaving the unspoken question hanging in the air between them.

Will you do me the honor of being my wife?

Elizabeth sat upright in her bed, her back pressed into the headboard behind her. Her shoulder was throbbing, a steady ebb and flow in time with her heartbeat, and a dull ache emanated from her ankle.

She understood her predicament well enough. What Georgiana had said was true. Even if everyone agreed to keep quiet, word would leak out somehow. When it came to gossip, news of a lady's disgrace would spread quicker than wildfire. It did not matter that she had done nothing to be put in this situation.

Yet, at the same time, she resented being forced into marriage. Being backed into a corner raised her hackles more than anything. Being backed into a corner and forced to marry an arrogant, overbearing man like Mr. Darcy only made the situation worse. Every instinct she possessed rebelled against allowing someone accustomed to obedience in all things to run roughshod over her.

She was forced to choose between the frying pan and the fire—to be scorched by the censure of society, or to spend her life struggling against a man who would expect her compliance as well as her gratitude for saving her from disgrace.

Even her mother, with her desperate desire for a good match, would not wish Elizabeth to marry Mr. Darcy. A marriage like this could only bring unhappiness to both parties. To enter into marriage feeling beholden to Darcy would be ill-fated. Already his stature in society was superior to hers. How could she make any claim to equality under such circumstances?

Pride held her back, pride and self-knowledge. She was far too outspoken, far too unrestrained, and sooner or later he would find her a liability. She could never be the kind of wife he required to be mistress of a large estate.

More importantly, she had always promised herself that only a deep and enduring love would prompt her to marry.

There were too many reasons *not* to marry Darcy, and only a single reason to marry him. The only inducement for marriage was to escape society's censure. From her vantage point at this moment, being censored by society appeared to be the better choice, far better than a lifetime of unhappiness.

Unless Mr. Darcy could convince her otherwise.

She looked towards him, wondering at his silence. He was leaning on the door, looking ill at ease. He did not appear to have anything to say. No doubt he, too, had many doubts about entering into the marriage. He had done the honorable thing and proposed, but now was thinking better of it.

The silence stretched on.

She did not wish to be the first to say something. His intentions were unclear. If he wished to withdraw his offer, he must do so himself. She would not assist him.

If only she could think more clearly through the pain that had settled into her shoulder like a clamp, biting into her flesh. She shifted, doing her best not to wince and alert him to her pain.

Elizabeth met his gaze questioningly. He was staring straight at her, his eyes following her every move. The steady gaze flustered her and she looked away. She could not help remembering that just a few moments ago he had been about to kiss her. Incomprehensibly, her heart skipped a beat and her hands trembled. She moved them under the cover to hide them.

Too unnerved now to bear the silence any longer, she took refuge in humor.

"You need not lean on the door as if you are hoping to escape, Mr. Darcy, though at least you have the advantage over me of being able to do it. I cannot run, because my ankle is injured. I am stuck in this bed and forced to deal with the situation at hand. However, if you have any crutches, I would be happy to oblige."

"As always, Miss Bennet, you choose to willfully misinterpret my actions," said Darcy, his lips twitching. "I do not desire to run *away*. If I wish to run in any particular direction, it is towards *you*."

His voice had a caressing tone that sent tingles down her spine. There was a peculiar warmth shining out of his eyes. Heat flooded her face. Who was the man standing before her? How could this be the same cold, haughty Mr. Darcy she had encountered at the Meryton assembly? Had she misjudged him, after all, as he had claimed? Were there hidden aspects to him she had not yet discovered? Had she been mistaken about him all along?

Suddenly Elizabeth felt out of her depth, swimming against a current that threatened to overwhelm her.

He approached her in three easy strides and with a quick movement took up a chair and moved it next to her bed.

"You have me at a disadvantage, Mr. Darcy," she said, trying to keep the conversation light. "With my back against the wall, I cannot escape you."

Darcy nodded. "I am sorry for that. I am sorry for everything that has happened today, your injury in particular, and most especially for Theo's careless actions which caused you the injury. I cannot help thinking that, if Mr.

Watling had aimed any lower, the bullet might have entered your heart."

The intensity in Mr. Darcy's tone unnerved her, as did the fact that he was sitting so close he could reach out and touch her.

"Oh, my heart is quite safe, Mr. Darcy," said Elizabeth with a little laugh, doing her best to diffuse the strange tension. "Besides, surely you cannot hold Theo responsible this time. It was Mr. Watling who fired the shot. Your brother had nothing to do with it."

"It was my brother's antics that brought this on. However, we need not discuss my brother, not unless you have a particular interest in him."

"I have told you, I do not."

"Then let us turn to the more crucial matter of how to resolve our situation."

Here it was. Elizabeth braced herself. There had to be some way out. She did not want to believe she had no other possibility than to commit her life to a man she hardly knew—a man she had despised until recently—a man she had considered the last person in the world she would have wished to marry.

If only she thought hard enough, she would find a solution. She could not think of one, not yet, but if she could stall him long enough, something would occur to her, she was certain.

Darcy licked his lips, which had suddenly turned dry. Oh, for a drink to quench his parched throat, or better still, several sniffers of brandy to loosen his tongue!

He was no good at words. It terrified him to think that his next few words would determine his whole future.

"Dearest Elizabeth—"

"Mr. Darcy," said Elizabeth, interrupting rather breathlessly. "I know you wish to renew your proposal, but I beg you to defer it for a moment."

Darcy did not know whether to be vexed by her reaction or relieved. The truth was, he did not have a clear idea what to say that would convince her.

"Please do not take it amiss," she said, a hint of laughter dispelling some of her pallor. "It is just that I delight in everything ridiculous, as you well know, and I find myself in a particularly ridiculous situation."

He loved the way her face glowed when she laughed. For a moment, he watched her, thinking how beautiful she was, admiring the sharp light in her fine eyes. Then the sound of voices outside the door reminded him that he did not have time to indulge in that luxury. Miss Bennet's reputation was at stake, even if she did not wish to acknowledge it.

"Ridiculous is perhaps not the right word, Miss Bennet," he said. "I do not believe you fully appreciate the seriousness of your position."

"I wish I had not been put in this position to start with," she said, with feeling.

So did he. Anne had not done him a favor by forcing Elizabeth's hand this way.

"Believe me," said Darcy, with equal emphasis, "if I could undo Cousin Anne's mischief I would."

"Oh, was it Miss de Bourgh who locked us in? I did not know. Though I cannot say I am surprised. She is rather odd."

"She is odd, but at least she did not do it out of malice."

Elizabeth seemed to reflect on that. She cocked her head sideways and considered him.

"Why did she do it, then?"

Darcy felt his face burning.

"She wanted to help me with my courtship."

"What courtship?"

Darcy was seized with an acute sense of embarrassment. He slipped his finger between his throat and his cravat, which felt as though it was suddenly beginning to strangle him.

"Anne would say, no doubt, that I was going about it too slowly."

"As far as I can tell, you were not going about it at all."

Was there laughter in her eyes?

"Are you mocking me?" said Darcy.

"Only teasing," said Elizabeth. "I had not realized you were quite so shy."

He had not wanted her to know that. It embarrassed him that she had put her finger on one of his weaknesses.

"I will admit it is a fault of mine," he said, stiffly. "I am not proud of it."

She put out her hand to touch his arm. The touch was very brief but it seared into his skin.

"You need not be ashamed, either," said Elizabeth. "I prefer to think you too shy than too arrogant."

He looked at her, half in hope, half in fear that she was laughing at him. His heart lurched at the grave expression on her face. There was sympathy there as well as under-standing.

There was hope for them, after all.

"I like to think that we can converse intelligently, at least, which is more than can be said of many married couples."

"Perhaps, but I do not know you yet well enough to be sure of even that much. Is it too much to wish we were not being compelled into a permanent state of marriage simply because we were found alone together in a room?" replied Elizabeth.

Under rather incriminating circumstances, Darcy recalled. *She could not have forgotten that, surely?*

"I was about to kiss you," murmured Darcy, his gaze moving to her lips.

He was no good at words, but perhaps there were oth-er ways to convince her.

She shifted as she guessed his intention, jarring her shoulder. The tiny whimper of pain was enough to stop him in his tracks.

With a sudden twinge of guilt, he realized he had forgotten about her injury.

Damnation! Where was that confounded doctor when they needed him? At the very least, Elizabeth needed some laudanum to ease her pain, but the wound needed to be examined as well. Was she looking paler than she had been earlier? He ran his fingers through his hair.

"This is the worst moment to have this discussion, but the fact is we have to reach some agreement. The longer we stay alone in the room, the worse the situation will become."

Elizabeth looked towards the door and the corner of her lips dimpled.

"I do believe there may be someone peering through the keyhole."

Startled, Darcy looked in the same direction. There was definitely movement there. He rose, went to the bedside table, took up the key lying there, strode over to the door and fitted the key into the lock but did not turn it.

"That should ensure our privacy at least," said Darcy, with a grin as he resumed his seat.

Their gazes met in perfect understanding. It was at moments like this that all his uncertainties disappeared. They were made for each, if only Elizabeth would see it.

He reached forward for the hand that was on top of the blanket. She resisted, then allowed him to hold it. He was surprised at how small and delicate it was, considering that Elizabeth was hardly a wilting flower. He ran his index finger across the sensitive tips of her fingers, relishing the feeling of them, one by one.

Her fingers trembled, just a little. A sense of triumph surged up in him. Perhaps she was not as indifferent to him as she would have him believe.

"Miss Bennet, I know I am not what you imagined in a husband. You consider me harsh and unfeeling," said Darcy.

When she made a gesture of protest, he gave a rueful smile.

"You need not deny it. You have made your opinion of me abundantly clear."

She withdrew her hand, looking agitated.

"I no longer know what I think of you, but that is not my only concern. You are asking me to abandon my principles. I have always said I would only marry for love."

"You are not abandoning your principles." He looked deep into her eyes, deep into her soul, willing her to understand the truth of what he was saying. "I love you, Elizabeth Bennet, and I wish more than anything else for you to be my wife. How can you say then that you are not marrying for love?"

"Now it is *your* turn to willfully misunderstand me, sir," she said.

"Please say you will give it a chance," he said, hoarsely.

She looked towards the window, considering his words. He dared not move, dared hardly breathe for fear of distracting her.

His whole being awaited her response.

Finally, she turned to him, her eyes full of conflict.

"You must give me time," she said.

"I will give you as long as you ask for. We could reach an informal understanding until you become more comfortable with the idea."

"No," she said, biting her lower lip, laughter once again springing to her eyes. "I meant I need more time tonight. I will give you an answer in the morning."

In the morning? Elizabeth would be calm and rational; in the cold light of day, she would reject him. He could not allow that to happen, not now he fully appreciated the depth of his feelings for her.

"Miss Bennet, if you will allow me to express—"

There was a loud knock on the door.

Darcy cursed the interruption. They had not given him enough time to convince her. They were hounding him.

"I am having a private conversation," said Darcy, as repressively as possible, hoping whoever was behind the door would go away.

It did not work. The door opened and Darcy quickly sat back in the chair, putting a distance between himself and Elizabeth.

"I am afraid I have to ask you to leave, Darcy," said Anne. "The doctor is here to examine Miss Bennet. Come on Georgiana. We must act as chaperones."

Darcy was on the verge of asking the doctor to wait, but the relief on Elizabeth's face was so obvious he felt guilty for even considering it.

"We will speak of this after the doctor leaves," he said.

She nodded, but already her thoughts were distracted.

As Darcy passed Georgiana, she looked at him. He shook his head slightly.

"You will bring her round. I am sure of it, William," she said.

He felt heartened by her words. Elizabeth Bennet would agree to marry him, inevitably, if only because it was the only way to rescue her reputation. Then he would have a lifetime to convince her that marriage to him was not such a terrible fate after all.

As the doctor entered, a harried-looking maid hurried forward to draw the bed curtains.

"You! Stop that this instant! How am I to examine the patient if I cannot see her?"

The maid cast a helpless look at Miss de Bourgh. When that lady shrugged, the girl backed away and whispered, "Yes, sir."

The elderly gentleman sniffed, then set his bag down on the bedside table. He frowned down at Elizabeth. "So, young lady, am I to understand you were foolish enough to put yourself in the way of a rifle?"

After her encounters with Mr. Darcy, Elizabeth's tolerance for overbearing men was approaching its limits. "Why, yes; I thought it would be a fine adventure to be shot. I have always wondered why only men should have the privilege."

"None of your nonsense, now. Where is the wound?"

Elizabeth gritted her teeth. "The wound? Why, it was just here a minute ago. Let me think… I remember now. It is just under the bandage."

The doctor glared at Miss de Bourgh. "Has someone dosed her with some ridiculous concoction or is she simple-minded?"

Anne coughed, perhaps covering a laugh. "She has had a trying day."

He harrumphed, then rummaged in his bag and produced a pair of scissors with the sharpest tips Elizabeth had ever seen. Without so much as a by-your-leave, he cut through the bandages and tugged them off, sending a sharp stab of pain into Elizabeth's shoulder. She clenched her fists to keep from crying out. And this was the doctor Mr. Darcy had praised so highly? Perhaps he was gentler when his patient was a man.

"Hmm." He probed at the wound with one finger. This time Elizabeth could not remain silent. "Have they given you no laudanum?"

"No." Her voice was hoarse.

"Fools." The doctor pulled a small bottle from his bag, poured the contents into a glass and held it out to Elizabeth. "Drink this."

At that point, Elizabeth would have accepted laudanum from the devil himself. "Thank you." She drank it down quickly, then coughed as the liquid burned her throat.

"It works best when mixed with brandy," said the doctor unsympathetically over the sound of her spluttering.

Anne hurried forward with another glass for her. "Buttermilk to wash it down. It helps. Believe me." With her free hand, she patted Elizabeth's back while she glared at the doctor.

Elizabeth, still unable to speak, nodded weakly. To think she had been glad when the doctor had interrupted them! She would be happy to trade him now, even if the only choice were Mr. Darcy.

"They should have given it to you sooner; then it would be working by now."

Frowning, the doctor began to set out a series of metal implements in a neat row beside her along with an incongruous violet silk ribbon. Was he planning to tie her wound in a bow? He picked up a particularly wicked looking forceps and tested it by picking up another instrument.

"Very good, then. I will examine her ankle while we wait for the laudanum to take effect. Once it does, I will need clean bandages and two strong manservants to hold her still while I remove the musket ball."

"That will not be necessary," said Elizabeth hurriedly. "I can remain still on my own."

He peered at her over his spectacles. "Young lady, when you have removed as many bullets as I have, you may decide on what is necessary. Until then, I require two men." He glared over at the maid. "Or do I need to fetch them myself?"

The maid scurried from the room.

Elizabeth closed her eyes. How much worse could this day get? Being held down by footmen—she really must start keeping a list of all the men who had compromised her today.

A hand slipped into hers. "I am so sorry, Elizabeth," said Georgiana. "You can squeeze my hand if you need to."

"Thank you. I might prefer a pillowcase over my head." At least she had one of the amiable younger Darcys now, not their stern elder brother. "Ouch!"

"Hold still, and it will not hurt so much!"

"Really, Darcy, she is in no danger at present," said

Colonel Fitzwilliam. "There is no point in scowling at the door as if it is your worst enemy."

Darcy turned his glare on his cousin instead. "She is in a great deal of pain, and I can do nothing to help her. Perhaps you think I should take that lightly."

Before Richard could answer, the door to Elizabeth's bedroom opened, but it was only the maid leaving the room. Darcy stepped in front of her before she hurried off. "What is happening in there?"

She bobbed a curtsey. "If you please, sir, the doctor looked at the wound, and he told me to fetch bandages and two footmen to hold Miss Bennet down while he removes the bullet."

"No." The thought of his Elizabeth in so much pain as to require such measures made his stomach clench. The image of her being pinned to the bed by his aunt's footmen was even worse. "Absolutely not."

"But sir, the doctor said most especially…"

Thankfully Richard stepped in. "There is no need. Darcy and I will handle it. All you need do is fetch the bandages."

"Yes, sir."

Richard cocked his head to one side. "I assumed you would rather not have footmen manhandling Miss Bennet, but you look rather pale. Are you certain you can manage this?"

"Will it truly hurt her so much? Is there no other option?"

His cousin sighed. "When a bullet goes in, it has to come out, no matter how much it hurts. He cannot just leave it there."

"I suppose not." He would never forgive himself for allowing this to happen.

"You must not go in there with such a worried countenance. If you wish to help Miss Bennet, you should appear calm and confident, as if this is nothing important."

"I am not that good an actor!"

"I know, but you could at least make the attempt." Richard clapped him on the shoulder. "Come, your lady awaits!"

Inside the room, Elizabeth still lay in bed, but everything else had changed. Her shoulder was now exposed, and beside her the doctor had spread out what looked like enough equipment to do surgery on a battalion of soldiers. Darcy's eyes were drawn to her wound like a magnet, the angry, red hole, now oozing blood again. He would have stopped in his tracks if Richard had not urged him onward.

Richard addressed the doctor. "I understand you require assistance."

"Ah, yes, Fitzwilliam. You will do nicely. Since you know what you are doing, you may take the shoulders."

The Colonel glanced over at Darcy with an amused look. "Best put me on the arm instead, or you may be operating on me next."

"Hmmph; if you insist. Darcy, I need you on the other side of the bed then. Left hand on the young lady's other shoulder."

Darcy hesitated. Would she not be angry if he put his hand on her? Decades of training fought against necessity.

Elizabeth said resignedly, "You might as well go ahead. He will just scold until you do it."

Tentatively, he placed his hand on her shoulder, being careful only to touch the fabric of her dress.

The doctor looked up. "And on my mark, your right forearm goes across her waist. When I give the word, you will need to use force to keep her still."

Darcy blanched. "I…"

"Well, can you do it or do we need a footman?" snapped the doctor.

Darcy's hand tightened on her shoulder. "I can do it. Miss Elizabeth, my deepest apologies."

"Do you know, this is the first time in my life when I have wished to be the sort of lady who could swoon. Think of how much more comfortable all of us could be!"

If Elizabeth was still teasing, perhaps her pain was not as bad as all that. He did his best to smile reassuringly. "Some day this may all make an amusing tale."

The doctor leaned down and peered into Elizabeth's eyes. "Very well; it appears the laudanum has taken effect, so we can begin. Fitzwilliam, do you have her wrist and elbow?"

Richard, damn him, seemed completely at ease as he complied with the doctor's orders. "With pleasure. It is not often I am given such a good excuse to hold the hand of a lovely young lady."

Elizabeth made a weak attempt at a laugh. "I would not receive such flattery from a footman, I think!"

Mr. Cox selected a long metal pick and held it up. "First, I will probe to find the bullet, then proceed with the extraction. If she does not remain still, this could worsen the wound, so pray hold her well. Gentlemen, are you ready?"

Surely he could not be planning to put that thing in Elizabeth's wound! Darcy tore his eyes away from the implement and leaned forward. Any trepidation about putting his arm over Elizabeth's body had disappeared at the idea that, if he allowed her to move, she would be hurt even more.

"I am about to begin."

Darcy felt Elizabeth's body stiffen abruptly, but she remained still without his assistance.

"Very good. It is not deep, and should be simple to retrieve."

Elizabeth whispered, "Simple. That is easy for you to say."

If only he could protect her from this! But telling Mr. Cox to stop would not serve any purpose. For Elizabeth's sake, it was best to get this done quickly, but it shamed him that he could do nothing to help her. Wait—what had Richard said? Calm and confident? It was worth a try. "Elizabeth, look at me. You can do this. I know you can, and I will be here with you the entire time."

She seemed to relax for a moment. "That is…" Then her face scrunched up and she began to breathe in short gasps.

He could not bear to see her pain, and her bravery in the face of it. If only he could take her pain onto himself! He would do so in a second, even were it doubly as bad. But all he could do was to hold her in place. "It will be over very soon."

Beads of perspiration formed on her forehead and she cried, "Stop, I pray you!"

"I am here with you, Elizabeth, and I always will be. You are doing very well." He hardly knew what he was saying, but somehow it was important to keep talking to her.

"Hold her tight now, gentlemen!"

Darcy braced himself just in time as Elizabeth's body arched against his arm. A low keening sound escaped her lips.

"There, I have it." The doctor held up his forceps, a small bloody ball held in the tips.

"Thank God," Darcy muttered, releasing Elizabeth's waist. "It is over, Elizabeth. The bullet is out."

Tears were leaking from the corners of her eyes. "Remind me in the future to stay far away from guns," she said, her voice just above a whisper.

"I promise." If he had anything to say about it, and he certainly intended to, no one would ever bring a loaded gun within a mile of Elizabeth. The next borough might be too close. "No more bullets."

When she almost smiled at him, he could not help himself. Taking her hand in his, he pressed a kiss on her forehead.

The doctor cleared his throat. "There is one more thing that must be done. This will burn. You need only keep her arms away now."

Even more torture? The doctor poured a vial of clear

amber liquid into the wound. For a moment Darcy thought it must not be too bad, then Elizabeth's hand clamped down painfully on his fingers. Who would have thought she had such strength? Her wide eyes darted from one side to the other. A drop of blood appeared on her lip where she bit down on it.

Richard said conversationally, "What was that you used?"

Beloved cousin or not, Darcy wanted to kill him for sounding so calm.

"Brandy," said the doctor. "It burns out the ill humors."

"My regimental surgeon swears by rum, but he says it strengthens the flesh."

"Filthy stuff, rum. Does it work?"

"Devil if I know, but more of his patients seem to survive. He leaves a bit of rum-soaked braid in the wound for the first few days, too."

The doctor picked up a strip of ribbon. "This is what I use. I never thought of soaking it in brandy. An intriguing idea."

Richard laughed. "I am glad our surgeon does not use violet ribbon! The men would be the laughingstocks of the army if word got out."

"No more brandy, I beg of you!"

To Darcy's relief, Elizabeth's voice was hoarse, but steady. She relaxed her death grip on Darcy's hand. "I hope I did not hurt your fingers, sir."

"Not a bit." Later he would check them for damage. For the moment, Elizabeth seemed disinclined to release his hand, and he was not about to object.

Anne touched his shoulder to get his attention. She held out a damp cloth, indicating Elizabeth with a movement of her chin.

Taking the cloth in his free hand, Darcy wiped it gently across Elizabeth's forehead, then dabbed at her lip to remove the spot of blood. "Is there anything I can get for your comfort?"

She shook her head wearily. "I thank you, but no. As long as he is done with my shoulder, I can manage. I am sorry to be such trouble."

"Trouble?" said Colonel Fitzwilliam jovially. "Far from it. You should have seen me the time I had a musket ball dug out from my leg. I would tell you how much trouble I was, but it would give Darcy far too much ammunition to tease me later."

"Now, Miss Bennet, this ribbon must remain in the wound, do you understand? Every day, you must have someone draw it out just a quarter of an inch, no more."

Elizabeth said sleepily, "That is the silliest thing I have ever heard."

Richard laughed. "I believe the laudanum is talking."

The doctor frowned at her. "Young ladies never understand anything. The ribbon must remain to allow the wound to drain as it heals. Otherwise, the skin will grow together and the poisons will be trapped inside. Then I will have to do all this over again to drain the abscess. You will not like it any better the second time, so keep that ribbon in place. And stay off that ankle for at least a fortnight."

Richard glanced at Darcy, then at Elizabeth's hand in his. "Would you like some refreshment before you leave, Mr. Cox?"

"No, I just wish to leave and not be called back again this time." The doctor scooped up his surgical tools and dropped them haphazardly in his bag.

"I will show you out, then. Cousin Anne, will you accompany us?"

"Of course. Darcy, I sent Georgiana out of the room. She was turning an unnatural shade of green."

"Thank you for your consideration. Doubtless she is much happier without witnessing the details."

Darcy turned back to Elizabeth as his cousins left the room. Now that the bullet was out, he could enjoy holding her hand, without even the presence of a glove keeping them apart.

Elizabeth wore a sleepy version of her arch look. "You do not choose your doctors for their amiability, I gather."

He laughed softly. "No. He can be quite acerbic and has no tolerance for what he sees as foolishness, but no one can match his healing skills. He saved Georgiana's life when everyone else had given up on her."

"What happened to her?" Her eyelids were fluttering down.

"She had pneumonia and was fading away before our eyes, until as a last resort we tried Mr. Cox. He threw out all the other doctors and told them they should not have bled her, and he started forcing her to move and cough. We had to take turns tapping her back—striking it, really—to loosen the mucus, then persuade her to take deep breaths and cough, every hour or two, day or night. She begged us to leave her alone and let her rest, but we could see she was improving."

"Mmm. Good." Elizabeth's eyes had drifted closed. "Glad…" Her voice trailed off, replaced by even breathing.

"By all means turn this into a social event, Darcy," said Mr. Cox from the doorway, "but I suggest you allow the young lady a chance to sleep and recover."

Darcy wanted to hold onto Elizabeth's hand forever, but he gently unwound Elizabeth's limp fingers from his own, rose, and tiptoed as quietly as he could from the chamber.

He vaguely heard the doctor giving instructions to the frightened chambermaid, who was to sit up all night with Elizabeth.

With a last look at Elizabeth's brave form lying quietly in the bed, he closed the door behind him.

❦ CHAPTER 11

GEORGIANA WAS WAITING anxiously outside the bed-chamber when Darcy emerged.

"Is the bullet—?"

"The bullet is extracted," said Mr. Cox. "No need to fuss over a minor wound, young lady."

"I am very sorry I had to leave," said Georgiana. "I am not very brave, am I?"

"Most delicately bred young ladies cannot endure the sight of blood."

"I cannot say I agree," said Anne. "I found the procedure fascinating. I think I should have liked to be a doctor."

"Ha!" said the doctor, "and I should have liked to fly. Now, Darcy, if you will show me the way out of this maze—"

"I will do it," interceded Fitzwilliam, cheerfully. "I am not sure Darcy can make his way anywhere at the moment. Anne, may I rely on you to ensure he has a stiff drink?"

"Very well," said Anne, "although I think what Darcy needs is something to eat. I am quite starving after all this exertion."

Darcy heard their words through a fog. Truth be told, he *was* feeling unsteady. Seeing Elizabeth in such a situation had shaken him to the core. He could still feel Elizabeth's shoulder stiffen under his hand as the pain tore through her. He could feel her pain as his own.

"Come on, Darcy," said Anne. "We cannot stand around all evening. Let us convene in the dining room. I will have some food brought up."

Darcy agreed readily that they needed to leave. Their voices were very likely disturbing Elizabeth. She needed badly to rest after what she had endured.

"I do not think I wish to have dinner," said Georgiana. "I still feel rather queasy."

"You really are a bit of a ninny, Cousin," said Anne. "You ought to toughen up."

As they made their way to the living room, Darcy balked. The last thing he wanted to do was eat, and he could not endure several of hours of idle chatter.

"Have someone bring up some brandy to my bedchamber," he said. "I wish to be alone."

A few sips later of brandy later, Darcy put down his snifter with a bang and rose to prowl his room. The peace he had sought eluded him completely.

Alone with his thoughts, he could think of all kinds of complications arising from the wound. What if she developed an infection? What if she was starting a fever? He reassured himself that Mr. Cox would have issued instructions if he thought there might be complications.

What was more important was to focus on the matter at hand, which was how to make Elizabeth agree to marry him. Even in this, he seemed unable to gather his thoughts together. All he could do was go over the whole disastrous proposal again and again in his mind. *Now* he could think of all the things he should have said. *Now* he could think of the right words. It was entirely useless, of course, because Elizabeth no longer required a proposal. She required logic and a strong argument to convince her he was the right person for her, and sadly, the more he thought about it, the less he felt he could convince her. If only he could persuade her that his feelings were strong enough to guarantee their happiness.

But what of *her* happiness? With a frown, Darcy glanced over towards the writing table below one of the windows. Then, he fished in his pocket for the slip of paper Georgiana had thrust upon him at some point during this incredibly stressful day—the direction for Jane Bennet in London. Sitting at the table, he quickly grabbed the necessary items and penned a short note to Bingley before calling for a servant. There was no need to send it *Express*, but he wanted it taken to the post at first light the next day.

The door closed on the footman as the hour struck ten, and Darcy accepted he could not remain in his bedchamber a moment longer. The doctor had ordered the chambermaid to sit up with Elizabeth through the night, but Darcy was too restless to stay away. He needed to know how she was faring. Besides, she did not know the maid. If she woke up, how would she feel to have a stranger looking down at her? Could he trust the maid to take care of her? What if she was in pain and needed more laudanum? Did the servant know what to do?

He set out in search of Georgiana. He found her in the parlor, engrossed in a card game with Anne and Fitzwilliam.

Thankfully, there was no sign of Lady Catherine.

"Ah, there you are, Darcy," said Fitzwilliam. "Care to join us?"

He could no more play a card game right now than dance a jig. He did not understand how they could be playing so callously when Elizabeth was suffering upstairs.

"No thank you. In fact, I am afraid my presence will

only interrupt your game. I have come to ask Georgiana to watch over Elizabeth with me."

Fitzwilliam frowned. "Surely there is no need for that? She will sleep through the night. Mr. Cox gave her a generous dose of laudanum."

Darcy glowered at his cousin. Really, Richard was completely heartless.

"Nevertheless, there should be someone there, in case something unforeseen should arise."

"Well, Cousin," said Anne, tossing down her cards, "you have quite ruined our game."

"Which is particularly aggravating," said Richard, "as I must rejoin my regiment tomorrow. I will be leaving early, and who knows when we will all meet again?"

Darcy did not register Richard's words. His only concern at this moment was for Elizabeth.

"I am sorry that you consider cards more important than a sick young lady," he said, coldly.

Georgiana put her cards down and jumped up. "I will be happy to stay up with you, Brother. It is the least I can do since I abandoned you at the crucial moment."

Dear Georgiana. At least someone here was concerned.

"Thank you, little sister," he said with a smile.

"Wait here for me, William." Georgiana hurried to the door. "I will just order us some tea to be brought up. It may be a long night."

❧━━✳━━❧

Candlelight dispelled the darkness of the room. Elizabeth opened her eyes drowsily. Was it morning already?"

"You," said a voice. "What are you doing, sitting around like that? Do you not have other work to do?"

There was no mistaking that voice. It was Lady Catherine. But what was Lady Catherine doing in her bedroom? Elizabeth dragged her heavy eyelids open. Oh, yes, now she remembered. She was at Rosings. She had been shot. Did Lady Catherine really want her to get up and work? If only she could think clearly! She struggled to sit up, but seemed quite incapable of doing so.

A figure sitting close to the bed rose up and moved quickly away. Elizabeth sighed with relief. Lady Catherine was talking to the maid, then, not to her. Elizabeth wanted to protest that the doctor had ordered the maid to sit there, but she was too drowsy for the words to form.

"There she is. Do your best for her, for I do not wish for her to use her injury as an excuse to remain in this house. The sooner she leaves Rosings Park, the better."

A short, rotund man bustled to her bedside and began to pull the bed curtains closed. "I shall do my very best, your Ladyship, and I dare say the young lady will be healthy in no time."

She was swimming in a sea of green velvet bed curtains, with only her injured shoulder outside. The sound of the bandages being snipped was followed by gentle pressure on the wound. Odd, it did not seem to hurt as much as it had earlier.

"Oh, dear me," said the gentleman. "This will not do. Whatever were they thinking to leave this ribbon here? How could she possibly heal with that in the way?"

"No doubt Darcy wanted to stop her from improving, just so he could spite me by keeping her here."

A sharp, painful tug on her wound made her flinch. She was so tired. Why could they not let her sleep?

"It appears clean enough, but it will need something to bind the flesh together. A few ground spider webs are ideal for knitting flesh."

She tried to draw her scattered wits together. "What are you doing? The ribbon is supposed to remain there." Not that she could remember why, just that it was important.

"Hush, now. Your job is to rest and heal, and mine is to make it as easy for you as possible." Whatever he was doing seemed to sting deep in her shoulder. "There we are. Now we must bring the skin together, yes, and just a little glue to hold it in place. You can see, Lady Catherine, it is practically healing itself already! You were quite right to call me. This young lady will owe you a debt of gratitude."

Elizabeth seriously doubted that. He had made her shoulder ache more once again, and why would no one let her sleep? She hoped Mr. Darcy would not be cross that she had allowed the ribbon to be removed.

"I will need to bleed her, of course. Perhaps your Ladyship would prefer to step outside while I do that."

"Nonsense. I am not troubled by the sight of blood."

No doubt Lady Catherine would be pleased if Elizabeth bled to death. The sharp sting of the lancet took her by surprise. The warm gush of blood over her arm made her stomach churn. Mr. Darcy would not be happy about this, either.

"There, that is enough for now." Something tight was wrapped around her arm, then the curtain was drawn back. "A few sips of this, and you will be as good as new." He held a cup to her lips.

She swallowed the bitter potion obediently. Maybe now they would let her sleep.

<hr/>

By the time Darcy and Georgiana finally arrived in the bedchamber there was no sign of the chambermaid.

Darcy quelled the surge of anger that rose up in him at the maid's negligence. There might be a perfectly good explanation. Perhaps Elizabeth had awoken and requested something and the maid had gone to get it. He would wait before passing judgment.

He examined Elizabeth's beloved face closely, admiring the perfect arch of her dark eyelashes, the pert angle of her nose, the decided angle of her chin. He avoided looking at her lips. They were too tempting.

"Perhaps it is a trick of the candlelight, but does she not look paler than she was earlier?" said Georgiana.

Darcy was startled out of his perusal.

He brought the candle closer to her face. Georgiana

was right. There were dark shadows under her eyes and her lips had lost some of their lush coloring.

Should he be alarmed, or was this merely the consequence of enduring the bullet extraction?

"I agree. However, we must simply watch and wait. If anything changes, I will send for Mr. Cox again."

Though perhaps Mr. Cox was now halfway to London. Darcy should have insisted he stay the night at Rosings before setting out.

The chambermaid did not return with a drink or anything else. Darcy made a mental note to seek her out the next day and make sure she understood the consequences of abandoning her post.

Meanwhile, he settled in, trying not to interpret every twitch, every movement, every sound that Elizabeth made as a sign that she was taking a turn for the worse.

"You should get some sleep, brother," said Georgiana. "I will wake you up if something changes."

As if he could sleep!

But as the clock ticked monotonously onwards and the house grew silent, Darcy found the fatigue of the day overcoming him, and he closed his eyes.

A scream awoke Darcy from the light doze into which he had fallen. Elizabeth was sitting up in the bed, her eyes wide open, pointing into the corner of the room.

"Take them away! I cannot bear the sight of them!"

She began to tear at her bandages.

"Hold her, quickly, Georgiana. We cannot allow her to undo the dressings."

Elizabeth fought against them. She was surprisingly strong.

"Is she feverish?" said Georgiana, following the direction of Elizabeth's frightened gaze. "I cannot see anything!"

Darcy hesitated, then put his hand to her forehead. "No, there is no sign of heat."

Elizabeth pointed to the corner. "Tell them to go away.

Why are they staring at me like that?"

With difficulty, both Darcy and Georgiana eased her back against her pillows and her eyes soon closed. Frowning, Darcy looked about the room. He could see no sign of the medicine which had affected Theo in the same way, but surely this could not be down solely to the laudanum?

Warm sunshine woke Darcy up. For a moment, as he shifted to ease the ache in his stiff back, he tried to remember why he was sleeping in a chair. Then everything came back to him.

How could he have fallen asleep when he had promised to stand guard over Elizabeth?

A panicked look at the bed revealed that Elizabeth was sleeping calmly. His heartbeat returned to normal as he watched her, lost to the world, resting innocently as if she did not have a care in the world. On the other side of the bed, Georgiana was dosing quietly, her blond curls disheveled around her face.

His heart swelled as a feeling of sweet happiness rose up inside him. The two women he loved most in the world were beside him. What could possibly be better? He sat there for several minutes, content to let the joy settle around him like a warm blanket.

Slowly his thoughts turned to the reality of his situation and the knowledge that, now the morning was here, he had to work out what to say to her. As he puzzled this over, an idea slowly began to form in his mind.

There was really only one solution.

As the sun fell upon Elizabeth's face, Darcy leaned forward to draw the bed curtain against the light. Her eyelids fluttered open briefly and then closed again, and he froze, not wishing to awaken her. He was relieved to see her face was not as pale as it had been the night before, but she looked so small and frail, lying in the big bed, surrounded by pillows and covers.

Then, Elizabeth's eyes opened again, and she gave a small smile as she caught him leaning over her.

"I see you are still here."

"It is morning. You slept through the night." He tried to rein in his suspicion over the medicine. She seemed perfectly rational.

Taking her hand, he held it tenderly. "Elizabeth."

"Yes, Mr. Darcy?"

"Are you feeling better?" he asked.

"I would nod my head but any movement at all and the room begins to spin." Her eyes drifted shut.

"That must be the laudanum."

"I am not certain which hurts the most—my head or my shoulder. But I am better than a few hours ago. I had some strange dreams. I feel as though I was in battle for hours." She frowned suddenly.

"How long have you been here?"

He looked away, embarrassed. "Not long enough. I am afraid my aunt seems to have found an opportunity to slip you some of Cousin Anne's medicine."

"Well, that explains it. You can hardly be expected to stand guard over me," she said, her eyelids sliding downward lazily.

Darcy sighed. "I feel responsible somehow."

"Oh, Mr. Darcy, you take too much upon yourself. You are hardly to blame."

Georgiana, hearing voices, stirred and sat up. Seeing Elizabeth awake, she gave a quick smile, rose, and tiptoed quietly out of the room.

He was silent. Her breathing evened out, seeming to indicate she was sleeping. If so, he could hardly talk to her about his idea.

Without opening her eyes, she said, "I expect you will now try to convince me of the necessity of accepting your proposal."

Leave it to Elizabeth to get right to the heart of the matter. "We both know the situation requires that we mar-

218

ry," he said. "I did not lock us in intentionally, nor did I hatch a plot for someone else to do it."

"I never believed you did. I just do not like being backed into a corner with no options available to me save one," she said.

"I am sorry if you feel you are being forced into something." He felt terrible about everything that had happened.

Her eyes opened, her focus more clear than before. "I assure you, no one will force me to do anything."

He smiled. "Very well, but you must allow me to try to convince you."

"Why, Mr. Darcy, I believe you are as stubborn as I."

This sounded more like his Elizabeth. Perhaps now was a good time after all to share his plan. "This is quite a tangle we find ourselves in, but I have an idea which might prove acceptable to you if you feel up to hearing it."

He noticed her already dark eyes were even darker because her pupils were dilated. Was it just from being in the darkened room or from whatever medicine she had been given?

"I am very tired, but I think I can listen for a little while," she told him. "You might have to remind me later what I have agreed to. My head is a little foggy."

"I shall try to be brief. I propose we announce our engagement now, but set no wedding date. In two or three months, if I have not been able to persuade you to marry me, you may quietly break the engagement, and I will not protest. You may say we did not suit or make up some other excuse." He put a hand to his chest. "Make it my fault entirely. Any gossip arising from what happened here will have died down by then, and your reputation will be untarnished."

She bit her lip as she appeared to consider his idea. If only she knew how unbearably endearing he found that little habit of hers. Uncomfortable with the silence, he continued anxiously, something that was uncharacteristic for him. "I do not expect you to love me, although I hope we might come to share a mutual regard. Sometimes, I am told, love grows from that."

"This is a very sorry state indeed—you do not expect me to love you? Why would you settle for that when you could have anyone? All those beauties in London! Any woman would be thrilled to receive your addresses. What about your cousin Anne or even Miss Bingley?"

"I do not want to marry 'anyone.' I wish to marry you. That is all I have desired for many months now. I have dreamed about showing Pemberley to you. I have imagined walking with you on the paths through the gardens and sitting with you beside the stream that meanders near the house. I want to share the place that is my life's blood. I believe you will come to love it as much as I do."

She looked confused. "You must forgive me, but I believe my injury and the laudanum have affected my brain. You are telling me you have admired me for a long time?"

Darcy nodded. "Almost since we first met."

"I do not know what to say. How can that be? We have hardly spoken except to argue. You even said I was not handsome enough to tempt you."

Darcy winced. "I have long owed you an apology for that remark."

Elizabeth tried to scoot up higher on the pillows, but even the slightest movement made her wince in pain.

"Let me assist you," Darcy said, but when he reached out to help her, she waved him away.

Feeling more uncertain than ever, he took her hand again and was relieved that at least she did not pull it away. "What can I say or do to sway you?" He wanted to hear her response and yet dreaded it at the same time. What if she would not agree? How would he bear it?

"You place a great deal of importance on your family. I have heard the way you speak of Georgiana and have seen how gently you treat her, but there is so much tension and misunderstanding between you and your brother."

"I care very much for Theo, but we have had our difficulties and misunderstandings. We are just…different." She certainly knew some of the complications, but there was so much that was broken between him and Theo.

"I know your brother cares deeply for you," she said.

Darcy's frowned. "He told you this?" If this were true, then she had certainly had rather intimate conversations with Theo. He was still not completely convinced she did not hold his brother in special regard.

"I had a difficult time convincing him that he should attempt to mend things between you, so we struck a bargain."

"A bargain?"

"Yes, he promised to talk with you if I would give you another chance to show me a better side of yourself— better than my impressions from when we met in Hertfordshire. I did not fully understand him then, but his meaning is much clearer to me now."

"But I never told him of my feelings for you."

"Apparently, you do not give Theo enough credit. He knows you well."

"And you agreed to this?"

Her eyes closed again. She seemed to be tiring. "Yes, another chance. It seemed simple enough at the time."

"So now you are asking me to do the same for him."

"That is what I wish," she said, her voice was becoming almost a whisper.

"What if he and I cannot resolve things? Our problems are complicated and of long standing."

"You must try. You are a man of your word, and if you promise to try, then I know you will give your best effort."

"And if I agree?"

"Then I will agree to your plan."

"I cannot tell you how delighted I am, dearest Elizabeth," said Darcy, fervently. "The first step is to remove you from this house and take you to London, where Mr. Cox will be close at hand."

"Not Mr. Cox," said Elizabeth, with a grimace. "I do not think I can endure another exposure to his charming manners."

"He means well," said Darcy, pressing her hand reassuringly. Her eyelids drooped.

Darcy sat for a few moments holding her hand before he realized she had fallen asleep again. A feeling of hope took root in his heart. Raising her hand to his lips, he kissed it as if to seal their bargain.

Darcy emerged from the room with a sense of purpose. His feet felt light, his heart soaring. He ordered the housekeeper to watch over Elizabeth and ensure no one disturbed her, including Lady Catherine. The housekeeper balked, but he gave her a look of such hauteur that he had her scurrying to obey.

It was only upon ordering his carriage to be brought about he discovered it had only just returned from Town. Normally, his brother taking it without permission, even though now safely restored to him, would have incensed him but it seemed even Theo's behavior could not disturb his present elation. He spent the next few hours sorting whatever must be dealt with, including riding over personally to the parsonage to request that Elizabeth's trunks be packed and ready to follow them to London.

"What, are you leaving so soon, Cousin?" said Anne, as his cases were carried down the stairs. "Surely Miss Bennet is not well enough to travel?"

"My fiancée," said Darcy, deliberately enunciating the words, "needs to be safe from the reach of your mother and her concoctions."

Anne gave a whoop of joy.

"Then I have succeeded!" To his absolute astonishment, she threw her arms around him and planted a noisy kiss on his cheek. "And to think that I was instrumental in your happiness!"

"Thank you," said Darcy, grinning suddenly as he realized he had much to celebrate. "Though I do not much approve of your methods. You must promise never to repeat such a thing with either Georgiana or Theo."

"I will promise no such thing," said Anne, running up the stairs and laughing like a giddy young girl and not at all like a woman of eight and twenty.

There was still Georgiana to alert about their departure. He regretted having to rush her, but he could not travel with Elizabeth without a chaperone, even if they were engaged.

He expected to find his sister in bed, exhausted after the long night's vigil, but she was fully dressed in a fresh set of clothes.

"Well," she said, her eyes full of expectation. "May I finally congratulate you on your engagement?"

Darcy tried hard to stay serious but a broad smile broke out of its own volition.

"You may."

She grinned with pleasure and clapped her hands in a surprising similarity to Anne and, for the first time, Darcy realized a family resemblance.

"I am so happy for you!" she said. "I am certain you are perfectly matched. I am glad you were able to talk Miss Bennet into it."

Darcy felt a stab of uncertainty. Perhaps he should take Georgiana into his confidence. After all, he could not be sure Elizabeth would not wish to leave him despite all his efforts, and he did not want Georgiana to be disappointed.

He tried to think it through, but he was too tired.

"I have asked the maid to pack my case. It is ready to be taken downstairs. When did you plan to set out?"

"How did you know—?"

"Brother, I knew you would not wish to spend another day under our aunt's roof," she said.

He felt a lump rise to his throat. "Thank you," he said, feeling humbled by his sister's perception.

As the carriage began to move, Darcy heard a shout from the house. He groaned. It was undoubtedly Lady Catherine, about to cause a scene. He had not taken leave of his aunt.

His first reaction was to ask the coachman to speed up, but years of good manners drilled into him intervened. Besides, he did not really wish to slink away like a coward, as if his departure was caused by something *he* had done.

With a sharp rap of the stick, he ordered the coachman to stop and braced himself for the inevitable.

However, it was not Lady Catherine who came into view but Anne, who ran down the steps and approached the carriage.

Darcy felt guilty at once. After years of never taking leave of his cousin because she was too sickly, he had not thought to seek Anne out again to say a formal farewell.

He opened the carriage door, ready to apologize.

"I am coming with you," said she, stepping into the carriage without so much as a by your leave, and before Darcy could react, Anne had reached over and pulled the carriage door shut.

"I do not think you should leave without informing your mother," he said sternly, striving to take control of the situation. "Besides, you need a maid. And what about your clothes?"

Anne gave a rather unladylike snort. "I do not believe *you* waited to take your leave of Mama! Besides, you really have a very poor idea of me, Cousin, if you think me unable to make arrangements to attend to my own comfort. The maid and the travelling cases will follow behind in the Rosings carriage. Richard says he will be soon after then; he has no intention of remaining behind."

Darcy swallowed hard and blinked at her.

"Shall I give the order for the coachman to set out? You cannot imagine how impatient I am to get away from this house. I have spent so many miserable years here that I can scarcely endure a moment longer. Now that I am free of my medication, I intend to enjoy my life to the full."

Darcy shuddered at the idea of this newly reborn Anne being let loose on London society. After so many years of inhibition and isolation, she had hardly more knowledge of proper behavior than a child. He was also uncertain about the prospect of sharing a carriage with such an unpredictable person when he was concerned for Elizabeth's welfare. It would be crowded with Elizabeth half-lying on one seat and three of them sharing the other.

"Anne," said Darcy, "I do hope you realize we are departing for Town because of Miss Bennet's health. Her condition is deteriorating. Your mother has been dosing her with the same medicine as you."

Anne leaned forward to take a closer look at Elizabeth.

"She looks very flushed. Do you think she is in danger?"

"I certainly hope not," said Darcy, refusing to consider the possibility.

"Perhaps it is only in contrast with her pallor yesterday," said Georgiana.

Anne put a hand to Elizabeth's forehead. "Miss Bennet is hot," she proclaimed. "She is developing a fever."

"That cannot be," said Darcy, seized now with a feeling of dread. "Mr. Cox assured me she would recover quickly."

"Then you must trust in his judgment," said Georgiana quickly, trying to catch Anne's eye to prevent her saying anything more.

"I do not trust in the judgment of any doctors," Anne muttered.

"Let us hope it is only a temporary setback," said Georgiana, soothingly.

It soon became apparent, however, that Elizabeth's condition was worsening. Her fever grew, as did her restlessness, and Darcy observed her every movement with desperate anxiety. He urged the coachman to hurry so many times the other two occupants of the carriage were soon clinging to their seats. He paced the courtyard of the inn when they were forced to stop to change horses. He refused all food and drink.

CHAPTER 12

WHEN THEY ARRIVED at the Gardiners' home in Cheapside, Darcy told his sister and cousin to remain in the carriage and insisted on carrying Elizabeth into the house himself, and set off up the stairs, ignoring the protests of her uncle and aunt who did not know what to make of the arrogant stranger who had invaded their home and demanded a chamber for their niece.

Thankfully, once over the shock of Elizabeth's sudden arrival, Jane Bennet quickly made the introductions as Darcy lay Elizabeth carefully onto the bed indicated by her aunt. With one lingering serious look at her, he turned and left, intent upon finding Mr. Cox without delay and thus taking Georgiana and Anne along with him.

Mr. Cox did not appreciate having his dinner interrupted, especially as he had company, and refused at first to accompany Darcy.

"She ought not to have developed a fever," said the doctor, severely. "If she has, it was no doubt caused by removing the bandages. Or by being jolted about in a carriage."

Darcy paled at the doctor's words. Elizabeth had torn at her bandages while under the influence of his aunt's medicine. It had to be that. Darcy would not forgive himself if he had contributed to Elizabeth's danger by moving her so quickly.

Mr. Cox, perhaps seeing from Darcy's expression that matters were indeed serious, took his leave of his guests and went upstairs to bring his instruments while Darcy walked up and down impatiently in front of the house.

"Well, what are you waiting for?" said Mr. Cox. "Are we to hang about until she grows too sick for help or shall we do something about it?"

Despite the urgency of the situation, however, Mr. Cox did insist on dropping off Anne and Georgiana at the Darcy townhouse before proceeding to the Gardiners, muttering that he did not need a whole gaggle of women watching him as he dealt with his patient.

By the time Darcy had returned with Mr. Cox, the Gardiners had realized Elizabeth required immediate attention. If they were taken aback with Mr. Cox's rough manners, they showed no sign of it. Mr. Darcy had already demonstrated sufficient concern over Elizabeth and her state of health; it was unlikely the gentleman would go to the trouble of bringing along a medical man who did not know his profession.

Mrs. Gardiner led the way back up the stairs to the chamber where Elizabeth lay, and Darcy's heart contracted as he saw the change that had occurred in her over the course of the last few hours.

Despite what Anne had said about doctors, he was forced to put his hopes in Mr. Cox. He had no choice in the matter, not if Elizabeth was to survive.

Mr. Cox bent over his patient, shaking his head and

making disapproving noises. He examined the bandages with a frown and began to peel off the layers, muttering under his breath. He had to tug to remove the last layer. With a frown, he bent down to examine the wound closely, then straightened. "Who, may I ask, did *that*?" he asked in a savage voice.

"What do you mean?" asked Mrs. Gardiner.

"I left the wound clean and open. Someone has closed it against my express orders." He pointed to the layers of stained cloth he had removed. "And those are not my bandages."

Fury rose in Darcy's chest. "It must be Lady Catherine's doing. She must have brought in her own doctor to attend Elizabeth. He must have interfered with the wound. How dare she?"

"How dare she indeed! This is why she is so ill. Can you not see how red and swollen it is become?"

Even if he had known, Darcy was uncertain what he could have done about it. With sick foreboding, he asked, "Is there anything you can do to help her?"

"Hmph. I will try, but I make no promises. She may be too far gone."

Jane let out a small sob as Mrs. Gardiner turned her face away, her hand covering her mouth.

Darcy's mouth was dry. "I pray you, do everything within your power for her."

"I always do," snapped Mr. Cox. "You there, woman— I will need some clean cloths. And open the windows."

"But it is chilly out," said Mrs. Gardiner.

"Just do it!" The doctor pulled a scalpel from his bag. "Darcy, hold her arm. Even unconscious, she may attempt to move away from a painful stimulus."

"I have it." If Mr. Cox asked him to pull the moon out of the sky to make Elizabeth better, he would die trying. Holding her arm was simple.

Mr. Cox made a quick incision, causing a moan to escape Elizabeth. No sign of opening her eyes, though.

Blood welled on her shoulder, followed by purulent yellow secretion oozing out.

Then the smell hit Darcy, the vile reek of putrefaction. Without thought he brought his arm up to cover his face. Jane fished desperately for her pocket and extracted a handkerchief, but Mrs. Gardiner gagged and stepped backwards.

"Hence the open windows," said Mr. Cox icily. He seemed unmoved by the overpowering odor. "This is why deep wounds should not be closed. It must drain for a time, then I will clean it out." He wiped off the scalpel on a rag, then glared at Darcy. "And this time, no one is to remove that ribbon!"

"You may be certain of it." If it took posting armed guards over Elizabeth's unconscious body, that ribbon would stay in place. He would never forgive Lady Catherine for the damage she had inflicted. And if Elizabeth died...he could not bear to think of it.

Both Jane and Mrs. Gardiner had regained their aplomb and as Jane took her sister's nearest hand in her own, the lady stepped forward to wipe away the secretions. "Will it hurt her if I put my vinaigrette by her face?"

Mr. Cox's expression softened momentarily. "It is unlikely to make a difference, but it will cause no harm. Perhaps you should make use of it yourself instead." Darcy could see the tears welling in Mrs. Gardiner's eyes as she shook her head and tucked a silver vinaigrette next to Elizabeth.

"She is young and healthy, and the wound has not had long to fester, so she stands a good chance of recovering."

A good chance was not good enough.

⊰ ⊱

"William?"

Hearing Elizabeth call out his name in her fevered state set Darcy's heart racing. Her pale face was in contrast to her fever brightened cheeks, while her hair formed a halo of dark, damp curls spreading out in disarray over the white of the bed linens. Even in this state, she looked beautiful to him. Although he knew he should not, that propriety forbade it, he kissed her hand and put it to his cheek. It was so small, so soft as he cradled it in his own.

"I am here." *I am here, my love,* he thought. Her fingers fluttered against his cheek as light as the wings of a butterfly as if she had recognized his voice. "Please, Elizabeth, what do you need?" he asked.

Her eyes still closed, she whispered, "Theo."

That one word jolted through him. She did not want him after all; she wanted his brother. Darcy tried to push away the hurt he felt, even as he recalled the promise he had made to himself. Well, if that was what he could do for her, then so be it. He would bring Theo here to comfort her.

"You wish for me to bring Theo here?"

Her eyes opened just slightly, and she shook her head. "Promise me."

"Anything. I would do anything for you." Darcy swallowed back the rush of unwelcome emotions that seemed to be stuck in his throat. Elizabeth needed him to be strong. He could not allow himself the luxury of tears now nor show weakness of any kind.

"Reconcile…Theo. No matter…" her voice trailed off as her eyes closed again.

"You wish for me to reconcile with my brother?" he asked, relief quickly spreading through him.

"No matter what. Promise me," she repeated, her voice losing strength with each word.

"I will. I promise I will, but you must promise to get well."

Darcy closed his eyes and brought her hand to his cheek again. As he thought about how he might honor her request, the one thing she seemed to want from him, he heard the soft swish of skirts and felt a presence beside him.

"You feel very deeply for her," said the low voice of Mrs. Gardiner.

Darcy nodded and looked at the lady as he clamped down the swell of emotions that rose inside. He would not lose the tight control under which he held himself. At least that was something he was good at. He was not good at understanding others; he was not good as a brother, but control—*that* he could do.

Mrs. Gardiner gave him a sympathetic look. "Mr. Gardiner and I consider Elizabeth as dear as our own children."

"May I stay? I could not bear to leave her now not knowing..." He was embarrassed by the pleading note that crept into his voice and hoped Mrs. Gardiner did not notice.

"Under the circumstances, you may stay as you are engaged. I will send Jane up. I believe she wishes to sit with her sister again."

He nodded his head. "Thank you."

Darcy sat in a chair on one side of Elizabeth's bed while Jane Bennet took a seat on the other. After several hours, Mrs. Gardiner came in to relieve her niece, and the ladies took turns that way throughout the night. This type of vigil was usually the work of women, its rhythms and rituals a mystery to him. How did they know when to wake? Perhaps they had some special sense that called them when it was time. He remembered his own mother sitting by his bed during childhood illnesses. She always seemed to know when he needed her. He would not think about that now.

Darcy kept up his watch, leaving Elizabeth's side only briefly. Once he splashed water on his face and took some tea. Another time, he stepped into the hallway so Jane could change Elizabeth's fever-dampened nightclothes.

Upon his return, he resettled at his post, putting his

head in his hands.

"Mr. Darcy?" Jane spoke softly.

He looked up into her kind, sincere face.

"Mr. Bingley has asked me to marry him," she said simply. "Just this evening."

"And you have accepted?" He actually felt a sense of relief at the news.

"Happily accepted. Thank you for telling him I was in Town. He called on me as soon as he received your letter."

Darcy did not know what to say. He had been so unfair to a lovely young woman who had been nothing but kind to him. His letter informing Bingley of Miss Bennet's presence in Town had also included a succinct apology for interfering in his friend's life. Now, he was doubly glad he had written. "Your and Bingley's happiness is all the thanks I require."

She smiled. It was not her usual small, shy smile. This one lit her face. "Then you should consider yourself well-thanked every day for the rest of your life."

After that, they fell into silence again, listening to Elizabeth's quiet breathing. At least she did not seem to be worse. Darcy watched as Jane dipped a cloth in cool water and ran it lovingly over her sister's face. Just before dawn, as Jane and Mrs. Gardiner were changing their watch again, Darcy saw Elizabeth's eyes lids flutter. "Mrs. Gardiner," he said, nodding his head toward the figure in the bed. "She seems to be stirring."

Jane stopped and turned in the doorway. Mrs. Gardiner moved to the bed, putting her hand to Elizabeth's forehead. She looked up and smiled. "The fever has broken. We should call for the doctor just to be certain, but I think she has turned the corner." This time he could not stop the tear that escaped from his eye and slid down his cheek.

The street outside the Old Bailey was crowded, peddlers jostling with pedestrians and men on horseback, and the usual riff-raff camped outside Newgate Prison. Darcy strode past them without a glance and went inside, nodding to the constable at the door. A roar went up from the direction of the courtroom. Someone must be putting on a good show for the spectators.

It was promising that Theo would subject himself to the chaos of the Old Bailey. It was hardly a pleasant environment, and Darcy would have thought his pleasure-loving brother would avoid it like the plague. But perhaps he actually was making some effort to learn his profession. He hoped so; with a frown, he recalled the cold letter Theo had so recently sent, telling him his allowance was no longer necessary. It was worrisome, for if the Pemberley coffers were not paying Theo's expenses, where was he proposing to get the money?

Most likely Theo would be on the courtroom floor assisting one of the barristers, but the simplest way to find him would be from the spectator's gallery. Darcy winced as shouts of disapproval came from the throng of onlookers, then pushed his way into the crowded space.

He could not yet see the floor, but he heard Theo's raised voice, speaking loudly to be heard over the jeers. "When did you see Harfield after that, Madam?"

Was *Theo* involved in the case? Darcy craned his neck forward, but could only see the Judge and the witness, a stout older woman who said, "I did *not* see him after that, 'til Tuesday night. Then he came home and sat down to supper, and he began to talk to me in a deranged state."

A robed and wigged figure with a slight limp approached the witness. "Kindly relate what he said." It *was* Theo.

The woman darted a glance at the judge. "He began to talk about the cobbler. Then I enquired who the cobbler was. He said his name was Trulock; he said the Virgin Mary was a bloody whore, Jesus Christ was a bastard, and God Almighty was a damnation thief!" Her voice rose with each blasphemy she uttered. "I am sorry, my Lord; but you said I should tell the whole truth."

The Judge folded his hands. "Yes, yes. Mr. Darcy, have you nearly finished your evidence?"

"No, my Lord; I have eight more witnesses to examine."

"I hardly think that necessary after the last two," said the Judge dryly. "Mr. Siles, can you call any witnesses to contradict these facts? With regard to the law, as it has been laid down, there can be no doubt upon earth; if a man is in a deranged state of mind at the time, he is not criminally answerable for his acts; *unless at the very time when the act was committed this man's mind was sane.* I confess, the facts proved by the witness bring home conviction to one's mind, that at the time he committed this offence, he was in a very deranged state."

The hubbub began again, with men around him shouting advice to the Judge. Theo turned to the spectator gallery with a triumphant smile, but his smile faded when he spotted Darcy, then he returned his attention to the courtroom floor.

The prosecutor approached the bench and consulted with the Judge, then turned to say something to Theo that was lost in the noise.

The Judge raised his voice, turning toward the jury benches. "Gentlemen of the Jury; the prosecutor's opinion coinciding with mine, I submit to you whether you will not find that the prisoner, at the time he committed the act, was not so under the guidance of reason as to be answerable for this act. If he was not, as seems to be evident, you must find him not guilty."

The men on the jury began to put their heads together, whispering, but Darcy's eyes were fixed on Theo, who spoke clearly. "My Lord, we, who represent the prisoner, are highly sensible of the humanity, justice and benevolence of every part of the Court; and I subscribe most heartily to the law as it has been laid down."

After no more than two minutes of discussion, the

foreman of the jury struggled to his feet. "We find the prisoner is not guilty; he being under the influence of Insanity at the time the act was committed."

"'E's mad as a hatter!" cried a man to Darcy's right.

Darcy's mind was buzzing as loudly as the crowd around him. Theo looked perfectly comfortable in the court. Was it possible he truly had been working as a barrister? If so, why had he said nothing of it? How could he have found clients? It made no sense. His eyes followed his brother as he cordially shook hands with the prosecutor.

The next prisoner was already being led in, and Theo was gathering his papers, apparently in preparation to leave. Darcy shouldered his way through the mass of spectators, then looked up and down the stone corridor. Where would a barrister go immediately following a trial? Even if he knew, it would not help, since he did not frequent the environs. He had only been in the Old Bailey once, and that in his student days when he had gone once out of curiosity to see what a trial looked like. That had been more than enough for him.

With a frown, he strode down the corridor toward the stairway. He would simply have to hunt until he found him. Judging by the look on Theo's face when he had spotted him, Darcy doubted Theo would be searching *him* out. And who could blame him? Once again, he had wronged Theo in believing he, like Wickham, had made no more than a pretense of studying law and that any career he may have forged had been by luck rather than talent.

After asking directions, he found his way to a wide passageway. For a moment, he thought Theo was not among the group of mostly bewigged men, but then he recognized the stance of one who stood with his back to him, speaking with an older gentleman who clapped him on the arm and laughed. Darcy carefully picked his way past the other junior barristers until he reached his brother.

"…was well done," said the older gentleman. "Particularly how you said nothing about his state of mind until it came time for the defense. When you said you were convinced that, in fact, he had stolen the horse, I thought Siles' jaw might hit the table! And then in less than a quarter hour, you destroyed his case." He turned a piercing look on Darcy.

Had he seen that face before? It seemed oddly familiar. Darcy cleared his throat. "Congratulations on your victory, Theo." It sounded hollow even to him.

"I thank you," Theo said coolly. "Mr. Garrow, may I present to your acquaintance my brother? William, you have no doubt heard of Mr. Garrow, the Solicitor General."

"Indeed. One could scarcely avoid it. It is a privilege, sir."

Garrow shook his hand with a firm grip. "You must be very proud of this young man. He has made a fine start for himself this last year. I admire a young barrister who is not afraid to take on the most difficult cases."

Darcy wished he could sink into the floor. "I was most impressed with what I saw today. It was well done, Theo."

Theo's expression was guarded. "It was not a difficult case."

"Not when you were in possession of the facts," said Garrow. "But had you done as many barristers would do, and not interviewed him and sought out his acquaintances, he would have been convicted without a second thought."

With a small smile, Theo said, "It would be a dull job if there were no puzzles to solve."

"Well, I must be off," Garrow said. "You will join us for dinner tomorrow night, Darcy?"

Theo inclined his head respectfully. "Of course, sir."

After Garrow had departed, Theo turned to his brother. "What are you doing here?"

He should have known Theo would not make this easy. So much had happened. Had his own withdrawal shaped Theo's life in some way? Had his lack of guidance as an older brother made Theo seek out Wickham's companionship? How could they mend the brotherly bonds they had ripped apart—that *he* had ripped apart—all those years ago?

"Do you have time to talk?" Darcy asked.

"I am rather busy at the moment," Theo replied, although clearly he was not. He simply stood there, wig and gown in hand, waiting.

Relieved his brother did not run from him, Darcy struggled to find a way to begin. He hesitated, and then the words tumbled out. "She was very ill with a fever. The wound became inflamed because of our aunt's incompetent idiot doctor. I thought I was going to lose her, that it was all over when I had just... just found her." He could feel himself crumbling, diminishing somehow with each sentence, as if he was folding in on himself. Finally, his voice faltered, and he turned away not wanting his brother to witness his pain, his weakness. What was wrong with him? He was in a public place. No one should see this.

Theo grabbed his upper arm and tried to turn him back. "Miss Bennet has been so very ill?"

Darcy nodded.

"But she is well now?" Theo asked, a shadow of concern crossing his face.

Darcy nodded again unable to speak.

"Thank God!" Theo exclaimed, tilting his face up, his eyes closed. "I have not seen you like this since..." Theo shook his head and ran his fingers though his untidy hair. "Even then you were so controlled, became so..." He stopped suddenly.

"Go ahead. Say it," Darcy told him through gritted teeth.

"So cold."

"Do you think I did not...that I *do* not grieve for Sebastian? Or our parents? I wanted to howl at the moon, but I could not. I had no choice. Someone had to hold the family together." The softness of his voice only served to emphasize the depth of his pain.

Theo stared at his brother in amazement. He had never seen him so emotionally raw, so exposed. "Come with me. I know a place more private."

Taking Darcy by the arm, he guided him away. Just a short distance down the hallway, they pushed through a set of doors into an empty courtroom.

"This is more private?" Darcy asked, looking around in disbelief.

"All trials in this court are over for the day. No one will come in. We can sit in the back." Theo made his way to an empty bench, checking over his shoulder to make sure his brother had followed. Darcy collapsed onto the seat and took a deep breath as if he had not been able to fully breathe in a long while. They sat in silence for a time.

"You were brilliant today, Theo. I had no idea you were such a skilled barrister. And Garrow is your mentor. What an honor!"

"In other words, you did not believe me when I said I was actually working in the law, trying cases. You thought I was like Wickham, who only played at it." He could not keep the edge of sarcasm from his voice.

"I could deny it, but that would not be fair. I admit I was wrong. It makes me wonder what else I may have been wrong about. I thought I knew you so well, but I see now I did not know you at all. I would like to change that."

"Offering an olive branch?"

"Of sorts."

"What precipitated this sudden change in you?"

"I do not consider it sudden. That night when you were so ill after taking Anne's medicine—that was when I realized how unfair I had been to you and how much I regretted pushing you away. I tried to mend my ways, but when I heard that gun fire and thought first you, then Elizabeth had been hurt, the old habit of being angry at you came back. I should not have said what I did. It was unfair. It was my fault." Darcy had a faraway look in his eye and seemed to be speaking about much more than just their estrangement.

"You are doing this for her. Am I right?" Theo asked.

"Family is very important to Elizabeth, and yes, I promised her I would attempt a reconciliation with you, but truly, it is not just *for* her. It is more *because* of her."

Theo's first reaction was to berate his brother, to push him away. If Darcy was only doing this to please Elizabeth, Theo did not want it. Examining his brother's face, he saw sincerity and honesty which made him willing to at least listen. "I am not certain I understand."

"I realized I cannot be the husband she wishes for, the husband she deserves, unless I make some alternations in my life. I may have been granted her hand, but it is her heart I truly desire."

"I have never seen you like this. I had no idea the depth of your affection for her." Theo shook his head in amazement. "You are certain she is going to recover?"

"I did not leave until the fever broke this morning, and the doctor had visited to confirm her recovery. I only went home long enough to clean up and then came here directly."

They sat in silence again, both uncertain what came next. They had shared more real truth in these past few minutes than they had in years, and now neither knew how to proceed, how to mend what had been broken for so very long.

"Will you come with me to see Elizabeth? I think it would relieve her mind to see us together," Darcy asked.

"It is not going to be that simple," Theo responded warily.

"I know, but could it be a start?" Darcy asked.

Theo blew out a deep breath. How did one respond when the world no longer obeyed its natural order? The sky was blue, the grass green and his brother angry. That was the way of things. Was it possible for such truths to change? Perhaps, in a single moment?

Pleasing though the thought might be, it was a great deal to take in. Now he was to face Miss Bennet? No—not quite yet. Surely it would not be too much to ask for some minutes to compose himself. His stomach pinched and grumbled. He raked his fingers through wind-tousled hair.

"I am sure you wish to be off immediately to see Miss Bennet," he said softly.

"It would be my preference."

Theo scuffed his boot along the floor. "I would like very much to oblige you. But the truth of the matter is that I have yet to break my fast today."

"But it is nearly—"

"I know." Theo shrugged, "but I find I cannot eat before Court."

Darcy cocked his head and looked at him. Not with a causal gaze, but with an almost soul-piercing intensity. Theo squirmed. Perhaps the angry brother was not so bad after all. This intense one would take some getting used to.

Darcy nodded slowly. "I can understand that."

Theo's eyes widened. "You can?"

He chanced a glance into Darcy's eyes and had to look aside a moment later. Dear God—he knew William as little as his brother knew him. There was feeling—other than anger and condemnation in Darcy's eyes. Had it always been there? Perhaps his brother was not the only one to have judged too harshly.

Theo pointed toward a window. "There is a good coffee house not far from here—"

"That you frequent after Court?"

"—yes, exactly."

"Then," Darcy paused and sighed, "then let us stop there first. I have eaten very little myself today and a meal would serve me well, too. Shall I arrange for the coach?"

"No, it is easier to walk from here."

"Are you certain, with your ankle—"

Theo shifted in his seat. It was pleasing to have Darcy trying to be civilized, but perhaps this was too much. "Truly, I do prefer to walk."

"Lead on then."

The walk to the coffee house was nearly as startling as their recent conversation. Darcy asked about Garrow and did the most bloody remarkable thing—he *listened*. Theo felt himself ramble on and on, but could not stop for such an attentive audience.

It was a relief to arrive at their destination and be forced to stop talking for a moment. What had Elizabeth done to him?

A serving girl recognized him and quickly settled them in, promising to bring his usual order. Darcy trained a raised eyebrow on him. There, that was much better. Perhaps all the laws of nature had not been so entirely over-turned.

"No, Brother, I am no rake. I have no line of bastards in my wake. I leave that to our cousin, the Viscount." Theo snorted. There was a connection to be managed very carefully.

Darcy tipped his head. "Forgive me, I meant—"

Theo waved his hand. "Leave it be. It is actually re-freshing—"

"Theophilus Darcy, as I live and breathe!"

Theo whipped around. "Monty!" He jumped to his feet and grabbed the outstretched hand. "I had no idea of your being in Town."

"Nor I you!" He pumped Theo's hand vigorously. "You are a sight for sore eyes."

Monty stood head and shoulders taller than Theo. He

also cut a fine form, impeccably dressed, though not quite so much as to be a dandy. Little did it matter, women were drawn to him as inexorably as moths to a flame.

"Have you been introduced to my brother?"

Monty shook his head. Darcy stood.

"Then allow me to present my elder brother, Fitzwilliam Darcy of Pemberley."

Monty tipped his hat. "My pleasure." He turned a raised brow on Theo, his lips pressing into a faint frown.

"Darcy, this is Sir Montgomery Preston."

Darcy bowed. "Did I not recently read of your father's passing?"

"Yes, just a few months ago."

"My condolences." Darcy closed his eyes and dipped his head.

"Thank you."

"Come join us, Monty." Theo pulled a third chair near the table.

"Thank you." Monty sat, tipped his head subtly toward Darcy and glanced at the door.

Theo blinked and shook his head marginally. "Are you still seeking that matched team for your four-in-hand?"

Monty settled into his seat and leaned the chair back on two legs. "Lord, yes. Have you any idea how hard it is to find a properly matched team?"

Darcy opened his mouth.

Theo cringed. Something utterly mortifying would surely come out.

"I have tried once or twice."

"You have?" Theo stammered.

"You are an admirer of horseflesh then, sir?" Monty leaned forward eagerly in his seat, eyes wide and flashing.

"After a fashion, I suppose, but not a true aficionado. I gave up the quest long before such a team could be found. I have settled for a few excellent hunters on the estate."

"Any as good as that brute your brother rides?" Monty laughed, a rich warm sound to match his nature.

"No, few could boast that."

What? A compliment now? Theo scratched his head. What might possibly be more unexpected?

"Indeed." Monty winked at Theo. "You should see my newest hunter, a fine, tall fellow—"

"He must be for you to ride without your feet scraping the ground." Theo nudged him with his elbow.

"You would need a ladies' mounting block to get into his saddle. I doubt he would even notice a little flea like you upon his back." Monty winked at Darcy, the corner of his lips turned up a bit.

"Is that a challenge?" Theo rapped the table with his knuckles.

Monty shrugged. "If you wish."

"Consider it accepted, as soon as my blasted ankle heals properly." Theo grumbled and crossed his arms over his chest.

Monty threw back his head and laughed. "Should have known, you, the great barrister—would find yourself a way out. You can be a slippery fellow, you know."

"I take exception to that."

Darcy cleared his throat, a dark flash crossing his face.

No! Darcy becoming defensive for him? That was almost too much to be borne.

Monty waved away Darcy's glower. "I said slippery— not slimy, like that bloke you used to keep company with, what was his name—Wickham, was it not?"

Darcy growled low in his throat.

"You do not think much of him either?" Monty snorted "I cannot blame you there. I was quite relieved when Theo finally told him what for and sent him packing."

Darcy stared.

Theo ran a finger around his collar. He had never mentioned that detail to his brother. "Yes, well it was some time ago and, I admit, it was perhaps too long in coming." He kept his eyes from his brother's. Surely Darcy would not gloat at a moment like this. But still—

"True enough. Sometimes it is difficult to rid yourself of that sort of vermin." Monty rubbed his fist along his jaw. "Speaking of which, did you know he is in Town now?"

Darcy leaned forward. "I knew he had been, but did not realize he was still here. He is in the Militia now, and his regiment is in Hertfordshire."

Theo blinked. *Wickham* had been in Hertfordshire? No wonder his brother had found those months so trying.

Monty shrugged. "Be that as it may, he is definitely here. I spoke to him myself; in fact, he asked after your sister."

Darcy drew a deep breath and clutched the edge of the table, murder in his eyes.

Monty raised his hand. "Not to worry. I told him quite directly a bit of pond scum like himself had no business thinking about a lady like your sister, much less asking after her. Told him I would see to him myself if he ever spoke her name again."

"And given your school championship in pugilism…" Theo muttered.

"I believe he found the threat credible enough."

"I am much obliged, Sir." Darcy said softly.

"Not at all. I have three younger sisters myself and the accompanying fortune hunters and rakes trying to attach themselves like apothecary's leeches."

"Then you well know the concerns." Darcy laced his hands together in front of his chest.

"Indeed I do, only last week…"

Theo leaned back and allowed the elder brothers to commiserate on the woes of protecting and providing for younger siblings who did not clearly understand the dangers of the world around them.

Though there were touches of insufferable arrogance scattered in and about their words, the theme was one of concern and protection, not control and criticism. Had it always been so? Theo chewed his cheek.

Maybe there was more to Darcy's edicts and demands than Theo ever considered. Was it possible that in his own clumsy and very imperfect way, Darcy has been trying to protect and care for his own?

Theo raked his hair again. He might have as much to learn as his brother after all.

.

CHAPTER 13

GEORGIANA PACED THE CARPET in front of the fireplace for what must have been the fiftieth time. Why was it that it was always the menfolk who were out doing things whilst the ladies waited at home? Her skin prickled and crawled. If she did not do something soon, she would run mad.

"Do be sensible," Anne looked up from her book. "What do you think you can do?"

"There must be something I can do to persuade Miss Bennet to—"

"Fall in love with your brother?"

"Yes, yes exactly."

"She is far too sensible a girl to have her head turned by romantic tales. Besides, there are none to tell. You must face the truth. He is one of the least romantic souls I can imagine. No woman would ever accept the notion of him as some gothic hero to sweep her off her feet."

"Are you saying that no woman would ever love him? How could you possibly…he is protective and caring and thoughtful…"

"—and taciturn, overbearing and given to offending everyone in a room given enough minutes to do so." Anne rose and walked to Georgiana's side. "I know you adore him, but you must confess, it would be hard for another to do so."

"Not if she knew his character."

"I grant you, his character is utterly sterling, and we all love him for that—at least when he is not grumping or sulking or criticizing. Surely you can see, those less redeeming of his traits make it difficult for his shining character to come to light."

Georgiana swallowed hard. There was a reason Fitzwilliam was not a popular man. It was such a shame though, if people only knew what he did for those he cared about.

Yes! Of course!

"That is it, Anne! Thank you." She grabbed Anne's hands and squeezed them.

"Are you well, dear? There is a wild look in your eye that I find quite unsettling."

"You have given me a splendid idea."

"What do you mean to do?"

"I am going to tell Miss Elizabeth about…about…"

"About what dearest?"

"Something very personal which will surely convince her of the true nature of Fitzwilliam's character."

"I suppose then I must come with you"

"No, you need not—"

"Yes, I do. If you need to have so private a conversation with her, you will need me along to distract her family so you might have privacy." Anne cocked her head and lifted her brow.

"I never considered that. My, you are full of unexpected insights."

"I heard that said before I became so ill. It is nice to be finding myself once again. Now, go get your things and we shall be off. We will stop for some flowers or perhaps some sweets or even both along the way. Trust me, an invalid always appreciates a bit of tangible good cheer."

They piled into Fitzwilliam's coach and gave direction to find a flower shop on the way to Gracechurch Street.

"Do you know, I do not think I have ever been shopping without Mrs. Jenkinson in tow, and not much of that either." Anne rubbed her hands together. "This will be such delicious fun."

"Do be serious. It is just a flower shop." Georgiana tried not to roll her eyes.

"Perhaps it is to you. But you have been to one or another shop often enough to find it common place. When you have been confined as much as I, any outing is an adventure and one with a lively companion is a capital one."

"I must take you at your word, but I do not pretend to understand."

"I do not require you to understand, simply humor me and allow me to have a spot of fun."

"Would you like to choose the flowers for Miss Bennet then?"

"Oh, yes, please! I already have something in mind. If only the flowers are available…" With great waves of her hands and flowing descriptions, Anne painted a picture of what she desired.

Who knew Anne ever could speak so many words together at once or be so…so vivacious? Georgiana pinched herself. No, she was not imagining it at all.

The coach stopped at a quaint little flower shop.

"Will this do?" the driver asked as he handed them down.

"I truly hope so," Anne said. "But if it does not, I am sure there are others."

"No, we must find something here. I do not wish to spend all day flitting from one shop to the next. I must see Miss Bennet today."

"Do not be such a kill joy."

"Anne, please. Let us go in and accomplish our errand." Georgiana led the way into the shop.

A number of other customers milled about, but the shop owner immediately hurried toward them. She probably saw the crest on the side of their coach. There was something to be said for a well-marked equipage.

"May I assist you, Ladies?"

Anne stepped in front of Georgiana. "Yes, I am looking for something very particular—a gift for her brother's betrothed who is recovering from –"

Several people stopped mid-step and turned to stare.

Botheration! Anne had never much dealt with gossip-mongers. She did not know how to keep her voice down or how to keep information to herself.

A familiar face caught Georgiana's eye from the far corner of the shop. Great heavens! It could not be. No! It was...Mr. *Wickham.*

She grabbed Anne's arm. "We must go now."

"But Georgiana—"

"Now." She dragged Anne away from the shop owner, ignoring the startled looks. She ordered the driver to take them elsewhere and hurried into the coach, pulling the curtains over the side glass.

"What was that disgraceful display about?" Anne bounced on the squabs and crossed her arms over her chest.

"There was someone in that shop who should not have been there."

"How exactly does one determine who is and is not to be in a particular shop? Is there some advanced formulae I have not been taught?"

"Anne, please. It is someone who has done...my brother great harm, and I do not wish to be anywhere near him, nor would my brother want me in proximity to him."

"Another of your brother's grudges?"

"No, no, not at all. In this, he is perfectly reasoned, and I am content with his pronouncements." Georgiana fanned herself with her handkerchief.

"You look very pale. Are you sure you wish to visit

Miss Bennet? Should I instruct the driver to take us home?"

"No, I am all the more determined to be true to my purpose now."

"If you say so." Anne patted Georgiana's hands.

How could it be? Was it possible she had only imagined it? The thought did little to soothe her racing heart. Enough of that. Even if it was him, she would never speak to him again, so he posed little danger to her.

She sighed. Now she simply had to convince her racing heart to slow and believe her own pronouncements.

Ultimately, they settled on a bundle of lavender and a box of lavender comfits to bring to Elizabeth. They were a far cry from what Anne wanted, but Georgiana could not tolerate yet another stop along their journey. At last they arrived at the Gardiner's.

The housekeeper showed them to the drawing room. The town home was far better appointed than Georgiana had expected for someone in trade. In fact, the house was nicer than some of her school friends' homes. With such refined taste, could their manners or company be nearly so shocking as Lady Catherine had intimated?

"Good afternoon, Mrs. Gardiner." Anne curtsied. "Please forgive our intrusion; there was no opportunity for formal introductions the other day. We came to inquire after Miss Bennet."

"We are honored by your visit, Miss de Bourgh, Miss Darcy." Mrs. Gardiner smiled a warm gracious smile that surely decreed her every bit as well-bred as the fanciest gentlewoman Georgiana had ever known.

Elizabeth shifted against the pillows and sighed. It was difficult to identify what was more vexing, the enforced quietude of her convalescence or the bewildering intelligence regarding the enigma that was Mr. Darcy. That man who was the very embodiment of all that appeared rude and unfeeling had not left her bedside until her fever had broken. Before that, he had declared his solicitude toward her and her family and how he longed for children to call his own, even to name their eldest son for her father. *What sort of man was he?*

Was three months, just *three* short months, going to be sufficient time? He would insist their betrothal became a bond then, but what if she was not certain? Could she possibly negotiate for more time? He did not seem the type of man to be gainsaid. Her chest tightened with a feeling that had become all too familiar recently. Was this how a caged animal felt?

An unfamiliar knock sounded at her door. It was not a man's hand, not Mr. Darcy. She breathed out a sigh and sagged into her pillows. Oh, that hurt!

"Miss Bennet, may I come in?"

That was Miss Darcy!

"Yes, please, come in." Elizabeth's heart sped up just a bit, the throb echoing dully in her wounded shoulder.

The door creaked and the girl herself appeared a moment later, a bundle of flowers and small box in her hands. Her smile was ready enough, if just a bit timid.

"I am so glad I have not woken you. Your aunt was concerned that you might not be up to company."

Elizabeth pushed herself slightly higher in bed. "No, no, not at all. You are very welcome. I am afraid I do not take to enforced quiescence very well. I am far too stubborn and troublesome a creature for that."

Georgiana pulled a chair closer to the bedside and sat down. "I can hardly imagine you being so troublesome. Here, Anne and I brought you these. She insisted an invalid always appreciates an offering from her guests."

Elizabeth took the gifts. "I dearly love lavender, in flower and in comfits as well. That was most thoughtful of you. I confess though, I am not so certain I much like the notion of being an invalid. I have little intention of allowing my confinement here to last a moment longer than it must."

Georgiana laughed. "Perhaps I must reform my opinion. It may be true that you are a stubborn—"

"—and troublesome creature. There was a reason why I said that." The tightness in her chest released just a bit. Georgiana was just the sort of company she needed.

"I shall learn not to question your judgment. Here, shall I open the comfits for you?"

"Only if you will share them with me."

"If you insist." She opened the box and passed it back to Elizabeth.

The faintly purple disks filled the room with a sweet perfume. She took one and popped it in her mouth. "I confess I had been recently considering how much I would enjoy something sweet. Thank you so much for coming to call." She held the open box toward her visitor.

Georgiana took one, put it in her mouth, and fell suspiciously silent. Long after the lozenge would have disappeared, the stillness lingered, becoming increasingly oppressive.

Kitty had worn that expression far too often to mistake it. "Forgive me, Miss Darcy, but I cannot escape the impression that there is something you would like to say, but are reluctant."

The young girl wrung her hands. "Well, yes, that is true. It is difficult to know where to begin, though."

"At the beginning?"

"I know that is good advice; I am just not sure where this begins."

"I am intrigued. If you would be so good as to help me adjust my pillows that I might recline a bit more easily, I shall be prepared to listen to however complex a tale you have to share."

Georgiana rose and fluffed her pillows, easing Elizabeth into a far more comfortable attitude.

"Thank you, that is far more agreeable. Now, your story?"

Sitting back in her seat, Georgiana returned to wringing her hands. "Yes, my story. I suppose, I must begin with an apology. If you do not already know, you will soon, I played a role in your current situation with my brother."

Elizabeth's eyebrows rose. "I imagine you want to explain that a bit further? It does not signify that you would come all this way for so simple a confession, then leave."

Georgiana giggled. "I suppose so." She chewed her lower lip. "I just hope you will not be very angry at me, and that perhaps, you might…"

"Might what?"

"Might understand, just a little bit, and even…even…oh!" She blinked furiously and fished a handkerchief out of her reticule.

What was troubling her so?

"My brother can be so difficult, I know. But that is not who he really is. I want so much for him to be happy, but for that to happen, he needs you to love him or at least like him very well. I want you to like him, for I love him so dearly. I want you to know what a good man he is, even if he can be utterly maddening at times. But I am afraid you will not…you will not listen to me…or you will be angry at me for my own foolishness and blame him for my mistakes instead of seeing how very well he has taken care of me…" She sniffled and pressed the handkerchief to her face.

The poor dear would soon be beside herself. She certainly felt very deeply for her brother and that was to his credit. A girl like Miss Darcy would not admire him so much if he were truly as hard as he sometimes appeared. What could have happened to affect her so?

"Please, I am happy to listen to whatever you wish to tell me." Elizabeth smoothed the sheets over her lap.

"My brother and Cousin Richard have been my guardians since our father died. They have tried so hard to care for me. They have been so good to me." She chewed her knuckle briefly, then in rapid, hushed words poured out a tale of secret assignations in Ramsgate which then led to a near elopement more fitting for a novel than a proper young lady of the *ton*. "It all happened just before he went to Hertfordshire with Mr. Bingley. That is why he was so very cross, I think. And it was made even worse when he saw Mr. Wickham there as well."

"I am afraid I do not understand, what has Mr. Wickham to do with—"

"Oh," Georgiana blinked, "did I not say? It was Mr. Wickham who, who…" she sniffled and covered her face with her hands.

Elizabeth gasped and pressed her hand to her mouth. "Gracious, I had no idea. He was so very—"

"Pleasing when you met him?"

"Yes, yes quite so." Elizabeth swallowed hard. How could she have been so foolish as to have believed Mr. Wickham so entirely when he railed against Mr. Darcy. Her cheeks heated.

"So many do, so do not berate yourself for it. But I fear that he may have said things about my dear brother…" Georgiana's brow knit.

"I…I cannot repeat the things that he said. I am ashamed—"

"That you believed him?"

Elizabeth screwed her eyes shut. "I should have never—"

Georgiana touched her hand. "I know too well how very persuasive he can be. Do not blame yourself. It is no wonder that you would have easily believed whatever calumny he might have spoken, particularly when my brother had already deported himself so infamously."

Even so, it was no excuse. She had been far too ready to accept Mr. Wickham's allegations with no proof to support them. Charlotte and Jane had tried to warn her, but no, she had been too proud to listen, for clearly she knew better. *What an excellent judge of character she was! Oh, it was too much to be borne!* She covered her face with her hands. What other mistakes—had she been equally wrong in her understanding of Mr. Darcy?

Elizabeth peeked up and met Georgiana's anxious gaze.

"I am sorry to have upset you. I can see that I have. But Fitzwilliam regards you so highly. Please forgive me if I have been too forward. I only wanted you to know what kind of man holds you in such esteem." Georgiana wrung her handkerchief until she could wrench it no further.

"I can see how much you care for him to share something so very personal with me. Thank you. I can see he takes his duty as your protector very seriously."

"No," Georgiana's hands shook in her lap. "I mean yes, he is, but there is so much more than that and that is what I am trying to convey. You see, after it all happened he would have been well in his rights to be so very angry with me, to treat me—"

"As he does Theo?" Elizabeth whispered.

"Yes...no, that is not at all what I mean. He has been so very kind and patient with me. He does not hold my transgressions against me, when I have been such a fool." She screwed her eyes shut and turned her face down. "If only I could convey to you how very good he has been to me when I have not at all deserved it."

"I am pleased to hear of his kindness to you. I am afraid that leaves me all the more confused though."

"Because he and Theo are at odds with one another?" Georgiana peeked up.

"It does seem difficult to reconcile the two very different images you present."

She shrugged. "I am not Theo."

"I do not have the pleasure of understanding you."

"Do you believe the tension between them is solely of Fitzwilliam's making?"

Elizabeth sucked in a sharp breath. "I...I cannot say I have given the matter a great deal of thought."

"Then allow me to assure you, they both carry their share of fault."

"Is not Mr. Darcy rather resentful—"

"Oh heavens, no! I do not find him resentful at all." Georgiana chewed her lip and looked up at the ceiling. "I understand he appears so, but the truth is far more complex. I believe what appears to be resentment is his own frustration with himself for being unable to manage and fix everything for everyone in his circle."

"And Theo?"

"Oh, Theo, my dear, dear brother. I know he is so much easier to like and keep company with. Theo is a delight, and I owe him nearly as much as I owe Fitzwilliam, do not mistake that. But, he is far from perfect…and that is perhaps the problem."

Elizabeth leaned in a little closer. "I do not—"

"Fitzwilliam is a difficult role model to follow. He is successful in nearly everything he attempts—"

"Except mixing in society—"

"Except for that. In many ways it is his only fault. I know Theo has suffered in comparison to Fitzwilliam, in school, among the family. He…" Georgiana plucked at her skirt. "Oh, please do not think ill of me, I do not wish to criticize either of my brothers."

"I understand, I have four sisters remember."

"Yes, I had forgotten. Then perhaps it will make sense that Theo has always resented the comparisons to Fitzwilliam."

"My younger sisters do get tired of being told of Jane's beauty and of failing by comparison to her graceful manners and gentle temper."

Georgiana sat up straighter. "Yes, yes! Exactly. Do they ever speak harshly or teasingly to Miss Bennet because of it?"

Elizabeth's brow furrowed. "Yes, I suppose they do."

"That is exactly the case with Theo. He has always delighted in vexing Fitzwilliam, I think because he is tired of being told how perfect his brother is. And lacking Miss Jane Bennet's disposition, Fitzwilliam—"

"Becomes defensive, angry and even critical?"

"That is exactly it. So you can understand why I feared you might not fully understand?"

"Perfectly. I…thank you for taking the time to explain so much. I have much to consider." *Was that the right thing to say to someone who had just shown you what an utter fool you have been?* Elizabeth hoped it was good enough.

"You are very gracious, Miss Bennet. Thank you. I should go now. I fear I may have overstayed my welcome."

"No, no, not at all. I am glad you have come. But I think you are right, I am tired. Please thank Miss de Bourgh for the lavender."

"I will. She will be pleased to know you liked it." Georgiana curtsied and ducked out of the room.

Elizabeth drew her knees up under the sheet and wrapped her good arm around her legs. How could she have been so utterly mistaken about this man who had offered her marriage? And what was she to do about it now?

Elizabeth might be recovering well, a fact for which Darcy was eminently grateful, but with the concern about her health receding, his worries about whether she would finally accept his offer had returned. He was not feeling optimistic. Elizabeth had seemed pleased when he and Theo had called on her together, displaying their tentative reconciliation, but she had spoken mostly to Theo, and her aunt only allowed them a few minutes with her.

"Lizzy needs her rest," said Mrs. Gardiner. "Only yesterday she was delirious with fever, and she has also had a long visit from your sister earlier."

Darcy returned the next day, in hopes of a favorable reception, but while Elizabeth was pleasant enough to him, she seemed to be avoiding his eyes. Apparently reconciling with Theo had not changed her view of him. But there was little he could say, since her sister remained in the room as a chaperone. Finally, after half an hour of painfully stilted conversation, he could no longer bear it.

"I must ask you if I have in some way offended you."

Finally, Elizabeth looked at him, her brows drawn. "No, sir, you have not."

"You seem uncomfortable with my presence." From the corner of his eyes, he could see Jane Bennet smiling encouragingly at him and nodding. At least someone seemed to approve of him.

"It is not you. It is…" She moved her hands around vaguely. "Everything."

"Everything?"

She looked down at the counterpane, picking at it with her fingers. "I am aware I have misjudged you, and much of what I thought I knew of you is not true. I am not proud of that."

Jane ostentatiously placed one of her hands over the other.

A month ago, Darcy would have ignored her hint as impudent and improper. Now he saw it for the kindness it was, and he was willing to take whatever help he was given. Tentatively he reached out and laid his hand over Elizabeth's. A rush of pleasure filled him as she tightened her fingers around his. How beautifully her hand fit in his! The delirious sensation of her skin against his momentarily robbed him of words, forcing him to struggle to put his thoughts together.

"The fault is more mine than yours. I did not make it easy for you to know me."

Her fine eyes lacked their usual sparkle when she finally raised them. "It was not only that Mr. Wickham told me lies about you. I believed him, for no better reason than that I wished to soothe my injured pride. There. Now you know how weak I can be."

He felt a smile grow on his face. "Is that all? If you believe it will make me think less of you, it will not. I have had years to learn that everyone always believes George Wickham, at least at first. Sometimes, I have wondered whether he might be possessed of the black arts, given his apparent ability to convince anyone of anything. You had no reason to disbelieve him, and he is extraordinarily persuasive."

"It does not trouble you that I believed him?"

"As long as you do not still do so, I am content. I should have warned you about him when he first came to Meryton. Your belief in him is just punishment for my pride in saying nothing of the history of our connection."

Elizabeth squeezed his fingers again. "Thank you for understanding."

Jane set aside her book. "If you will excuse me, I must check on my cousins. I will return shortly."

"Of course," Darcy said. Bingley just might have been correct when he said Jane Bennet was an angel. As she left the room, he turned back to Elizabeth. "Is there anything else troubling you?"

She bit her lip. "Nothing to speak of. I still dislike being told I have no choice about this engagement, but as Jane says, none of us can choose to abstain indefinitely from eating, either. That does not mean food is not enjoyable, or that we would not choose to eat it if we could. I am trying to bring myself around to that way of thinking, but I fear it is in my nature to resent compulsion."

"I hope you know that, despite my wishes, I would not have chosen to force the issue in such a way." He held his breath waiting for her response.

To his relief, Elizabeth smiled. "Yes, you are fully acquitted on that count."

Thank heavens for that! "While I am making great progress with understanding my brother better, I admit I am still angry with my cousin, Anne, for locking us in at Rosings. Theo has done more than his share of annoying pranks, but that was all they were—annoying. I am thankful he was not the one who put you in the situation of being obliged to marry."

Elizabeth laughed ruefully. "Yes, Anne may take all the credit; she told me about it herself and seems quite proud of her success."

"There are moments when I could almost sympathize with my aunt's desire to keep Anne in a more compliant state!" Darcy shook his head. "My cousin is quite the liability. This evening we are due to attend the theater with her, and she has had a vast deal to say upon the subject—and the performance—before she has set foot in the building!"

Elizabeth smiled. "Can you imagine the arguments the two of them will have now? Rosings Park may not be large enough for two such opinionated women! I suppose I should be grateful Pemberley is so far from Kent."

Darcy sucked in his breath. *Did she realize what she had just admitted?* "I hope Pemberley will suit you in all ways."

She gave another rueful smile, acknowledging his point. "All I know of Pemberley comes from Miss Bingley, though my aunt tells me the grounds are particularly lovely."

"Your aunt?" *Not the horrible Mrs. Philips from Meryton, please God!*

"Yes, Mrs. Gardiner spent her youth only a few miles from Pemberley, and speaks of it fondly."

"Did she? Where did she live?"

"In a small village called Lambton. You would not have known her; she was merely the doctor's daughter, not part of the gentry." There was a touch of bitterness in Elizabeth's tone. "I hope that will not be an embarrassment for you."

"Not at all." He hesitated, then plunged in. "Perhaps we could invite your aunt and uncle to come to Pemberley at Christmas." He would happily invite the entire populace of Hertfordshire to Pemberley if Elizabeth was willing to marry him.

"I think…" she said slowly, then straightened her shoulders and smiled. "I think I would like that very much."

Elizabeth woke the next day feeling well rested for the first time in ages. Mr. Darcy had promised to call upon her again on the following morning, and she was determined to show him a marked improvement when he did. As such, though she felt sufficiently well to get out of bed and submit to the maid's ablutions, she allowed Jane to help her into a simple dress to accommodate her bandages. Then, she then lay back on top of the counterpane under Mrs. Gardiner's watchful eye as Jane took her usual place on a chair at her side.

The sudden clang of the doorbell drew her aunt from the room, but raised voices shortly followed, and to Elizabeth's surprise the door flew open to reveal Lady Catherine de Bourgh who swept in, closing the door with a snap on the anxious face of Mrs. Gardiner.

"That is your sister, I suppose," the lady began.

"Yes. Jane, permit me to introduce Lady Catherine de Bourgh, Mr. Darcy's aunt. Lady Catherine, this is my eldest sister, Jane, who is to marry Mr. Bingley, Mr. Darcy's friend."

"I suppose that is a suitable match, since both families have connections to trade. Though I understand you bring little to the match beyond the clothes on your back."

Jane blushed, at a loss to know how to answer, completely unaccustomed to being addressed in this manner.

"Since Mr. Bingley has no objection, I hardly think that concerns anyone else, Lady Catherine," said Elizabeth. She waved a hand towards an armchair. "Do please be seated."

Lady Catherine threw the chair a scathing look before perching upon it, smoothing her skirts and then raising her chin as she met Elizabeth's eye.

"This is a better house than I would have expected,"

she said. "Though situated as it is in a commercial district, it must experience an unpleasant amount of traffic."

"Coming as I do from the country, I find I enjoy the hustle and bustle of town," said Jane, making an effort to be agreeable.

Lady Catherine did not deign to reply. She sat silently, looking about the room as if to find fault.

Let her try, thought Elizabeth. It will be difficult for her to see aught amiss. Her aunt and uncle took great pains to keep the house superbly maintained and impeccably furnished in the latest style.

"You may leave us, Miss Bennet. I wish to speak to your sister alone."

Elizabeth signaled for Jane to stay, but her sister was too intimidated to oppose Lady Catherine. She gave a small shake of the head and mouthed an apology.

Lady Catherine stared fixedly at the door until Jane had closed it, then turned fiercely to Elizabeth.

"You can be at no loss, Miss Bennet, to understand the reason for my journey hither. Your own heart, your own conscience, must tell you why I come."

"I find myself afflicted with a curious lack of curiosity, Lady Catherine. However, I am sure you have every intention of telling me."

"Impudent girl!" Lady Catherine stood and went to the window to look out. "This is my reward, for welcoming you into my home, for condescending to treat you with civility!"

"I hope I have shown you every civility in return, your Ladyship."

Once again, Lady Catherine lapsed into silence. Elizabeth did not entertain any hopes it was going to last, and she braced herself for more.

"I see that your wound is much improved. I never thought much of it. *'Tis just a flesh wound,'* my nephew, Colonel Fitzwilliam, informed me. However, it served its purpose very well, did it not? You were able to insinuate yourself not only into my home but into my nephew's life."

Elizabeth was incensed by Lady Catherine' wholly inaccurate accusation.

"As you well know, your nephews both witnessed not only the shot but the depth of the wound itself. I find it highly unlikely to believe the Colonel would refer to it as just a flesh wound!"

Lady Catherine waved her hand dismissively.

"I will concede the wound may be genuine enough, though why you were shot and how is not as clear to me as it should be. However, the fact remains you contrived to compromise my nephew. He would never have proposed to you otherwise."

It was a thought that had occurred to Elizabeth, and there were moments—though they were growing fewer—that she grew convinced that he had only offered for her out of duty, because he was enough of a gentleman to wish to shield her from scandal.

"I beg your pardon, Lady Catherine, but may I remind you it was your daughter who locked the door and forced Mr. Darcy into a situation whereby he must propose? And may I remind you further, your Ladyship, you were a witness to the fact I turned down Mr. Darcy's first proposal?"

"I am wiser to the world than all that. Your refusal was nothing more than an artful allurement intended to draw him in."

"No doubt your Ladyship will have it, too, that I arranged to have myself shot in order to draw his sympathy."

"It would not surprise me to learn it. However, that is neither here nor there. I am here to give you one last opportunity to redeem yourself in my eyes—to prove that you are possessed of a sense of honor and decorum. It has come to my knowledge that you actually intend to go through with this farcical marriage. If you care anything for my nephew, you would not embroil him in such a situation. No good can come from it. Do you wish to subject him to the censure and condemnation of his friends and family? To alienate him from all that he is accustomed to? Do you really think for one moment that marriage to you can bring him *anything* but unhappiness?"

Lady Catherine's words would have been more easily dismissed if Elizabeth had not wondered such a thing herself. Confined to her bed with little to do, she had spent many hours wondering if agreeing to marry William—she blushed even as she thought the name—was not in fact the utmost folly for both of them.

She would not for anything acknowledge this to Lady Catherine, but she did not feel quite as sure of herself as before when she answered the woman who—if the marriage took place—was to become an aunt to her.

"I do care for him, which is precisely the reason I wish to marry him. It is quite absurd to expect me to claim affection for your nephew while at the same time relinquishing any claims on him."

"This, then, is your answer? Unfeeling, selfish girl! Do not think you have heard the last of it. I intend to do everything in my power to prevent my nephew from persisting in this folly. I will see to it that he withdraws from this engagement. I have the means to do so and I shall; you may depend upon it."

"Your nephew is a man of his word, your Ladyship. I do not think it likely that he will withdraw his offer."

"The engagement is not yet official. The papers have not been drawn up. It is no more than an informal understanding, and I intend to ensure it goes no further."

With that she swept towards the door. Elizabeth rose from the bed and tried to follow, hoping to contain the damaging effects of Lady Catherine's anger. She did not wish the Gardiners to bear the brunt of it.

She need not have troubled herself. When Lady Catherine reached the bottom of the stairs, Mr. Gardiner emerged from the drawing room and invited her to partake of some tea and cake.

"I will not honor the family with my presence," she replied, brushing past him. "I have been most grievously insulted by your niece."

As Lady Catherine's carriage drove away, Elizabeth made her way back to the bed slowly. She felt as if all the energy had been drained from her. The encounter had left her far more shaken than she was willing to admit. Worse, it had awakened many of her fears and uncertainties. What if Fitzwilliam changed his mind? What if, despite his words, he had proposed only out of duty or honor?

Elizabeth could not bear it. So much for believing herself indifferent. She had convinced herself she gave in to Mr. Darcy's persistence because, ultimately, she had little choice in the matter. Now suddenly, for the first time, she began to wonder if there was more to it than that.

CHAPTER 14

IT HAD BEEN A long day, and Theo was contemplating the mess of papers spread across his desk, when he detected the unexpected sound of Monty's voice outside his chambers. Not that his presence was unusual, but he had rarely heard Monty speak in such a grim, commanding tone. Known for his easy disposition. it took a great deal to kindle his friend's wrath.

"In with you!" snapped Monty.

The door to Theo's chambers was flung open, and Monty propelled a young man inside.

"There is no need to be so rough, Preston!" The dandified young man glared at Monty, rubbing his wrist.

Monty slammed the door shut, then leaned back against it, his arms crossed over his chest. Monty the Mountain—that was what they had called him at school when he did that. He was unshakeable.

"Tell him," he growled.

Theo cocked his head to one side as he eyed the sullen-looking young man. "Duxbury, is it?" he asked mildly. He had been part of the crowd Theo had run with during his student days.

Duxbury straightened his waistcoat with a tug. "You know perfectly well who I am."

Theo gave Monty a questioning glance, then said dryly, "I do not suppose one of you might be persuaded to tell me the purpose of this call, delightful as it may be."

"He made me come! It was not my idea. I was having a private conversation when…"

Monty said, "And as soon as you repeat that private conversation to Darcy, you may go on your way."

Theo sat back in his chair. "It is hard to imagine what could be so urgent, but it is generally unwise to argue with Monty. Those fists, you know."

Duxbury sniffed. "It is none of his affair. He was eavesdropping."

"Perhaps I might refresh your memory," said Monty. "You were telling your friend about your recent drinking bout with Wickham."

"It is not against the law to drink with a friend!"

"And Wickham said…" Monty prompted inexorably.

"Oh, very well! He said his fortune was made because that pompous jack…"

Monty cleared his throat loudly.

Duxbury gave him a poisonous look. "Because the elder Mr. Darcy is now engaged, and he will dig deep in his pockets to spare his beloved's family from shame. Wickham said he would be set for life."

Theo sat up straight. "And how did he plan to enact this pretty little blackmail?"

He had not intended to use his cross-examination voice, but it came out naturally.

The dandy swallowed hard. "He did not say exactly, just that there was a comely bird who would sing whatever tune he chose."

Theo's eyes narrowed. He had heard more about Wickham's wenches than he cared to recall. "Did he happen to name this particular bird?"

"No, it was some girl he had met in Hampshire. Or maybe Hertfordshire. I cannot recall—wherever his regiment was stationed. He was about to return there, as he said, and would see his little bird right away."

Miss Bennet's family was from Hertfordshire—and Wickham knew them, or knew of them? This was not good, not good at all.

"Did he say anything else?"

Duxbury shook his head sullenly. "Not about that, no. Just crowed about his good fortune."

Theo cast a glance at Monty.

His friend shrugged his broad shoulders. "That was all I heard," he said.

"When did this conversation with Wickham take place?"

Licking his lips, Duxbury counted on his fingers. "It was just after the prizefight, so certainly less than a se'nnight."

Seven days. Wickham could create a great deal of mischief in that time.

"Very well," said Theo. "You can go, as long as you promise to let me know if you hear anything else."

The dandy dusted his sleeve resentfully. "Or what? You will send your friend here after me?"

"Rest assured that I will," said Theo, grimly.

Duxbury shrugged. "If either of you had cared to ask before I was dragged here without so much as a by-your-leave, I would have told you I feel no loyalty towards Wickham in any case. He owes me a large sum of money."

Having felt that he scored a point, Duxbury cast a self-satisfied look at the two of them and strolled casually from the room.

Theo jumped up as soon as Duxbury was out of sight.

"We have to find Fitzwilliam right away," he said, striding out so quickly that most people would have had difficulty following. Monty's long legs, however, unfolded easily as he rose gracefully and in seconds he was at his friend's side.

"I say, times truly have changed," said Monty, amused. "A month ago, your brother would have been the last person you would turn to with a problem. Now you go straight to him."

Theo scowled. "It is not that simple. This directly affects him, and, unlike me, he knows Miss Bennet's family."

"I did not mean to criticize. He is a more decent fellow than I expected, I grant you, but you have had your disagreements."

"Oh, he is indeed a decent fellow, and I am glad he has stopped assuming the worst of me at every turn. Now I still have the task of convincing him that I do not need him hovering over me constantly to protect me from the wicked world! He seems to have forgotten I have made my own way in it for some time now."

"He does seem to be one to go to extremes. I am deathly afraid to insult you in his presence, since he would probably take it into his head to challenge me for it. As if I have not been insulting you many times a day for years!"

"So that explains your uncharacteristic politeness at the theater last night! And there was I thinking you were sparing my sister's innocent ears."

"Well, I would not wish to add to her troubles, since she already has to deal with you, your brother, and that eccentric cousin of yours. I swear I lived in terror of what would come out of that lady's mouth next!"

"Oh, yes," said Theo dryly. "I could see you quaking in your highly polished boots. I must remind you it was your idea to invite us all to join you so you could finally meet Anne de Bourgh."

"That was before I learned how terrifying she is! All you had told me was that she had changed dramatically as her health improved and would likely be taking her place in London circles. Given she is a considerable heiress, it was practically my duty to meet her at the first opportunity. But even if she were inheriting the throne of England, it would not be enough to tempt me!"

"Anne is not so bad. She means well, but she has been ill for so long that she has lost the sense of how to behave in society."

"I find it hard to believe she ever knew! Staring openly at total strangers, saying anything that popped into her head. She even asked me who had tied my cravat!"

"Ah, *now* we get to the heart of the matter! Your vanity has been pricked. She had likely never seen such an intricate style before and was amazed by its complexity."

Monty harrumphed. "If she wishes to succeed in society, she had best learn to leave the subject of gentlemen's cravats alone, unless she wishes to pay a compliment. Can you not teach her to tame her outspoken tongue?"

Theo laughed. "You have not met her mother if you think Anne is outspoken."

"It is worse than that! Your cousin reminds me of *my* mother." Monty shuddered. "I say, I hope she is not staying long at your brother's house. As it is, perhaps I should wait outside this evening."

Theo clapped him on the shoulder. "Never fear, my friend! You may depend upon me to protect you from the fearsome Miss de Bourgh."

Georgiana hurried to meet Theo as soon as he arrived at Darcy House. "I am so glad you are here! We have had the most horrible day."

Theo exchanged a glance with Monty. "What happened?"

"Aunt Catherine came to Town early this morning and called unexpectedly on Miss Bennet. Then, she came here in such a fury, hurling insults about the lady and the Gardiners before storming upstairs to poor Anne's room where she had the most frightful argument with her as well, all about the Dower House and Sir Lewis's Will and disinheriting Anne. That was when Anne accused her of deliberately drugging her for years to keep her from claiming her property. We could hear them shouting from downstairs. William told me to go the music room and practice the piano when the strong language started, but even when I was playing I could hear what they were saying."

She seemed to realize for the first time that Theo was not alone. "I beg your pardon, Sir Montgomery," she added softly. "I should not have mentioned a family quarrel in front of you."

Monty made a courtly bow. "Be not alarmed, Miss Darcy. You have my confidence."

In truth, it was unusual for Georgiana to speak this freely in front of a relative stranger, for she was normally quite reserved. Theo reflected that he would have to warn her not to take Monty seriously. She needed to be told his friend tended to flirt with every female he met.

The warning could wait, however. It sounded like he had more than enough on his plate at the moment. "It sounds like quite the disagreement," said Theo. "But I need to speak to Fitzwilliam. Where is he?"

Georgiana gestured toward the window. "He is gone to Rosings but an hour since. Fitzwilliam took Aunt Catherine to task over her visit to Miss Bennet, but she would not listen, continuing to rant about the conditions of the Will; then, she stormed out of here, and Anne insisted on going with her. They were both in such a rage, he felt it incumbent upon him to head to Kent directly, and he spent the rest of the day in preparation."

Theo narrowed his eyes. "Naturally. Our brother went to Kent to solve a dispute of law, leaving behind the one person in the family versed in legal matters."

Placing her hand on his arm, his sister said, "I am certain he did not mean to slight you! He would have been glad to send someone else in his place. He was not at all happy about leaving when he was due to call on Miss Elizabeth on the morrow."

"Nevertheless, this leaves me with a quandary. I will have to seek counsel from Miss Bennet."

"What is the matter?"

Theo hesitated, reluctant to raise Wickham's name to Georgiana in Monty's presence. But she was as frustrated with William's protectiveness as he was and he should not add to that.

"Our old friend Mr. Wickham has apparently decided to create a scandal within the Bennet family, in hopes of persuading Fitzwilliam to pay him off. Since our brother is away, it falls to me to stop him. I will call on Miss Elizabeth in the morning in the hope she holds any information which might help thwart Wickham's intentions."

Georgiana paled. "Theo, William says he can be dangerous. What if he tries to hurt you?"

Monty cleared his throat. "Miss Darcy, I believe your brother meant to say that *he and I* would pursue Wickham together."

"Oh, thank you, Sir Montgomery. That would be a great relief to my mind."

"Just what I needed," grumbled Theo. "Another nursemaid."

"Your sister is correct, my friend. When dealing with Wickham, you need someone to watch your back."

While the journey to Rosings was never pleasant, this time Darcy had hated it in an entirely new way. Each step of the horses, each rut in the road, each mile traversed was one more away from Elizabeth. He had not even been able to see her before he left. Just a quick note dashed off with the hope she would understand. But there had been so much misunderstanding; this only seemed to beg for more. But why now, just as there were glimmers of hope with her?

What choice had he though? Anne and her mother were Sisyphus and his stone. How could so much stubbornness exist in one house? Perhaps the ease with which Anne might be managed encouraged Aunt Catherine to insist on Anne's tonic long after any true need might be argued.

Despicable though the practice might be, Darcy understood the temptation. Anne was so, so—what did one call a person who acted on every whim and allowed each loose word to fall from her mouth without restraint? Impulsive, uncontrolled or was it just untutored? He rubbed his fist along his chin.

In all fairness, Anne behaved much like a girl ten years her junior, untaught, untrained and thereby unrestrained. So many of the years Anne should have been mentored in the ways of society were spent deep in tonic-induced lethargy. Perhaps there was hope, in time, and with an appropriate, active companion, she might become a…a what? At least not an embarrassment to the family. She might never truly be accepted by the best circles, but she might be able to mix in some company without scandal following her.

The coach pulled up outside Rosings' imposing entrance. With a bit of good fortune, he might handle this as he had so many tenant disputes. Hear both sides, recommend a compromise, shake hands and share a pint—well perhaps not a pint, but a glass of sherry would be more appropriate. Still, it was conceivable that it might all be done in time to return home the next morning. He sat up a little straighter and smiled. He might even be able to see Elizabeth, albeit a little later than planned.

What a delightful thought that was. The sooner he attended this disagreeable business, the better. Why wait for the carriage steps? He jumped down, tugged his coat straight and marched up the stairs to the front door. Rosings would come to order. He would see to it.

The butler admitted him. His normally implacable countenance was lined and shadowed. Even his livery was—rumpled as though he might have slept in it. The house did not smell right. Darcy cast about. Where were the flowers? Normally every room sported large vases of cut flowers in their season and the house smelt like a garden.

"Where?" Darcy pointed to an empty table that usually held a large ceramic urn.

"Just been taken downstairs into storage, sir. We took the liberty of placing the larger items and the more expensive pieces there for the duration."

"Duration of what?"

The butler opened his mouth, but paused, drew a breath and released it. "The current…tensions, sir."

Oh, dear God. Darcy pinched his temples. "Take me to Lady Catherine."

The butler took him to a small sitting room that overlooked the garden. Aunt Catherine sat at a small desk covered in documents and books. How odd, her desk never held either before.

"Darcy!" She rose, knocking a book to the floor.

Darcy entered and the butler shut the door behind him.

"I am glad you have come. Perhaps you can speak some sense into that daughter of mine."

"For what is she in need of sense?" He sat down near the fireplace. It too should have been filled with flowers, but was dark and empty instead. That was hardly more surprising than Aunt Catherine asking anyone else for sense and good judgment. Such a request was wholly astonishing.

"Everything! She is complaining about everything—the menus, her companion, her gowns, me… If she would simply take her tonic as she should—"

"No!" Darcy sprang to his feet and towered over her. "Let us settle that matter completely now. She will not have any more of that tonic—or any like it—now or ever again."

"But can you not see what it has done to her—she is unmanageable and out of control."

"And you desire to control her?"

"I am her mother. I know what is best for her." She tapped her chest.

"She is a grown woman. She may decide what is best for her."

"But she knows nothing—"

"Because you have taught her nothing!"

"How dare you? What would you know of her education or the education of young women?" She snorted and tossed her head. "Anne demands nothing less than Rosings Park. She believes herself the owner of the estate and wishes to condemn me to the dower house."

"Is it true?"

"Certainly not."

"How do you know?" Why did he bother to ask?

"Because—"

"What does Sir Lewis' will say?"

"I have no idea. Legal gibberish is best left to scholars, solicitors and barristers. The relevant point is that Anne is not capable of—"

The door flew open and slammed against the wall behind it. "I am not capable of what, Mother? Not capable of making a decision? Or today is it that I cannot know my own mind, or even form a rational thought? What is the incapacity of which you accuse me now? Surely you have something new to add to your ever-growing list."

"Good evening, Anne," Darcy said though his teeth.

Several of Anne's curls had escaped their pins and bobbed around her flushed cheeks. Her eyes flashed with an energy he hoped not to have turned against him. Perhaps a lethargic Anne was not so bad—

"You see! You see!" Lady Catherine threw her hands up. "This is why she needs her medicine."

Anne flew at him. He raised his hands and staggered back several steps.

"Is that why you are come, to force me—"

"Nothing of the sort. I would never wish to see you take that vile brew again."

"Good, at least we need not repeat that argument, for I have already had it with Mama and would be most happy to rehash it if necessary." She stamped and crossed her arms over her chest. "Why are you here?"

"To assist you and your mother in coming to a compromise—"

"I have no desire for compromise and indeed I will not. I will not accept anything less than what I am promised in father's will."

"You see!" Lady Catherine stomped to Anne and leaned into her face. "She does not care for what I have done for her—what she owes me for all the care I have lavished upon her."

"*Care?* What kind of care keeps one a prisoner in her own home?"

Lady Catherine turned a dangerous shade of crimson. "Prisoner! You consider yourself a prisoner? If it was so terrible, why did you never complain before? I will tell you why: you had every comfort, everything you might desire—"

"Everything *you* desired, Mother, not I. You never consulted me nor cared one jot for what I wished for. And as for why I never complained—"

Darcy stepped between them. "Both of you, stop!"

They turned on him, fangs bared and claws at the ready.

"How dare you speak to me that way! Have you forgotten who I am?"

"I will not stop. I have only now found my own voice—"

Lady Catherine whirled on Anne. "Your own voice? You might learn to use it to express proper gratitude instead of complain and make ridiculous demands."

"Ridiculous demands, is that what you call them?"

Darcy stepped back. Tenant disputes were one thing, but this—this was entirely another creature all together, one of truly mythic proportions.

He glanced across the room. Perhaps there was a simpler answer to be had. He slipped away from the warring harpies and stole to the desk.

Sir Lewis' will was the uppermost document. How fortunate. He sat down and lifted it into the light. What language was it written in? At first glance, it appeared to be the King's English, but no. This was some strange alien dialect—it must be.

Legal documents were hardly foreign to him, even wills, but this…this monstrosity was in a class unto itself. He would never decipher its secrets. He needed a practitioner of the same dark arts that had drafted the tome.

Theo.

Oh, bloody hell. He should have sent Theo in the first place and remained with Elizabeth.

Something flew across the room and smashed into the opposite wall. All he could do now was separate these two until he could enlist Theo's aid. He skirted the two women, made it to the door and called for the butler.

The next day, the post brought ill tidings to Gracechurch Street and, having read the letter thrust upon her by Elizabeth, Mrs. Gardiner looked up at her niece in dismay.

"This is most unfortunate," she said, shaking her head despondently. "More than unfortunate. What could Lydia have been thinking? Surely she must know elopement is wrong."

"That has never stopped Lydia before," said Elizabeth bleakly. "Most likely she thought it was more romantic and never considered the risk."

Mrs. Gardiner handed the letter back to her. "I must send for your uncle. He will wish to know of this immediately." She hurried out of the room, and Elizabeth opened Mary's letter up and read it through again. Was this the third time or the fourth? Somehow she kept hoping her first reading might have made matters look worse than they were, but in this case, her first impression turned out to be true. It was hopeless. Lydia was lost forever.

The repercussions were clear. The Bennets were disgraced. No one respectable would have anything to do with her family. No gentlemen would ever court Kitty or Mary. Their whole future hung on the balance. Would Mr. Bingley honor his promise to Jane? How would Mr. Darcy react?

How was she even going to tell Mr. Darcy what Lydia had done—that she had not only behaved shamefully, but done so with a gentleman he rightly despised? What would Georgiana think, after she had been so brave as to share her own experiences with Elizabeth?

She could just imagine the disapproving look that would cross his face when Mr. Darcy knew the truth, how he would draw back into himself. She could hear the cold tone he would use with her. How could he respect her after this proof of her family's disgrace? Hot tears pooled in Elizabeth's eyes and began to run down her cheeks.

The worry over the repercussions of Lady Catherine's visit and the attendant anxiety of her succeeding in preventing the marriage was nothing to this… this *damage*! To think she had been so looking forward to seeing Mr. Darcy today!

Dropping the letter onto the table, she fished out her handkerchief and pressed it to her face. Her tears were for Lydia, of course, not for the gentleman. It would hurt when he turned cold and disapproving, but it was not as if she had ever sought his good opinion. Even if she had accepted she must marry him, it was more out of a sense of responsibility than anything else, was it not? She might like him better now than she had previously, but he was still too grave, too resentful in temper for her tastes. Heavens—he had disapproved of his own brother, who was as amiable a young man as she had ever met. She would be in good company if Mr. Darcy decided to think less of her because of Lydia's behavior.

Elizabeth drew in a shaky breath. Yes, she must push aside this unaccountable feeling of regret, of sadness. Like her tears, they were for her lost sister and naught else—how could they be?

Instead of brooding on his disapproval, she should be turning her mind toward the best way to inform him of the present developments. *Mr. Darcy, I have received grave news from Longbourn which is likely to distress you as much as it does me.* No. She should not anticipate his distress. *Mr. Darcy, I am grieved to inform you my youngest sister Lydia has disgraced herself by agreeing to an elopement.* No, too formal. *Mr. Darcy, I have received dreadful news from Longbourn...*

The sound of the front door closing reached her. Perhaps it was Jane, returning from her drive with Mr. Bingley, still happily oblivious of the disaster that had befallen them. Elizabeth braced herself for the unpleasant conversation, but it was her aunt who entered the sitting room.

"Another letter from Mary," she said, holding it out to Elizabeth.

Elizabeth quickly broke the seal and scanned the letter. This one was shorter than the previous one, so it did not take long.

"Any news?" asked Mrs. Gardiner.

Elizabeth shook her head, a tear sliding down her cheek. "None, except that Colonel Foster says he is now certain they did not go to Scotland. Apparently Wickham told one of his fellow officers he intended to take Lydia to London. It is as I said before. He has no intention of marrying her. She is lost forever."

Mrs. Gardiner sank heavily into an armchair. "Let us not give up hope quite yet," she said. "I have sent word to your uncle. Perhaps he will think of something." She sighed. "Poor foolish girl! How could she have done such a thing?" She fell into a glum silence as they both reflected on this matter. "Have you thought how you will tell Mr.

Darcy about this? If you would prefer for your uncle to inform him of it, I am certain he would be willing to do so."

Sorely tempted, Elizabeth hesitated before saying flatly, "Thank you, but I must do it myself. I will simply tell him the truth and offer to release him from any obligation to me." Her breath caught in her throat.

"I cannot believe he would accept such an offer."

"We will know soon enough. He told me he would be calling on me at eleven."

Her aunt gave her an odd look. "Are you certain he said eleven? It is nearly half past twelve."

"That late already? It cannot be." As she said it, Elizabeth glanced up at the small mantle clock. Her aunt was correct.

Why was Mr. Darcy late? He was always prompt, if not early, for his appointments with her, as if he could not bear to stay away a minute longer than necessary. She had teased that she could set a watch by his comings and goings. What could have delayed him so long?

Her chest tightened, and she closed her eyes. She knew perfectly well what had prevented his attending her.

"He must have heard the news already, and that is why he has not come." Despite her best efforts, her voice trembled.

Mrs. Gardiner's brows drew together. "Surely he would not... Lizzy, there may be a perfectly reasonable explanation for his absence."

Elizabeth looked down at her hand, the one which would now never be graced by a wedding band. "He would have sent me a message if he had been delayed."

Mr. Darcy could not marry her, even if he wished to—even if *she* wished it. It would ruin his family and spoil any chance of Georgiana making a respectable match. She could not even condemn him for it.

But the sick feeling in the pit of her stomach gave her a different message as his defection made her understand her own wishes for the first time. She had been acting the part of a resentful child who did not want to be forced into marrying him, but *he* was not the part she objected to. Lady Catherine's visit had first made her realize there was more to her feelings than that, but now she began to comprehend he was exactly the man who, in disposition and talents, would most suit her. When she had first read Mary's letter, his presence had been the one she had wished for, because he represented security, hope, and, above all, love. What a cruel trick fate had played on her, that she should recognize her love for him only when all must be in vain!

She would never see him again, or if she did, it would only be for a brief, cold meeting to formally put an end to their understanding. He would never know of her true feelings for him. It would be her secret, to suffer with in silence.

Her tears could no longer be held back. "Pray excuse me," Elizabeth said in a strangled voice, and fled for the privacy of her bedroom.

Instead of being admitted immediately to the presence of the Gardiners, Theo was directed to wait in the small sitting room. Of all the times for them to take on the airs of the *ton*! Impatiently, he glanced at the long case clock in between the two long windows fronting onto the street. The day was progressing far too swiftly, his plan of calling in Gracechurch Street that morning thwarted by an urgent summons to attend Mr. Garrow in his chambers. Time was of the essence, he knew; he must reach Elizabeth's home in Hertfordshire before nightfall.

Finally Mr. Gardiner joined him, his step heavier than usual. "Pray forgive our lack of hospitality today. We are somewhat in disarray owing to some unfortunate news we have received. I do not suppose you know where your brother might be? Elizabeth was expecting him to call on her today, but he never made an appearance. I sent a messenger to Darcy House, but he came back with the information that the master was away. Elizabeth says he told her nothing yesterday of any travel plans."

Fitzwilliam was not going to be happy about this. "He had to go late yesterday to Rosings; an unexpected family matter."

Mr. Gardiner's brows drew together. "So he did not decide it would be best to keep his distance?"

"I have not the honor of understanding you, sir. He went, as I understand it, to resolve a quarrel of my aunt's making."

"Your aunt! Yes, we have heard first hand of her views on your brother's engagement, and then your brother failed to keep his appointment with Elizabeth, and now he is out of Town." He wiped his brow. "Still, I suppose *you* would not be here if you knew anything of this matter."

"If you are implying my brother might have changed his mind, I can assure you that is untrue." Theo took a deep breath. He did not want to be caught in a quarrel about Fitzwilliam's intentions. "I was looking for him myself earlier, and came here in the hope Miss Elizabeth might be able to provide me with some information in his stead."

"She is not in a state to receive visitors at the moment. Is there perhaps a message I could give her?"

Theo chewed his cheek. He could hardly ask about her family without an explanation. "I received some information earlier that a certain thorn in my brother's side is threatening to make mischief towards Miss Elizabeth's family, and in my brother's absence, it is my responsibility to try to stop him. He is an officer in the Militia stationed near Miss Elizabeth's home, but I do not know where her home is. I hope to gain that information from her so I may pursue him."

Mr. Gardiner dropped heavily into a chair. "Mr. Wickham." It was a statement, not a question. "I fear you are too late."

A coldness gripped Theo. "Too late? What has happened?"

Mr. Gardiner sighed. "I might as well tell you. It will be known all over Town quickly enough. My niece, Lydia, has eloped with Mr. Wickham. They found her gone just yesterday."

Theo sank into a chair. "I am so sorry!" He would have liked to express himself much more vehemently, but did not wish to offend Mr. Gardiner. "Please, tell me everything."

"We received intelligence earlier today from Longbourn. Lydia left a note hinting they were traveling to London where Wickham would be collecting a debt he was owed. Then they would be able to marry. Do you know what he is talking about?"

Theo's anger rose. "I found out only yesterday Wickham has somehow heard about my brother's engagement to Miss Elizabeth Bennet and planned a scandal and then to ask for money in order to keep it quiet."

"What kind of man is he to do something like this?" Mr. Gardiner asked incredulously.

"A man without scruples. A man who is so desperate for money, he would use another innocent girl to achieve his aim."

"Another? He has done this before?"

Theo nodded. He could not share Georgiana's story with Mr. Gardiner, but surely Darcy had told Elizabeth or she had worked it out. She must be beside herself with worry. "Perhaps Miss Lydia did not know what he had in mind and had no idea he was using her to extract his vengeance on my family."

"So your brother knows nothing about the elopement?" Mr. Gardiner's brow was furrowed with worry.

Theo shook his head. "I am certain he does not."

Just then Elizabeth appeared in the doorway. "Uncle, I heard voices. Has there been news?" Upon seeing Theo she blushed deeply. "Mr. Darcy, I thought you were..." She stopped suddenly and fixed her eyes on the floor.

The gentlemen stood. "Lizzy, it seems your Mr. Darcy is not avoiding you. In fact, in all probability, he has no knowledge of what has occurred," said Mr. Gardiner.

Elizabeth's gaze flew to Theo. "He does not know?" she said so softly that Theo almost did not hear her.

"He was called away last night on an urgent family matter. Did he not send word to you?" Theo asked.

Elizabeth's face was pale, and Theo was certain the cause was more than just her recent illness. "I have not heard from him. When he did not come today as he promised, I thought he...well, I thought..."

Seeing the uncertainty written on her face, Theo went to her and took both her hands in his, squeezing them lightly. "Please, Miss Elizabeth, do not doubt my brother's loyalty. He would never abandon you. He is the most honorable man I know. If he knew of the elopement, he would already be out searching for your sister."

Elizabeth looked up, her eyes rimmed with tears. "Thank you for that. I did not want to doubt him, but the situation is such that I could understand his need to protect Georgiana."

Theo gave her what he hoped was a reassuring look. "You must never doubt him."

Elizabeth lowered her eyes. "Can you send word to him?"

"Yes, but I will do even better. Time is of the essence in matters like this. Now he appears to be in Town, I will begin looking for Wickham myself. I know many of his haunts and may be able to find him before Darcy even returns."

"Is there anything I may do to assist you?" Mr. Gardiner asked.

"No, thank you, sir." Theo gestured toward the window. "I see my friend is waiting outside for me, and we will begin the search immediately. He knows Wickham, too, and will be only too glad to help me track him down." Theo smacked his fist into the palm of his other hand. He ached to connect that fist with Wickham's jaw. "In fact, my friend is the one who brought me the intelligence that something was afoot. Now I should be off."

"Thank you for your assistance," Elizabeth said, with a grateful smile. "I believe some people underestimate you, but I do not."

Just then, they heard noises in the hallway and one of the maids appeared at the door. "There is a messenger here for Miss Elizabeth. He says he was instructed to put his letter directly into her hands."

"Please show him in, Jenny," said Mr. Gardiner.

The girl disappeared and returned in a few seconds followed by a rumpled and dusty boy. The way he played with his hat betrayed his discomfort at his state of dishevelment.

"Excuse me, Miss," he said, holding out a letter to Elizabeth. "Mr. Darcy told me to give this directly to you and no one else."

Elizabeth took the letter from him and fingered the seal.

The boy, who had not seen Theo in the room yet, nearly jumped when Theo said, "Thank you, Danny."

Danny's eyes grew wide, and he touched his hand to his forelock. "Mr. Theo! I did not expect to see you here."

When Theo stepped forward and put a coin in Danny's hand, the boy said, "Thank you, sir, but I am not certain I deserve it."

"What do you mean?" Theo asked.

"Mr. Darcy gave this letter to me last night before he set out on his journey, with strict instructions I deliver it at first light, but on my way here, the horse I was riding went lame, and I had to walk him all the way back to Darcy

House. Then all the horses were in use, so I had to make my way here on foot. I did not realize it was so far. I am very sorry. I hope my delay has not caused you any concern, Miss," he said, turning to look at Elizabeth hopefully.

Elizabeth took pity on the poor young man whose appearance reflected the difficulties he had experienced that day. "No, there was no inconvenience at all. Do not worry," she said. "If you go to the kitchens, Cook will see that you are fed before your return journey. I thank you for your efforts."

When Danny left the room, Mr. Gardiner turned to Theo. "If the staff at Darcy House knew where your brother was, why did they not inform my messenger?"

"The servants are well trained not to give out any information about our family," Theo said. "They must not have realized from whom the inquiry came. I am so sorry this caused you to worry, Miss Elizabeth."

Looking up from Darcy's letter, Elizabeth gave the gentlemen a small but genuine smile. "It is as you say; Mr. Darcy was obliged to go to Rosings at short notice and begs my forgiveness for not being able to see me today."

"Now that has been settled, I must be on my way. I promise I will find Wickham and make this right," Theo said.

"But how will you do that? How can this be fixed?" Elizabeth asked.

"You said earlier that you have confidence in me, did you not?" Theo asked.

Elizabeth nodded. "Yes, I do. Please forgive my momentary panic. I trust you will do everything in your power, Theo."

He was startled at hearing her address him by his first name.

"I may call you that now, may I not, as we are to be brother and sister? And you must call me Elizabeth."

CHAPTER 15

THEO SWUNG HIMSELF up into the curricle and settled himself beside Monty. "I had not expected you to arrive so quickly."

Monty looked pleased. "At your service. Now, where are we going? The Great North Road?"

"No. It turns out Wickham is here in London. He convinced Miss Elizabeth's youngest sister to run off with him."

Monty swore under his breath. "Poor girl. What now?"

"I say we find him. I know several of his usual haunts."

"And when we find him? Do we force him to marry the girl?"

Theo's eyes narrowed. "I think not. He is clearly hoping my brother will pay him to wed her, but even without that incentive, he would still take this opportunity to marry into the family and keep his hand in William's pocket for the rest of their lives. No, I say we stop the marriage and teach Wickham a lesson instead."

Monty's expression brightened. "This is starting to sound enjoyable."

Once Theo had left, Elizabeth pleaded exhaustion and stole away to her room to reread her letter from Darcy.

With everyone in the drawing room looking at her, she had not been able to give it her full attention, and from her first glance at the message, it was clear this was more than just an apology for missing their appointment for that day. Now alone in her room, she fluffed some pillows and curled up on the bed. Carefully, unfolding the pages, she began to read.

My Dearest, Loveliest Elizabeth,

A family matter has arisen which requires my immediate attention and will take me to Rosings for a day or two. The unfortunate result is I will be unable to call upon you today as I had promised. I am certain you will understand my absence, as family is of the highest importance to you as well as to me. I shall send word as soon as I return.

I hope I have not been too forward in addressing you as "my dearest, loveliest Elizabeth" for it has been many months since I first thought of you this way. Although you have been gracious enough to accept my proposal, I know you are not entirely pleased with the circumstances of our engagement, nor even with the engagement itself. I can only promise to do everything in my power to assuage that concern and make you as happy as you have made me.

I am looking forward to taking you to Pemberley, as I have imagined you there so many times. I have known you belong there from almost the first moment I met you. I cannot wait to show you all the pathways and gardens on the estate where you will be able to ramble to your heart's content. I am anxious to share each season and its special gifts with you—the warmth of the summer's sun, the changing colors of the leaves in the autumn, the first dusting of snow that signals the beginning of winter, and most especially the spring, as trees and flowers burst forth with new life. Just like spring, you have brought new hope and joy back into my heart for the first time in more years than I care to count.

I wish I could be more eloquent when it comes to telling you how very much you mean to me, but whenever I am in your presence you seem to steal away not only my breath, but my ability to form a coherent sentence. In time, I hope I will be able to show you what I cannot easily express in words.

I was very serious in my suggestion to invite the Gardiners to Pemberley for Christmas. Your aunt and uncle are very fine people, but even more importantly, I know how much you love them and that makes them dear to me as well.

My Heart Is Yours.

FD

Elizabeth closed her eyes and held the letter to her heart for a moment. Did this count as her very first love letter? She reread some parts again, especially the paragraph about Pemberley. Did she belong there as he said she did? She hoped so. Darcy might have difficulty expressing himself in conversation, but there was no mistaking his eloquence with the written word. Every day revealed new layers to this man and with each one, she saw more to like.

Just then, she heard sounds outside her door.

"Aunt Lizzy? Are you sleeping?" It was her niece, Ella.

"No, come in."

The door opened and Ella's bright face appeared. "Would you come and read to us, please?"

Elizabeth smiled and straightened her legs. "Of course I will."

When the child did not move, Elizabeth added, "Now off with you! I shall be there in just a moment."

Ella grinned back and disappeared in a flash of skirts.

Elizabeth stood and carefully placed the letter in the pocket of her dress where she could touch it any time she wished. She was getting married. She would be mistress of Pemberley. She and Darcy would have children together. For the first time, she began to believe that those very things just might be exactly what she wanted.

Theo and Monty ran Wickham to ground at the second place they stopped, a seedy tavern with several shabby rooms to let. Wickham must have wanted William to be able to find him; he had used this place often in the past.

Fortunately, the man behind the bar did not recognize the wild lad Theo had once been in the soberly clad young barrister, but he was happy to answer questions in return for a few coins.

"Wickham? Yes, he is upstairs, and as much a rapscallion as ever."

"Did he bring a girl with him?"

The man guffawed. "Of course he did. She were dressed too fine for a place like this, but she weren't complaining. Doubt she been wearing many clothes since then, if you take my meaning."

Theo had no doubts as to his meaning. In an attempt to save the poor girl further embarrassment, he told Monty to remain below while he approached Wickham.

"I will call if I require assistance."

"Be sure that you do!" said Monty.

Theo climbed the narrow, uneven steps, noting the dirt in the corners. He rapped with his cane on the door the barkeeper had indicated.

Wickham's voice came from inside. "In a minute, in a minute!"

He took a deep breath and held it. The familiar voice brought back a flood of memories. For years he had considered Wickham more his brother than William. It had started after William had rejected Theo following Sebastian's death; it was George Wickham who had been there for him and had provided desperately needed comfort. And when their father had passed away, Wickham had been Theo's only remaining tie to Pemberley at Cambridge, since William never wrote to him and Georgiana was far too young. They had shared so many memories—it was difficult to believe they had parted ways so completely.

The door flew open, revealing Wickham in his shirt-sleeves, no sign of a cravat and his hair disheveled. His countenance brightened when he saw his visitor.

"Theo! Now this is the best surprise I have had in months." He took the hand Theo had not offered and pumped it enthusiastically. "I so hoped your anger would run its course so we could be friends again. I hope you know I never intended to hurt Georgiana in any way. I would have treated her well; you must have known that. She was your sister, after all."

Wickham seemed so pleased to see him that for a moment Theo was tempted to return his warmth, but his mention of Georgiana put an end to that. He could manage little more than a nod of acknowledgement. Had he said one word, he would have said far too much. He was not here to pay back old debts, but to recover Elizabeth's sister.

"Come in, come in! The place is not much, of course, but I have a bottle of wine we can share." Wickham paid no attention to the young girl in the bed, covered with a blanket.

Managing the difficult feat of bowing in her direction while keeping his eyes elsewhere, Theo said, "Miss Lydia Bennet, I presume?"

"How did you know?" she said coyly.

Wickham's face grew dark. "I see you are not here on your own behalf, but an emissary from Prince William. Pray forgive me for assuming old friendship meant something to you."

Goaded beyond wisdom, Theo blurted out, "You were the one who put an end to our friendship, not I!" He cursed himself as soon as the words were out of his mouth.

An unbecoming expression marred Wickham's face. "A man must have money to live, at least those of us without brothers to give us an allowance. So, how much is His Highness offering me this time?"

Theo gestured toward Elizabeth's sister. "Surely you do not wish to discuss this here."

"It does not matter. Lydia knows all about my plans, do you not, my Dove?"

Theo was shocked enough by this that he turned to look at the girl. "Is that true? You know he ran off with you with the intent of blackmailing my brother into paying him to marry you?"

"Your brother? Lord, no wonder you are so stiff!" she said. "Of course I know. Why should I care? Mr. Darcy has plenty of money and will not miss it; and I will be married before Lizzy is."

Even though Mr. Gardiner had warned him Lydia was different from her sisters, Theo had not expected this. He put on his best barrister face and ignored her words. "You seem to have found yourself a kindred soul this time, Wickham."

"She will do, and you and I will be brothers after all. Perhaps then you will see your way to forgiving me."

Theo's skin crawled. "That is not the point."

Wickham tossed off a glass of wine and smirked. "But it is the point—I see it all now! That is why you are being so cold to me. Let me guess. His Highness has threatened to withdraw your allowance unless you cut me. You have no choice. I understand completely, and would do the same in your shoes. But we need not play that game when it is just the two of us, not after all our years together. I will tell the Prince that you were very harsh towards me. I have missed you, Theo!"

It was like a knife in Theo's side. He had watched George Wickham lie his way through a hundred scrapes over the years, and he knew when his old friend was lying. He was not doing so now. God help him, George had truly been hurt by his defection.

"You may think that, if it gives you comfort," Theo said brusquely. His initial plan, to convince the Bennet girl to return to her family and turn her over to Monty while he dealt with Wickham, was not going to work. "If we are such friends, perhaps you might want to explain something to my satisfaction. When you were planning to run away with my sister, why did you steal Georgiana's ring and necklace?"

"Me? I never touched anything of hers." Now he was lying.

"I wanted to believe that at the time. I wanted to blame the servants when we found they were missing, but having trained as a barrister, I needed proof. You should not have taken them to old Grimby to pawn, because it meant I knew where to look. I knew your habits. Grimby told me you had brought them." It had taken half a year's allowance for Theo to redeem his sister's jewels and quietly return them to her. Now he was paying for his unwillingness to have his old friend arrested at the time.

"I needed a few pounds to tide me over, since my plans to wed Georgiana were exposed. I could hardly ask you for them."

Theo hardened his heart. He was not dealing with his boyhood friend, but a man who had chosen to take advantage of his family again and again. "Indeed not. But perhaps I was not clear enough. Grimby is willing to testify against you."

Wickham's cocky grin faded. "Theo, you would not do that to me. Not after everything we have been through together."

"I will charge you only for stealing the ring. Its value is less, and you will be transported, not hung." There were some things Theo could not bear to have on his conscience, and being the cause of George Wickham's death was one of them.

"Transported! That is as good as dead. You are joking, Theo. Tell me you are joking."

The pain was twisting inside his chest, but he told himself to remember Georgiana, to remember William, to remember Elizabeth's anxiety.

"I am not joking," he said calmly. He turned to the door and opened it.

"Where are you going?" Wickham sounded panicked.

"To fetch a constable, of course."

"You will give me time to escape, will you not? I prom-ise you, I will go to the Continent and you will never hear from me again."

"Not good enough, George."

An ugly expression marred Wickham's handsome face, turning it into an unfamiliar mask.

"I thought you were different from the rest of them, that you were the only decent one of the Darcys. I see I was wrong. You are just as willing to punish me for the crime of not being as well-born as you are—and it is not even your money I am asking for, but your brother's. You will never see a penny of it, you know!"

There was no point in arguing further. Theo started down the steps, but was knocked to the side when George Wickham pushed past him, racing ahead in hopes of reach-ing freedom. Theo struggled to catch his balance and hur-ried after him, damning himself for a fool in warning Wickham of what he had planned.

He need not have rushed. In the tavern, Monty leaned back against the door to the street, his arms crossed. Monty the Mountain. Wickham looked small in front of him.

"Going so soon?" Monty drawled. "I believe Theo is not quite finished speaking to you."

His mouth dry, Theo slapped a silver coin on the bar. "Fetch a constable right away. That man is guilty of theft."

He had barely turned when the sound of a blow reached him. He turned to find Monty still leaning against the door, while Wickham nursed his knuckles.

"That was a foolish thing to do, Wickham," said Monty. As Monty's fist shot out, there was a cry of pain from Wickham, and he slumped to the floor.

Theo stepped over the sprawled figure and opened the door for the barman, who rushed into the street in search of a constable. Monty stooped down to drag Wickham to his worthless feet.

As Theo cast a look outside, the neighborhood looked much as it had when they arrived, its inhabitants ignorant of the drama unfolding behind the inn's door. Theo shuddered; even now before nightfall, it was a dismal place, with drunkards arguing loudly, a beggar wailing on the corner, and several children in ragged, dirty clothes fighting over a much cherished object. The only solace in this gloomy, grey-brown world was the bright basket of flowers on the arm of a girl offering posies to indifferent passers-by.

Stepping inside, Theo closed the door on the unwelcome scene only to find himself face to face with Wickham, who was testing his chin gingerly with one hand and holding the other out to Theo in supplication.

"Have some mercy, Theo; for heaven's sake, you cannot simply cast off all our years of friendship. We went through so many things together—you cannot do this. I see you mean to caution me, and I have heard you. Now let me go, and we will say no more of this matter."

Theo shook his head and brushed past Wickham, ignoring the outstretched arm. "It is out of my hands. A constable will be here directly."

Wickham's countenance turned ugly. "You choose to send me into exile? For the love of God, Theo, Prince William has influenced you too strongly. Though he has long earned his title, neither of you are of Royal blood, and you would do well to remember it."

Turning about, Theo glowered at him, conscious of a spark smoldering in his breast. "And you would do well to remember Darcy's caution to you after you tried to ruin our sister!"

Wickham returned Theo's glare with a sneer. "And you have only *her* word that I did not succeed!" Then, he laughed mockingly.

The spark flamed fiercely as angry bile rose in Theo's throat and without further thought he aimed his fist at

Wickham, whose head snapped backwards as he dropped to the floor like a rag doll.

"Ouch! Damn it," Theo bent over, cradling his aching hand.

"You are not made for fist fights, my friend!" Monty pushed him gently onto a nearby settle and inspected the hand. "You will do—no broken bones, though it will smart for a while." He walked over and bent down to inspect Wickham's prone form. "His brow will bear the evidence longer, I suspect."

Theo glanced at Wickham, rage still throbbing within. "An hour ago, I could not bear the notion of death for him, but for a moment, I wished to kill him by my own hand."

"Understandable." Monty straightened up. "He lives, though he has not much of a life remaining. He will wish for death before too long, I fancy."

Not wishing to dwell upon this, Theo turned his attention to the pain in his hand, and he flexed the fingers tentatively. He would have to forego the pianoforte—his escape, his relaxation, his comfort—and he sighed. In the short term, he would have to find another outlet…

He looked up as the barkeeper returned with a constable in tow and, as Theo outlined the charges against Wickham, a wooden jail cart pulled up outside and two large and menacing men clambered down from the bench.

Wickham began to stir, and Monty, who was using him as a footrest, crossed his legs and winked at Theo. "Have no fear—he goes nowhere." He waved a well-manicured hand towards the constable. "Finish your duty, and then we may wash our hands of the scum."

Within a few minutes, the necessary paperwork was complete, sufficient time for Wickham to come round fully and appreciate his situation. The steadily blackening eye and bruise on his chin were in stark relief to the paleness of his countenance as he took in the cart through the grimy window, Monty having hauled him to his feet once more.

Theo refused to look at Wickham, brushing past him as he began to beg him once more to let him go. He could not bear to hear his pleading and, angry though he was with him, his heart ached at such an outcome for one who once was very dear to him. Swallowing hard on a restriction in his throat, he shot out into the street as the burly men entered and drew in some air, then wished he had not.

Coughing, he covered his mouth with his uninjured hand, then turned to speak to the constable and shake his hand as Wickham, now trussed like a turkey, with ropes about his ankles and wrists, was man-handled into the cart and secured behind the padlocked door.

As it rattled away slowly along the cobbles, Monty turned to Theo.

"What do we do now to assist the young lady?"

"I promised Miss Elizabeth Bennet I would do all I could to try and put things right, so we must restore her sister to the family as soon as possible."

Monty frowned. "It is fortunate Miss Bennet did not follow Wickham downstairs to witness what just took place, but I am surprised she did not. Could aught be amiss?"

"Perhaps she awaits Wickham's return." Theo sighed. "We have done all we can now to aid the family and have only to take her to them." He gestured towards Monty's curricle. "Will it suffice, do you think? Speed is of the essence."

Monty smiled ruefully and shook his head. "Do you not recall our journey hither? You are nearly as broad as I, yet you propose we squeeze her in between us? It would not be very fitting, my friend." He looked up and down the street. "I shall see if I can find a willing lad to take word to Gracechurch Street, that Miss Bennet's aunt and uncle can come and claim her. It is but a mile distant." Monty glanced about the street, then grimaced. "Though it is another world, thankfully. I may have to spread my search; I shall return directly."

Theo nodded and threw one last glance about the street before turning to re-enter the inn. Little had altered since he last viewed the scene other than the young flower seller had moved on, taking with her the only splash of color in the grime-filled corner of London.

Closing the door, Theo tried hard to let go of his last sighting of George Wickham. The fear writ upon his countenance as the cart set off would likely haunt him for some time, but he pushed it ruthlessly aside and walked quickly over to the barkeeper and shook his hand.

"Your timely assistance is much appreciated, sir."

The man inclined his head and touched a hand to his forelock. "A pleasure, sir; 'tis not the first time and 'twill no doubt not be the last I see a fallen man dragged from the building."

"I assume there is a bill to settle."

The man's air became disgruntled. "Aye, there is. An' who be paying it now, I wants to know."

"Have it drawn up and presented to this address," Theo handed him a card. "I will arrange for it to be settled. In return, I ask one further favor."

Pocketing the card, the man nodded. "At your service, young sir."

"Would you be so good as to send a girl up to the room to assist the young lady within to dress and to pack up her belongings?"

As the barkeeper turned to hail one of the serving wenches, the door to the street opened and Monty strode into the room.

"These streets are full of nothing but reprobates; look who I encountered!"

"Richard!" Theo's smile widened as he recognized Monty's companion. "What the devil are you doing in this God-forsaken part of Town?"

"On maneuvers, old chap." Colonel Fitzwilliam tapped

the side of his nose. "Covert; undercover; top secret stuff."

They shook hands and then walked over to stand near the empty hearth.

Monty grinned. "Routing out the miscreants who were too in their cups to find their way back to barracks, more like."

With a reciprocal grin, the Colonel nodded. "Indeed. So—what have I missed? I could not have been more surprised to see Sir Montgomery Preston's noble features, nor to learn that you were in this…" he waved a hand, "charming establishment."

It did not take above a few minutes to acquaint the Colonel with all that had happened, and, as Theo's narration drew to a close, Richard Fitzwilliam released a low breath and shook his head.

"I am not surprised at such an end for Wickham. Man only has so many narrow escapes, whether by wit or good fortune, and he has surely taken his share." His gaze narrowed as he met Theo's eye. "And how do you fare, Cousin?"

Theo shrugged. "Other than a sore hand, I do not know. I am saddened by it, but like you, I am not surprised his chances ran out. He has angered me too, yet I would have given a deal not to be personally involved in this outcome."

Monty clapped his friend lightly on the shoulder. "Do not take on so, Theo! You cannot assume the blame for his misdeeds; besides, we are equally liable for catching the toad in his final leap."

He flexed his hand, and the Colonel grinned. "That I should have liked to see! Long have I wished to plant one on Wickham myself, yet always I was restrained by one more tolerant than I. Talking of whom, how is your brother and what of the enchanting Miss Bennet? Is she well recovered from the accident?"

Theo barely had time to enlighten his cousin when the door to the staircase was pushed aside with a bang and

Lydia Bennet flounced into the room. Though she had received some assistance to dress, she remained somewhat disheveled, her curls haphazardly tied with a ribbon and her gown creased.

With little concern for propriety, she marched straight over to where the gentlemen stood.

"What have you done with him? Where is he?"

It seemed ludicrous to adhere to any form of civility in the circumstances, but nevertheless, Theo made the attempt.

"Miss Bennet, may I present to you my cousin, Colonel Fitzwilliam and my friend, Sir Montgomery Preston." He turned toward them, but before he could present the lady to them, Lydia tapped him on the shoulder.

"I do not care who *they* are," she pointed rudely at his companions, "I wish to know only where Wickham is. I will not be parted from him."

Could this creature truly be a sister to Elizabeth? Theo could feel his temper rising once more, but as his desire was to restore the girl to her family at the soonest opportunity, he drew in a calming breath and swallowed the retort he longed to utter.

"If you will please take a seat, Miss Bennet, then perhaps I can explain."

Throwing herself into the nearest chair, Lydia pouted as Theo sat opposite her. "You may talk all you wish. I shall only listen to that which interests me: where my Wickham has gone and how soon we can be reunited."

"May I ask what you presently understand?"

Lydia shrugged. "How should I know? I did not bother to listen to what business you discussed; I was admiring the light from the window upon my dear Wickham's hair. He has quite the softest hair I have ever known."

Theo stared at her incredulously; then, he rushed into a rapid explanation.

"George Wickham stole some pieces of jewelry and sold them to a pawnbroker. The stolen items were identified and returned to their rightful owner; however, the family concerned wishes to press charges. The pawnbroker is prepared to testify. It is a clear case of theft. Wickham is only fortunate the family is prepared to overlook the more valuable piece in favor of the smaller, permitting a sentence of transportation rather than death." Lydia sat up in her chair, her countenance bewildered. "He is presently in custody and will be charged with the crime and duly tried. You cannot see him."

She frowned. "But we are to be married!" Lydia looked bemusedly at each of the gentlemen in turn. "Will he be there for very long? I had hoped we could set a date. The summer is such a fine season for a wedding, is it not?"

Catching his cousin's eye, the Colonel slightly shook his head before addressing the lady.

"Miss Bennet. Mr. Darcy has outlined the situation precisely as it is." He paused as Lydia let out an unladylike snort.

"Mr. *Darcy*?" She let out a short laugh. "Oh yes, I forgot—I have met his brother. Mr. High and Mighty Darcy, soon to be *my* brother. Lord, I find I cannot think of *this* one as 'Mr. Darcy' too."

The Colonel glared at her. "Let me summarize the situation: Wickham has committed a crime and will be sentenced, either to death or transportation. He is incarcerated with immediate effect. The next, and likely the last, time you see him will either be on the gallows or boarding a ship; in either case the journey has no return passage."

Lydia stamped her foot. "But what about the *wedding*?"

The Colonel sighed. "He faces a sentence far worse than marriage, Madam." He turned to Theo and shook his hand before repeating the gesture with Monty. "I have tarried too long and will take my leave of you both; I must return to my duty."

"It was good to see you, Richard, albeit so briefly." Theo raised a hand as his cousin did likewise before closing the door, and he turned back to face Lydia who was curling a strand of hair about her finger with studied interest. She seemed like such a child at that moment, and he felt the first stirrings of sympathy for her. What chance had she in the face of Wickham's practiced arts?

"Do you believe Wickham would have married you?"

She looked up and then shrugged. "In time. It did not signify when it would take place, but I am certain it would have." Lydia sighed dramatically. "Now I must begin anew, but I shall soon succeed. After all, every man is in need of a wife, is he not?" She giggled, then looked from Theo to Monty and back again. "You are both very handsome. Do either of you seek a wife?"

His empathy faded in an instant. Was the girl deluded? Monty was staring at Lydia in blatant disbelief, but opportunely, the serving girl appeared with a cloak and bonnet, followed by a young man carrying a small trunk, and Theo got to his feet

"I think we have said sufficient on the matter; your aunt and uncle will be here directly. They have been most concerned for you."

"Oh la!" Lydia jumped to her feet. "They are *such* fuddy-duddies. And they will make all manner of fuss about this, which Mama never would."

The servant held out the cloak, but Lydia merely raised a brow before turning towards the gentlemen, a coy smile upon her lips. "Would you be so kind as to assist me?"

Theo grasped the cloak and held it out, staring at the ceiling while Lydia made a performance of settling it on her shoulders.

"Where is my bonnet?" The serving girl thrust it into Theo's unsuspecting grasp and disappeared through the scullery door and hastily he passed it to Lydia.

"Will you tie my ribbons for me?" She peeped up at him from under her lashes.

Theo shook his head. "I am afraid you will have to do it yourself, Miss Bennet. I have sustained an injury to one of my hands and am unable to assist you."

Lydia pouted, then laughed. "Lord, you are becoming stiffer by the minute! I begin to see a resemblance to your lifeless brother." She walked over to a mirror on the far wall, though the layer of dust upon it hardly made it fit for purpose, and made a show of tying her ribbons, adjusting the rim of her bonnet this way and that. Then, she turned back to face Theo.

"Your cousin is not wed, is he? I have always had a preference for a man in uniform—though I do prefer a red coat over any other." She smiled as she walked back to where the men stood. "My dear Wickham has such a fine figure and wears his regimentals better than any other I have seen." Her face fell for a second. "Though I must think on him no more." Then, she glanced at Theo again. "Yes, your cousin would do nicely, for though he is old and his countenance is quite ordinary, he has broad shoulders and thus wears his coat well."

Before he could muster a response to this piece of absurdity, Theo jumped as the lady squeezed his arm. "And you, sir. You are a gentleman of means, if you are Mr. Darcy's brother; yet you must have a profession, and as you wear no uniform nor dog collar, might I essay you have chosen the law?"

Theo removed her hand from his arm. "Indeed. I am a barrister, and I have no time for seeking a wife as I have a career to make."

Lydia let out an exaggerated sigh. "My poor, dear Wickham. He was intended for the law, you know? Well, he was first intended for the church, but your unprincipled brother put paid to that!"

The desire to defend William, something he seemed to be making a habit of lately, rose within him, but though his acquaintance with Lydia Bennet was in its infancy, he knew when to save his breath.

Salvation arrived in the form of a carriage pulling up outside the inn, and Monty strode to the door, swinging it open. "I believe your aunt and uncle have arrived, Miss

Bennet."

Mr. and Mrs. Gardiner were clearly relieved to find their niece safe from harm, but her unabashed manner soon drew their censure. They tried to curb her tongue as she delighted in retelling her story, but their obvious discomfort in her evident pleasure over her escapade elicited the gentlemen's sympathy, and in a bid to end their torment, Theo and Monty urged the party out to the carriage as Lydia continued to spout inanities.

"My adventure will be the envy of my sisters, for I return to them a married woman in all but name." She laughed. "What a fine jest! I have come closer to being wed than them all, for all Jane's beauty and Lizzy's fine wit!"

"That will do, Lydia!" Mrs. Gardiner took her hand and dragged her to the carriage steps, quickly urging her inside.

Mr. Gardiner smiled apologetically at Theo and Monty as they made their farewell. "We cannot thank you enough for returning our niece to us, and can only hope you will overlook her foolishness. She is full young, and the years she has attained thus far do not appear to have admitted much sense."

Monty laughed, and Theo smiled as he shook Mr. Gardiner's hand. He liked the Gardiners, and he liked Elizabeth too. He could not account for how Lydia was part of the same family, but if they could tolerate her, then he would strive to do likewise.

"We are thankful we could be of service, sir." He bowed. "Please send my best wishes to Miss Elizabeth; I hope to call upon you all in the near future."

With that, the gentlemen turned towards Monty's curricle, and Mr. Gardiner joined his wife and niece for the ride back to Gracechurch Street.

CHAPTER 16

DARCY SHIFTED AGAINST the soft carriage squabs and peered out the side glass. The same farmhouse he had been staring at stood resolutely on the horizon, no closer than the last time he had looked.

Perhaps he should take to the box himself? Surely he could get more speed from the horses. He groaned and flexed his hands into fists. What was he thinking? He would probably make excellent speed to London, until the beasts dropped dead half way there.

He threw his head back against the seat, his mind racing as it was once more filled with the contents of Theo's *Express* that morning. What a fool he had been. With Anne contesting the terms of her inheritance, Theo was the one to handle the matter, not him. But could he see that—no. No, he had to rush off blindly to the rescue only to discover he lacked the necessary understanding to do anything but stand between the two screeching harpies and prevent their claws and teeth from drawing blood.

Had he only been at Darcy House where he should have been, he would have been there for Elizabeth and her family when they needed him. Instead it was Theo who stepped up to do what should have been his duty.

Theo.

Thank God he had been there and been willing to put aside the past. He had not only found the scoundrel Wickham, but had taken him to task. Granted, Darcy would probably not have resorted to such…physical… tactics. But no one could question that Wickham was entirely deserving of every consequence, including sitting in gaol and contemplating transportation.

Darcy sniffed. He probably would simply have bought the man off and forced him to marry Lydia Bennet. He shuddered. Then he would have faced a lifetime of calling Wickham brother and wearing him like an albatross around his neck. No, Theo's way was better. Perhaps it was best Darcy had been away. And Theo was the best suited to deal with Anne and Lady Catherine.

The corner of Darcy's lips rose. He might learn to enjoy sharing responsibility for the family with Theo.

At last, the dreaded farmhouse left his view and the sights of London rose before him. Soon, though not soon enough, he would see her.

⁂

The housekeeper admitted him and led him to the parlor—the empty parlor. How ridiculously unfair, just plain bloody wrong to keep him waiting a moment longer—

"Mr. Darcy?"

He whirled about, unable to breathe. "Elizabeth…" He crossed the room in just two steps, hands outstretched.

She smiled and the room brightened. Her fingers entwined in his and his knees threatened to melt.

"You look very well—" His voice was an odd squeak.

"I am feeling much better, thank you. How was your journey?" She gestured toward the settee.

Darcy sat with her, not relinquishing her hand. He had endured far too much distance from her. Oh, her eyes were lovely, simply enchanting.

"Your journey?"

"Oh, yes. Forgive me. It was not a good trip, to be entirely honest. The matters under dispute would have been better handled by my brother. I should have sent him in my stead."

She stared at him with that peculiar glint in her eye, the one he had not seen nearly enough of. Elizabeth, his Elizabeth, was pleased with him.

"I think he would be pleased to hear you say that."

"I will make it a point then to tell him so when I see him."

"You have not seen him yet?"

"No, I came directly here as soon as I had word of what had happened."

"Oh." The gleam left her eyes and her smile faded.

"I cannot forgive myself for—"

"Stop, please, do not say that. Is that not the very thing that has caused you so much trouble already? That you could not forgive yourself or your brother..."

"That is not what I meant—"

"But out of the overflow does not the mouth speak? Forgive and think upon this affair, and on the past, only as it gives you pleasure."

"Pleasure? I do not take your meaning. How is there any pleasure to be found in the unspeakable actions of that...that..."

She pressed a finger to his lips. Oh, he would rant and rail far more often if that was to be his reward!

"I concede I cannot find pleasure in Mr. Wickham's actions, but in their outcomes, I may." She met his gaze with one so compelling he might never look away again.

"I cannot image your meaning. I await your instruction. Enlighten me with your great wisdom."

"First, my sister was rescued, through a Darcy's intervention." She tapped the tip of his nose.

With such remonstrations, she could continue this lecture the rest of the afternoon and he would voice no complaint.

"News of her…" She cleared her throat. "…unexpected travel…has been contained, so the damage to her reputation may be minimized. And you," she trailed her fingertips along his brow.

Hopefully she would not require him to remember what she said later. There was only so much distraction a man could endure with his higher faculties intact.

"Have discovered afresh how useful your brother can be."

He chuckled.

"And I…" she swallowed, her eyes glistening. "I am embarrassed to say that when you did not come to call the day we learned of Lydia's…"

"You thought I did not call because of her."

She bit her lower lip and nodded.

"And the thought distressed you?"

"Very much so. It was in that moment that I realized…realized…how very much…"

"I love you."

She gasped. "Exactly…how very much I love you and how I did not think I could bear it if—"

"Do not say it and do not think it, for it shall never be." He cradled her cheek in his palm.

A throat cleared from across the room. "Excuse me, Madam."

They jumped and turned. The housekeeper stood in the doorway, a tall figure shadowing behind her.

"Mr. Darcy to see you." The housekeeper curtsied and ducked aside.

The figure removed his hat and stepped inside. "Forgive me, Elizabeth, Darcy. I seem to have selected a very inopportune—"

Darcy and Elizabeth rose.

"Not at all, Theo." She stepped toward him.

"Theo?" She did not even call him—

"Yes, William, he is to be my brother after all and I have no desire for so much formality among those closest to me. Do you not agree?"

There she was, smiling that smile at him again. He tugged his cravat. "I do not know, it is not something I have experience with."

She tucked her hand into the crook of his elbow. "Just because it is unfamiliar does not mean that it will be disagreeable."

He slipped his hand over hers and she laced her fingers with his. For such enticements there was little he would outright reject.

Theo stared.

Darcy cleared his throat.

"Oh, yes," Theo twitched his head. "I came to inquire after Miss Lydia Bennet. Is she much shaken after the...ah...events of this week?"

Elizabeth huffed and rolled her eyes. "I fear she is not nearly so shaken as I would like her to be. At first, she accepted your story of the stolen jewelry as you told it—"

Theo grumbled under his breath. "But has since reformed the tale in her mind as one with Wickham as the victim."

"How did you—"

Darcy and Theo shared a dark glance.

"I fear this is not the first time he has manipulated an innocent." Darcy tried to catch Elizabeth's eyes.

She rewarded with him with a gaze not nearly as troubled as he expected.

"Or not so innocent." She lifted an eyebrow. "I have little faith in Lydia's ... blamelessness."

Theo stroked his chin with his fist. "Perhaps it might be useful for me to have another conversation with her? If you like, I may speak to her far more...ah...plainly than I did before."

"My uncle and I spoke of that very thing. We both thought it might be helpful to her, but hesitated to ask yet another favor of you. Since you have offered though, I will most gratefully accept on behalf of my family. If you will excuse me a moment, I will fetch her." She curtsied and departed.

Darcy and Theo stared at one another for a moment that went on far too long and became more awkward as it did.

"Thank you for what you did in my stead. I am grateful. You handled the matter perhaps better than I would have."

Theo raked his hair back and blinked several times. "I confess, that is not what I expected to hear you say."

"I can surmise all too easily what you expected, and I regret that too. I am grateful for having this opportunity to make a fresh start of things."

"I am too." Theo looked aside and scuffed his boot along the edge of the carpet.

"And I am not nearly so reluctant as Elizabeth—" How lovely her name felt on his tongue. "—to ask a favor of you."

"Indeed, what would that be?"

"I need—I would like for you to go to Rosings and sort out the details of Anne's inheritance. She and Aunt Catherine are embroiled in an epic battle over it and I—"

"You took one look at the documents and—"

"Felt like a schoolboy who did not prepare for his lessons." Darcy rubbed his forehead.

"I should have expected those documents to have been drawn up in the most cryptic manner possible. I shall leave for Rosings on the morrow." Theo turned aside and traced the edge of the carpet with his boot tip again. "Thank you for your faith in me."

Darcy tugged his sleeves beneath his coat cuffs. "There is one other favor I would ask of you."

"What else can I do for you?"

"Stand up with me, when Elizabeth and I marry." Darcy caught Theo's gaze.

Theo's eyes widened. "Truly?"

Darcy nodded.

"I…I would be honored." Theo extended his hand.

Darcy took it and pumped it hard.

A small sniffle startled him. Elizabeth stood in the doorway. The fist she pressed to her mouth did not conceal her smile and her eyes sparkled.

Elizabeth opened the door to Mrs. Gardiner's small sitting room and ushered Theo inside. He had no notion what he could say to Lydia Bennet to help matters—what in all this did she still fail to comprehend?—but the offer had been made and thus so must the attempt.

"Oh Lord! Not you again!"

"Lydia!" Elizabeth gave her sister a resigned look, but Lydia merely turned her back and stared out into the street. "*Please* try to show some manners."

"Good afternoon, Miss Lydia." Theo bowed as Lydia threw a bored-looking glance over her shoulder. "I came to enquire after your well-being, and your sister suggested I speak to you once more about what has happened."

Lydia let out a huff of breath before walking across the room and throwing herself into a fireside chair. "You may speak all you wish." She waved a hand airily. "They all do a vast deal of *speaking*, though I have long tired of listening."

Theo exchanged a glance with Elizabeth, who sighed, shook her head at him, and walked to the opposite end of the room to take Lydia's place at the window. Turning around, Theo walked over to where Lydia sat.

"May I join you?" He indicated the chair opposite and, taking Lydia's dismissive shrug as acquiescence, sat down. "How are you?"

"What is it to you?"

Theo merely raised a brow at this and, after a slight pause, she sniffed and said, "Oh very well. If you will make conversation… I am in an ill temper. I am come to Town, with all there is to enjoy, yet I am not allowed to go out. My aunt drones on and on the whole day long and both she and my uncle make it plain naught I do is to their taste, yet *then* they say I cannot return to Longbourn!" She threw an angry glance over at Elizabeth. "And my sisters treat me abominably. Look!" She pointed at her sister who met her angry gaze with apparent calm. "I am watched over at all times as though *I* have committed some crime."

Elizabeth made as though to walk over, but Theo shook his head at her. At least Lydia had acknowledged there had been a crime—this was an improvement on when he last spoke with her. "Miss Lydia," Lydia refused to look at him. "Would you prefer it if your sister left the room?"

Raising her chin, Lydia nodded before throwing a smug glance in Elizabeth's direction. Theo got to his feet and met Elizabeth by the door, saying quietly, "Perhaps if you wait just outside—I will leave it slightly ajar?"

Elizabeth bit her lip then nodded, whispering, "I am so sorry, Theo," as she slipped out into the hallway.

Drawing in a calming breath, Theo turned back and resumed his seat opposite Lydia, who was curling her hair round her finger, much as she had done the last time he saw her. Again, he was reminded she was only just beyond childhood, of an age with his own sister, and he felt his frustration diffuse a little.

"What of your parents, Miss Lydia? Have you received word from them?" He knew that recognition from Mr. and Mrs. Bennet would, in the circumstances, be critical in repairing any taint remaining upon the family's reputation.

"Papa is to come here, but I am told he refuses to take me home with him." Her eyes flashed. "And he has insisted on Mama remaining at Longbourn, for he must know she will be my only support in this, as is ever the case!"

"But did it not occur to you there would be repercussions by fleeing from your family's protection?"

Lydia frowned as though genuinely confused. "Why

should there be? Eloping is not uncommon and it is *so* romantic—to be certain, it deserves far less censure than this!"

"Regrettably, it cannot be deemed a successful elopement with no marriage taking place. Your reputation has been damaged and, in turn, it has brought shame and distress to all your family. You cannot blame them for your present circumstances; by falling in with Wickham's scheme, you must accept some culpability, and—"

Lydia rounded on him. "No, I will *not*! It is not *my* fault, and it is not Wickham's—it is *your* fault. You and your self-righteous brother, who is more a criminal than Wickham ever was and who should be brought to task over it!"

Theo almost bit his tongue, his sympathy fading and his defenses rising as soon as Lydia spoke ill of William. How soon had it come to pass he wished to protect his brother so? He was unable to pursue this intriguing thought, however, for Lydia rose to her feet and thus so did he.

"Had *he* not robbed my dear Wickham of his due, stolen his inheritance from him, he would not have had to resort to other means to fund his way in life. And besides, what of it? The rich have more jewels than they could possibly ever want!"

"That is hardly the point, Madam!" So she *had* taken on board the theft. "It is also erroneous! I believe your sister has already explained to you the truth of the circumstances around what was and what was not Wickham's due from the Darcy family."

Lydia stamped her foot. "Pah! I do not believe it for a moment. And I have done no wrong either. I did what all my other sisters have yet failed to do and found myself a husband." She sighed dramatically. "But it has all come to naught. I suppose I must let them all have their say and then I shall just go home to dear Mama."

"You cannot just go home to your Mama. Because you remain unmarried, you have to go elsewhere."

"That is what my aunt believes. She wishes to send me to a place quite northward. *Why* must I?"

Theo ran a hand through his hair in frustration. "We are going round in circles, Madam."

"Then why do you not cease speaking?" Brushing past him, Lydia flung the door aside and ran from the room.

Theo winced as he heard a door slam and then blew out a breath, shaking his head at Elizabeth and Darcy as they came into the room.

"I fear I have made matters worse."

Elizabeth smiled, though her countenance remained sad. "You have tried, Theo, as have we all. There is little else we can do."

He shook his head. "I shall not give it up yet. Which way did she go?"

Darcy stepped aside as Theo made for the doorway. "She ran down the hall and out of the rear door."

"It gives access to the garden," Elizabeth added.

Straightening his coat, Theo brushed a hand quickly through his hair and smiled at Elizabeth. "Then I shall take some air." He paused, then glanced at his brother. "Please tell me I was not this unreasonable at the same age?"

Darcy shook his head with a smile. "No—you were cleverer."

Theo laughed and set off into the garden in pursuit of Lydia. With a small amount of persuasion, she allowed him to seat her on a stone bench before perching himself on a convenient tree stump.

"This situation is what it is. What must be decided is how to manage it. What is it that you wish to happen?"

Lydia stared at him in surprise. "Why, I wish to be Mrs. Wickham, and hear all my friends call me such. Indeed, that is what I wrote Maria Lucas of, for I knew she would envy me more than any other. And then I wrote Althea Long, for she would have been grieved had Maria known more than she." She paused, the aggression she had shown earlier fading quickly. "You are the only person to ask me this question."

Theo reflected it was likely no one anticipated a sensible answer, and he had not been disappointed. He was done with trying to be polite; it was time to be plain in his speaking, as he had suggested to Elizabeth earlier.

"You wish to be the wife of a convicted man, transported to the other side of the world?"

"No—I wish to be the wife of Mr. George Wickham, the man whose life you ruined. If I am to be sent away, I would rather be on the other side of the world with him than in the wilds of the north with a load of sheep!"

Theo was tempted to point out that even shepherds need wives, but he did not. No unsuspecting yeoman farmer deserved to come home to Miss Lydia Bennet after a hard day on the moors.

"It is an arduous journey. Do you think you could bear it? Many do not survive its trials."

"Oh la!" Lydia waved his concern aside. "I am perfectly hardy; I have never had a day of ill health, and have grown quite the tallest of all my sisters." She paused and stared dreamily into the distance. "I would be able to walk ahead of all the single young women into every drawing room in the country. Oh it could be delightful!" She clapped her hands together, smiling, all trace of the petulant child gone. "No longer would I be compared with my elder sisters. I should have my own establishment. Do they have balls there? I should so like to lead the dance at a public assembly, and—"

At this point, Theo acknowledged defeat and tuned out her voice. Balls there may be, but he would not waste his breath explaining that where Wickham was headed they were made of iron.

"Theo!" Glancing over his shoulder, he saw Darcy on the steps to the house beckoning him. Never had Theo responded more gratefully to a summons from his brother.

"Excuse me, Miss Lydia." He turned to her and bowed. "I shall return directly."

Lydia shrugged. "Do not hurry on my account. I am sure I have little else to do but wait around."

Theo walked quickly towards his brother who turned and preceded him into the house.

"Intelligence of Miss Lydia's flight may not be as contained as you hoped. She says she has written of it to both a Miss Lucas and a Miss Long?" Theo shook his head. "It may be that marrying her off to a convicted man is the best we can now hope for."

Darcy's countenance became grave as he too shook his head. "I am afraid it is no longer possible. Here," he opened a door and ushered Theo inside Mr. Gardiner's study.

"What is it?" He frowned at Darcy. "What has happened?"

"The circumstances remain a little unclear as yet, but we have just received a visit from a constable. Apparently, early this morning Wickham was viciously attacked—"

"But he is under lock and key!" Theo interjected. "How can this be?"

"I know very little other than he has been badly injured."

"He lives?"

"For now; they do not anticipate he will last beyond eight and forty hours for his wounds are too severe."

"Have they apprehended the attacker?"

"No. They have been unable to identify who it was or how they got into Newgate as yet."

Theo frowned again. "A veritable mystery." Then, he shrugged. "Though one must suppose Wickham has his fair share of enemies. Perchance one of them is incarcerated in the same place?"

"Perhaps. There is little we can do; he is in the hands of others now. I am more concerned with Lydia Bennet and what we can do to minimize the damage to the family. Elizabeth will be distressed to learn her sister has written to her friends."

"I wish I could have done more than relay even further disturbing news."

"Nonetheless, I thank you for offering to help; I know Elizabeth is exceedingly obliged to you for making the attempt."

Theo sighed. "What will you do now?"

Darcy shook his head. "I know not; but do not concern yourself further with either of them, Theo. You have done more than your share by restoring Lydia to safety and ensuring Wickham is behind bars. Let me try to resolve the consequences of the situation." He smiled slightly. "Why do you not turn that legal brain of yours to the other pressing family matter? I have, in my turn, done little in Kent other than make things worse; I will gladly pass the burden over to you if you are still prepared to take it."

"I shall attend to it directly." Theo followed Darcy out of the study and they walked along the hallway to the front door. "I shall see if Richard is available to accompany me." He grinned as he shrugged into his greatcoat. "I may need a second if I am to duel with Aunt Catherine."

"Take a helmet too," Darcy cautioned with half a smile. "Anne is truly her mother's daughter at times."

Theo laughed, then his expression sobered. "I do not envy you trying to resolve matters with Miss Lydia Bennet."

Darcy sighed. "No more do I." He glanced down the hallway to the door into the garden. "The first step is to break this news to her. I do not think she will take it well."

Theo sat at his uncle's desk, his head bent over the legal documents Lady Catherine had presented to him. Although the language and provisions of the Will were not unusual, he read slowly, carefully, making notes from time to time. He could not understand why all of this had not been made clear at the time the Will was originally read. Perhaps it was because it was in Lady Catherine's best interest not to say anything, and Anne was too ill or too young to raise any questions. She would have undoubtedly accepted what her mother told her.

At first, his aunt and cousin had insisted on staying in the room with him while he worked. Lady Catherine had an annoying habit of clearing her throat all the time, as if she wanted to make sure everyone knew of her presence. Honestly, how could he forget? Theo was very glad he'd brought along some reinforcements. The Colonel had accompanied him on this trip partly to keep Theo from losing his mind and partly to help keep his aunt and his cousin from coming to blows.

"Really, Aunt Catherine, Anne, you should go to your sitting room where you will be more comfortable," Theo suggested as politely as he could manage.

"Hrumph! Comfort? What will make me comfortable is for you to finish and tell me what that... that document has to say," Lady Catherine demanded.

"I agree," said Anne, folding her arms over her chest defiantly.

"If time is of the essence, then I insist you leave me alone to work!" Theo shot his aunt and cousin his most terrifying look. Although it was the same look that had caused grown men to break down on the witness stand, neither of the ladies seemed impressed. Behind them, Theo could see Richard trying in vain not to smirk, and he glared at him, too.

"That look will not work on me," Anne said indignantly. "You forget. I have known you all your life, and you do not frighten me."

"Then I beg you both to leave me in peace while I read this." He stood and brought his fist down on the desk. "Now!"

"There is no need to have a tantrum, Theo dear. I have seen you do that before, and I am not impressed," said Lady Catherine indignantly.

Theo came out from behind the desk and took his

aunt's arm and then his cousin's. Escorting them to the door, he ejected them out into the hallway with a little push.

"Richard, would you escort the ladies to the sitting room and make sure no one disturbs me again?"

The Colonel calmly gave a nod of his head and smiled. "I will post a footman outside the door," he said as he ushered his aunt and cousin off down the hallway before they could regain their senses and protest.

Theo closed the study door and turned the key in the lock. Leaning his back against the cool wood of the door, he ran a hand through his hair. Thank goodness he had not inherited the Fitzwilliam temper. His mother had not been like that but the rest of that clan...well, you definitely did not want to cross them.

About an hour later, Theo finished his examination of the documents. It was fairly straightforward, but he could see there would be problems when he revealed the provisions. Neither his aunt nor his cousin would be happy. Rising from the desk, he stretched his legs. The thought crossed his mind that a glass of brandy might be in order despite the fact that it was just a little after noon. He and Richard had left London at dawn in the hopes that they could settle things here and return before it was too dark to travel.

He strode over to a cabinet at the side of the room and extracted a bottle of brandy and a snifter. Pouring himself a glass, he swirled the liquid around lazily. When his uncle had been alive, he had kept only the finest brandy in his cellar. Lady Catherine did not like brandy, but Theo was hoping this might be one of the bottles left from his uncle's stores. He sipped and felt the warmth of the liquor spreading though his body. Yes, it was some of the good stuff.

There was no sense in delaying. He would have to confront the ladies sooner or later. Savoring the fiery liquid for a moment, he thought about how best to manage the situation. Once he decided on a course of action, he finished the brandy in a few gulps, stepped out of the study, and headed toward the sitting room. Feeling a little like he was about to face a firing squad, he took a deep breath and nodded to the footman to open the door.

Two pairs of female eyes turned and simultaneously bore into him. Their looks were so fierce he was surprised he did not burst into flames on the spot. Richard stood near the fireplace looking very relaxed as usual. Leave it to a military man to be calm in the heat of battle.

Before Theo could even open his mouth, he was bombarded with questions.

"What does it say? Can I make Mother move?" Anne asked.

"I will not move to the Dower House!" said Lady Catherine vehemently. "That would be completely unacceptable."

Taking a deep breath, Theo said, "I could give you a long explanation of all the technical, legal aspects of the Will, but you would be bored to tears. The short answer is, Rosings becomes Anne's when she either marries or turns twenty-five, whichever comes first. As she is now over twenty-five, there is no doubt the entire estate belongs to her to manage as she sees fit. She also inherits the house in Town. Aunt Catherine, the Will states you shall be allowed to live here in the main house until Anne marries. You have been left a generous stipend. I am certain it will more than meet your needs."

"No, that cannot be!" Lady Catherine shrieked. "I want another opinion!"

"Father told me he was leaving everything to me, but you would not believe me!" yelled Anne.

Theo put a hand up to stop them, and much to his astonishment, they quieted. "There are several other important provisions. First, if for some reason Anne is not able to take charge of the estate due to illness, the property can be held in trust for her. During that time, Lady Catherine would be responsible for managing the estate until such time as Anne is able to assume control or she marries and her husband takes over. But then I am certain you already knew that." Lady Catherine would not meet his eye.

"Ah, ha! Is that why you kept me drugged for years?" Anne turned on her mother.

"Anne, my dear child, I was only taking care of your inheritance until you were well," said Lady Catherine sweetly.

At the same moment, Theo and Richard both saw Anne's hand reaching for a small porcelain figurine. Richard reached her first and removed the delicate object before it went the way of some of the other treasures of the house.

"Anne, you are not ten years old any more. There will be no more throwing things. You are frightening everyone. I am surprised half the servants have not given notice." Theo was not going to tolerate any more nonsense from either his aunt or cousin.

Anne turned away from her mother, sniffed haughtily, and put her nose up in the air. Lady Catherine made that noise again in her throat, the one that drove Theo nearly mad. Richard rolled his eyes.

"There are two more provisions to consider. If Anne does not marry and produce heirs—either male or female—the property reverts to one of the de Bourgh cousins. The second is that Lady Catherine must approve of any gentleman Anne wishes to marry."

Lady Catherine smiled triumphantly. Anne started to reach for something to throw again, but Theo stopped her with just a look this time.

"Anne, would you take a walk with me in the garden?" Theo asked.

"This is an odd time for a stroll, Cousin," she replied.

"I thought perhaps we could talk as we walk. Will you join me?"

Once in the garden, Theo guided Anne to a stone bench near the roses. "What is it that you want, Anne? I think there is more to this than just who owns the property," he began.

"Strange, no one has ever asked what *I* want."

Theo blinked; it was a strange echo of Lydia Bennet's words to him. Then, he roused himself. "Let the past go and turn toward the future. What is it you see for yourself?"

She paused to consider the question. "I want to meet people. I wish to marry, but not some stranger my mother picks out for me! And I want a new maid and a new companion."

"Very well. The new maid and companion can easily be done. Would you like to open the London house and move to Town for a while? Your chance of making friends there would be much greater."

"Yes, I think that would be a lovely idea." She hesitated.

"What is it, Anne?"

"I believe I shall need a little 'polishing' before I am ready to meet people," she responded.

"Polishing? What do you mean?"

Anne looked at her hands which were clenched tightly together on her lap. She spoke softly. "I have been out of society for so long that I fear I no longer know how to behave among people. I do not want to embarrass myself."

"You are being very brave. There are special ladies who do nothing but prepare young women for their come out. Perhaps that is the kind of companion you need."

"Truly? Someone who would help me learn how to walk, how to perform *something* for company, tell me what to talk about." She hesitated. "How to flirt?"

"Yes, those very things."

Anne, who had seemed hopeful just a moment before, was now subdued and focused on something far away as she spoke. "I am afraid people will make fun of me or talk behind my back about how old I am. I am not very pretty either."

Theo was unsure how to respond. It was true that she was not traditionally pretty, but with the right clothes, a new hairstyle, she would certainly be noticed. She was an heiress after all. The problem would not be too few suitors, but perhaps too many. "I believe an ordinary come out will not do for you. What you need is to be introduced to people at small parties and soirees."

"That sounds much better, but who would invite me?"

"Ordinarily, your mother would manage that for you, but..."

Anne jumped to her feet. "No! Absolutely not! She would ruin everything!"

Theo's heart went out to his poor cousin. "I was going to say—if you had not interrupted me—that we should ask our aunt, Lady Matlock, for assistance. She would be just the person to introduce you around. She knows everyone in the *ton*. Perhaps she can even recommend a special companion for you or teach you what you need to know herself. Would that meet with your approval?" Theo held his breath while she considered.

"Would you talk to her for me? Please, Theo."

"Of course, I will. Now, what about your mother? Do you truly believe she kept you drugged for her own self interest?"

Anne looked at her hands again and shook her head. "No, I think she did it because she believed it was the best thing for me. She loves me in her own strange way. That doctor is the one who gave her the medicine and told her I required it daily. I am angry with her for not knowing better, but I do not believe it was entirely from her desire to control me."

"Then you will try to stop fighting with her?"

Anne nodded. "But I am afraid she will disapprove of any man I meet so she may be able to continue living here in the main house. What am I going to do about that? Or if she does allow me to marry, she will choose some ridiculous man she can manipulate."

"I have an idea about that, too. Will you trust me?"

✿CHAPTER 17

THEO AND COLONEL FITZWILLIAM took some refreshments with the ladies before returning to London. The scene proved a bit awkward, so the gentlemen told funny stories which kept at least Anne smiling. Lady Catherine was not as cheerful, but she did make an effort at politeness.

"I do not understand why you must hie off to Town again so quickly, Theo dear. It would be only polite to stay the night," Lady Catherine complained.

Theo shifted uncomfortably. "It would give me great pleasure to spend more time with you, my dear Aunt, but I have matters which require my attention and so must ask your pardon." Lady Catherine responded with one of her little disapproving noises.

At some point during the day, Theo had become aware that it was likely Lady Catherine had known about each and every provision of the Will, but was choosing for her own devious reasons to feign otherwise. As such, he chose his next words carefully.

"Before I depart, there is one last matter to be settled.

It is about the provision that you must give your approval of anyone Anne wishes to marry."

"Ah, yes. What about it?" Lady Catherine smiled like a smugly satisfied feline.

Theo felt a shudder run down his back, but he pressed on. "Anne is concerned you will not approve of anyone no matter how eligible just so you will be able to stay here in the main house."

"Well, of course, I am very concerned that no one take advantage of her," said Lady Catherine at least sounding sincere. Theo was not convinced of his aunt's innocence.

"Do you trust Darcy's opinions?" Theo asked. He noticed Anne was trying to take an interest in the biscuit on her plate.

"He has not shown much good sense in marrying that Miss Elizabeth Bennet."

Theo let the comment about Elizabeth go. "But generally, you would agree he is a good judge of character, am I correct? After all, you have entrusted many estate matters to him over the years which is definitely a sign of your trust." Now he had her trapped. She could not easily say she did not trust Darcy without calling her own judgment into question.

Lady Catherine sighed and conceded. "You are correct. Generally."

"Then would you agree that, if the gentleman is someone of whom Darcy approves, you will also approve without question?"

Lady Catherine set her teacup aside and considered. Anne watched her mother hopefully while Richard looked menacingly at his aunt.

"I will approve, but only if Darcy *and* my sister, Lady Matlock, both agree."

Anne started to speak, but Theo put his hand on her arm to silence her.

"Very well, if Darcy and Lady Matlock approve, you give your word of honor not to interfere?"

Lady Catherine sat up in her chair and sniffed the air cautiously. "Oh, very well, I give my word."

Anne, Theo and Fitzwilliam were so relieved they simultaneously slumped back in their chairs.

"I will hold you to that," Theo said.

"You are becoming more and more like your mother every day, Theo," his aunt told him with a hint of both resentment and approval.

"As my mother was the kindest, warmest, most loving person in the world, I shall take that as a great compliment."

After finishing their tea, Theo and Richard prepared to depart for London. Lady Catherine skulked off to her private sitting room, but Anne walked out to the waiting carriage with her cousins.

"Good bye, Theo, Richard. I cannot thank you enough for coming to my aid. I do not know how I will ever repay you."

"You will repay me by behaving like a lady," Theo said, tapping her affectionately on the nose. "No more throwing priceless vases and figurines."

"I promise." Turning to Richard, she said, "You will speak to your mother on my behalf? I will need her support to enter society."

"We will both speak to her," said Richard, "and I am certain she will agree. She has worried about you over the years, but has not visited because of the enmity between your mother and my father. They are too much alike, I suppose."

"The Fitzwilliam temperament," Theo added. "But of course, none of us has inherited it." They all laughed.

Anne threw her arms around Richard and then Theo. "I wish you a safe journey. I love you both so very much and shall see you in Town very soon."

❧━━━❧━━━❧

Theo was surprised by how good it felt to return to the

Darcy house in London. The greeting exchanged by the brothers held a hint of warmth long absent between them, and though Theo could tell William was yet a little awkward in making such overtures, it was a beginning.

They repaired to the study at the back of the house, sending a request for some tea with an obliging footman, and Theo quickly set before his brother all that had happened in Kent, warmed once more by William's quick approbation of Theo's handling of the matter and his heartfelt gratitude for resolving what to him had seemed unfathomable.

The arrival of the tea tray drew the discussion to a close, and as they each took a seat before the hearth, Theo's mind quickly turned to the matter of Wickham.

"Have you seen him? Does he live yet?"

Darcy nodded. "Yes, and he lives, though it is only a matter of time. Do you –" he threw his brother a keen glance. "Is it your wish to see him before—well –" he waved his arm as if unsure how to express the words.

Did he wish to see Wickham one final time? Theo stared at his booted feet. He had mulled over precisely that question more than once during the past four and twenty hours. They had been such friends in their youth, and there had been a time when he considered Wickham more a brother than William.

Frustrated with himself, his blindness, Theo blew out a breath. He had been a fool at times under Wickham's influence. Yet now the reality of the man's death was upon them all; what did he want to do?

"Theo?" He looked up and met his brother's serious gaze. "It is not obligatory."

Theo shook his head. "No—I know; and I will own to having thought of it." He sighed. "He is unworthy and has caused us all much anger and despair, and transportation was as likely to have ended in his demise as anything. Yet now his end is upon us…" he left the sentence hanging in the air between them. They both had so much to resent

Wickham for.

"Despite his injuries and his imminent fate, he is George Wickham yet."

Theo raised a brow at Darcy, then reached for his teacup. "Then he is not cowed by his circumstances? He looked fearful enough when bundled into that prison cart."

"Oh I think he understands the end is approaching, yet he is not of a relenting or forgiving nature. When I saw him, he was quite unrepentant of what he had done. I believe he still lays the blame for his lot in life firmly in our—and more specifically my—hands."

A feeling of distaste rose within Theo as he recalled Wickham's slur upon Georgiana the other day. He had no desire to see him again. "Even in such circumstances, how can he…"

Just then, a loud rap on the door drew their attention and Colonel Fitzwilliam strode in.

"Well—what news? Has the scoundrel relinquished his hold on life yet?"

Darcy shook his head, but before he could speak the Colonel frowned. "Yet you were speaking of him," and at Theo's surprised look he added, "It is not often you share the same air and countenance. Thankfully, I might add, for it is quite intimidating!"

Darcy smiled slightly. "Is there any further word on the attack?"

The Colonel nodded, then espied the platter of biscuits near the tea tray and grabbed a handful before throwing himself into a nearby chair. "I have just spoken to an acquaintance close to the investigation and thought I would drop by and share what little there is. Apparently, there is no trace of the assailant though the weapon was left behind—a small pair of shears."

Theo winced. "An unusual choice! And what of Wickham? Does he claim to know who wielded them?"

"That is the oddity." The Colonel munched on a biscuit for a moment and Theo and Darcy exchanged an amused glance. "According to my source, Wickham refused to provide a name. Whether he knew the attacker or not therefore remains unknown. Of course, in his condition, there is nothing anyone can do to force him to reveal what he may know."

Darcy frowned. "If they are known to him, this must be the one noble gesture of his selfish life."

Letting out a slow whistle, Theo placed his cup on a side table. "A fine time for him to suddenly show some moral backbone. This has all the markings of a wronged woman."

The Colonel snorted. "Indeed—and we can assume from her weapon she was intent upon pruning him once and for all. And this weapon was not the only thing she left behind—a small nosegay was found on the floor."

For a fleeting moment, something tugged at Theo's memory, but he shook it aside. "I do not understand how she could have gained access to his cell."

"Inside help, apparently. It is supposed one of the jailors let her in under cover of darkness in the early hours. As the jailors of Newgate are all as thick as thieves with each other, no one is letting on as to who assisted or why." The Colonel popped the last biscuit into his mouth and got to his feet. "I must away; duty calls."

Theo sighed, and he too rose from his seat. "It goes against my training to own it, but if it is a woman he has wronged, I confess I hope she is not caught and tried."

Darcy sent him an understanding look as he joined them. "It is good to see you, Richard; thank you for accompanying Theo to Rosings."

"It was my pleasure, Darce. You know I like nothing more than a little skirmish before dinner! Always whets the appetite!" He winked at Theo, and they shook hands before he turned for the door. "I will see you both anon."

The door closed upon the Colonel, and Darcy turned back to face his brother.

Theo had resumed his seat. "And what of Miss Lydia Bennet? Please tell me you had more success than I in that quarter?"

"I am not sure whether it could be deemed a success, but a solution has presented itself. She is to be wed to Wickham."

Theo rolled his eyes at Darcy as he sat down. "Then she will be happy—it was all she desired, and she could see nothing beyond it. How is it to happen? And will the stigma of being the widow of a criminal not stain the Bennets' name yet?"

Darcy hesitated. "The elopement, such as it was, is all about the Bennets' neighborhood. Thankfully, no word of Wickham's incarceration has followed it. Yet without marriage to him, there is little we can salvage. Even a swift marriage to another, should such a thing be possible, could not answer so well."

"But?"

A raised brow was the only response to Theo's question.

"There is something you have not yet revealed."

Darcy gave a rueful smile. "You are not in Court, Theo."

Theo grinned. "So there is something—tell me."

Releasing a heavy sigh, Darcy nodded. "Wickham is intent upon making things as difficult as possible for everyone but himself." He shifted in his seat, his recollection clearly troubling him. "Despite his condition, he finds amusement in finally having something to bargain with."

"What could he possibly demand? You cannot give him back his life!"

Darcy got quickly to his feet and walked over to the window. Then, he turned to face his brother. "He does not wish to die in Newgate. Unless the charges against Wickham are dropped, he will not consent to wed Miss Bennet and afford her the protection—such as it is—of his name."

Theo blinked. "But the charges are registered. We cannot just—"

"In principle, no, we cannot. But as no trial can now take place, nor a conviction gained, I am informed—as I am sure you are aware—a little oiling of the Clerk to the Court's palm will see the case dropped if we are *all* in agreement." He met Theo's eye, his air and countenance reflective of his concern. "It is down to you, Theo. I am prepared to do this for Elizabeth, for her peace of mind. If Lydia Bennet is wed to George Wickham, outside of Newgate and with no pending charges, her reputation will be somewhat restored and thus the stain upon the Bennet family is considerably lessened."

Theo drew in a deep breath. It had taken all his will power to send for that constable, to have Wickham arrested. He had known it was necessary, but he had suffered for doing it. Yet here was a compromise that seemed as though it suited everyone, and he knew what the right thing to do was. Getting to his feet, he walked over to join his brother, meeting his anxious gaze firmly.

"Then of course I agree, though yet again he has cost us dear."

"Thank you, Theo. I know there is a legal process to these things, but I am assured it can be expedited at some expense. I believe it is one worth the bearing."

"And the marriage to Miss Lydia Bennet?"

"Once Wickham is permitted to leave Newgate, he is to be transferred to a small chapel of rest nearby where the ceremony is due to take place at first light on the morrow. A special license was the only choice, and I have already put it in motion," Darcy paused and glanced at his pocket watch. "I must be at my attorney within the hour to finalize things.

"Special license?" Theo shook his head. "It is not right; yet more expense to correct Wickham's wrongs." He looked at Darcy who shrugged his shoulders. "And the lady—no doubt she is delighted at the need for one."

Darcy almost growled his response. "Be thankful we are not privy to *Mrs.* Bennet's thoughts upon the matter."

Theo released a short laugh. "Yes—I gathered from Miss Bennet the other day that she is close to her mother. It does not surprise me to learn that they are alike. Mrs. Bennet does not attend the ceremony, then?"

Darcy shook his head vehemently. "When Elizabeth put the suggestion of it taking place to the Gardiners and her father, who arrived in Gracechurch Street yesterday, they agreed not to inform Mrs. Bennet until after the event."

"A wise move, it would seem. And Miss Lydia Bennet? She is not too distressed by the news of Wickham's fate?"

"From what I understand, the only distress caused to the lady was that of not having time to order wedding clothes. All else, I believe she finds to her liking."

Theo patted Darcy on the shoulder. "I do not know how your Elizabeth—or Jane Bennet either—became such delightful—and dare I say, rational—ladies, but I am thankful for you it is so!"

"I am only thankful Hertfordshire is a long way from Derbyshire!"

"Speaking of Elizabeth—is she well despite the present situation?"

Theo suppressed a smile as his brother's features softened instantly. "She is remarkably well. She will be here later with her father; I will introduce you. The one concession to wedding finery he has permitted is for his daughter to carry a small posy of flowers; Elizabeth and Mrs. Gardiner were to visit a nearby florist to order it this morning."

Theo frowned as once again something pulled at his memory.

"What is it?"

"Nothing," Theo shrugged the notion aside. "It is a great deal to take in over a short space of time!"

"Indeed. Well, I must prepare for my appointment." They both turned to walk towards the door. "Let us trust to hope Wickham survives another night, and we can finally bring this sordid business to a close."

The following morning, Darcy arrived at Gracechurch Street as soon as the hour was acceptable; indeed, it was perhaps a little earlier than would normally be tolerated for a call, had the purpose behind it been nothing more than politeness.

As it was, his determination to ensure the marriage took place whilst Wickham maintained his tenacious grip on life was entirely overridden by the desire to see Elizabeth again. Every day it became harder to leave her, and he longed for this sordid business to be over, that they might contemplate their own future—a life together as Mr. and Mrs. Darcy, living at Pemberley.

A wave of happiness filtered through him whenever he allowed his thoughts to roam in such a direction, taking him by surprise even yet, and he smiled as he stood at the window of the Gardiners' drawing room waiting for someone—again, the name Elizabeth whispered through his mind—to come and greet him.

How much more at peace did he feel? These past weeks, not only securing Elizabeth as his wife—his smile widened—but also the first steps of rapprochement with his brother, foretold a whole new beginning, and…

Darcy started as a horse and rider pulled up sharply outside the Gardiners' house—Theo! What the devil was he doing here? He had decided against seeing Wickham again and, as a consequence, had no role to play in the wedding that morning. He frowned as his brother dismounted and wound the reins around the railings before turning to the pack attached to his saddle.

Turning on his heel, Darcy left the room and walked quickly to the front door, swinging it aside as Theo came bounding up the steps.

"What on earth are you doing?" Darcy exclaimed,

"And why are you carrying those?"

Theo grinned in his usual engaging fashion.

"Good morning, William!" He bowed extravagantly and thrust a delicate bouquet of flowers into his brother's hands. "May I present a small token of my affection?" He winked, and Darcy could not help but laugh as he stood back to allow his brother entry into the house.

Placing the flowers carefully on the hall table, Darcy pointed towards the drawing room door, and Theo preceded him into the room.

"This is an unexpected visit?"

Theo nodded. "Indeed, it is. And until all of three hours ago, I had no plan to do so."

Darcy glanced at the clock on the mantel as they took seats near the hearth. "As it is but a half after nine, I assume there is a story to tell?"

For a moment, Theo's handsome features darkened, his air and countenance quickly losing their animation. He stared into the fire crackling merrily in the hearth and, fingers of wariness tapping gently on his shoulder, Darcy prompted, "Theo?"

With a start, Theo looked up. "Forgive me; I am lost to thought." He sat back in his seat and met Darcy's concerned look. "You are right, I have uncovered something I wish to share with you."

The fingers took firmer hold, and Darcy moved his shoulders uneasily but said nothing as Theo got to his feet and grabbed the poker, giving the logs a hefty shove. Then, he turned to face his brother, the poker yet in his hands.

"I went in search of Wickham's assailant."

"What!" Darcy stood up, the wariness turning into fear. "Are you out of your mind? Why must you court danger, Theo? *When* will you curb your reckless…"

Darcy stopped as Theo threw him a fierce look, holding up a hand to stall his words. "Do not judge me! Do not always suppose I have been reckless!"

"I am sorry." Darcy bowed his head and drew in a shallow breath. Damn it, he had done it again—instinctively assumed the worst of his brother, not given him credit for the man he had become. He raised solemn eyes to meet Theo's. "Forgive me? I am still learning to curb my own faults and should not forget it."

Before Theo could respond, the door opened, and they both turned about.

"William!" Elizabeth walked quickly to him, offering her hand in the presence of company, which he placed a firm kiss upon and then retained hold of. Blow whatever etiquette he should follow, he needed her calming presence. "Theo, how lovely to see you! I did not expect the pleasure of receiving *two* Mr. Darcys this fine morning!"

Elizabeth smiled, her eyes sparkling, but then her expression sobered. "Is there," she looked from Darcy to Theo and back again, "is aught amiss?" She gasped and raised a hand to her mouth. "Tell me, is it Wickham? Are we too late?"

Darcy quickly reassured her to the contrary. "Theo and I were just about to discuss some business—nothing for you to be concerned about, Elizabeth."

"Precisely," Theo added with a smile as he replaced the poker. "Incredibly boring, hence our disgruntled air! I do not suppose there is chance of a cup of tea? I am quite parched." He glanced at Darcy. "It does not usually take much persuasion for William to indulge either."

Darcy met his brother's eye and nodded, pleased to see the spark of anger gone.

"Would you be so kind, Elizabeth?" He squeezed the hand he held gently. "If one of your aunt's maids could oblige, we would both appreciate it."

"Of course! I will see to it directly." She turned towards the door, pausing on the threshold to smile reassuringly at Darcy. "I shall leave you to your business and return to aid my aunt. Lydia is—well, Lydia still."

There was silence for a moment after the door closed,

and Darcy tugged uneasily at his neck cloth before glancing at Theo. Then, he waved a hand at the seats they had vacated. "Shall we continue? Perhaps you had best share your tale. And Theo," as they took their seats, Theo looked across at him. "I promise to hear you out, and apologize now for any further exclamation I am driven to. You do try a man, you know."

Theo smiled ruefully. "Indeed, I do. I will attempt not to shock your sensibilities too often." His smile faded. "Only hear this, William. There is no other I would relate these facts to, and I am trusting to your absolute confidence in doing so." He moved to the edge of his seat and held out his hand. "Do I have your word, whatever you hear from me now, it will go no further than these four walls? Do you trust me sufficiently to make such a promise?"

Without hesitation, Darcy reached out and shook his brother's hand firmly. "You have my word, without question."

"I have found the person who attacked Wickham; I have discovered her motive, such as it is, and have heard how it came to pass."

Darcy released a slow breath. "So it is as we thought: a woman."

Theo shrugged lightly. "Perhaps; she is little more than a girl." He paused, staring into the distance as though recalling something, then shook his head. "It is a sorry tale, and—"

Just then, a light rap upon the door heralded the arrival of the tea, and nothing further could be said until the maid left them in peace once more.

Darcy took a welcome sip of the hot liquid before placing the cup on a side table, and Theo began to talk.

"I passed a bad night; sleep would persist in evading me, and as I lay in the darkness, my mind began to weave together the threads lingering in the recesses of my memory." Theo paused. "Do you recall a couple of weeks ago, Georgiana and Anne calling upon Miss Elizabeth—here, in Gracechurch Street?" Darcy nodded, unsure of the connection. "They called at a flower shop on the way to purchase a gift for the lady, only for Georgiana to see George Wickham lurking in the establishment's shadows."

Biting back the desire to demand why he had not known of this, Darcy grabbed his tea again and swallowed a mouthful so that he could not speak, but Theo was continuing.

"Georgie was not overly distressed when she spoke of it to me, more concerned her instinct had been to bolt like a rabbit and would he ever affect her thus. I thought no more upon it, until last night." Theo stopped to take a sip of his own tea. "Richard said yesterday that the assailant left two things behind: some pruning shears—identified as the weapon—and a discarded nosegay."

Theo flexed his hand, and the now almost faded bruising on his knuckles was sufficient to indicate to Darcy the direction of this thoughts.

"On the day of Wickham's arrest, there was a flower girl on the corner of his street—an incongruous location, with no hope of any trade—and she disappeared once Wickham had been removed in the jail cart. It occurred to me this morning the scoundrel must be known to her, and I felt certain the small pruning shears would be traced back to the very same flower shop Georgiana visited."

Darcy sighed. A young girl—probably much the same age as Georgiana, and much the same age also as Lydia Bennet, merrily preparing for her marriage, still seemingly oblivious to the appalling circumstances.

"But she will face the gallows if apprehended."

Theo stared at Darcy for a moment. "Aye, perhaps—*if* she is apprehended."

Narrowing his gaze at his brother, Darcy nodded slowly. "Pray continue; forgive the interruption."

Theo inclined his head gravely in acceptance of this, and Darcy endeavored to conceal a smile. There were times when his brother could not help but assume the mantle of his profession and this was surely one of them. Well, he was prepared to let him present his case.

"I rose as soon as first light came, keen to determine the location of the flower shop, yet I knew only that it lay between Mayfair and Cheapside. It was too early to consult Georgiana—and I was reluctant to do so—but I paid a quick call to the mews behind Darcy House where the coachman was able to assist."

"You did not reveal your purpose?"

Theo threw Darcy an exasperated look. "Of course not, you dunderhead!"

Darcy blinked, then choked back a laugh. His younger brother had never called him names—at least, not to his face. He found it strangely endearing.

"Why do you think I appear thus?" Theo waved a hand at his state of dress, which Darcy had not paid any mind to. Now he noted the poorly tied neck cloth and, amusingly, the ill-matched gloves he had discarded. "I dressed hurriedly in near darkness, not wishing to disturb my man. The fewer who knew of my purpose, the better."

"And you found her, this flower girl? At the shop?"

"After a fashion," Theo rubbed his chin thoughtfully, and Darcy noted for the first time the shadows beneath his eyes. "I had not thought my plan through before turning Theseus in that direction. I could not swear to recognize the flower girl even if face to face with her. I paid her little enough attention at the time, my eye caught by the colorful basket she held; all I could attest to was her being full young and of slender build." Then, he shrugged lightly. "And truth be told, she found me!"

"What on earth do you mean?"

"I arrived at the shop's location and though the hour was early, all was a-bustle with delivery carts from Covent Garden being unloaded by young lads, and a woman giving orders as to what to place where. I tethered my mount, and took up a position just across the street, tucked into a passage where it joined the main thoroughfare, prepared to watch and wait until any possible likely figure appeared."

"And she did."

"Indeed. A voice behind me spoke—it seemed I was blocking access from the passage, and I stepped aside only to behold a young girl whose cap and apron clearly showed her connection with the flower shop opposite. Before I could consider if this might be the person I saw near Wickham's lodgings, her face went white, she let out a faint cry and all but fell to the floor."

"Good grief! She recognized you from that day! Her reaction surely confirms her guilt!"

Theo got to his feet and walked over to one of the long windows fronting onto Gracechurch Street. Then, he turned to Darcy, his expression grave.

"Yes; she has confessed the whole to me, yet the attack was not premeditated."

Darcy stood and walked to join Theo at the window and they both stared into the street for a moment.

"Damn Wickham," he muttered, and Theo threw him an understanding look. "Damn him for the lives he has ruined. What is her story, Theo, and how came you to discover the whole?"

"I offered my arm to aid her, walking back the way she had come. At the other end of the passage was a quieter thoroughfare and on its corner a small area of greenery with some seating. She fell upon a bench, her pallor yet indicative of her disquiet. She was trembling, William," Theo ran a hand through his hair and drew in a long, deep breath. "She shook like a frightened deer upon my arm, her eyes wide with trepidation, yet she did not speak, nor try to run. I felt for her in her distress—who could not?"

A little awkwardly, Darcy patted his brother on the shoulder. "I do not blame you."

Theo stared out of the window, though Darcy suspected he saw little of the bustle of Gracechurch Street. He was unused to such solemnity in his brother and was not sure he liked it. Then, Theo cleared his throat and took up his story again.

"Wickham was her lover—whenever he was in Town, that is. He seduced her with his smiles and his words, said he loved her, promised to marry her when she found herself with child."

Darcy bit back on an expletive, and Theo once again sent him a sympathetic look.

"Who knows whether he would have stood by her had he not received intelligence of your engagement? He saw his opportunity to prosper from the Darcys yet again, promptly detaching himself from the young flower seller and setting off in pursuit of Miss Lydia Bennet."

"This girl was familiar with his hangouts, so soon tracked him down to the lodgings where Monty and I found him; she had planned to call upon him, beg him to reconsider, but saw the activity at the inn and hesitated to act, hovering on the corner for a while. Thus she saw Wickham's removal to Newgate."

"And also saw you."

Theo nodded. "Indeed. She has an uncle who is a jailor at the prison—it did not take much for her to persuade him to let her visit her beloved—she did not reveal he had cast her off—she took the nosegay as an offering to Wickham, knowing the stench inside would be dire."

Darcy shook his head. "Why did she wish to take him back?"

"She loves him—or she did; and the child has been born, but ten days ago. She wished him to acknowledge his son."

"Damn him."

"Yes, yes—you already said that, William. Wickham cannot be more damned than he already is, scarred of face and facing his Maker."

Darcy growled. "Even that is too good for him."

"Most indubitably," Theo agreed. "Well—he got his comeuppance. She set off for the prison before going to work the other morning, and under cover of the predawn greyness, she was allowed into his cell, where she begged him to stand by her and their child. Admittedly, he could have done little for her, incarcerated as he was—but it was his constancy she desired more than pecuniary comfort, the reassurance she remained dear to him."

Theo looked troubled and turned from the window to face Darcy. "He refused—not only to having any affection for her, but even had the gall to question whether he truly was the father of her child. She says she became distraught, hysterical; she grabbed the small shears from her apron and lashed out at him in her grief, marking his face and, as you know, badly lacerating his arm as he tried to defend himself."

Darcy shook his head, saddened by all he had heard. "Dear Lord. What a disaster Wickham has made of his life; what ruin and despair he has brought upon others."

"Indeed. As for the girl, Wickham's screams brought her to her senses once more and, horrified at what she had done, she dropped the shears and fled." Theo breathed heavily. "There you have it; a sorry tale, with no happy ending for either party."

"And the young girl," Darcy narrowed his gaze. "You asked me to remain silent, to say naught of any of this—you do not intend to take the matter further?"

"It is what I wish. She does not deserve, despite what she has done, to end on the gallows, and her child does not deserve to end in the poor house. I am no law enforcer, William. My purpose is to see justice done, and I believe it has been."

"And the uncle? He will no doubt keep his silence to protect his niece."

Theo nodded. "Apparently, she later found out he threatened Wickham as he lay on his sick bed—that if he spoke of his assailant to anyone, his remaining hours on this earth would be all the more painful. As you know, Wickham is not the bravest of men and has a low pain threshold. It was sufficient to keep him quiet."

"I still cannot believe you managed to track the assailant down with such ease when the law enforcers seem to have admitted defeat."

Theo rubbed his eyes, his weariness almost palpable. "They have lost interest with no one baying for answers or for justice to be done, I suspect; there is crime far more worthy of their interest than that of a prisoner attacked in his cell. Yet, I have an enquiring mind. I would have it satisfied."

Darcy huffed out a breath. "You have damned excessive curiosity, you mean! Ever it led you into scrapes as a child—you are fortunate this did not end differently. Had the assailant been of different inclination, or taller stature…"

Theo raised a hand in protest. "Hey, steady on, Fish! I am no defenseless weakling!"

"No—I know you are not. I am just…" Darcy swallowed hard on the lump that arose from nowhere into his throat. "I have perhaps more regard for your safety than you credit me. I have no wish to lose you, when I feel I have only just found you again."

They stared at each other, but just then there was a loud clatter from the floor above followed by a burst of laughter.

"It seems Miss Lydia Bennet's spirits remained unimpaired as her nuptials approach." Theo shook his head. "It is a poor contrast to the young girl I saw this morning."

Darcy glanced at the ceiling. "Miss Lydia will not perhaps find things so amusing when she lays eyes upon her intended. He is not a pretty sight." Then, he frowned. "How did you come to bring the bridal flowers?"

"Ah—yes; by delaying the girl's arrival at work, she was behind in her duties, the first of which was to deliver a wedding bouquet. I offered to take this on, Theseus being to hand, and you can imagine my surprise when I was given the address!"

"And what of her welfare? Will she cope?"

"I believe so. The proprietor, though she scolded her roundly just now, seems a steady woman. The girl says she supported her through her confinement and is prepared to continue employing her. There is an elder sister who is helping care for the baby."

Darcy sighed. It was indeed a sorry tale, though likely less common than one would hope in that there was a chance for this girl to make a future for her son. Like his brother, he believed she deserved that. He glanced at the clock. "It is almost time to depart. Will you not reconsider? It may help you to accept the inevitable if you see him."

Theo chewed his lip. "I do not know."

Before they could say more, the door was tapped and Elizabeth came in, and Darcy walked to meet her.

"It is time we made our way to the chapel. My aunt is bringing Lydia down now."

"Theo?" Darcy turned to look at him where he remained by the window. "Will you not come?"

Releasing a long breath, Theo nodded. "You are right, William; I shall regret it later if I do not." He glanced at his discarded gloves as he joined them at the door. "Though you will have to forgive me for not being more suitably dressed."

Darcy allowed Elizabeth to precede them out of the door as Lydia and the Gardiners came down the stairs, then turned to Theo.

"You will be considerably more presentable than the groom. You must prepare yourself."

Theo nodded, his expression grim. "I am ready; let us be done with it."

CHAPTER 18

IT WAS WITHOUT QUESTION the most pathetic wedding ceremony Theo had ever seen, starting with Lydia's gasp of dismay on beholding her bridegroom, followed by clapping her hand over her mouth. The fetid stink of rotting flesh in the room made Theo wish he could do the same. The sight of the jagged wound running across Wickham's cheek and across his lower lip almost caused his stomach to rebel. Lydia garbled her vows, her eyes fixed on Wickham's feet and never meeting his eyes. Darcy put the wedding band in Wickham's good hand, but still needed to assist him in pushing it onto Lydia's finger and in signing the register which was brought to his sickbed.

Lydia was out the door as soon as it was over, though Elizabeth stayed a moment longer to apologize for her sister's behavior and to thank him for his cooperation. At least she had no difficulty looking Wickham in the eye. As she spoke, Theo sidled up to Darcy and said quietly, "Go ahead without me."

With a serious look, Darcy nodded, then escorted Elizabeth from the darkened room, leaving Theo alone with

Wickham.

Theo tried to see some likeness of his childhood friend in the wasted figure lying before him, his face turned toward the wall. In an attempt to lighten the atmosphere, he said, "Who would have thought you would be married before me?"

Wickham grimaced. "Who would have thought *you* would be the death of me?"

Theo shook his head. "This was your own doing. I did not wrong that poor girl in the flower shop."

"Wrong her? She was a very active participant in being wronged, as I recall it. And you—*you* would have had me transported. You. The one I called my friend."

It was Theo's turn to have a bad taste in his mouth. "The friend whose sister you tried to seduce. That is not how I treat my friends."

"I…" A fit of coughing wracked Wickham. He reached out for his glass, and Theo placed it in his hand and helped to raise it to his cracked lips. "I thought you would be pleased to have me marry Georgiana. Then we could be brothers in truth, and I would not have to scrounge for every penny. I could have lived the life your father wanted for me. But in the end you were just like the rest. It might have amused you to keep company with me, but I was not good enough for your precious little sister. You could not stand a mere steward's son aspiring to marry a Darcy."

"No, I could not stand a wastrel marrying Georgiana for her money. Remember when you threw away the living my father had left you, and I tried to persuade you to study with me? But you would have nothing to do with anything that resembled work, not when there was gambling and loose women to be had instead." Theo sucked in a long breath of air. Why was he bothering to explain himself? Wickham would never admit the part he had played in his own ruin. His troubles were always someone else's fault.

And in this particular case, one of his problems truly was Theo's fault. If Wickham had not been in Newgate, he would have seen a surgeon for the wound in his arm before it had festered, but apparently in gaol he had been left to rot until it was too late. The stink of the pus oozing from his bandage told its own story. That arm should have been amputated days earlier.

Wickham had gone to gaol because of him. He knew better than to steal when he might be caught, but he had counted on Theo never allowing him to be punished if he stole from a Darcy. Wickham had never truly known him.

He realized Wickham was watching him closely. Wickham had always known how to read his moods. "There is no point in quarreling now. It is all over anyway. You and Prince William will be great successes, and as for me—" Wickham gestured down at himself . "I will not be here to trouble you much longer. But you could still do me one last favor."

"What is it?"

Wickham lowered his voice. "Bring me some opium. Let me leave this world with a little pleasure."

"Opium?" For a moment, all Theo could think of was Anne's medicine, but then he recalled those times years ago when he and Wickham had visited the opium dens together. A few times had been enough for him, but Wickham kept returning as if he could not stay away. That was when they had begun to grow apart. Suddenly a great many things began to make sense to him. "I will see what I can do."

"My thanks, Theo. I knew I could count on you."

Theo gave a short nod, then left. Outside the room, he took a deep breath of the clean air, untainted with the stench of rotting flesh.

The attendant hurried up to him. "Are you done, sir?"

Theo took a coin from his pocket and pressed it into the woman's hand. "Fetch a surgeon to see if anything can be done for him. Tell him he is an opium addict, and have him send his bill to me." He handed her his card.

"Yes, sir, and thank you kindly."

Darcy sat back, watching his brother and sister engaging in conversation. This had been a good idea of Georgiana's, to have a family dinner, just the three of them. How many years had it been since they had shared a meal without other company? It certainly had not happened since Georgiana had left school.

"I wish I could meet your Mr. Garrow," said Georgiana. "He must have the most amazing tales to tell."

Theo flicked his eyes in Darcy's direction before replying. "Perhaps it could be arranged some day, after you are out, of course. He does not often go out in society, but might accept an invitation for dinner."

"I do hope so." Georgiana took a deep breath, then turned toward Darcy with a determined look on her face. "William, is it true you would slit Theo's throat if he took me to observe a trial at the Old Bailey?"

Darcy choked on a sip of wine and glared at his brother. "No," he said darkly. "I would not slit his throat, though I might give the idea serious consideration."

Theo said nothing, only watched with an amused smile dancing on his lips. Georgiana was the one to respond. "I do not see why. I think it would be educational for me."

He recalled the crowded gallery, full of pungent odors and crowded with commoners. "You would find it most unpleasant, I fear. It is thronged with the sort of person you have never been exposed to, and the matters discussed in the trials are shocking and quite unsuitable."

His brother clapped his hand over his eyes, shaking his head. "You may as well tell him all of it, Georgiana."

Georgiana squared her shoulders. "It would not shock me. Theo tells me all about his trials, and if he does not, I pester him until he does. And he did take me there once, after I begged him to, but said he dared not do it again because you would slit his throat if you found out."

Theo leaned back in his chair. "Guilty as charged, my

349

Lord. I fear our little sister has developed a taste for lurid melodrama, and cannot get enough of it."

"I cannot believe you would tell her of such matters!"

Theo shrugged, his expression suddenly guarded. "She is interested, and she chafes at the bonds society places on a young, well-bred girl. I would rather tell her of the evils of the world than have her go out to discover them herself. Besides, she has a clever mind, and has been known to give me useful suggestions."

Devil take it, how was he supposed to remain on good terms with his brother if Theo insisted on going behind his back and exposing Georgiana to all sorts of riff-raff? This was how the trouble in Ramsgate had started, and look what had happened there! "I am still Georgiana's guardian," he said icily, "And I would prefer to discuss these things in advance, rather than after the fact."

Theo set down his fork with unusual care. "Indeed, you are her guardian—or her gaoler, depending upon how you look at it."

"Do not be ridiculous!"

"Ridiculous? Tell me, O Great Guardian, what sort of book does she like to read?"

Darcy huffed. What was Theo trying to prove? "Poetry, travelogues, and books about music."

His brother's eyes narrowed. "Gothic mysteries and romances. Which of us is correct, Georgiana?"

Georgiana pushed back her chair and jumped to her feet. "Neither of you." Her voice trembled. "Why do you have to turn everything into a battle? Theo, you are among your family, not in a courtroom. William, why must you speak to Theo as if he is a child who needs discipline? Elizabeth would be ashamed of both of you."

Elizabeth. The one accusation that could stop Darcy in his tracks. What would she wish him to do? He cleared his throat. "I assume this visit happened before our recent reconciliation. Perhaps in the future we could discuss such matters together."

The corner of Theo's mouth twitched. "It is England's loss that you cannot become a judge, Georgie. Very well, William; I will keep you apprised of any plans concerning Georgiana."

"I thank you," Darcy said heavily. Why must this be so difficult?

"In the spirit of this new agreement, you should be aware I intend to continue supplying our sister with novels you may think beneath her, as well as discussing my cases with her when she wishes, and offering my sympathy to her on how painful it can be to know your beloved elder brother would disapprove of you if he were aware of what you were doing." More gently, he added, "It can be very difficult to live up to your standards, William."

Unexpectedly, Georgiana giggled. "Elizabeth says even he cannot live up to his own standards."

Darcy tugged at his cravat. "There is a certain amount of truth to that." Was Georgiana truly frightened to admit her interests to him? What did she think he would do to her?

Then he realized the truth. The answer was sitting at his table. Georgiana thought he would reject her as he had rejected Theo for so many years. Somehow he must make her understand that would never happen. "Georgiana, I would be happy to escort you to observe the courtroom proceedings. Perhaps we can find a day when Theo will be arguing a case, so you can see what a fine barrister he has become."

Georgiana's eyes grew wide, then she jumped up from her chair to throw her arms around him. "Thank you, William," she said, her voice trembling. "That would mean a great deal to me."

With a lazy grin, Theo said, "Let us be careful to select a day when I am arguing a case I have at least some hope of winning! I would not care to disappoint both of you at once."

His sister's face lit up. "But you have a chance of winning every case, so we might as well go to the first one. When would that be?"

Theo's grin faded. "On the contrary. There are cases I cannot win because someone has paid the witnesses to testify against my client. And others where my client did in fact commit the crime, but it is my job to defend him to the best of my ability. It is hardly a victory when my efforts mean a guilty man goes free. The worst cases are those where the defendant is found to be innocent, as indeed he is, but merely having been taken to prison and then to court is enough to soil his reputation forever, or the slow pace of justice means his business has gone bankrupt and his family hungry in the meantime. I may succeed in keeping him from being transported or hung, but I cannot give him his old life back. There are some cases where no one wins."

Darcy met his brother's eyes, and knew they were both thinking of a particular case no one had won. George Wickham had fooled them all once more. As soon as he had hope of a future outside prison or transportation, his strength had begun to return, and the surgeon who had taken his arm now said it was more likely than not he would survive long enough to make his new wife regret her hasty marriage to a man with one arm and a visage scarred enough to scare children. Wickham might be free and in England, but he would never be able to employ his charm again, nor would he ever gain the riches he longed for. Instead, Mr. and Mrs. Wickham would be forced to live in seclusion on whatever allowance her family allowed them, an outcome none of them could take pride in. No doubt Darcy would end up settling some sort of income on them simply to ease Elizabeth's worries about her sister.

That raised another question, one which might be safer discussed in front of Georgiana rather than alone, where he and Theo might fall to quarreling again. He had not yet addressed that cold letter Theo had sent him at Rosings

352

telling him to stop sending his allowance. "Very true. Sometimes no one wins. And speaking of your practice, Theo, while I am pleased to know it is thriving, there is no reason to stop your allowance from Pemberley. Our father set it up with the expectation it would continue throughout your life."

"No doubt he thought I might need it! But as it is, I am earning enough money to provide for my needs. I have been for some time, in fact, and have only kept accepting the allowance because of a debt I needed to pay."

No doubt he had many debts from his wilder days. Darcy caught himself before that thought went any further. He was not supposed to condemn Theo out of hand, but look for the good in him. At least he believed in paying off his debts. That was something. "Should you require assistance in paying your debts, I hope you will apply to me."

"I appreciate your generosity, but there is no need. The debt is paid now."

"Theo." Georgiana's soft voice interrupted.

"Yes?"

"Perhaps you should tell William about your debt, lest he misunderstand the reasons for it."

Devil take it, why did Georgiana know so much more than he did about Theo's life? "Theo's private affairs are his own business."

"Not always." Georgiana's direct gaze was on Theo.

"Chief Justice Georgiana Darcy, at the very least," said Theo with a rueful smile. "Since she insists, I will explain, but I would appreciate it if you would withhold any commentary on my actions. I am well aware there were flaws in my reasoning."

Good God, what sort of trouble had Theo got himself into? "I will do my best."

"After Wickham left Ramsgate, Georgiana discovered her ring and the diamond necklace our mother had left her were missing. On a hunch, I visited a pawn shop I knew

Wickham had employed in the past. I found them there and purchased them back. That is why I was in debt. The necklace is valuable."

"That was the theft you charged him with? I thought it was a ring of yours."

"I saw no harm in allowing everyone to make that assumption, and it was simpler that way."

Darcy could hardly fault his brother for attempting to keep Georgiana's name out of a criminal charge. "I am glad you did so. But as I said, the allowance is still yours. You may not need it now, but someday you may wish to marry and purchase a home of your own."

"William, just because you cannot get to the altar soon enough does not mean I am longing to be leg-shackled! Keep the money in the Pemberley coffers. I can take care of myself." His voice was distinctly cool now.

What had he done now to anger Theo? Was it wrong to be generous to his younger brother? Bewildered, he said, "I did not mean to offend you."

Theo blew out a long breath. "No, I am sure you did not. I appreciate you are trying to help, William, but I do not wish to be your financial dependent."

"But it is not my money. Our father bequeathed the allowance to you in his Will. I owe it to you."

"It comes down to the same thing." Theo turned to Georgiana. "Chief Justice Georgiana, perhaps you can explain this better than I to our stubborn brother."

Georgiana glared at him. "As if you could not do it yourself! William, taking the allowance places Theo in your debt. Even if it was originally from our father, you are giving Theo money, and he cannot give you anything in return. You would not like to be in that position, either."

"I suppose not." But devil take it, he was supposed to take care of his younger brother! Why did Theo have to be so stubborn? "Very well."

"Of course," Georgiana continued thoughtfully, "There is nothing to stop you from setting aside the money you would be paying him, and if someday Theo wants to avail himself of his inheritance, you can give it to him then, rather than doling it out to him over the years."

Now that was a sensible solution! "An excellent thought. I will do that."

Georgiana smiled apologetically at Theo. "A good judge must be impartial, you know," she said.

He laughed. "That will teach me why we should keep knowledge of the law from young ladies! You will make some fortunate gentleman a formidable wife someday, Georgiana."

"Only if he permits me to visit the Courts," she said. "And now, Theo, you no longer have an excuse when I want to bring home one of your law books to read."

Theo lifted his wineglass to her with a smile. "No one can ever say obstinacy does not run in our family!"

Darcy could certainly drink to that.

A few nights after the family dinner, Theo met Monty at their club for a drink. He was drained from all the turmoil of the past few weeks and looking forward to a quick drink and an early night. The recent nuptials between Wickham and Lydia Bennet—now Mrs. Wickham—had been especially difficult for him. In spite of Lydia's stubbornness, Theo almost felt sorry for the girl. What kind of future would she have tied to a dishonest rake like George Wickham?

It could not have been the wedding of her dreams. There had been no wedding breakfast or celebration, and the consummation had occurred before the ceremony instead of after. He doubted Lydia would even let her new husband anywhere near her, as her disgust for his condition could not have been more clear. He assumed she had gone to stay with the Gardiners.

"How was that cozy little family dinner you were dreading?" Monty lowered himself into the leather chair next to him, his long legs stretched out before him. His broad muscular frame never quite fitted the club chairs.

Theo smiled. "I was surprised how much I enjoyed it."

"Your little sister is turning into a lovely young lady. When will she be making her come out?"

Theo gave his friend a sideways glance at the reference to Georgiana and saw Monty's eyes were twinkling with mischief. Instead of reacting as his friend had clearly hoped he would, Theo said, "Of course, I always love time with my sister, but it was good to be with William, too."

"Theo, I am truly shocked!" Monty said in a mocking voice. "Are you feeling well? Developing a fever perhaps?"

"Be serious for a moment. If you are able, that is. My brother is making an effort to be more agreeable. Elizabeth has had an astonishing effect on him."

Monty raised a questioning brow. "The man formerly known as Prince William? Agreeable? I will own I found him civil enough when we finally met, but this is a stretch from your usual assessment of him as a proud, stiff-necked fellow!"

"You would not believe the changes in him. And by the way, I have made a vow not to call him that anymore so I would appreciate it if you would desist also."

"What sort of changes are we talking about?" Someone caught Monty's attention across the room, and he raised a hand in greeting just before the young man disappeared into the card room.

Theo waited until Monty's attention was back on him before responding. "Well, for one thing, he is trying very hard not to order every one about as he has always done."

"A complete reformation then!"

"Hardly that, but I do give him credit for trying. It is as if now he is thinking about having a family of his own, the one he has is even more important to him," Theo said.

"I have never seen anyone so besotted with a woman as he is over Miss Elizabeth Bennet." Monty swirled the brandy around in his glass. "But then she is a beautiful and charming creature."

"Do you know he spent an entire day going from one jeweler to another looking for just the right wedding gift for her?"

"An entire day?" Monty looked incredulous.

Theo massaged his temple. "He asked me to go along, and I foolishly agreed thinking it would give us some time together. I thought trying cases was exhausting! Let me tell you, court is nothing compared to traipsing around after my brother when he is in search of something. He is relentless and very particular!"

Monty laughed. "So have your brother and the lady set a date yet for their wedding?"

"I am not certain. They are discussing a double wedding with Bingley and Elizabeth's sister Jane." Just the thought of another wedding was enough to make Theo groan, and he reached for his glass again.

"Good heavens. A double wedding? You told me there were five girls in the Bennet family? Are they all as pretty as the ones I have met?"

"I do not believe you! What are you doing even looking at them? The ones you have met are either married or soon to be married," Theo exclaimed.

"You must admit that, though Mrs. Wickham is a bit empty headed, she is quite a treat for the eyes," Monty responded, waggling his brows.

"Good Lord! You noticed something like that?"

"You know me. I never could turn away from a pretty face with a sweet little pout or a tempting…"

"Stop! Please stop! I will never be able to look that poor girl in the eye again. Maybe you should have married her instead of Wickham."

Monty snorted and plunged on. "So do tell. What about the other two sisters?"

"I have not met them all, but my brother tells me Mary is very serious and reads sermons all the time. Kitty is apparently attractive enough but not much better behaved than Lydia," Theo responded.

They sipped their brandy in silence for a few minutes listening to the reassuring, familiar sounds around them in the room. The clink of glasses, an occasional outburst of laughter, the crackle of the fire, and the snap of cards being dealt in the next room.

"So now your brother is getting leg-shackled, you cannot be far behind."

"Me? Marry? My dear man, you are out of your mind! You are the one who must marry to carry on your family title, but fortunately, I am under no such obligation. I do not believe I shall ever marry." Theo took another sip of the warm amber liquid.

"So you say now!" Monty told him. "Mark my words. Some young lady will turn your head and all your protests will be forgotten."

"I am looking forward to our evening at Vauxhall," Theo said. "Who will be in attendance?"

"Very well, we shall change the subject, as I can see any talk of marriage makes you uncomfortable."

Normally Theo loved it when Monty laughed. It was a deep, rolling sound that seemed to set the entire room to vibrating. Tonight, he was finding his friend very irritating. "So what about Vauxhall?"

Monty finally stopped laughing and rattled off the list of the invited guests.

"That sounds like a very agreeable group. I am looking forward to it."

"Theo, I warn you! Whatever you do, do not invite your cousin, Miss de Bourgh."

Theo looked at his friend solemnly. "I would not think of it! Even though I love my cousin, I know she has much to learn before she is ready to attend an event like this. Honestly, I will be relieved to have some time away from her. She was about ready to invite herself to our family dinner the other night, but we were able to head her off. In the end, she only returned to Darcy House this morning."

Monty lifted his glass to Theo. "Here is to getting away from annoying cousins!"

Theo sat up and leaned close enough for them to touch glasses. "Here is to an entertaining evening."

The day they were to go to Vauxhall the weather held, which meant Theo and Monty could make use of the curricle. The whole party had agreed to set out from Darcy House together, with Mrs. and Mr. Gardiner chaperoning the young ladies in separate carriages. As it turned out, the young gentlemen were the first to arrive. Theo left his friend to lord it over everyone from the high perch of his curricle and, taking the steps two at a time, ascended to the front door and beat a rhythm on it with the knocker. The door opened almost at once.

Georgiana threw her arms around him.

"You look very pretty," he said, and she did, with her hair done up into ringlets under a pretty blue bonnet that matched her eyes.

Then, Anne appeared at top of the stairway, clearly dressed for an evening out.

"Do not tell me Anne is coming with us?" he said in a fierce whisper to Georgiana. "She was not even invited."

"I heard that," said Anne, sternly. "Georgiana has already raised some objections, but I assured her there would not be a problem. I have met Sir Montgomery and we took to each other exceedingly well. I am sure he will be delighted to find I am joining the party. In fact, I rather think it will be a pleasant surprise."

Sometimes, thought Theo, *Monty was too polite for his own good.* He had clearly left Anne with the wrong impression. Theo could not correct this, of course, but he was obliged to do what he could to dissuade Anne from coming.

"I would advise against it, Anne," he said as firmly as he could. "You cannot invite yourself. It is simply not done. Besides, Sir Montgomery has only bespoke nine places for tonight. It will be quite impossible to request an extra setting at the last minute."

Anne waved his objections away.

"Pooh! As to that, I am certain we can grease some-one's palm for an extra setting, Theo. I am as rich as Croesus. Now that we have sorted out the terms of Papa's Will—thanks to you—I find I am very well endowed."

Theo sputtered. Georgiana turned pink.

"Perhaps well-endowed is not quite the right word, Cousin?" ventured Theo. "It has certain—connotations."

He refrained from mentioning that greasing someone's palm was not a phrase delicate females were accustomed to using, either.

"Nonsense," said Anne. "*You* comprehended my meaning, did you not, Georgiana?"

"Yes— however, I do believe Theo is right," said Georgiana, rather timidly.

Anne turned an unsmiling gaze on Georgiana and looked about to object, but apparently relented. "Very well, I will avoid the phrase."

"Shall we wait in the drawing room?" said Theo, "that way we can spot the others when they arrive."

They did not have to wait long. Theo had no sooner taken up a place near the window when two carriages drew up to Darcy House—the Gardiners' landau and Darcy's barouche.

"Ah," said Theo, relieved, looking out of the window. "Here comes Darcy with the rest."

Theo felt like a traitor as he accompanied his sister and cousin to where Monty stood waiting next to his curricle. The polite expression on Monty's face turned to an accusation as he spotted Anne. He controlled it, however, as he greeted Anne and Georgiana, bowing and greeting them with perfect civility.

"Is that your curricle, Sir Montgomery? It is quite dashing. I shall go in the curricle," announced Anne.

Theo only just managed to conceal his dismay. It was

bad enough imposing Anne on his friend, but to oblige him to have her next to him all the way would be certain to try the patience of a saint, and Monty was no saint.

"I will need all my wits about me to negotiate the crush outside Vauxhall Gardens," said Monty, "so I would prefer not to have the distraction of a young lady next to me. However," he added, seeing a stubborn look settle on her face, "I would be delighted to drive you in Hyde Park one day next week."

"Very well," conceded Anne. "I will hold you to your promise."

"I thought I told you not to invite her," he growled once everyone was settled in the other two carriages and Theo swung up to the seat beside him.

"I could as soon stop her as prevent a thunderstorm from happening."

A glum mood seemed to have settled over Monty as he drove off in silence, saying no more. Theo felt a qualm of conscience. He should have made more of an effort to stop Anne from coming, but he had not really insisted because part of him felt sorry for her. He would never forget the transformation that had occurred at Rosings as Anne had slowly emerged from the medicine-induced haze she had suffered all those years. He did not have the heart to deprive her of the pleasure of tonight's outing.

However, that did not mean he had to saddle his friend with her.

"I am sorry, Monty," said Theo, contritely. "I should have tried harder to stop her. I did not mean to destroy your night's pleasure."

"Pray continue to grovel, Theo," said Monty, his lips curling as he drove the curricle skillfully through a narrow space between two fruit carts. "It does not undo the damage, but I am deriving some amusement from it."

Theo's contrition evaporated instantly. "If you are looking for amusement, then do not expect me to provide it. You must wait until we are at Vauxhall. Though I still do not understand what possessed you to invite my family."

"It was a fit of generosity that I am rapidly coming to regret."

"I am perfectly serious, Monty."

"I was hoping to spend the evening flirting agreeably with your sister."

"You know very well, Monty, that my sister is off-bounds."

"There is no harm in a little light flirtation, is there? Do not tell me you have taken on your brother's role now and are turning into a Prince Theophilus? I never thought I would see the day."

"You are not going to provoke me, Monty, so do not even try. I am determined to let nothing mar the pleasure of this evening, particularly since you are to foot the bill."

"I cannot believe we are truly at Vauxhall," said Georgiana. "I have heard so much said about it that it is like a dream come true."

"I hope you find it lives up to its reputation," said Monty, smiling at Georgiana's palpable excitement as they paid their three-and-sixpence to enter.

"I am sure it will," she said. "It is so kind of Fitzwilliam to allow me to attend, even though I am not yet officially out."

"It is very generous indeed of your guardian," said Mrs. Gardiner, giving Darcy a warm smile even though he was standing too far away to hear their conversation. It was obvious that Darcy had rapidly become a favorite of hers.

Oh, so now it is Darcy who is receiving the credit for this, then? Considering how long it had taken Theo to convince Darcy that it would be unfair to exclude Georgiana from the invitation, he thought she could at least have thanked him too.

Still, seeing her enjoyment was reward enough.

They were greeted by a troop of acrobats performing circus acts and juggling. Anne watched for a few minutes, then stopped the jugglers and requested them to teach her how to juggle. Amiably surprised, they were happy to oblige. Not for long, however. It soon became clear that she would not be leaving until she became a competent juggler, whereupon they became far less inclined to be complimentary and more inclined to grumble. Theo was obliged to slip them a coin to appease then. However, nothing the other members of the group said could drag Anne away until Monty, employing his legendary powers of persuasion, described far more appealing sights they were yet to encounter, and managed to intrigue Anne enough to forget the jugglers.

It was a warm dry evening and the Gardens were crowded. Darcy, who was uncomfortable with the good natured jostling and press of people, was anxious to reach the relative privacy of the supper boxes, but there was no making fast progress, even if Anne were not with them, hindering their progress. Theo was stopped and greeted by several barrister friends and by a client he had defended. Monty seemed to know a prodigious number of handsome ladies who all wanted to talk to him on one pretext or the other. Darcy's expression, meanwhile, was growing increasingly constricted.

Sensing Darcy's discomfort, Monty offered to take Darcy, Elizabeth, Bingley and Jane through a shortcut behind the buildings straight to the pavilion, allowing the rest of the party to proceed at a more leisurely pace.

"I am not certain that it is quite proper to split the party," said Mrs. Gardiner. "After all, Mr. Gardiner and I are here to serve as chaperones."

"Let them go, my dear," said Mr. Gardiner. "There is no cause for alarm. Your nieces are with their fiancés, after all. And with so many people always promenading to and fro in front of the boxes, there can be no suggestion of impropriety. You will have your chance to put your eagle eye to good use later, when we are strolling amongst the trees. Besides, I cannot imagine Mr. Darcy conducting himself in anything but the most exemplary manner. I am sure Sir Monty will be happy to replace us as chaperone, will you not?"

Theo had to refrain from laughing at the idea of Sir Monty playing nursemaid to Darcy.

"Shall I don a matron's cap?" said Monty. "I wonder if it would suit me?"

"You, sir, would look far better in a bonnet, with a large peacock feather as trimming," said Elizabeth, laughing.

"You flatter me, Miss Elizabeth," he said, with a grin, "but I do agree that it would complement my green eyes."

Darcy was looking restless. Theo wondered how it was that his brother was so different from him. Theo thrived in the midst of crowds or in the center of the public eye, while Darcy avoided them whenever he could.

"Enough nonsense, Monty," said Theo. "Just go. My brother is impatient to be seated."

Mrs. Gardiner watched them uneasily as they walked away. "Oh, dear, perhaps I should go with them."

"I wish you to stay with me, Mrs. Gardiner," said her husband, drawing her arm through his and patting it. "We will take our time exploring the place. We do not come here every day, after all—it has been a long time since our last visit."

When they arrived some time later at the dinner box, however, Mrs. Gardiner's fears were confirmed. They found the two couples seated alone in the box, while Monty was leaning negligently against the entrance of another box some way down, engaged in conversation with a handsome lady in tall ostrich feathers.

He took his leave from the young lady as soon as he saw the group and came over.

"I hope you have enjoyed the garden so far, Miss de Bourgh, Miss Darcy?"

"Oh, yes," explained Georgiana. "The vaulted colonnade seemed to go on forever, and I loved the flowers and lanterns hanging from the trees. I cannot wait for dark to fall so we can see the lights."

"I was splashed by one of the fountains," said Anne. "It took me by surprise."

"Mrs. Gardiner, how about you? Did you enjoy the sights?" said Monty, smiling engagingly at her.

"I did," replied Mrs. Gardiner. "However, you will not charm me into forgetting that you abandoned your post."

"Have I let you down?" said Monty, "I beg your pardon most humbly. Tell me what I must do to earn your forgiveness, and I will perform it devotedly, madam."

At his hang-dog expression Mrs. Gardiner could not help laughing. "It would be ungrateful of me to be unfriendly to my host," said Mrs. Gardiner. "So I suppose you must be forgiven."

"You are a cunning young puppy," remarked Mr. Gardiner. "You must give me lessons on how to avoid being in Mrs. Gardiner's bad books."

At that point, the arrack punch arrived and the group took their seats in the box. As soon as it had been served, Elizabeth tapped on the edge of her glass with a fork.

She waited until she had everyone's attention.

"I know this is unconventional for a lady, but since we are mostly family here, I will not hold back. I would like to propose a toast. If everybody could stand up, please," said Elizabeth. She raised her glass. "To my brother Theophilus Darcy, the hero of the day! We owe you an enormous debt of gratitude."

"Hear, hear!" came the responses.

"To Theophilus Darcy!"

Theo looked over to where Darcy was sitting, wondering how that had gone down with him. He sincerely hoped there would be no jealous misunderstanding of Elizabeth's gesture. He knew Darcy had been convinced for a long time that Elizabeth harbored some feelings for Theo.

There was no danger of that. Darcy was smiling, a be-sotted look on his face. No one who saw him now would think he had for a long time held the title of Prince William. *She is very good for him*, Theo thought. Darcy's gaze shifted and met his. Then Darcy did something unprecedented. He winked.

Theo almost dropped his glass in astonishment. He did not remember the last time he had seen his brother make such a gesture. Monty winked often enough, but Darcy?

"And to Sir Montgomery Preston," added Elizabeth, "Who, as I understand it, put his boxing skills to good use by apprehending Wickham when he tried to get away."

General laughter followed.

"To Sir Monty," said Anne, loudly, after the others had already sat down and put down their glasses. She gulped down a mouthful and promptly choked on it.

There was some good-natured laughter at her reaction, then the waiters arrived with the food and everyone's attention was distracted as Georgiana exclaimed at the famed wafer-thin ham and wondered how they were able to cut it that way.

Monty, who was next to Anne, was forced to minister to her by walloping her on the back.

"This drink is remarkable," she said, her eyes taking on a marked shine. "I like it. Far better than the swill mother used to douse me with."

"It is not exactly medicinal," said Monty. "The arrack punch here has a reputation for potency. It is made from the best ingredients."

Anne turned to give Monty her full attention. "You know," said Anne, staring at Monty's cravat. "I do wish you would let me tie that cravat for you. There is something not quite right about it."

She reached for the cravat. Theo observed his friend's discomfort in amusement and waited to see what would happen. Monty was rarely at a loss for words when it came to the ladies, but he was clearly thrown off guard by Anne.

"My dear Miss de Bourgh," said Monty, in a drawl. "I am quite accustomed to having ladies take off my cravat, but not generally in public. If you insist on doing so, may I suggest we go somewhere else?"

Anne blinked, thinking this over. It was impossible to know what was going on in his cousin's mind. Did she understand Monty's insinuation?

"I knew it," she said with a satisfied nod. "I am *not* the only lady who objects to your knot. Never underestimate what a lady has to say when it comes to fashion. I believe the fair sex has a decided advantage over men when it comes to these matters."

Monty, who was unwisely taking a sip of his arrack, promptly choked on it. It was now Anne's turn to thump him on the back, which she did rather more vigorously than was necessary.

"I see that you, too, find the arrack punch much stronger than expected." She gave him a kindly smile. "I have discovered that sipping it more slowly makes it much more agreeable. I would advise you to do the same."

Theo could not help laughing. "Really, Anne, you cannot expect to give Monty any useful advice about drinking. I am sure he must have been drinking alcohol at his mother's apron strings, for in all my years of knowing him, I have never seen him truly foxed. He is quite a wonder. Every gentleman I know has succumbed to the bottle, one way or the other, but not Monty."

Monty was about to reply, but Anne interrupted. "I have worked out what is wrong with that cravat. I do not understand why you object to having it corrected. You will look a great deal less unkempt if only you would listen to sense."

Unkempt? Monty? Theo gave a bark of laughter. This was really too much, particularly when Monty prided himself on the exquisite tailoring of his clothes and impeccable taste.

"You cannot let my cousin get away with that, surely,

Monty. That is a low blow indeed."

Under the table, Monty gave him a kick to the shin. Theo bit down an exclamation.

"I am sorry that my tie disagrees with you, Miss de Bourgh," said Monty, with the carefully polite tone of someone rapidly losing patience. "I would not wish to have you suffer any further. Since you are quite the expert at tying gentleman's cravats, I would be happy to succumb to your tender ministrations. You may make any corrections you deem fit." At this, Monty bowed and offered his neck up to Anne with an eloquent gesture of the hand.

Theo waited for Anne's reaction. Monty had issued a challenge, expecting Anne to retreat. He did not know Anne.

Anne's eyes flashed. "Very well," said Lady Catherine's indomitable daughter, promptly reaching for the guilty cravat and unraveling it.

Theo grinned at Monty's shocked expression.

From across the table, Darcy frowned at Theo in disapproval.

Theo raised his brow and wagged his eyebrows.

"What do you expect me to do?" he mouthed.

"Stop her," mouthed Darcy back.

Considering that Darcy had turned tail and ran when faced with the harpies at Rosings, it was rather much for him to expect Theo to control Anne.

"How do you find the food, Anne?" said Darcy loudly, in a misguided attempt to distract her.

"I am busy with something else, Darcy, as you might have noticed if you bothered to look. I have not yet had the opportunity to try the food."

Elizabeth laughed. "Your cousin certainly does not mince her words!"

Anne's fingers twisted and turned the cravat in different directions. Monty, stuck in an awkward position with his neck bent backwards to avoid contact with Anne's fingernails, gave a beseeching look to Theo.

Theo ignored it cheerfully.

"Help!" yelped Monty, still hoping for rescue.

"I have no intention of helping," said Theo, "I know now there is justice in the world. After all the times you outsmarted me with the ladies, I am enjoying every moment of your discomfort."

"I wish you would stop talking, Theo," said Anne in a quelling tone. "You are distracting me."

"I beg your pardon, Cousin Anne," said Theo, with mock humility. "I will endeavor to keep as silent as a mouse."

Finally, Anne appeared to be satisfied. She leaned back to survey the results.

"That will do," she said. "Much better."

Theo peered at the knot she had tied, preparing to tease his friend mercilessly about it, but to his astonishment the cravat was tied in what was called a Waterfall, and it was a definite improvement over Monty's original.

"Well, Cousin, I do believe you have outdone yourself. Where did you learn to do this?"

It would not have surprised him at this point to hear that Anne had been leading a double life.

"I have had little to do over the years but pore over the fashion plates. I have memorized every detail of men's as well as ladies' fashion."

Monty looked at himself in one of the booth's reflecting mirrors and gave an exclamation.

"Good heavens!" he exclaimed. "A perfect knot!"

It was absurd to think that Anne of all people could best Monty at tying his own cravat. Discovering this unknown side of his cousin only served to emphasize that they had done something remarkable when they had weaned their cousin off that terrible medicine. Something else to thank Elizabeth Bennet for. If she had not come to Rosings, that might never have happened.

He looked at his friend's astonished expression in the mirror and began to laugh. Monty, catching his eye, began to laugh, too, and then Anne threw back her head and embarked on a strange kind of neighing laugh, which only served to set off Theo again.

Darcy frowned. What the devil were those young whelps up to, encouraging Anne to behave so badly in public? She was making a proper spectacle of herself and Theo was doing nothing to prevent it. He had always known Monty was a bad influence on his brother and it was more than obvious now.

"William," said Elizabeth gently, taking hold of his hand under the table. "You need not scowl so horribly, you know. Remember, you have forgiven Theo his past sins and Anne is enjoying herself, probably for the first time in her life. You would not wish to deprive her of that, would you?"

Darcy heard what she said as if from far away. Her thumb was stroking his palm in such a deliciously sensual manner that he was having difficulty staying still. The stroking sent shivers of anticipation through his body and he found his gaze drawn to her smiling lips.

"I believe you wished to say something to me, Darcy?" remarked Anne, breaking into his trance.

Darcy dropped Elizabeth's hand like a hot potato and struggled to draw himself back to the present. For the life of him, he could not recall what he had wanted to say.

"It was nothing of importance."

"Do you know when the orchestra will strike up?" asked Georgiana. "I really do not want to miss anything."

"They start promptly at eight o'clock," said Mrs. Gardiner.

Elizabeth's fingers crept over Darcy's hand and caught it again. Her eyes were full of mischief.

So she was playing the seductress, was she? He would show her what that meant—soon enough. The wedding day could not come too soon for him.

Darcy tried to slowly pull his hand away. The next course would be arriving soon, and he would need both hands to grasp the knife and fork. Everyone would notice.

He gave another gentle tug. Elizabeth held on fast.

"Though we will hear the orchestra from here," said Anne, "I do not intend to listen to the whole performance. There are far too many other things I would like to see."

"You have been here before, then, Miss de Bourgh?" asked Monty.

"Yes, Mama brought me here once, but I do not remember anything distinctly. Only the lights sparkling and swaying and being obliged to sit and listen to the orchestra for what seemed like hours before Mama whisked me away, saying I was growing tired, before I had any opportunity to discover the gardens."

"I cannot imagine anyone whisking you away if you did not wish it, Miss de Bourgh," said Monty.

Theo elbowed Monty. "It is a rather sensitive subject. Kindly do not set her off."

Fortunately, Jane spoke before Anne had the opportunity to respond.

"This is such a beautiful place. Now that darkness is falling, the colored lamps are so magical." She sighed wishfully. "I cannot help but wish that Lydia could have been here to see them. She would have enjoyed the sight so much."

Elizabeth's hand withdrew quickly. This was not a conversation anyone wished to have at this moment in time.

"She could hardly have come here, Jane, under the circumstances," said Elizabeth, mildly. "Her husband is by no means fully recovered. With a severed arm, anything could happen. Infection could still set in. He is lucky to have escaped with his life."

"I cannot help wishing it could have been otherwise," Jane sighed. "Poor Lydia. She has taken the news of Wickham's injury badly."

"She would have been a great deal worse if he had been

deported," said Elizabeth. She was not quite as forgiving in nature as Jane.

Across the table, Theo had stiffened. Darcy felt a wave of sympathy for him as he noticed the dark shadows under his brother's eyes. Theo had taken this whole affair very badly. He did not need to be reminded at this moment of anything to do with this whole debacle.

Darcy spoke up, seeking to divert attention from the subject. "I have heard that you see the good in everyone, Jane, which is a very agreeable quality," said Darcy. "It must account for the reason you were willing to overlook all the faults of my friend Bingley here and agree to marry him."

"Oh, I say, Darcy!" said Bingley. "I protest. Although I do agree that Miss Bennet—Jane—is my superior in so many ways, I do think I have one or two positive things in my favor."

Jane blushed and lowered her eyes. "I must protest as well, Mr. Darcy," she said, shyly. "I find Charles perfect in every way. I cannot think of a single thing I would wish to change in him."

At this declaration, Bingley turned to her, took up her hand and kissed it.

"That is because you are an angel," he said, ardently.

"Enough of this." Anne broke in. "You are forgetting that there are unmarried ladies here." She looked pointedly at Georgiana.

"You need not look at me, Cousin," said Georgiana. "I am not the only unmarried lady here."

Anne looked surprised and everyone laughed.

Monty rose to his feet. "Well, ladies and gentlemen, if you are all finished with the business of eating, perhaps we can take the opportunity to stroll around the garden and discover what entertainments are on offer tonight before the fireworks start."

Darcy was relieved when they finally turned away from the main area where the buildings were housed. The crowds thinned out here, and the semi-darkness gave a sense of privacy away from the bright glow of the burning lamps. They strolled slowly, Elizabeth's arm wrapped around his, tantalizingly close. He drew Elizabeth stealthily a few inches closer, aware that behind them Mr. and Mrs. Gardiner were watching.

Elizabeth giggled softly. "William! I am shocked! Are you not being rather too daring?"

"Not daring enough, my love," whispered Darcy. "I long to take you behind those trees over there and kiss you as that couple in the shadows is doing, but I cannot."

Elizabeth was silent. Darcy's heart sank. Had he spoken out of turn? Had he offended her? Elizabeth was so outspoken he sometimes forgot that she was still an innocent young lady.

"I— would like that, too," she said, in a shy unsteady voice that was very unlike her.

He trembled as he realized there was a note of passion in her voice. His self-control was fast slipping away.

"Would you excuse me a moment, please?" said Darcy. "I need to do something."

He strode over to where Monty and Theo were engaged in an argument over horses. "Theseus is a glorious beast, Monty. Admit it. You know he could outpace Thunder any time."

"Never mind about that vicious beast of yours, Theo. I need your assistance. I need you to divert the Gardiners' attention. I swear I will go insane if I do not have a moment alone with Elizabeth tonight."

Theo whistled. "How the mighty have fallen! I would not wish to be in your shoes, Darcy, for anything, begging for assistance from the like of us."

Monty grinned. "A man consumed by passion is something I understand very well. I will do what I can to help you, Darcy, but what will you give me in return?"

"Knock it off, Preston," said Darcy. "This is no time for levity."

"On the contrary, dear brother," said Theo, "I thought that was exactly what you were after. A moment of "levity" with your betrothed?"

"Perhaps if you will allow me a little harmless flirtation with Georgiana..." remarked Monty.

"No!" said both Darcy brothers together.

"I rest my case," said Monty, spreading out his hands in a helpless gesture. "How can you expect me to risk life and limb to divert the Gardiners when you will give me nothing in return?"

"Just find a way," said Darcy, gritting his teeth against their raillery and striding back to where he had left Elizabeth alone on the path. Bingley gave him a questioning look as he went past.

"Anything the matter, Darcy?"

"Nothing that cannot be put to rights with a bit of determination."

As he took up Elizabeth's arm again, she smiled at him.

"I can see you are up to something."

He smiled back. "You already know me well." He could not believe how lucky he was to have found the one woman in the world who truly understood him. He felt humbled by his good fortune. "I am the luckiest man alive, Elizabeth Bennet. I wish I could find the words to tell you how ardently I have come to love you."

"I am certain you will, by and by," said Elizabeth, laughter brimming in her eyes.

As they reached the viewing area, Elizabeth was jostled by people coming from different directions, all intent on finding a good spot from which to watch the fireworks.

Elizabeth was alarmed to find herself being pulled away. She tucked her reticule tightly under her arm, holding firmly onto the string. She had heard there were sometimes pickpockets in the gardens, intent on robbing the unwary.

Another shove. She held onto Darcy's arm tightly, not wishing to be separated from him. It would be easy to be lost in the crowd.

"Is that the Prince Regent over there?" said a voice loudly behind her. "I believe it is."

The voice sounded familiar, but as Elizabeth tried to place it, someone tugged her again.

Elizabeth turned to confront her assailant and found Monty behind her. He winked at her and signaled silence, then gestured for her to follow.

Confused, she glanced at Darcy. He was looking at Monty and nodding.

There was a narrow walkway lined with trees leading to a fountain and behind it, situated in a secluded alcove, there was a bench.

"Go," said Monty. "I will cover for you."

Before she could say anything, he had slipped away and disappeared into the crowd.

Elizabeth swallowed a nervous impulse to giggle as Darcy led her to the bench and they both sat down.

"I am sorry for the subterfuge," said Darcy. "Who would have thought the Gardiners so obsessed with propriety?"

"After what happened with Lydia—"

"Hush," said Darcy, putting his forefinger to her lips. "I did not contrive to have us alone to discuss Lydia, or anyone else for that matter. Only us."

Elizabeth shivered as his finger moved to trace the outline of her lips. It was exquisite torment to sit there in the darkness, quite still, feeling his touch, wanting desperately for him to move closer, but knowing he needed to do this his way. Her breath quickened and her lips parted of their own avail.

Darcy took a deep shuddering breath as a firework exploded and cascaded into the sky, showering him with orange light. He drew her suddenly into his arms, crushing her against him, his heartbeat quivering alongside hers. His scent enveloped her—a heady mix of shaving soap and something essentially Darcy. He hesitated for one last second, his eyes boring into her with scorching intensity, then his lips came down to hers in a fierce craving that overwhelmed her senses.

She could no longer breathe. The world melted around her and there was just him, his body trembling against hers, his mouth roving over her face then back to her lips. Her hands went out to touch him on the face, to sink her fingers into his silken hair, to feel the masculine breadth of his shoulders and back—shyly at first, then more confidently as she lost herself in the sensations awakening inside her.

"Elizabeth, my love." She hardly recognized his voice as he murmured endearments to her in a hoarse voice. "I have waited so long for this. I never imagined I could feel this way for any woman."

A particularly large explosion sounded close by. Darcy drew back, startled. Taking a deep breath, he reluctantly pushed her away from him.

He ran a shaking hand through his hair.

"Oh, Elizabeth! What have you done to me? To make me forget myself in a public area when anyone could stumble against us? You have bewitched me, body and soul."

She took his trembling hand and held it against her cheek. "I love you, William Darcy," she said, and at the leap of pure joy in his eyes, she repeated it again. "I love you. You have made me the happiest woman alive."

For a long moment, they looked into each other's eyes. Then Darcy bent forward and planted a gentle kiss on her lips—a soft petal touch that reached into her and plucked at her heartstrings, one at a time, playing the most beautiful melody in the universe, so beautiful she thought she would shatter.

She had never dreamed she could have felt anything like this.

She gazed at him in wonder.

They belonged together. They had always belonged together, only she had not known it. And to think she had almost let him go!

"We have to go," murmured Darcy, his eyes promising more, much more.

As if one, they stood up together in unison, hands clasped together, a hundred tiny lights dancing across their faces, and went in search of the others.

"So tell me again, why am I along on this trip?" Theo stretched his long legs across the floorboards of the coach until his feet were not quite touching his brother's boots.

Darcy grunted and shifted in his seat until his feet were free once more.

"I asked you a question, Brother dear."

"Apparently you are here to punish me by making this trip as unpleasant as possible."

Theo grinned and tapped his boot against Darcy's.

Darcy kicked back. "There is plenty of room in this coach without you crowding me."

Theo chuckled. "So touchy. One might think you were anxious about something." He tapped Darcy's boot again.

"It is not every day that one is on his way to be married."

"I suppose that is true enough." Theo pulled his feet back and crossed his arms.

Not so very long ago, he would never have done that. They would have ended their exchange in a huff of prickled feelings and tart words. How very much had changed since then.

Theo slid down in the seat and parked his feet on the squabs beside Darcy.

He swept Theo's feet off. Boot heels thudded on the floor boards. But some things would not change. Perhaps that was for the best. Theo would not be Theo without a bit of mischief in him. Darcy chuckled.

"What are you laughing at? A man about to be noosed has little to laugh at, or do you take lightly tying a knot with your tongue you cannot untie with your teeth." Theo snorted.

"I do not take it lightly at all." Darcy ran his knuckles along his jaw. "Particularly when I consider how easily none of this might have ever been."

"You are truly and utterly besotted, Brother. I never thought to see you in such a condition."

"I confess, I did not either. But I cannot repine for it." Darcy looked directly into Theo's eyes. "Or anything that has come as a result.

Theo scratched his head. "It is rather remarkable, is it not? Whilst it was uncomfortable, I never truly appreciated how…"

"Ill-suited?"

"Yes, that will do. Ill-suited our family situation was. I believe our mother would be very pleased were she with us today."

Darcy glanced out the side glass. The church was barely visible in the distance. "You are right. I think she would have liked Elizabeth."

"No doubt, she would. You are a fortunate man, to have found a woman—"

"Willing to put up with my disagreeable and taciturn nature?" Darcy laughed. "I do not deceive myself. I will never be truly agreeable like you and Bingley." *Was it wrong to so enjoy Theo's look of astonishment?*

"Perhaps not. But she has smoothed many of your rough edges and made you far more tolerable."

"Tolerable enough?"

"I suppose."

"But not enough to tempt one for more than brief spells in company?" Darcy's brows twitched.

"Georgiana and I have noticed. It is a good thing." Theo leaned his head back. "Georgiana will be receiving suitors before either of us is ready for it."

Darcy huffed. "I do not care to think about it. I am merely thankful that I will have Elizabeth by my side when that happens."

"I believe Georgiana is even more pleased by that."

"What of you?"

"What do you mean? I have a promising career before me, a bevy of good friends…"

"A wife, Theo, what of that?" Darcy steepled his fingers in front of his chest.

Theo coughed. "What need have I for a wife? My housekeeper is efficient and without one I need not worry about hosting company, only enjoying the hospitality of others. I have companionship enough and should I desire—"

"I do not need to know."

"Perhaps not."

"Still, I think you are in need of a wife yourself."

Theo jerked upright. "Do not even think it. What is more, do not mention the possibility to Elizabeth."

"I have no need; she has already mentioned it herself. She has already identified several ready candidates."

"I have no interest—"

"Anne for example."

"I would sooner shoot myself—wait, I would shoot you first, then myself. And surely, Elizabeth would not approve of that outcome."

Darcy fought to keep a straight face. So this is what Theo found so amusing for all those years. No wonder his steadfast persistence in the sport. *A man reaps as he sows, does he not?* "Your friend, Sir Monty, has several sisters does he not?"

"I have no interest in Monty's sisters. They are…not suitable."

"Do not forget, Fitzwilliam's sister."

"She is only slightly less dreadful a prospect than Anne."

Oh this was too rich! Darcy forced his smile back. "But she is very proper."

"Indeed she is that. I hardly consider myself proper enough for her and she would happily make me aware of that every moment of my life. No, I do not need a woman bent on reshaping me into her image of a husband."

"It is not so very bad a thing..." Darcy's brow's flashed up.

"For one as flawed as yourself, I would have to agree. But I am quite content with who and what I am. There is no need for a woman to come in and improve upon what I already consider—"

"Perfect?"

"Hardly. Satisfactory, I consider it satisfactory." Theo ran a finger along the inside of his collar.

"As would I."

Theo stared. "I am not sure I will ever get used to that. I might even come to miss grouchy old 'Prince William'."

"Do not ever tell Elizabeth you called me that."

Theo snorted. "Ah-ha!"

"Or I shall unleash *her mother's* matchmaking proclivities upon you."

Eyes bulging, Theo threw up his hands. "You have my word."

"I thought that enough to convince you."

"Indeed. We are nearly there, you know. In just a few minutes, nothing will ever be the same again."

Darcy swallowed hard. "A daunting thought; but I have no doubts. This is one change I can embrace wholeheartedly."

"And I am sure you will." He winked

What could he do but reward Theo with the sour look he so desired.

The coach rolled to a stop. They jumped out and ascended the steps to the church.

"Do not look so fierce. Why else did you ask me to stand up with you but to have me cheer you with my good humor?"

"Because you are my brother…and I am glad of it."

"And I too." Theo extended his hand.

Darcy took it and shook it firmly. "I hope, one day, to see you as happily situated as I."

"I will stand up with you, but that is as close to priest-linked as I intend to be. You may keep the parson's mousetrap for yourself."

EPILOGUE

London, 10 June 1812

Dear Mrs. Reynolds,

Hah! I knew you could not rest without a full description of William's nuptials. I doubt you will ever get a satisfactory account from my brother, since apparently he saw nothing but his bride during the entire event. I never thought to see him so besotted!

I will refer you to Georgiana for any detailed description of the lace and silk involved, but I will tell you the bride looked lovely. I suppose I should say the brides looked lovely, since Elizabeth's eldest sister, Jane, wed William's friend, Bingley, in the same ceremony. A double wedding was a wise choice in this case, since I doubt the mother of the brides could have survived such excitement twice. Such a fluttering of nerves and handkerchiefs you have never seen! You would have dosed her in an instant with your special tincture of lemon balm.

Mrs. Bennet, I am sorry to say, was sufficiently recovered by the time of the wedding breakfast to consider the fate of her remaining unmarried daughters. You might think marrying off three daughters in two months, she could rest on her laurels for a time, but no. That woman is terrifying! At every turn, she would push her unmarried daughter Miss Katherine in front of me, apparently in the hope that William's condition might be contagious to me. Alas, the new Mrs. Darcy is by far the most interesting of Mrs. Bennet's brood, and Miss Katherine is merely a washed-out version of her elder sisters.

I must confess I flirted a little with the other Bennet daughter, Miss Mary, who earned my sympathy via the misfortune of being the only plain one in the family and generally disregarded by the rest. It was most satisfying to see a little color in her cheeks afterwards as a result, but I had to take to my heels when Mrs. Bennet approached yet again with Miss Katherine. Mr. Bennet, in the meantime, seems to be determined to take on my old avocation of needling William for his own amusement. As an expert on the subject, I must say he shows some promise!

Naturally our family provided its share of the entertainment as well. Colonel Fitzwilliam was in attendance since, as he said, unless he witnessed it with his own eyes, he would never truly believe William had taken on a leg-shackle.

Cousin Anne insisted upon coming as well, which was hardly surprising as she has taken to insisting upon going to any event any of us attend. I live in fear she will turn up in my club one of these days! But she was well behaved, at least by her own standards, which is to say she only made half a dozen outrageous utterances. While she did stare fixedly at my friend Monty's cravat, she managed to restrain herself from taking any direct action.

As for Monty, he could not miss the wedding because he is determined to put in an appearance anywhere Georgiana might happen to be. He is only doing so to annoy me, I believe, but I had my revenge. I told Mrs. Bennet he was a wealthy baronet and unmarried. He could not turn tail and run quickly enough!

Then it was all over. William and Elizabeth departed, still starry-eyed. I rode back with Monty and the Colonel, where we proceeded to enjoy an evening you would disapprove of, thanks to two bottles of William's finest port which Richard had been clever enough to liberate from Darcy House the previous day.

As for William and me, our truce remains in effect, and I anticipate his new bride will not permit any change in that status. You will be amazed when I return to Pemberley at Christmas—at William's insistence, I might add, although your plum pudding may have something to do with it as well—at how civil we have become, something I once thought quite impossible. I can see you shaking your head and murmuring, "I told you so, Master Theophilus!"

Yours, etc.,

Theo Darcy

Postscript—You are not under any circumstances to allow the cook to leave before she has written down her receipt for ginger cakes!

Want more of Theo Darcy?
Read his letters at:
http://thedarcybrothers.com

ABOUT THE AUTHORS

✣MONICA FAIRVIEW

A confirmed Jane Austen addict, Monica Fairview used to be a literature professor, but her compulsion to write something other than scholarly articles pushed her over the edge, and resulted in her first published novel, the Regency romance, *An Improper Suitor.*

Now she dedicates whatever time she can spare from raising a very active daughter to writing and reading –and more writing. Born in London, Monica lived in the USA for many years. She loves to chuckle, read, and visit historical places. Sometimes she enjoys doing nothing at all. When she has the time.

So far Monica has written two Jane Austen sequels. *The Other Mr Darcy* focuses on Caroline Bingley and introduces Mr. Darcy's American Cousin Robert, while *The Darcy Cousins* on Georgiana Darcy. A short story of hers appeared in Laurel Ann Nattress's anthology *Jane Austen Made Me Do It*, featuring a number of your favorite Austenesque authors, published by Ballantine. She has written one neo-Victorian/futuristic novel based on Pride and Prejudice, *Steampunk Darcy*, and a traditional Pride and Prejudice Variation *Mr. Darcy's Pledge* (Vol. 1)

Visit her website at: http://www.monicafairview.com/

ℳ MARIA GRACE

Though Maria Grace has been writing fiction since she was ten years old, those early efforts happily reside in a file drawer and are unlikely to see the light of day again, for which many are grateful. After penning five file-drawer novels in high school, she took a break from writing to pursue college and earn her doctorate in Educational Psychology. After 16 years of university teaching, she returned to her first love, fiction writing.

She has one husband, two graduate degrees and two black belts, three sons, four undergraduate majors, five nieces, sewn six Regency era costumes, written seven Regency-era fiction projects, and designed eight websites. To round out the list, she cooks for nine in order to accommodate the growing boys and usually makes ten meals at a time so she only cooks twice a month.

Visit her website: http://randombitsoffascination.com/

CASSANDRA GRAFTON

A fan of Jane Austen since having to study Pride & Prejudice for her English Literature O Level examination in 1978, Cassandra has been indulging her passion for all things Austen for many years. Having long wanted to be a writer, the two came together in recent years, and she is now publishing her endeavours in the hope that readers will enjoy delving into her stories as much as she enjoyed creating them.

A former college lecturer and then PA, she is British born and bred (though she did live in the USA for five years). Cassandra has two grown up children and splits her time between Rafz, Switzerland, where she lives with her husband, and Regency England, where she lives with her characters.

Visit her website at: www.cassandragrafton.com

✤SUSAN MASON-MILKS

You might be surprised to learn that when Susan read *Pride and Prejudice* for the first time in the eighth grade, she was not impressed! That changed when she saw the now famous 1995 mini-series version of the story. Deciding to give Austen another chance, she read all the novels and fell in love. Her favorite Austen book is *Pride and Prejudice* with *Persuasion* a close second.

She says, "Writing stories inspired by Austen's books offers a way to spend more time with characters I've grown to love. Just because the book ends, it doesn't have to be the end of the story." Her first novel was *Mr. Darcy's Proposal* with another in the works for 2015. She was also co-editor and contributor to *Pride and Prejudice: The Scenes Jane Austen Never Wrote.*

When people catch her day dreaming (which is often), she always says, "Oops, gone to Pemberley, again."

In addition to writing, her other loves include singing, reading, walking, and yoga. She currently lives in Seattle with her husband, two very naughty cats, and Lucy, the Tibetan terrier, occasionally called the Tibetan terror.

Visit her website at: http://austen-whatif-stories.com/

ABIGAIL REYNOLDS

Abigail Reynolds may be a nationally bestselling author and a physician, but she can't follow a straight line with a ruler. Originally from upstate New York, she studied Russian and theater at Bryn Mawr College and marine biology at the Marine Biological Laboratory in Woods Hole. After a stint in performing arts administration, she decided to attend medical school, and took up writing as a hobby during her years as a physician in private practice.

A life-long lover of Jane Austen's novels, Abigail began writing variations on *Pride & Prejudice* in 2001, then expanded her repertoire to include a series of novels set on her beloved Cape Cod. Her most recent releases are the national bestseller *Mr. Darcy's Noble Connections*, *Mr. Darcy's Refuge*, *A Pemberley Medley*, and *Morning Light*, and she is currently working on a new Pemberley Variation and the next novel in her Cape Cod series. Her books have been translated into four languages. A lifetime member of JASNA, she lives on Cape Cod with her husband, her son and a menagerie of animals. Her hobbies do not include sleeping or cleaning her house.

Visit her website at: www.pemberleyvariations.com

Made in the USA
Lexington, KY
27 December 2015